# LOVE ON A DIME

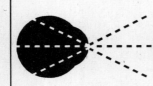

This Large Print Book carries the
Seal of Approval of N.A.V.H.

# A LADIES OF SUMMERHILL NOVEL

*Book #1*

# LOVE ON A DIME

## CARA LYNN JAMES

**THORNDIKE PRESS**
*A part of Gale, Cengage Learning*

GALE
CENGAGE Learning™

Detroit • New York • San Francisco • New Haven, Conn • Waterville, Maine • London

GALE
CENGAGE Learning

Copyright © 2010 by Carolyn James Slaughter.
Scripture quotations are from the Holy Bible, King James Version.
Thorndike Press, a part of Gale, Cengage Learning.

**ALL RIGHTS RESERVED**
This novel is a work of fiction. Names, characters, places, and incidents are either products of the author's imagination or are used fictitiously. All characters are fictional, and any similarity to people, living or dead, is purely coincidental.
Thorndike Press® Large Print Christian Romance.
The text of this Large Print edition is unabridged.
Other aspects of the book may vary from the original edition.
Set in 16 pt. Plantin.

**LIBRARY OF CONGRESS CATALOGING-IN-PUBLICATION DATA**

James, Cara Lynn, 1949–
   Love on a dime : a Ladies of Summerhill novel / by Cara Lynn James.
     p. cm. — (Thorndike Press large print Christian romance)
(Ladies of Summerhill ; 1)
   ISBN-13: 978-1-4104-3087-8
   ISBN-10: 1-4104-3087-1
   1. Women authors—Fiction. 2. Rhode Island—Fiction. 3.
Large type books. I. Title.
PS3610.A4284L68 2010b
813'.6—dc22                              2010024172

Published in 2010 by arrangement with Thomas Nelson, Inc.

Printed in the United States of America
1 2 3 4 5 6 7 14 13 12 11 10

*Love on a Dime* is dedicated
with all my love
to my husband, Jim. Thank you
for your help, support,
encouragement, and patience.
You're my hero!

# Prologue

Jack slowed his pace, his courage once more waning at the sight of the Westbrook home across the way. Anxiety twisted his stomach in a knot. But in the dusky light, Lilly's glow of confidence reignited his own flame. She understood her parents far better than he did. Since she believed her father would agree to the marriage, why should he hesitate?

Arm-in-arm they strolled across the road. Among the row of fine brick townhouses facing them, the Westbrook house stood three stories tall like all the rest, with long, paned windows overlooking Washington Park.

Mr. Ames, the ancient butler, opened the front door. Jack and Lilly entered the dimly lit foyer.

"Where is my father this evening?" Lilly asked the butler.

"In the back parlor, miss."

7

"Shall I go with you, Jack?"

"No," he whispered, squeezing her hand, "I'd rather do this on my own. Say a prayer all will go well."

Jack strode toward the parlor, determined to plead his case. Every nerve ending in his body fired with life — and more than a few with apprehension. He'd calm himself and then ask Mr. Westbrook for Lilly's hand in a respectful tone, solicitous, but not fawning. He'd restrain his usual brash attitude and hope Mr. Westbrook would consent to a marriage most would deem unsuitable. If he weighed the odds of success, he wouldn't even try.

Jack inhaled a steadying breath and increased his pace down the narrow hallway leading to the back of the house. Gas sconces threw a pale light along the Persian runner that muffled his footsteps to a soft shuffle. The house lay silent except for the noise of a sledge hammer beating against his chest.

*Lord, I need a large dose of Your strength. Don't allow me to cower. I've never been a quitter and I don't want to start now.*

He hadn't asked God for much in the past, but this was too important to rely on his own untested powers.

Jack paused before he came to the door of

the back parlor, straightened his bow tie, and squared his shoulders. Voices stopped him before he moved forward. He recognized Mrs. Westbrook's high, girlish tone. He'd wait for a lull in the conversation, excuse his entry, and then ask to speak to Mr. Westbrook. Jack waited for several minutes before he heard his name.

"Thomas, I noticed Jackson Grail seems especially fond of Lilly. You don't suppose he wants to marry her, do you?"

Jack winced at the worry in her voice. With his back to the wall he stepped closer to the parlor.

Mr. Westbrook chuckled. "No, my dear, he's George's friend, not Lilly's. She's hardly more than a child."

"For goodness' sake. Lilly's nineteen, certainly old enough to catch the eye of a young man."

"All right, she's not my little girl anymore. But ready for marriage? No, Nessie, I don't believe so. She has lots of time to choose a mate. There's no rush."

"Hmm. I wouldn't want her to delay too long. I've given considerable thought to her future."

"I'm sure you have," Mr. Westbrook murmured. Jack pictured his wry smile.

"Well, it's my duty as her mother to guide

her. Oliver Cross or Pelham Mills come to mind as possible suitors. Maybe Harlan Santerre. He's such a polite young man and his mother and I have been friends since childhood. Yes, he's most definitely my first choice."

Jack let out the breath he'd been holding, knowing he should break away, cease his eavesdropping —

"They're all acceptable to me. But what about young Grail? You say he might be interested in her. He's got a good head on his shoulders."

"But no money in his pocket. Need I say more?"

Jack frowned and tried to swallow, but his mouth was dry.

Mr. Westbrook sighed. "No, my dear. You're absolutely right. He's not suitable, though I do like him."

"I do as well. And now he's as finely educated as our own George. But he would have to strike it rich quickly in order to court Lilly," Mrs. Westbrook added. "And that's highly unlikely."

"Nearly impossible, I'm afraid. So I hope you're wrong and young Grail hasn't set his heart on Lilly." Her father sighed. "He's an intelligent boy. I'm sure he'd know better. Especially when she has an ambitious mama anxious to make her the perfect match."

Mrs. Westbrook laughed. "Thomas, do stop your teasing."

Jack bumped his shoulder against the curlicues of a large gilt picture frame. Turning to give it a hard shove, he stopped himself. He wouldn't let his temper get the better of him. Leaving the oil painting crooked, he stumbled down the patterned runner, away from the awful voices. When he came to the foyer he dropped into a rosewood chair and ignored the curious stare from Mr. Ames.

Jack buried his head in his hands and tried to gather his wits before he had to face Lilly. But the Westbrooks' conversation resounded through his mind. *Poor. Unsuitable.* Why had he ever thought they'd accept him as a son-in-law? His love for Lilly had banished all reason. He'd lived in a fog of hope these last several months, but now it cleared.

At the sound of light footsteps he looked up. "What did Papa say?" Lilly asked, grasping his hands.

He glanced at her without speaking and then saw his own anguish reflected in her eyes. He so wished his answer could bring her joy. She gently pulled him into the dimly lit sitting room. The sheers and heavy velvet curtains blocked all but the final rays of daylight from seeping through the windows overlooking the park. They faced each other in front of the unlit marble fireplace, his arms tight around her slim waist, her hands lightly touching his vest.

"Tell me," she said in a rasping voice, barely audible.

"I never had the chance to ask, Lilly. When I got to the back parlor your parents were already discussing appropriate husbands. And my name wasn't on the list."

"That's because they don't know we love each other. Papa has never refused me anything. It might take some persuasion, but you can do it. We can approach him together."

Lovely, pampered Lilly, who owned her father's heart — except when it came to marriage partners. And marriage among the rich was certainly a business transaction. Their kind never married Jack's kind. He'd gone to St. Luke's and Yale with the wealthy, but as a scholarship student, he didn't belong to their set no matter how hard he tried to fit in. Maybe he would've accepted the impenetrable barrier if Lilly hadn't swept into his life.

He gazed at her, drinking in her passion, memorizing her large, expressive eyes and flawless skin, her tall, slender form and thick brown hair framing her face.

Her eyes blazed like blue fire. "Come. We'll speak to Papa. Right now."

Jack caught her wrists. "No, I can't. I'm so sorry. He won't change his mind. It's pointless to even ask." *Save me the humiliation.*

Her strangled cry pierced his heart. "You won't even try? We love each other. Isn't that worth fighting for?" Lilly's voice rose with disbelief.

How could he explain he couldn't abide her father's rejection? He refused to hear again that he wasn't good enough to court Lilly — once was enough. And he didn't want her to elope with him without her parents' approval. Jack groaned. As much as he adored Lilly, he wasn't acceptable to the family. The daughter of a prosperous banker, Lilly couldn't marry a man without a family fortune.

"We can marry without their consent. You'll find a good job. I know you will. Don't you see, Jack, we don't need my parents' permission."

"But I want their respect." And he'd never gain their esteem by stealing their daughter away. He turned from her, running a hand through his hair. He'd been fooling himself. How could he provide for Lilly, care for her in a manner in which she was accustomed? What could he promise her? A one room apartment in a dingy part of town while he made his way in the world, if he ever made it at all. How long before his beautiful, young and idealistic bride would realize she'd sacrificed too much for an improbable dream? He'd harm her if he stole her from her family.

He glanced at her and could see in her face the stubborn, naïve hope that lingered there. But he understood reality as she never would. He'd let his love blossom before he should have.

Jack slowly moved away, steeling himself for the hurt yet to come. "Your parents are right. I'm in no position to marry. I should never have proposed, because I have nothing to offer."

Lilly rushed to him and flung her arms around his neck, tears spilling down her cheeks. "What about our love? Why do you need more than that?"

"Lilly, we can't exist on dreams. I have to earn a living. And I can't support you on a clerk's salary. You'd miss your old life."

Her lovely, soft features hardened. "You must think my love is too weak to withstand hardship. It's strong enough to survive anything. Why do you doubt me so?"

Jack shook his head. "I doubt myself, not you." What if her confidence in his abilities weren't warranted? What if he never rose above petty clerk, despite his fancy education? A girl from a society family, proud and successful for generations, could never be content washing laundry, cooking meals, and scrubbing floors on her hands and knees. She'd grow bitter and resentful.

"I can adapt to less. I don't care about a beautiful home. I only want you," she said, her voice rising with frustration.

He wouldn't argue about the effects of poverty and how it wore on a person. She wouldn't understand. "If we came from the same background, I wouldn't hesitate to speak to your father. But we don't."

"But you will. I know it. I'll wait until you feel ready to marry me. There's no hurry. I'm patient. I can wait forever." She pleaded with beautiful eyes glistening with tears.

"No, please don't wait for me." Jack's voice cracked like ice.

He wanted her to wait, but he couldn't ruin her chances of making a suitable, maybe even a happy marriage. The odds of succeeding in the business world without connections were small. If and when he'd proven himself, he'd return and hope she'd still want him. And forgive him. But he couldn't ask her to wait.

He blotted her tears with his handkerchief, but they kept streaming down her face. Her slender shoulders heaved with soft sobs. He kissed her again gently and then retreated to his bedroom before he was tempted to crush her in his arms and beg her to elope. He'd planned to stay for the week as George's guest, but now he needed to leave quickly.

Within ten minutes he was gone.

Jack's heart slammed against his ribs. The past two weeks had been a misery. He couldn't sleep. He couldn't eat. *Go back, go back!* his mind and heart screamed. *You've made a terrible mistake!*

His stomach roiling, Jack fought to keep a dignified pace and not run all the way to Washington Square. At last, he stood before the Westbrook home and tapped the front door knocker against the heavy wood.

He'd explain he couldn't manage without her and his infernal pride had blocked his common sense and their tender love. Would she accept his apology? They'd work something out. He didn't know how exactly, but they would. He knew their union was sanctioned, indeed designed, by God.

Mr. Ames pulled the heavy door open.

"May I help you, sir?"

"Yes. Is Miss Westbrook at home?"

The hunched-over butler shook his head. "They've all gone abroad. They sailed yesterday."

Jack's cautious optimism collapsed in a heap of despair. "And when will they return?"

"Next spring."

*Next spring.* Jack groaned. "G-Good day," he mumbled, turning from the door.

*I'm too late. I've lost her.*

# One

## NEWPORT, RHODE ISLAND — JULY 1899

*Six years later*

With a deep sigh of satisfaction, Lilly Westbrook whipped the last page of her manuscript out of the Underwood typewriter. Carefully she shredded the carbon and threw the messy strips into the wastebasket. No meddlesome maid could possibly reconstruct her work and tattle to Mama.

For a moment, a wave of sadness overshadowed the pleasure she felt at finishing another story. How she longed to share her secret with her mother, but as much as Lilly hated deception, she knew Mama would never understand. Mama was proud of her for dabbling in poetry, but this?

No. It was best to stay behind closed doors to write her dime novels.

Lilly shuddered to think of the disgrace she'd bring upon herself and, even worse, upon her family, if her secret was revealed. The very notion of social ostracism weakened her knees and left her legs wobbly. A twinge of guilt pinched her conscience as it often did when she considered her concealment. Yet why look for trouble when her work was progressing so well?

Lilly scrubbed her hands until all evidence of the carbon paper and inky ribbon disappeared into the washbasin near her bed, then covered the typewriter Mama had given her as a birthday gift a few years before. Mama thought a typing machine unnecessary for a poet, but she wasn't one to begrudge her children anything within reason.

Lilly withdrew a letter from her skirt pocket and smiled as she re-read the last lines.

My dear Lilly,

I want to again express my thanks for all you've contributed to the Christian Settlement House of New York. We so value the time and effort you have devoted to assisting our young ladies with their sundry life skills and English fluency. Your exceptional generosity and financial support have enabled us to continue our work in accordance with the Lord's purposes.

Sincerely,
Phoebe Diller, Director

Miss Diller's kind words sent a rush of warmth to Lilly's heart and strengthened her resolve to continue writing. For without the profits from her novels, she couldn't afford to donate more than a few dollars to her favorite charity. How could she possibly quit writing when her romance novels provided so many blessings to others?

Lilly locked the final chapter in the roll-top desk by the bay window and hid the key beneath the lining of her keepsake box. Time for a well-deserved walk by the sea. She removed her reading spectacles and placed her straw hat decorated with bright poppies squarely on top of her upswept hair. After a last furtive glance toward the desk, she left her bedroom to the morning sunshine that splashed across the shiny oak floor and floral carpet.

All the way down the staircase she congratulated herself for typing "The End" of her story, though it was only a few days before deadline. That was much too close for comfort. She sighed. Too many social events had disrupted her normal writing routine this summer. But she had no choice but to force a smile and attend the functions, even though most of them bored her to distraction.

She wouldn't think of that now. At least she'd finished the manuscript before the deadline and for that she'd treat herself to a few minutes out of her room. With a light heart, she strolled through the deserted foyer, past Mr. Ames, the butler, and out the front door. A beautiful day greeted her with its sun-blessed smile.

As she crossed the veranda, her sister-in-law Irene Westbrook, seated at the end of the porch, peered over a small, familiar book. The lurid cover of Lilly's latest novel, *Dorothea's Dilemma,* popped out in garish color. Lilly stopped short and pressed her palm over her gyrating heart.

"Oh my," she murmured. She'd never expected to see one of her novels in her own home, let alone in the hands of her brother's wife.

Irene smoothed her halo of silky blonde curls caught up in a loose pompadour. She laid the slim paperback on her lap, her eyes gleaming with curiosity. "Why hello, Lilly. Where have you been on this beautiful afternoon? Cooped up in your bedroom again? My goodness, what do you do in there all day?"

"Sometimes I enjoy a few hours of solitude." Lilly's nerves seized control of her voice and it rose like the screech of a seagull. "I'm sorry I interrupted your reading." Heat crept into her skin as Irene watched her, face aglow with interest.

"Do sit down, Lilly."

She slipped into a wicker chair opposite Irene. A gust of salty air, typical of Newport's summer weather, blew in from the Atlantic and brushed its cool breath across her cheeks. She prayed it would fade the red splotches that came so easily when embarrassment struck.

Irene cocked her head. "Is something wrong? You look positively ill."

"No, I'm fine." Though every fiber of her body continued to quiver, Lilly steadied her breathing. She folded her hands in the lap of her charcoal-gray skirt and willed them not to shake.

"You aren't shocked by my novel, are you?" Irene smirked.

"Of course not." Lilly squirmed around on the soft chintz cushion and avoided Irene's skeptical stare. "Why should I be shocked?"

Irene leaned forward. "Some people claim dime novels are trash, and from your reaction I thought you might be one of those faultfinders. Of course they're wrong. These books are filled with adventure and I *love* adventure." She rolled the last word around her tongue like a stream of honey.

Irene, the niece of Quentin Kirby, one of San Francisco's silver kings, fancied herself an adventuress, but Lilly inwardly disagreed. Irene merely appreciated fun and frivolity more than most. That hardly made her a woman like the heroines of Lilly's books. "I'm so sorry, Irene. I didn't mean to criticize your choice of books. I just wondered where you obtained your copy."

"I discovered it in the kitchen while I was searching for a blueberry tart." Irene grinned as if Lilly ought to admire her cleverness. "One of the scullery maids must have left it there."

"You took it without asking permission?" Lilly could scarcely believe Irene had wandered downstairs to the basement kitchen, the domain of servants who strongly disapproved of visitors, even the family.

"Why yes. Well no, not exactly. I *borrowed* it. As soon as I finish reading, I'll give it back. Of course."

Irene tapped the big, red letters spelling out the author's name across the cover. "Fannie Cole. She's a splendid writer, the very best. Have you ever read any of her books? I devour them like chocolate."

Lilly's heart lurched. "Naturally I've heard of her. I believe her stories are rather popular."

"They're enthralling."

At the sound of the front door squeaking open, Lilly looked away with relief.

Mama bustled onto the veranda, a frown knitting her eyebrows. "What's that about Fannie Cole? She's quite infamous, I hear." Glancing from Lilly to Irene, Mama's eyelashes fluttered, a sure sign of agitation. "Oh, I see you have one of her books . . ."

Lilly knew her mother couldn't let this breach of propriety pass without comment. On the other hand, the kind and ever tactful Vanessa Westbrook would hate to offend her new daughter-in-law.

"Mama, Fannie Cole writes harmless fiction. You needn't worry." Lilly smiled her assurance, hoping she'd veer off to another topic.

Her mother sunk into a wicker chair beside Irene. "Perhaps, my dear, but you must admit, there are so many more uplifting novels." She patted Irene's arm, which was robed in a cream silk blouse that matched the lace of her skirt. "Lillian is a poet, you know. Her work is delightful. You must read it. I'll go fetch you a copy."

Lilly cringed. "No, Mama. I wrote those poems years ago. She wouldn't be interested in the meanderings of an eighteen-year-old ninny. It's sentimental tripe."

"Nonsense, my dear. You've always been much too critical of yourself."

"Nevertheless, I'm sure Irene would prefer Fannie Cole." *Who wouldn't?* Lilly thought. Still, she appreciated her mother's enthusiasm for her meager literary efforts.

Irene tossed her a wide, grateful smile. "There, that's settled."

Mama's round, girlish face tightened with distaste. "I wish you wouldn't read dime novels because . . ." She looked toward Lilly for support.

"Really, Mama." Lilly softened her voice, not meaning to scold. "While some of the dime novels are sensational, others are written to help working girls avoid the pitfalls of city life. They're moralistic tales that encourage virtue. Nothing to be ashamed of reading." *Or writing.*

"Exactly." Irene beamed. "I couldn't have said it better myself. Of course, I read for the story, not the moral lesson, but I'm sure it's beneficial for those who enjoy a good sermon."

Lilly suppressed a sigh of resignation. "No doubt Miss Cole hopes and prays her words

26

touch the hearts of her readers and bring them closer to the Lord." Lilly looked at Mama and Irene, hoping they'd somehow understand her purpose and approve. But both looked puzzled over her words.

Irene's gaze narrowed. "An odd way to spread the gospel, don't you think?"

"Not at all. The Lord is more creative than we are." Lilly bristled and then glanced away when she found her mother and sister-in-law still staring at her.

She'd spoken up much more forcefully than she intended. With a sinking heart, Lilly realized Mama would never accept her viewpoint; it flew in the face of beliefs and opinions ingrained since childhood.

Irene picked up a sheet of paper resting on a small table between two pots of ferns and waved it like a flag on the Fourth of July. Lilly immediately recognized *Talk of the Town,* a gossip rag published by that scandalmonger, Colonel MacIntyre, the bane of Newport society. He shot fear into the hearts of all upstanding people and others who weren't quite so virtuous. Lilly swallowed hard.

Mama gasped. Her pale skin whitened. "Oh my dear, that's hardly appropriate for a respectable home."

Irene shrugged. "Perhaps not. But if you

don't mind my saying so, it's great fun to read. I'm learning the crème de la crème of Newport are up to all kinds of mischief." She laughed with pleasure.

"Listen to this." Irene leaned forward. *"One hears that Miss Fannie Cole, author of wildly popular dime novels, has taken up residence at one of the ocean villas for the season. The talk about town claims this writer of sensational — some might even say salacious — stories, belongs to the New York and Newport aristocracy. Which of our fine debutantes or matrons writes under the nom de plume, Fannie Cole? Speculation runs rampant. Would the talented but mysterious author of* Dorothea's Dilemma, Hearts in Tune, *and several other delectable novels please come forward and identify herself for her public?"*

Lilly's throat closed. She clamped her hands down on her lap, but they shook like a hummingbird's wings. Had a maid or a footman stumbled across her secret and sold the information? Colonel Rufus MacIntyre of *Talk of the Town* paid handsomely for gossip. No one was safe from his long, grasping tentacles, including some of the most prominent people in society.

"The colonel has mentioned Miss Cole in his column for the last two weeks, so I expect we'll hear more about her during the summer." Irene grinned as she studied the sheet. "I wonder who she is. I'd love to meet her."

Mama's mouth puckered into a small circle. "Undoubtedly someone from the wrong side of the tracks. No one we'd know." She punctuated her words with a firm nod.

Irene persisted. "You must have an idea, Lilly. You seem to know everything that's going on in society."

Lilly turned away, sure that a red stain had again spilled across her pale skin. Her sister-in-law was right. She did listen to all the tittle-tattle, but she prided herself on her discretion. The foibles of her set provided grist for her novels, not for spreading rumors and innuendo.

"You give me far too much credit, Irene." She hated to dodge questions to keep from lying, but what was her option short of confessing? She twisted the cameo at the neck of her tailored shirtwaist.

Mama wagged her finger. "Mark my words. By the end of the summer someone will discover Fannie Cole's true name and announce it to the entire town. Oh, my. What humiliation she'll bring upon her family. They'll be mortified."

"How delicious," Irene murmured.

Lilly groaned inwardly. Her subterfuge gnawed at her conscience, worsening day by day, but she couldn't turn back the clock and reconsider her decision to write in secret.

She rose. "Will you excuse me? I need to take my walk now."

With her head held high and as much poise as she could muster, Lilly descended the veranda's shallow steps. She strode across the wide, sloping lawn that surrounded Summerhill, the old twenty-two-room mansion the Westbrooks rented for the season.

Once she reached the giant rocks that separated the grounds from the ocean, she picked her way over to a smooth boulder that doubled for a bench. As she'd done every day since her arrival three weeks ago, Lilly settled onto its cold surface. Instead of watching the breakers pound against the coast and absorb the majesty of nature's rhythm, she rested her head in her hands and let the breeze brush against her face.

What would happen if her beau, Harlan Santerre, discovered that she and Fannie Cole were the same person? The wealthy railroad heir, a guest of the family for the eight weeks of summer, miraculously seemed ripe to propose. Her mother kept reminding her how grateful she should be that such a solid, upstanding man as Harlan Santerre had shown interest in a twenty-five-year-old spinster with no grand fortune and no great beauty. Mama and the entire family would be humiliated if her writing became public knowledge and Harlan turned his attention elsewhere.

Yet the Holy Ghost had urged her to compose her simple stories, and as she wrote, her melancholy gradually faded. Her enthusiasm never waned thanks to the joy she received from doing the Lord's work.

Why would He allow someone to ruin her and end the good deeds she accomplished? He should smite her enemies instead. All her life she'd trusted the Lord to guide her and protect her, but never had she needed His help more than now. But would He continue to shield her?

Trembling, Lilly tossed a stone into the roiling surf and watched it sink into the foamy white waves. What if the surge of curiosity aroused by Colonel MacIntyre didn't fade away and everything she held dear was threatened?

# TWO

Jack Grail's blood coursed through his veins as the matched pair of grays gained speed. With daring abandon, he urged the horses forward as they pulled the carriage around the twists and turns of Ocean Drive. Manorial homes set on windswept lawns rushed by. He glimpsed the deep blue Atlantic crash and spit against boulders and cliffs. A steady breeze raked through his hair and whistled past his ears. How he loved the exhilaration that increased with every hoofbeat, the stimulant of speed.

"We're here." George Westbrook leaned across Jack and pointed to a winding driveway tucked behind a low stone fence. Jack slowed the horses to an easy canter before turning into the pebbled drive.

Directly ahead, Summerhill crowned a gentle rise. With white shingles and gingerbread trim, it looked like a wedding cake set against the sprawling acres of bright green grass. Yet the awnings and wrap-around porch won his approval for their refreshing simplicity. This seaside home, called a cottage — despite its numerous rooms — appealed to him far more than the Italianate palazzos and French chateaux that lined Newport's Bellevue Avenue, one of the country's most exclusive addresses.

Jack lifted his chin toward the house. "What a grand home you have here."

"We rented it for the summer. The doctor thought a few months by the ocean might improve my father's health. His asthma has worsened this past year."

The Westbrooks weren't nearly as rich as the Astors, the Vanderbilts, or the Goelets, but leasing a mansion still made them plenty rich, in Jack's opinion. They certainly had enough to remain in great comfort.

A familiar and unwanted prick of envy punctured his good humor. Someday, he hoped to build a villa boasting thirty spacious rooms and sweeping views of the rocky Rhode Island coastline. If he expanded his business and achieved the success he expected, he might have a place like Summerhill, commodious, though unpretentious by Newport standards. In a few years a summer house could easily be within his reach — if all went well.

As they neared the cottage, Jack slowed the horses. Then he saw her glide across the lawn, back from the sea. Lilly. His heart clenched. She looked the same as she had six years before, only more mature, less girlish. Tall and slender, she walked with a grace he'd never noticed while they were secretly courting. Her dark skirt billowed out in a gust of ocean wind as she grabbed onto her straw hat piled high with too many red flowers. Gone was the debutante. In her place strode a young woman some might consider past her prime, but whom he suspected was just coming into it. As Lilly approached, he noticed the years had softened her sharp features and added curves to her slender frame. But she never once glanced in his direction before she disappeared into the house.

He halted the carriage when they reached the veranda and turned the reins over to a stable hand. With an occasional glance toward the porch, hoping Lilly would appear, Jack unloaded his trunks containing everything he'd need for a three-week visit.

"I'd like to pay my regards to your mother and sister."

"No doubt they can be found in the library. Follow me." George instructed a footman to carry Jack's luggage up to a guest bedroom and then headed through the foyer and down a wide hallway lined with paintings of seascapes and still lifes in gilt frames.

Jack's heart raced when they entered the oak-paneled room lined with bookshelves rising to the coffered ceiling. He inhaled the smell of furniture wax mixed with the fragrance of roses.

He saw her carefully climbing the ladder set against the shelves, apparently too intent on retrieving a book to hear their loud entrance. She stretched up, grasped a volume, and then gingerly descended the rungs.

"Lilly, look who I've brought home." George jerked his thumb toward Jack. "Remember Jackson Grail?"

She halted, wrenched her head around, and glanced down. Her blue eyes widened as the color drained from her face. The hefty tome slid from her slim hand and thudded to the floor. She didn't seem to notice.

Jack scooped up the Jane Austen volume and tucked it under his arm. "Hello, Lilly." His muscles tensed. Would she ignore him or slap him in the face for leaving her so abruptly years before? Apprehension slithered down his back. He deserved anger for the abominable way he'd treated her, but he hoped she'd found the compassion to forgive him, though he'd never had the decency to even ask.

After a brief nod, she continued her descent. Dainty boots reaching the floor, she lifted her chin and came forward with an uncertain smile. He recognized the light floral scent enveloping her, flooding him with warm, unforgotten memories. She pinched a smile. "How delightful to see you. George didn't tell me you were coming."

Her frown settled on George, but was her hint of reproach also directed at him? He hardly expected her to welcome him. "I hope my presence won't cause you any inconvenience. If it does, I'll be happy to move to a hotel."

"No, indeed. We should all be upset if you didn't stay." Her words were more generous than her tone of voice indicated. "But I must say I never expected to see you again after so long an absence."

From her stricken look, that was an under-statement.

"Sorry I forgot to tell you about Jack's visit, Lilly." Her brother's long face sported the same rueful grin that had maneuvered him out of trouble for most of his life.

"You're forgiven, George, as usual." She cleared her throat and half-smiled at Jack.

"Are you here for business or pleasure?"

"A bit of both. I'd like to buy a boat, maybe a yawl or a sloop. I also brought work along." He searched her eyes, looking for some semblance of encouragement, hope, that she might welcome his pursuit again. Was she still hurt? Angry?

She nodded politely. "Well, I'm not surprised you'd combine business and pleasure. You always were full of ambition and boundless energy."

When she smiled, he accepted her remarks as complimentary, though he couldn't be sure.

"Do enjoy yourself in Newport and don't work too hard." Lilly looked as though she hoped his vacation would soon be concluded.

Jack shook his head, realizing she had no idea how hard he had struggled to return here, as a worthy potential suitor. "Don't you approve of a strong work ethic?"

"You misunderstand me. I certainly believe in commitment and diligence." Frowning, Lilly glanced at George, who was eyeing escape to the billiard room across the hall. "Yet, too much labor is as destructive as too much recreation. We need to strike a balance."

Jack gave a small bow along with a sheepish smile. "I'll try to remember that."

"See that you do." She laughed and so did he, cracking the ice, though not melting it.

This wasn't the passionate reunion he'd yearned for, but he'd known a cordial welcome was the most he could expect from the woman he'd jilted. And more than he merited.

"Jackson Grail, do come here and let me properly welcome you to Summerhill." Mrs. Westbrook and a young woman descended onto the settee at the far end of the library and waved him forward, like a small, plump queen to one of her people. Mrs. Westbrook exuded the friendliness George had inherited but Jack could see the matron's eyes flit between him and Lilly. He followed the Westbrooks over to their mother. Lilly squeezed in next to her while he and George took the leather chairs that afforded a clear view of the back lawn and ocean beyond.

Jack gaped at Mrs. Westbrook's companion, a stunning woman with brassy hair, a small, stubborn chin, and full lips curled into a seductive smile. She glanced up at him with half-closed eyes, then coyly tilted her head. She looked vaguely familiar, but since he'd traveled to so many places over the last several years, he couldn't place her.

When Mrs. Westbrook introduced her as

George's wife, Irene, his heart sank. Poor, sorry George. From the adoring gaze George bestowed upon her, his old friend didn't even harbor a doubt about her character. Jack hoped he was mistaken about the flirtatious woman, but her blatant interest rubbed him the wrong way.

Irene continued to scrutinize him as a maid served tea.

Mrs. Westbrook stirred several spoonfuls of sugar into her delicate cup. "George tells me you've settled down now and bought a newspaper and a magazine."

"Yes, a few months ago. After I left the Klondike, I stayed in San Francisco for a while. I thought I might like to live out West. But when I heard of several business opportunities in New York, I couldn't pass them up." He dared to glance at Lilly; was she gathering that he was a self-made man now? And Mrs. Westbrook — clearly, George had told his parents of his success in the Klondike.

Irene cocked her head. "Why publishing?"

"My father was the editor of our hometown newspaper — in Connecticut where I grew up." A universe away from the city and society people like the Westbrooks. "I worked there until I left for college. I've always been interested in the business, so it was a natural choice."

Mrs. Westbrook sent him an approving smile. "That's commendable, Jackson. So many of the young men who make their fortunes out West come home and squander them on meaningless pursuits."

Wine, women, and song, that's what she meant. For him, there'd only been one woman . . . "I've wanted to own a newspaper since I was a boy." And to build a publishing empire. "Luckily, both the *Manhattan Sentinel* and the *New York Monthly* magazine were available. I also might purchase a publishing house — Jones and Jarman."

Lilly choked on her tea, setting off a coughing spell that doubled her over. When her chest finally quit heaving, she glanced up at Jack with watery eyes. "Pardon me."

"Are you feeling all right?" he asked.

"I'm perfectly fine," she rasped. "Thank you."

Apparently convinced Lilly had sufficiently recovered, Mrs. Westbrook returned her focus on Jack. "And what exactly does Jones and Jarman print?"

He leaned forward, surprised at her curiosity and interest, although she'd treated him graciously in the past — other than dismissing him as a worthy suitor for her daughter. "Several types of books including dime novels, both western and romance." Cheaply made fiction for the masses and often highly lucrative.

Beaming as if they shared a secret, Irene lowered her voice. "I've read them all." She lifted a copy of *Dorothea's Dilemma* from the folds of her dress. "Fannie Cole is extraordinary. Do you happen to know her?"

Jack shook his head. "No, I've never met Miss Cole. In fact, being new to publishing, I don't even know who she really is. Most of the Jones and Jarman writers use pen names."

"How clever," Irene cooed.

"My daughter has been writing poetry this summer." Mrs. Westbrook smiled with maternal pride. "She spends countless hours in her room composing verses."

"They're unimportant little rhymes, Mama." Lilly blushed just as he expected she would. Shy and introspective, she disliked anyone calling attention to her achievements.

He couldn't resist. "Are you in need of a publisher, Lilly? Perhaps I can introduce you to Mr. Jarman."

"No, my little rhymes are merely works in progress. Besides, they don't publish poetry, now do they? Tomes of poetry hardly mesh

41

well with westerns and romances. Am I not right?"

"You are, but I would like to read your poems at any rate."

"Sometime, perhaps."

He knew she would never show him one word of her verses, not now. When they were courting he'd read several of her poems. Her sentiments were highly emotional, unlike the decorous and reticent Lilly she presented to family and friends. Was that passionate woman still there, right beneath her carefully guarded surface? "You seem to know quite a lot about Jones and Jarman," he said. "Have you ever read any of their books?"

She picked invisible specks of lint off her skirt. "My taste runs more toward literature, but I've heard some of my friends mention their dime novels."

He nodded. "They're quite popular. Do you write anything besides poetry?" he asked.

Lilly blinked. "Nothing of significance." She abruptly set aside her teacup and rose.

"Please excuse me. I have correspondence to attend to." Her small smile showed a slight thaw of her reserve. "I do wish you an enjoyable stay at Summerhill."

"Thank you. I hope it will be."

# Three

Lilly rushed up the carpeted staircase, anxious to vanish into the sanctuary of her bedroom. Her heart tumbled end over end. She stopped before she reached the landing and forced air into and out of her lungs as rhythmically as she could manage. Still, her bosom heaved as if she'd run several miles in a tightly laced corset.

After six years, she never expected to see Jackson Grail again. What nerve to show up on her doorstep when he surely must know his appearance would upset her. Her heart burned at the memory of him declaring his love and then casting her aside with only a lame explanation.

"You left so suddenly." Jack's deep voice startled her. She turned her head and spotted him at the foot of the stairs. "Did I say something to offend you, Lilly?"

She clutched the stair rail. "Not at all," she fibbed. Why was he following her? The item in *Talk of the Town* coupled with Jack's sudden appearance stripped her of every ounce of composure. She needed solitude to think and absorb all the bad news of the day.

"Then I'm sorry for my mistake. I thought you seemed distressed." Jack inclined his head, but he didn't turn to leave.

Lilly hesitated, and then regained her manners. "I'm afraid I haven't been particularly welcoming, and I apologize for my behavior. Will you forgive me?"

"Yes, of course. Is there anything I can do to help?"

"No, but thank you for your concern." She waited for him to bow and depart, but he continued to stare at her, his eyes brimming with — what? Embarrassment? Regret? She couldn't tell.

He nodded as he shifted his weight from one foot to the other. "Would you mind stepping outside for a few moments? I have something to tell you that I should have said long ago."

Lilly shook her head but felt her resolve weakening. "No, I'm sorry. I do have letters to write . . ."

She wasn't ready for any more revelations today. Was he about to apologize for his departure or offer an explanation for why he failed to maintain any sort of relationship since then? Later, when she prepared herself to accept his account calmly and without bitterness, she'd listen. But not yet.

"Can't your correspondence wait? I promise I won't take up much of your time."

Curiosity overcame her better judgment. Slowly she descended the stairs, clutching the rail for support. When she reached Jack, she refused to slip her hand into the crook of his arm. He raised his brows, but she ignored his questioning look. Her knees shook as they passed through the veranda and out onto the lush back lawn.

"Shall we walk to the beach?" he suggested.

Lilly nodded and pointed to a small sandy cove hollowed out between mounds of granite that jutted into the surf.

They strolled silently across the lawn and stopped where the grass edged a narrow strip of wet, silvery sand. Wisps of downy clouds floated across an azure sky which touched the royal blue ocean. A breeze shook the leafy skirt of a nearby elm tree and stirred the wild red roses blooming all along the shore. Their perfume blended with fresh, salty air, heavy and humid. With her hand shielding her eyes from the glare of the noonday sun, Lilly lifted her gaze to Jack.

Her heart fluttered, just as it always had when she looked at him. The years faded away and she saw the same broad-shouldered man who towered above her and moved with an athletic agility. A lock of his raven hair blew across his forehead. He pushed it back unsuccessfully, obviously unaware of his boyish appeal mixed with a strong, masculine allure. He'd grown more handsome now that he was approaching thirty, though age had crinkled the laugh lines around his dark brown eyes. Instinctively, Lilly knew to guard her heart.

"What did you want to tell me, Jack?"

"I'd like to clear the air since I'll be at Summerhill for a while." Taking a wide stance, he paused, as if he was unsure how to continue. "Hmm. This is harder than I expected." A grim expression replaced his buoyant self assurance. "All right, I'll come directly to the point. I regret that I left you so suddenly. I couldn't be the husband you deserved and I was wrong to propose when I was so financially unprepared." Jack stepped closer. "I made a mess of things and I'm terribly sorry, Lilly."

Jack narrowed his eyes, obviously seeking a reaction. To look at him was like staring at the sun, brilliant and blinding. She glanced toward the waves relentlessly crashing against the craggy coast, but still, she felt the penetration of his intense stare.

She raised her palms. "There's no need to say any more. I believe it would be best if we let the past lie buried." She blinked back tears welling behind her eyelids. She wouldn't let him see her cry.

At first he looked as if he'd protest, but then he gave a curt nod. "Yes, perhaps you're right — although I hope we can be friends."

Lilly half-smiled, suspecting that a couple once in love could never become just friends no matter how hard they tried. "Of course, if you wish."

Relief ironed out the worry lines that had gathered at the edges of his eyes. "I'm thankful you're not still angry with me. Or are you?"

"I don't carry grudges from the past. I look toward the future." That wasn't completely true. She hadn't forgotten Jack; his shadow loomed in every corner of her mind. And try as she might, she hadn't quite forgiven him.

He moved closer. "I also look forward to the future. That's why I bought the newspaper and magazine. No more hunting for treasure."

Lilly couldn't suppress a grin. "I heard you found all the gold you could ever want in the Klondike."

Tales of his enormous achievement had filtered back to New York society and caused quite a stir. Once he returned to the city he'd garnered countless invitations from the best of families who were anxious to introduce him to their unmarried daughters. Or so she'd heard. "You're a very rich man, I understand."

He tucked his chin to his chest. "I've been blessed with enough funds to buy a newspaper and a magazine — and possibly a publishing house. In the coming years I hope to make them grow larger and more successful." He smiled. "But I'm not as wealthy as people think — especially after my purchases."

Then his lips curved downward and Lilly thought he might say something more personal, but instead he merely paused as if he wanted to speak but couldn't find the words.

Lilly glanced over her shoulder and squinted. Harlan, thin as a quill, was standing on the back veranda talking to George. Should she feel grateful for his timely appearance or fearful he'd misinterpret Jack's presence? She took a deep breath and waved. Although he raised his hand in return, the grim set of his mouth sent a jolt of apprehension through her chest.

"Who's the gentleman walking toward us? Is that Harlan Santerre?" Frown lines cut into Jack's forehead.

"Yes. He's a friend of the family." Lilly eased away and strolled across the lawn toward her beau.

Jack followed. "The railroad man?"

"The very same. His father owns the New Jersey and Washington line, among others." Why had she added that? Did she hope that Jack would be jealous?

"You're among illustrious company, aren't you? The Santerres are powerful people."

Lilly shrugged, trying to soften her stance. "I suppose they are. Now that my brother has returned from the West, he expects Harlan will offer him a good position at one of his railroads." And that gave her parents hope that their son might amount to something after all. "Harlan and George were friends at school, you know. Perhaps you remember him too?" Lilly asked.

Jack's cocky grin pulled downward and vanished. "Indeed, I remember him well."

"He's our houseguest for the rest of July and August."

Jack strolled close to her, scarcely a hair's breadth apart, as Harlan sauntered across the grass to meet them. "It must be grand to take the summer off, but some of us can't afford to." A hint of bitterness crept into his deep voice.

Lilly chuckled. "Come now, Jack, with your success in the Klondike, you'd never be forced to work another day in your life. You're choosing to do so."

He exhaled a long, mournful sigh. "I want to succeed as a businessman, not as a lucky prospector."

"I understand." She smiled.

The years hadn't diminished Jack's single-minded ambition and need for material success and recognition, though she did respect his determination. And perseverance. It wasn't easy to make a fortune out of nothing except a good education.

But she wished he'd stayed away. How could she bear to see him day after day and pretend he was merely a casual acquaintance? Already their conversation dredged up memories of the good times they'd had together, her dreams of becoming his wife, and the children they might have had.

No, having him at their summer cottage, running into him in the hallways and sitting with him at meals would be anything but what she needed right now.

Yet what choice did she have?

She shoved the hurt deep inside and watched Harlan strut forward with his hand outstretched. "Jackson Grail, isn't it? Don't I know you from St. Luke's? We were in the same class, but you were a day student, as I recall." Harlan reached for his palm and Jack shook it firmly.

Slight of build, Harlan looked small and hardly robust. He tilted his head back, appraising Jack with frosty eyes. "I never forget a face." His nostrils flared, as if his memory of Jack reeked with an unpleasant odor.

"That's right," Jack said steadily. "I worked in the dining hall as a busboy at Yale, so you probably remember me from there as well." Jack straightened to his full height — well over six feet, half a head taller than Harlan.

Lilly tensed. Hostility soaked the air. She felt a slight headache coming on.

"Shall we return to the cottage? It must be time for luncheon." She pulled her mouth into a smile so tight and so bright, her jaw began to ache.

It seemed that the charmed days of her golden summer in Newport had drawn to an abrupt close.

■ ■ ■ ■

Throughout the meal Jack and Harlan glared at each other, yet they maintained a façade of congeniality that frayed Lilly's nerves. She said little while the others gossiped about yesterday's yacht race, the latest tennis match, and the van Patten's upcoming ball. She nibbled at her salad and sipped only a spoonful of consommé.

Jack captured her thoughts although she tried not to glance in his direction. His sudden appearance threw her off center, thrust her buried memories into her consciousness, and worse, exposed emotions she thought she'd conquered. She tried hard to focus on Harlan, but with warmth rising past her tight collar into her neck and cheeks, she knew she must look flustered. Harlan tilted his head, obviously bewildered, but continued to chatter politely.

Deeply buried feelings for Jack were surfacing against her will, bubbling like a hot spring. *But I'm practically engaged to Harlan. I can't allow myself to think of Jack. Not now, not ever again.* Yet a seed of doubt broke through the scarred surface of her heart. She had to tamp it down before it grew and spread. She couldn't allow Jack's sudden return to so profoundly affect her.

Three years ago she'd finally swept him to the far corner of her mind and let his memory turn to dust. Until then she'd held out the foolish hope that he'd return and offer his hand in marriage. But she never heard one word from him.

To recover from Jack she began to dabble in poetry and short stories. When she learned the Settlement House needed additional support, she scribbled dime novels hoping for a few extra dollars to contribute. Much to her surprise, the popularity of her stories grew until Fannie Cole became a sensation. Writing reawakened her interest in life until she gradually pulled herself from the quicksand of despondency caused by Jack's desertion. The Lord gave her a purpose and saved her from despair. He was right beside her when she needed help.

She settled back in the chair and tried to refocus on the conversation which had turned to tomorrow's yachting party she had no desire to attend.

Luncheon dragged on until Lilly thought she'd faint from the strain — not that she'd ever succumbed to a gesture as dramatic as fainting. Her life was normally quiet and she wanted to keep it that way. Unlike many of her more outgoing friends, she hated to draw attention to herself. An incurable introvert, she enjoyed her privacy and solitude away from the bustle of society.

After they all finished their fruit course, footmen pulled back the heavy chairs for the ladies, and the group finally dispersed for the afternoon. Hoping to steal an hour for writing, Lilly headed for the doorway, but Harlan blocked her exit.

"May I speak to you for a moment?" His expression looked grim. But Harlan was a serious man, so his countenance might not signify displeasure. He lightly touched her forearm.

"Yes, of course."

Lilly followed him down the hall and into the empty drawing room. She paused before the marble fireplace, her face stiff from smiling. He appraised her and she squirmed beneath his scrutiny.

"Is there something wrong?" she asked.

He looked more puzzled than angry, but the set of his features, hard as a plaster mask, left her with a sense of foreboding. He dismissed her question with a shake of his head. "There's nothing wrong with me, I can assure you."

She gave his hand a reassuring pat. "I'm glad to hear that." The ticking of the mantel clock measured several seconds of silence.

Harlan tweaked the corners of his sparse blond mustache. "This is awkward." He cleared his throat. "It's Mr. Grail. He seems to be unusually — devoted — to you."

She gave a shrill laugh. "I hardly think so."

"Do you know him well?"

She'd never seen Harlan's jealous side before and she didn't like the change.

"I've known Mr. Grail since he and my brother were students at St. Luke's. Of course, he was mainly George's friend, not mine." Another misleading denial that speared guilt into her heart. But she couldn't admit her past with Jack without creating a melodramatic scene too distasteful to even contemplate. "I haven't seen him in years."

Harlan's face relaxed. "Mr. Grail's attentions disturb me. However, if it's only interest on his part and not yours, then I'm satisfied."

Lilly smiled. "Please don't be concerned about him."

Harlan's lips curled upward. "Then I shan't worry."

"Good."

She couldn't forget how her family's long-time friend had brought her contentment when she believed only her writing could provide satisfaction. When he began to court her and suggest they might share a future together, her pipe dream of Jack returning to claim her as his bride finally faded. She needed Harlan's affection and enjoyed it — until today. She pushed that thought away.

He rubbed his hands together. "Now, I have something for you. It's only a trifle, but I think you'll like it."

"Thank you, but there's no need to shower me with gifts."

"But I *like* to spoil you."

Harlan strode out of the drawing room. Lilly collapsed into one of the antique chairs, newly upholstered in white brocade threaded with gold. A pool of sunshine flooded through the wide windows facing the front lawn. It cast a glow throughout the loveliest room in the house, but it certainly didn't reflect her darkening mood.

How could she reassure Harlan of her love and loyalty? And how could she reassure herself? She'd begin by staying far away from Jack and close to Harlan. Such a simple solution might work if she stayed in her bedroom and wrote her dime novels.

Harlan returned, followed by Irene. As usual, her sister-in-law's eyes glinted with secret amusement.

He thrust a book at Lilly, red-faced. "It's merely a small token of my esteem."

Irene snickered at his discomfort. "Don't fret, Mr. Santerre. We women adore gifts, large and small."

Lilly accepted the volume. "Thank you so much. *Sonnets from the Portuguese* by Elizabeth Barrett Browning. I'll treasure it."

"Perhaps we can read it together." His voice held a note of vulnerability and hope that touched her heart.

"Yes, if you'd like." Lilly feared she might choke on the intimacies of sentimental poetry, but if he insisted, she'd try her best. She'd never admit his kind gesture had failed to quicken her romantic feelings. That was her failure, not his.

Irene murmured, "She'd also enjoy any one of Fannie Cole's stories. Perhaps next time . . ."

Harlan glowered. "You don't mean those trashy dime novels, do you?"

"I do, indeed. What's trash to some is treasure to others." Irene turned on her heel and sauntered out the door with a smug smile Lilly found tiresome.

"That woman is insufferable. I can't imagine why your brother ever married her." Harlan sniffed, shaking his head.

Lilly silently agreed.

# FOUR

Jack climbed the staircase two steps at a time to catch up with Lilly. "What book are you holding? One of Jones and Jarman's dime novels?" He hoped his light tone of voice would bring on a genuine smile. Or at least relax her squared shoulders or the clench of her jaw.

When she halted and flashed a grimace, he knew he'd made a mistake by mentioning the stories she disdained. Like so many in her set, she probably disapproved of popular fiction with minimal literary value — although Fannie Cole's books did have a moral and spiritual dimension most in society refused to acknowledge publicly.

Her hand trembled as she held up *Sonnets from the Portuguese*.

Jack's heart flipped over. "I gave you that book on your eighteenth birthday, didn't I?" They'd spent a glorious spring afternoon reading it together beneath the shade of a chestnut tree. He'd read one verse, she the next until the sun began to slide into evening.

Her cheeks reddened. "This copy is a gift from Harlan." She continued up the stairs and glanced over her shoulder.

The thought of Lilly with Harlan made Jack's throat tighten. He hadn't expected to encounter a rival, but of course he should have known many gentlemen would wish to court her.

"Don't look so crestfallen. I still have yours. I can't bear to part with a book." She gave him a sad smile, turned abruptly, and disappeared into her bedroom.

Jack wondered if she ever read it and thought of him with fondness. Or did she picture him and hurl the book across the room? He winced at the thought. How could he capture her love once again? How could he earn her forgiveness?

He pondered their past relationship, growing less and less hopeful for reconciliation. Yet a few discouraging words wouldn't halt his pursuit. All he needed was a large dose of tact and patience, both difficult for him to come by. But he didn't wish to scare her away and right into the open arms of Harlan Santerre.

Left alone, Jack wandered into the library.

He skimmed through several articles he'd brought from New York as the rest of the household scattered for their afternoon activities. The ladies followed their normal routine of paying calls upon neighbors along Ocean Drive and Bellevue Avenue while Mr. Westbrook dozed nearby in a corner of the library, a mystery novel resting on his lap. His asthmatic wheeze ended the quiet but didn't disrupt Jack's concentration. They'd both declined George's invitation to gather at the Reading Room, Newport's male bastion where women weren't allowed but cigars and whiskey were.

After several hours of studying financial reports Mr. Lewis Jarman had given him, Jack borrowed a golf club and several balls from the game room storage closet and stepped outside into the bright afternoon. On the side lawn, he located the putting green beside the vacant tennis court. He took a few practice swings and relaxed.

"Grail, may I join you?" Harlan appeared at Jack's side a few minutes later, a club in one bony hand and bucket of balls in the other. "I thought I'd practice awhile before my round this afternoon at the golf club."

Jack tapped the ball too hard and it rolled down the hill onto the rocks.

A smirk lifted one corner of Harlan's

mouth. "So sorry, old boy. You can't expect to become proficient overnight. Golf's new to you, I see."

Jack clenched the handle of his club. *Lord, give me patience. Don't let me swing at this supercilious fool.* Jack answered through gritted teeth, aware he must look like a gargoyle, but unwilling to soften his expression. "I learned how to play at St. Luke's. But you're right, I'm a bit rusty." Golf was a gentleman's game of leisure, but he noticed other men mixed business with pleasure at the golf links. He had little time for hobbies and only a modicum of patience for such a slow, plodding pursuit.

Harlan squinted as he gauged the distance to the hole. "That should be an easy putt. I enjoy playing in Newport, but my favorite course is St. Andrews." He paused. "In Scotland."

Jack bit back a smart retort. There was no point in taking umbrage or bickering with Santerre. He watched Harlan's ball roll right into the hole. After years of practice, Harlan played well and, Jack suspected, he played to win.

"I believe I'm finished for the day," Jack said. He gathered a few stray balls, hiding a scowl beneath his cap pulled low over his forehead.

"With practice you're bound to improve," Harlan said.

Jack tried not to react, but his body stiffened. He remembered Harlan's barbs all too well, as if they were back in school, one the son of privilege, the other the son of poverty. Jack tossed several balls into his bucket.

"Do you have a chance to coach?" Harlan continued.

Coaching, indeed. A favorite sport of the rich, racing coaches required an expensive equipage and fine horses, plus time to learn how to drive the thing. Jack shook his head.

Harlan tapped his ball into the hole. "Miss Westbrook adores coaching. It's very exciting for a young lady."

Jack stifled a chuckle. He couldn't imagine Lilly finding enjoyment perched high atop a vehicle with only a thin rail to keep her from plunging to the ground. He could picture her. With knuckles and face white with fear, she'd hold onto her hat and pray for physical deliverance.

"Well, Harlan, I'm shocked. It seems I don't know Miss Westbrook as well as I thought." *And you don't know her at all.* Jack smiled to himself.

"Yes, indeed. She thrives on entertainment only the best society can provide. Sailing, dancing —"

"That's odd," Jack interrupted, the mockery of his frown barely contained. "I thought Miss Westbrook loved books and writing poetry. Perhaps I'm mistaken again. Until today I haven't spoken to her in many years. Perhaps she's changed." With a reserved, yet strong personality, Jack knew Lilly might adapt to new circumstances but never truly alter.

"She was brought up in society, so naturally she appreciates its pleasures. Her books and writings are merely a quaint diversion. A hobby, at most."

"Of course you understand her quite well." Jack bobbed his head in a nod.

"I do, indeed. We spend quite a lot of time together. We're very close."

Every nerve in Jack's body sparked. From the smug look on Harlan's face, he'd just delivered an important message. Lilly belonged to him.

"I must be off. Good day, Harlan."

Jack strode back to the cottage, annoyed that he'd allowed Santerre to sour his mood. The man obviously thought he had a lock on Lilly's affections, but Jack refused to believe she had such bad taste. Only time would tell if he still had a chance to redeem himself.

Before he'd come to Summerhill he thought he could win back her love if she forgave him for his stupid and painful desertion. But now he realized he'd also have to defeat Harlan, a formidable opponent.

Climbing up the veranda steps two at a time, Jack found George seated on a rocker beside a pot of red geraniums. He dropped his newspaper to his lap. "Nothing much going on at the Reading Room, but I did get a tip about a sailboat. I heard she's a real gem. Shall we take a look?" George asked.

"All right. Is she small and affordable?"

George looked surprised. "I seem to remember you always wanted a boat big enough to require a crew, not something 'small and affordable.' "

Jack laughed. "I still do, but I won't be able to make such a purchase for quite a while."

"You'll have to judge this craft for yourself. Shall we go? It never hurts to see what's available."

They rode in a horse and buggy for three or four miles into town and stopped at one of the long piers that jutted into Newport harbor. George found the captain of the *Osprey,* a sleek, two-masted yawl, and altogether, they toured the vessel. Owning such a boat would bestow tremendous prestige, for among the ultra-rich it symbolized belonging and acceptance. But as much as Jack admired the shiny mahogany woodwork, solid brass fittings, and fair price, he knew he shouldn't buy the craft.

"What do you think, Jack? She's a beauty." George appraised the boat from stem to stern with a yearning in his eyes that Jack recognized matched his own.

Jack thanked the captain before they stepped onto the dock. "Definitely worth every dollar. I'm sorely tempted."

He could afford the sailboat, though prudence dictated he wait until his businesses grew into a force to be reckoned with. But he'd never been able to indulge in rich men's toys before and owning the *Osprey* would proclaim he'd arrived.

He remembered sailing with his uncle on a small boat cutting through the waves of Long Island Sound. The salt had permeated his veins forever. The force of wind raking through his hair, the smell of skin tanned by the sun, even the stench of seaweed drying on the rocky beach — he loved it all as a boy. And he wanted to feel those sensations again.

Jack sighed. Realistically, when would he find the time to sail? Now was the time to put his talents to work building a publishing enterprise through his own skill and ingenuity. He couldn't spend his days in idle play like Harlan Santerre or even George. They headed down the long dock toward the carriage. Jack hated to pass up the opportunity to own such a vessel. "It's such a bargain, George, I'll have to give it more thought. Unless you wish to make an offer."

As they stood at the end of the pier and admired the thirty-two-foot boat rolling gently at its mooring, George became quiet as if lost in his own worries. "I'd love to purchase the *Osprey,* but Irene comes first. As it is, I can barely pay for her ball gowns, let alone jewels. I'm afraid I've failed her. She expected a rich New Yorker, but she got me instead." He stroked the point of his goatee.

"She was lucky to snag you."

"Life's ironic, isn't it? When my sister weds Harlan, she'll have endless means but no social ambition. Irene, on the other hand, has little money and a craving for the society that demands it. Life can get all mixed up." George shook his head mournfully. His long jaw sagged into his flagpole neck.

Jack's heart slammed against his ribcage. "Is Lilly engaged to Harlan?"

Despite Harlan's not-so-subtle warning, Jack hadn't realized they were considering marriage. During those hardscrabble years in the Klondike he'd counted on winning Lilly back once he'd made his fortune, though if he'd been honest with himself, he'd have known the odds were slim. How could he have been so arrogant? Of course she wouldn't pine away while he struggled to become a gentleman of means. He hadn't even written her one letter since his spineless departure.

To show her he'd turned opportunity into success, to gain her forgiveness, to win her affection once again — those were the primary reasons he'd come to Summerhill. This news about Lilly and Harlan caught him by the throat, unaware.

"They're not officially engaged, but we're expecting Harlan to pop the question any day now. They've been courting since spring." George cast a suspicious eye at Jack. "Are you surprised Lilly has a beau?"

Jack glanced toward the harbor crowded with sailing ships underway in the brisk wind. "No. She's a lovely girl. I expected as much."

But he really hadn't expected anything of the kind. Abruptly, he turned and boarded the buggy. Just talking about Lilly and

Harlan in the same breath scorched his soul. Disappointed in her taste in men, he was shocked she'd taken a liking to the haughty Santerre. But then again, he'd assumed he still understood Lilly, even after a long separation. Apparently he didn't know her at all anymore.

George climbed into the leather seat next to Jack and took the reins. "I never thought anyone would fall in love with her. She's too standoffish. Not flirtatious like most of the ladies."

"No, she's certainly not like most of them," Jack agreed.

Porcelain skin, intelligent eyes reflecting an honest heart, a direct manner. Lilly possessed a womanly beauty Jack hadn't found in anyone else. He couldn't erase her image from his mind, not that he wanted to.

"Harlan claims she's smart and sensible. She listens to him." George snorted. "He's a solid, dependable man, but he prattles on and on about his railroads. I imagine Lilly is bored to tears. But she's polite, and Harlan, no doubt, mistakes good manners for a keen interest."

"Does she want to marry him?" *Could she possibly love him?* The words adhered on the roof of Jack's mouth, impossible to dislodge.

He still couldn't believe Lilly could fall for a smug, shallow fellow like Harlan Santerre with nothing more to recommend him than an inherited fortune. Though money was more than enough for most young women, he'd thought Lilly would rise above greed and social position. Ha! He'd so hoped she'd wait for him, a poor boy made good returning to her in triumph. He'd certainly miscalculated.

George yanked the sides of his fedora as the breeze threatened to lift it off. "If Lilly didn't want to marry Harlan, she would have dropped him months ago. They're a fine match, one that suits the entire family."

Did the match suit Lilly as well as it satisfied the rest of the Westbrooks? Jack thought she'd willingly sacrifice herself to benefit her brother and her parents.

"How so?" Jack tried to keep the edge out of his voice.

"Harlan has impressive connections in both the business and the social world. Irene adores her new friends who come from the richest families in New York and Newport. And Lilly seems to like all the entertainment as well, though I'm never sure what she really thinks."

"What about your father?"

"He appreciates tips about real estate

coming on the market."

"And you?"

George's face lit up. "Harlan has practically promised me a job."

"I can't imagine you'd enjoy working in an office with Santerre."

George shrugged. "I'd prefer teaching at a preparatory school for boys, but Irene and I need the salary Harlan will provide. He hasn't proposed to Lilly yet, but we're all quite sure he will."

Jack looked away and scowled. Should he step aside like a gentleman or try to win Lilly back? Wouldn't it be wrong to disrupt her plans for an advantageous marriage? Yet he couldn't imagine the self-centered Harlan bringing her one iota of joy.

Like it or not, he'd keep his feelings to himself — at least for now.

# FIVE

The next morning Lilly strolled across the back lawn toward the sea. Chilly from the stiff breeze, she pulled her shawl around her arms.

*Lord, I need You to settle my nerves and bring me through this nightmare. Please don't let me fall in love with Jack all over again. He'll only bring me misery.* She couldn't deny how his presence fluttered her heart and sent her mind reeling. But the Lord would strengthen her to battle her powerful emotions.

The Lord had never failed her. He'd comforted her through the agonizing days after Jack left and eventually guided her into writing. Yet now He seemed so distant, so invisible. *I trust You, Lord. It's not easy at the moment, but I do believe You'll watch over me.* She certainly didn't trust herself. The words of her favorite verse came to mind. *Trust in the LORD with all thine heart; and lean not unto thine own understanding. In all thy ways acknowledge Him, and He shall direct thy paths.* Her spirit calmed.

When Lilly came to the rough boulders that jutted into the surf, she noticed her father standing on the edge, fishing rod in hand. A shabby old vest strained against his round form; baggy pants and a tattered shirt completed the outfit her mother would have discarded had she known it existed. Lilly hiked up her ecru skirt and picked her way across the craggy surface.

As she approached the water, the wind freshened, sweeping her hair out from its topknot and carefully pinned sides. She held on to her skirt before it billowed like a bell.

Papa glanced sideways. "Lilly! Have you come to fish?"

"No, I'm out for some exercise and a bit of solitude."

Papa grunted his approval. "The rest of the family thrives on constant activity, but I can see you still treasure your rare moments of peace and quiet. As do I. This bracing sea air is certainly good for my lungs." He demonstrated by taking deep breaths without his usual wheeze.

"It's a blessing your health is improving."

He sidestepped and made room for her on the giant rock. "I'm glad you joined me,

Lilly. I've been meaning to speak to you but haven't had a chance. Or maybe I just hate being the bearer of bad news."

When she noticed Papa's somber expression, Lilly's muscles tightened. "Is something the matter?"

Papa sighed. His jowls sagged and he looked older than his sixty years. "I'm afraid I've had a financial setback. I'll have to stop contributing to the Christian Settlement House, at least for the time being. Perhaps by the first of the year things will improve, though commerce is always uncertain." He glanced at her sideways, empathy in his eyes.

Lilly swallowed hard. "Oh no, Papa. That's very bad news, indeed."

A sheepish look flickered across his face. "You're upset, aren't you? I can't blame you one bit. The Settlement House counts on me for much of its support, so this was quite a blow to their budget. I know how important their mission is to you and your dear friend Miranda. This morning I telephoned Miss Diller to explain the situation as best I could. The poor woman was almost too distraught to speak."

"I'm sure Miranda will be as well." Friends since childhood, they volunteered together during much of the year. "Does she have other donors in mind?" Lilly refused to think of the consequences of Papa's devastating news. "You couldn't be the only one. Surely there are many other contributors."

Papa's mouth pulled down in a frown. "According to Miss Diller, I'm their primary sponsor. They operate on a shoestring budget with the help of volunteers like you and Miranda. Even with my support they barely make ends meet. I didn't realize my help was so vital." He shook his head. "That makes it all the worse."

"I wish I could contribute more," Lilly murmured. The slap of the wind on her face seemed sharper and wetter than before.

"My dear, you give so much of yourself already — in addition to your donations from your trust fund."

Her monthly stipend was too small to provide much assistance, but she gave it willingly along with significant proceeds from her dime novels. She'd hoped to write less for a while until Harlan settled her future and the disturbing Fannie Cole comments in *Talk of the Town* died down. But obviously this news changed her plans.

Papa looked her straight in the eye. "I'm afraid the place will shut its doors within a month unless they receive a generous contribution."

Lilly sighed. "No, Papa. Not close! What will the poor women do?" She dropped down onto the boulder and winced as the jagged edge tore her white silk stocking.

Papa lowered himself, too, groaning as he awkwardly positioned himself beside her. "I'm so sorry, Lilly. Perhaps we could ask someone to assist with a financial gift. Harlan might oblige."

"Harlan?" Her heart soared for only a second before it plunged downward. "If I ask him, I shall be in his debt. You know how I detest begging for favors."

Papa nodded. "Yes, I know. But if he's to be your husband, he won't mind. Goodness knows he has the money to spare. And the kindness, too, I trust."

There was no point in reminding him that Harlan hadn't proposed as yet. Despite her reservations about marriage, Lilly mustered a modicum of enthusiasm. "I don't think he favors the Settlement House, but of course I'll speak to him — now, if I can find him."

"Good luck, my dear." Papa brightened and then turned back to his fishing.

Lilly strode toward the cottage. No question about it, she needed to pound out more dime novels, though she had hoped for a short break. If she mustered the nerve, she'd ask for more money.

Before she reached the veranda she saw Harlan striding across the grass. She quickened her pace and greeted him with her warmest smile.

"Good morning. You're just the man I hoped to see. May I have a word with you?"

Harlan helped her up the veranda steps. "Of course."

Strolling through the French doors and into the back hallway of Summerhill, Harlan looked more amiable than usual. Her courage bolstered, Lilly plunged ahead. "I hope you'll do me a very important favor, Harlan. Papa is one of the major supporters of the Christian Settlement House, but unfortunately, circumstances require him to cancel his contributions in the foreseeable future. This is catastrophic for them. They'll be forced to close if another donor isn't located."

She stopped, caught her breath, and glanced into Harlan's glacial eyes. "I was hoping, perhaps, you'd see fit to take over for Papa. It's such a worthy cause. And they'd be so grateful for your generosity." She was pleading and she loathed herself for it. But what other option did she have?

Harlan's lips thinned. "Ah, the Christian Settlement House — my cousin Miranda's pet project. Ordinarily I'd say no. I already

76

support all the charities I care to." He gave her arm a condescending pat. "But since you're so fond of the place, for some reason, I'll give it serious consideration." A weak smile flit across his face, bypassing his eyes. "Now if you're not too busy, maybe we can golf today."

Between gritted teeth, Lilly answered, "I'd be delighted." Any sacrifice for the Settlement House seemed small and worth the effort. Harlan knew she disliked golf, but he played well and enjoyed it immensely. "As soon as I change my clothes, I'll be ready to go."

Several hours later, after nine holes in the brisk wind of an approaching storm, Harlan's mood seemed to plummet. On the manicured course of the Newport Country Club, both Jack and George beat him soundly in front of his friends and Lilly, a most unfortunate occurrence. Jack's jaunty step and ear-to-ear grin aggravated Harlan's sour disposition. On the drive back to Summerhill, Lilly avoided the subject of his donation, but Harlan wouldn't be deterred.

"I've come to a decision, Lilly. I'm quite impressed with your loyalty and dedication to New York's poorest. Heaven knows they need all the help they can get." He turned toward her, his face crushed with false regret. "Yet in all good conscience, I cannot advocate a cause which encourages dependence upon the good will of others when self-sufficiency is required. So I must regretfully decline."

Lilly fought to retain her composure. "They're worthy young women, not parasites."

Harlan held up his hand to stop any further discussion. "Nevertheless, my funds are allocated elsewhere."

"I'm" — she paused, searching for an appropriate word — "disappointed." Lilly turned away before a flood of inappropriate words drowned her good manners. She'd try again later when his mood improved.

In the meantime she'd ask Jack, though she doubted with his possible purchase of Jones and Jarman he'd be able to offer any assistance. Yet perhaps he could help in some small way. She'd wait for the right opportunity to broach the subject.

That night Lilly and Harlan conveniently followed Jack into the musicale held at Belcourt Castle. The Louis XIII–style mansion was set atop a first floor stable, which housed Mr. Belmont's horses and collection of fine carriages. An unusual design to say the least, but quite grand, Lilly mused while the violinists tuned their strings.

"What's wrong, Lilly? Did Harlan do something to upset you?" Jack asked, leaning toward her as the three of them took their seats on delicately carved chairs. "You look distraught."

"That's quite enough, Grail," Harlan said. But then a woman on his far side engaged him in conversation.

From behind her open fan Lilly explained the plight of the Settlement House and ignored his subsequent gibe about Harlan. "So you see," she concluded, "they desperately need your assistance."

Harlan, situated on her other side, twisted the end of his mustache and cocked an ear again.

Jack shook his head with obvious regret. "Unfortunately, I plan on using all available funds for my business enterprise. But rest assured, I'll make a small donation first thing tomorrow morning." Jack leveled a gaze at Lilly. "And I'll ask some of my business acquaintances if they'll help too. I'm familiar with the fine work done there." His voice softened to velvet. "The Settlement House is fortunate to have you as an advocate."

"Thank you." Her blush deepened as she lowered her gaze and ignored Harlan's penetrating stare.

Jack leaned across Lilly and tapped Harlan on the wrist. "Say, Santerre, why don't we both contribute to the Settlement House and ease Lilly's concern?" The twinkle in Jack's eyes sent a smile to Lilly's lips which she quickly hid behind her feather fan. "What do you say?" Jack asked and squinted at Harlan. "You're not speechless, are you?"

Harlan sputtered, "Don't be absurd." His mouth twitched in a frown. "I will gladly cover a month's worth of expenses if you'll do the same. That should tide them over until they locate a permanent sponsor for their most worthy endeavor."

"Excellent," Jack said, through gritted teeth.

"Better yet, why not make it two months, until they find a permanent sponsor?" Harlan looked toward Lilly, obviously looking for her approval.

"Fine," Jack said.

"Splendid! I'm very relieved. Thank you so much." Lilly tossed a grateful smile to Jack and then to Harlan. Jack grinned broadly while Harlan seemed to force his small smile. "If both of you search for a benefactor, I'm certain the Settlement House will stay open."

But until that happened, everything the volunteers and staff had worked so hard to achieve stood in jeopardy. This was only a stopgap measure to temporarily solve a chronic financial problem.

She trusted Jack to contact everyone who might donate to such a worthy cause, but she feared he wouldn't have the proper connections. His short time in society provided some rich and influential acquaintances, though probably few who would owe him a favor.

Harlan knew the prominent society players in New York and Newport, so he could raise funds with just a letter or personal visit. Perhaps after more thought he'd reconsider and write a generous check to cover expenses for six months or a year. She hoped they'd both continue their support.

As she fanned herself against the stuffy, humid air, she wondered why Harlan couldn't bring himself to donate an even more generous sum to such a worthwhile institution so desperately in need of assistance. What good was an abundance of money if you didn't use it to eliminate the suffering of others? Yet she was grateful he'd decided to help.

The next morning on her way to the library to find a research book, Lilly was stopped in the hallway by Mr. Ames, the butler.

"You have a telephone call, miss. It's Miss Reid. Do you wish to speak with her?" His ancient voice quaked as his narrow shoulders hunched, caving his chest inward. A devoted servant since Papa wore knickers and slid down banisters, Mr. Ames refused to retire.

"Yes, indeed."

He tottered away while Lilly slipped into the study. The telephone rested on Papa's oak desk. Unaccustomed to using Mr. Bell's marvelous new invention, she studied it for a moment before raising the receiver to her ear, thinking it looked rather like a fancy candlestick.

She cleared her throat and shouted into the mouthpiece. "Miranda, it's wonderful to hear your voice. I do miss you so much — and working at the Settlement House as well. Papa told me he's had to discontinue his support for now. How is Miss Diller reacting?"

Miranda's voice crackled. "She's dreadfully upset. It was an awful shock, but your old friend Mr. Grail and Harlan telephoned earlier to donate funds which will help for a while. That was very thoughtful of Harlan, especially since he doesn't approve of immigrants." She paused for a second. "You asked him to contribute, didn't you?"

Lilly laughed. "Yes, I did and he agreed." She left out the fact that he said no at first.

"You must be terribly persuasive," Miranda murmured. "I wonder why Jackson Grail suddenly donated funds. How odd."

"No, not really. He's staying here for a few weeks as George's guest. I asked him to contribute too."

Miranda chuckled. "Good thinking. But having him at Summerhill must be rather unpleasant for you."

"It's a bit awkward at times. Very awkward, actually. Anyway, is there something I can do to help the Settlement House?" Lilly asked.

Her best friend didn't hesitate. "Yes, that's why I telephoned. I'm so sorry to trouble you while you're in Newport, but to be blunt, we need you here. Miss Diller hopes we can assist her in developing a long-term solution to this financial crisis. Together, perhaps we can come up with a plan. And Florence is out with some lung trouble. Miss Diller was hoping we might be able to cover her English lessons this week."

It felt good to think she might be of some assistance. "I'll gladly come to New York. I've been half-sick here, missing you and the girls. Unless you hear otherwise, I'll arrive tomorrow afternoon — if I can convince

Mama to let me go."

"That's splendid." Miranda sounded relived. "Thank you so much. Do come straight to the Settlement House. I'll meet you there." She paused and then asked the next question so quietly, Lilly barely heard her. "May we speak freely? There's something else you need to know."

The office door was closed, but anyone in the hallway could overhear. "I'm afraid not. Will it keep until tomorrow?"

Miranda replied with a tentative, "Of course. And don't worry. It's probably nothing but my overactive imagination."

Lilly dismissed the tone of her friend's voice and rushed off in search of her mother. She found her on the back veranda with George, Irene, and Harlan lounging on wicker chairs set among a jungle of potted plants.

"Come join us, Lilly." Her mother gestured to a vacant chair, half-concealed by ferns waving in the breeze.

"Thank you, but I don't have much time to chat. Mama, I received a telephone call from Miranda. She asked me to come to New York for a few days to work at the Settlement House. You don't mind, do you?" Of course she knew her mother would mind, very much.

Mama's eyelashes fluttered. "Now isn't the best time." She glanced toward Harlan, whose glower distorted his normally pleasant features, and then she pursed her lips. "You volunteer countless hours during the rest of the year, so you should take time off to enjoy yourself during the summer. Stay here with your family and friends. Miranda is sensible. She'll understand."

Lilly toyed with the lace at her neck. Though she usually followed Mama's wishes to keep peace in the household, this time she couldn't. "Miranda wouldn't summon me unless they truly needed my assistance. So I must go for a short time. I'll return by the end of the week." Lilly excused herself and stepped toward the door.

"Wait a moment, Lilly." Mama's pale skin reddened from the tight collar of her pearl gray dress upward to her hairline. "I suppose if you must go," she sputtered, "it would be all right for a day or two. But you must return for the van Patten's ball. You've accepted their kind invitation, so it would be unforgivable to decline at the last moment."

"Of course."

Before Lilly could escape, Mama added, "The Carstairses are leaving for the city, early tomorrow morning. I'm sure Beatrice would welcome you along. I'll make the arrangements. And do ask Miranda to return with you for a visit."

"Thank you," Lilly said, surprised Mama didn't insist she remain at Summerhill where she could keep an eye on her. But naturally Mama wouldn't argue in front of guests. She simply had to make it appear that it was her plan too.

# Six

The next morning Jack held the telephone receiver to his ear. "Good morning, Mr. Jarman. It's a pleasure to hear from you, although I didn't expect we'd be in contact until I returned to New York. I've been giving serious thought to making an offer."

"I'm delighted. But just yesterday I received another proposal. I wanted you to know since you were the first to show an interest."

Jack's pulse quickened. He'd counted on a few more weeks to study the financial statements for the publishing house. "Oh? May I ask from whom?" His stomach tightened. He could see his hopes slipping away.

"Atwater Publishers."

Their well-established star, Mrs. Elna Price, rivaled Jones and Jarman's rising newcomer, Fannie Cole.

"We're to meet tomorrow morning," Mr. Jarman said.

"I'd also like to discuss a purchase as soon as possible. Would it be convenient if we met late this afternoon in the city?"

They agreed on a four-thirty appointment before hanging up. Jack quickly stacked his clothes in his valise and searched for the Westbrooks. Gathered for a late breakfast, Jack found them lingering in the dining room over oatmeal, poached eggs, and bacon served on fine china plates.

Mrs. Westbrook blotted her mouth with a linen napkin. "Do eat some breakfast, Jackson."

"I already have. Thank you. I'm taking the next train to New York. I need to take care of some pressing business that came up unexpectedly. I'll return in a few days."

A sly smile turned up the corner of Irene's pouty lips. She wore a red frock, guaranteed to garner attention at the casino. An overblown American beauty rose amidst a garden of pale pink and white blossoms.

"How coincidental. Lilly's also in the city. No doubt she'll be thrilled to see you. Don't you agree, Harlan?" Irene asked.

His face hardened, as did Mrs. Westbrook's. He paused and then said in a cool tone, "What are you implying?"

Irene shrugged and fingered the cameo at her neck. "Why, nothing."

"If you'll excuse me, I'll be on my way." Jack bit back a grin as he exited the dining room.

He left within the hour. Traveling comfortably in a first class compartment, he skimmed two Fannie Cole novels he'd borrowed from Irene. Much to his surprise, he enjoyed the misadventures of her brave heroes and sassy heroines. The train pulled into Grand Central Terminal late in the afternoon and Jack disembarked.

He hailed a carriage and rode directly to the Jones and Jarman offices on Broadway. As usual, the city was hot and steamy, teeming with people and all types of horse-drawn vehicles. His cab wove through the tangle of traffic.

When Jack arrived at the publishing house, the long and lean Mr. Jarman led him into his inner office crowded with books and manuscripts piled high on tables, shelves, and floor. A small oil painting of the late Mr. Jones, cofounder of the business, hung on the wall beside Mr. Jarman's picture. He and Jack sat on soft leather chairs as a secretary poured two cups of coffee. Cold lemonade would have suited Jack far better.

The publisher frowned and ran his fingers over his shiny oval head edged with salt-and-pepper hair. Sideburns and a trim beard semi-circled the rest of his face. "Before we begin to negotiate, I think you should read this item." He handed Jack a copy of the scandal sheet *Talk of the Town.*

Jack scanned the paragraph, nothing more than baiting to try and get Fannie Cole to reveal her identity.

With his hands folded on the desk top, Mr. Jarman leaned forward. "I suspect if Miss Cole doesn't reveal her name, Colonel McIntyre will up the ante." His sallow face blushed. "My wife shoves this scandal sheet under my nose quite often, I'm afraid. And since it is in regard to Miss Cole . . ."

Jack stifled a grin. He'd met Trudy Jarman several times socially during the last several months. She was a sweet-tempered busybody who never seemed to miss a word of gossip. But this gossipy item about Fannie Cole certainly was troubling.

Jack leaned forward. "What's Rufus MacIntyre's purpose in revealing her identity?"

"He might have a grudge against Miss Cole or her family. But I suspect he'd rather blackmail her than expose her. He's done it before. If she pays, he'll keep silent, at least for a while."

This complicated the purchase. "Have you spoken to Miss Cole about this?"

With a sigh of frustration, Mr. Jarman

shook his head. "No, she hasn't come into the office in quite a while. And, if *Talk of the Town* is correct, she's summering in Newport. So she probably won't return until autumn."

"Don't you know who she really is?" Jack asked.

Mr. Jarman shook his head. "She comes here from time to time, but she leaves almost as fast as she appears. I hand her revisions, pay her in cash, and then she's off like a scared rabbit. She's heavily veiled, and I've never caught more than a glimpse of her face."

Jack groaned. "I'd like to speak to the mysterious Fannie before I purchase Jones and Jarman. It's imperative for this company that she doesn't quit writing. She needs to know I'll help her deal with that scoundrel, MacIntyre."

"Believe me, I understand your concern."

"How about if I make my offer early tomorrow morning? Will that be soon enough?"

"Excellent." Mr. Jarman rose. "Eight o'clock sharp?"

"I'll be here. Also, would you like to stay on for a while? I'd appreciate your help while I learn the business."

Mr. Jarman nodded. "I'd like that."

They shook hands and Jack started for the door. "I have an acquaintance who volunteers at the Christian Settlement House. A Miss Lillian Westbrook. Do you know her?"

"Haven't had the pleasure, I'm afraid."

"I was visiting her brother in Newport when you telephoned. She's part of the New York and Newport set. It's possible she may even know how to put me in touch with Miss Cole."

"That would certainly be helpful. If you're going to the Settlement House, would you mind delivering a box of books? Miss Miranda Reid ordered several Fannie Cole dime novels for the young ladies."

"I'd be glad to. Do you think they'll still be open at this hour?" It was already past five o'clock.

Mr. Jarman chuckled. "Oh, yes. Miss Diller resides on the premises along with several university students who are dedicated to helping the poor."

Lilly would think he'd contrived this unexpected visit, but he'd gladly endure her displeasure if she assisted him in locating Fannie. She knew so many society people, he felt sure she had some idea of Fannie's real name. And why wouldn't she help unless she felt duty bound to keep the authoress's secret? He'd employ all his powers of persuasion to enlist Lilly's assistance. Jack sighed. If she refused, he doubted anyone else would help him.

He lifted the book carton, hurried down two flights of stairs, and hailed a hansom cab. Tossing the box onto the seat, he climbed inside the carriage and exhaled a long breath. He really wanted to purchase Jones and Jarman, but he needed to know how their most valued writer was reacting to *Talk of the Town*'s veiled threat. He assumed she'd seen the item. Everyone in society read the colonel's scandal sheet, whether they admitted to it or not. But if he couldn't speak to her, did he dare proceed with the purchase? What if Fannie Cole refused any additional contracts?

Jack groaned as the horse wove through the knot of traffic toward the Settlement House. He needed both Lilly and Fannie to cooperate, but he couldn't be sure either one would agree.

When Lilly arrived at the Settlement House mid-afternoon, she hoped to find Miranda alone. But her best friend was busily preparing soup for the evening meal, when dozens of the city's poorest inhabitants would descend upon them, seeking a hot supper. They'd join with the residents and create quite a crowd.

Absorbed in cutting vegetables, the tall, slender Miranda didn't look up when Lilly entered the room. Her abundance of thick black hair was neatly piled on top of her head and covered with a net. A few unruly tendrils escaped on the sides of her pale face splashed with a handful of freckles. Her hair was one of the few things which defied her discipline.

Several other helpers, college students and society women, worked side by side in the tight confines of the kitchen, chatting as they sliced and diced. They often bumped into each other as they moved about preparing the supper. One saw Lilly and called out a greeting.

Hearing her name, Miranda grinned and then hurried over to squeeze Lilly in a hug. She handed her an apron. "Thank you so much for coming on such short notice."

"Believe me, I was happy to escape Summerhill for a few days." Lilly leaned closer over the chopping block and whispered, "I'm anxious to know the news we couldn't discuss on the telephone."

Miranda glanced about the crowded space. "I'll tell you when there aren't so many ladies around to overhear."

Lilly nodded reluctantly. "All right." A

blast of heat from the large black range hit her in the face when a helper removed loaves of bread from the oven. But the delicious aroma made Lilly yearn for just a small piece. With butter and strawberry jam. She wiped beads of perspiration from her brow with a clean linen handkerchief and rolled up the sleeves of her navy blue shirtwaist.

Miranda grinned ruefully. "This is a far cry from Newport, isn't it?"

Laughing, Lilly diced an onion for the vegetable soup. Tears stung her eyes and trickled down her cheeks. Several more of the little domes awaited her. "I haven't even seen the kitchen at Summerhill, though I imagine it's much cooler. But at least here I can help and do some good."

While several other volunteers washed potatoes and carrots, Miranda chopped the celery. Her normally pink cheeks grew rosier as she bent over the opposite side of the chopping block from Lilly. "Only a thousand more pieces to slice and I'll be done."

Making soup for the large crowd expected for supper in the dining hall required a lot of food and preparation. After an hour's steady labor, Lilly tried to hide her weariness behind a smile. Unlike Miranda who helped out nearly every day, Lilly assisted only once or twice a week. If she had a choice, she'd volunteer as often as her friend, but Mama insisted on only the occasional foray into the seamier side of life.

Yet even Mama had to admit assisting at the Settlement House had lifted Lilly's melancholy moods after Jack's defection, though Lilly never confided the cause behind her sudden gloominess. Here she discovered how truly blessed she was despite her misfortune at love.

Miss Phoebe Diller, wiry and quick, swooped into the kitchen, heels tapping like castanets against the wooden floor. She greeted each of the women, thanking them all, encouraging each of them, and then looked toward Lilly and Miranda. "Would you two please come to my office after the soup's on the stove?"

Half an hour later they joined the directress, a pint-sized lady of indeterminable years, though Lilly guessed her age to be somewhere around forty. Miss Diller wore a plain brown dress without adornment, a tight bun scraped back from a plain, heart-shaped face. She never seemed to perspire or lose an ounce of energy, despite the heat. While Lilly and Miranda sat on hard chairs in front of her desk, Miss Diller glanced out the window at a vegetable patch in the back yard. A true Garden of Eden in a rat-infested neighborhood.

Miss Diller turned back to the pair. "Lilly, I'd like to thank you for interrupting your vacation to come back to New York." Her voice rose above the outside clamor of horse cars and voices shouting in foreign tongues.

"My pleasure," Lilly said.

Miss Diller smiled her appreciation, but then her face grew serious. "Your father has been a most generous benefactor for many years and I quite understand why he has to halt his donations. We hope he's suffered only a short-term setback. But if not, I'm obliged to develop a new plan for raising funds." Her face brightened. "We've received contributions from Mr. Santerre and Mr. Grail and we're enormously grateful. Yet their funds won't last indefinitely." She looked at Lilly, then Miranda.

"I'm hoping you ladies might have an idea how to garner more money. I'm at a dead end. Miss Reid, I suspect you know Miss Fannie Cole, the authoress who gives so much to this institution. Would you be able to contact her?"

"I believe I could get a message to her, if you'd like," Miranda answered, unflustered.

Lilly looked away as her face heated, more from the turn of conversation than the humidity. If Miss Diller knew Fannie's true identity, she didn't let on.

"I would so appreciate your assistance. Please ask Miss Cole if she would open her heart once again and donate a bit more, at least until we find other sponsors. I hate to ask her since she's always been tremendously generous, but I must. I'm not too proud to beg when it comes to the Settlement House."

"I shall make inquiries," Miranda said.

"Splendid." Miss Diller clasped her hands at her narrow waist for only a moment before her fingers began to fidget. She paced behind her desk and halted at the bookcase, found a cloth, and began to dust. "Do either of you have friends or acquaintances I might contact?"

Miranda nodded. "Maybe a few. And I'd be glad to canvas the churches near my home. Maybe we could organize a charity ball in the fall."

"The needs are immediate. Perhaps we could even bring together a charity picnic in Newport," Lilly put in. "I can ask Mr. Grail to write an article about the Settlement House in his newspaper. It could feature the girls' wonderful accomplishments and, of course, our need for support."

"A splendid idea. Thank you." Miss Diller

beamed. "I knew you two would be of great assistance."

Lilly steepled her fingers. "And I'll speak to my mother's friends. And some of my own who might have trust funds or willing husbands. And we can all pray the Lord will find a way to keep this place open and solvent."

Miss Diller's eyes brimmed with tears. "You two are God sent."

For the next hour the three planned a picnic to be held at one of the farms on the outskirts of town, often rented for social occasions. Society loved casual picnics where they shed their formalities and relaxed.

"We have a good start," Miss Diller said as the girls rose.

A wave of muggy air carried in the stench of cabbage mixed with rotted garbage from the neighborhood. Lilly breathed easier once she and Miranda hurried down the narrow hallway to a classroom where a group of girls and women gathered for an English lesson. Immigrants from all over Europe chattered in foreign languages. They dressed in dark colors, and some of the older Polish and Russian women wore head scarves tied under their chins.

"Ladies, may we begin?" The room quieted to a hum. Distracted by the sound of heavy footsteps in the hall, Lilly glanced toward the door.

Jack stood there, in business attire, with a top hat resting on a box. He bowed to the group and stepped back into the hall, obviously waiting for her to emerge.

# SEVEN

"I'll take over if you'd like to speak to our visitor," Miranda murmured, obviously recognizing Jack from years before.

Lilly nodded. "Yes, thank you — I think."

Lilly strode into the hallway and found Jack waiting for her. "What a surprise. What brings you here?" Lilly pushed stray pieces of hair behind her ears and patted her chignon, hoping it wasn't askew. She tried to sound collected, but shock rattled her voice.

"I'm looking for Miss Phoebe Diller. I came to New York to meet with Mr. Jarman. He gave me this box of Fannie Cole books to bring over. I was happy to do it."

"How kind of you. I believe Miss Diller is in her office."

"Truth be told, Lilly, I also came to speak to you."

"Oh?" Lilly swallowed hard. "What would you like to know?" She walked briskly down the hall with Jack following close behind.

"I was wondering if you could put me in contact with Miss Fannie Cole, the dime novelist. According to *Talk of the Town* she's in society, so I thought you might know her or at least have an idea of who she is."

"I'm so sorry, but I'm afraid I can't help you. *Talk of the Town* could very well be mistaken."

"I don't believe so."

"No?" She said nothing more as they approached the office, but Jack's raised eyebrow expressed his skepticism.

They entered the directress's cramped room and found her cleaning a window with ammonia and newspaper. After Jack deposited the box on the floor, Lilly introduced him to Miss Diller. She wiped her messy hands on her apron and then reached out a hand to greet him. "I'm so happy to meet you, Mr. Grail. Please thank Mr. Jarman for sending over the books so promptly. The ladies will certainly appreciate them. They love the Fannie Cole stories."

"Ah yes, Fannie Cole." Jack gave her a rueful smile. "When I meet her I'll mention how much the ladies here enjoy her books."

"You intend to meet Miss Cole?" Lilly struggled to keep panic from raising her voice into the upper octaves. *Lord, please don't let Miss Diller mention that Miranda knows her.*

Jack's curious brown eyes angled in her direction. He gave her a little shrug. "I'm her new boss. At least I will be tomorrow morning, when I buy the publishing house." His gleaming smile sent shivers spiraling down her back.

Lilly leaned against a file cabinet, her legs weak. She had so hoped Jack wouldn't purchase Jones and Jarman.

"May I congratulate you on your new acquisition," Miss Diller said. "I wish you every success. Please sit down, Mr. Grail, and tell us more about your new endeavor."

He talked for five minutes without pausing. When he finally wound down, Miss Diller said, "Mr. Grail, I'd like to thank you for assisting us in our hour of greatest need."

"I'm glad to help. If there's anything else I can do . . ."

The directress nodded. "If you happen to know of any potential contributors, perhaps we could ask for their support. We're able to continue operating for the time being, but in the future — well, that's in the Lord's hands." She sighed, the first real sign Lilly had seen that the responsibility of keeping the institution functioning weighed heavily upon her.

Jack rose. His lips pressed tight as he stood still, apparently lost in thought. Finally he said, "I'd like to make a sizable donation, one to give you breathing space for more than a few months."

Lilly's eyes widened. "Where will you get the money if you're buying Jones and Jarman? I thought — I'm so sorry. I shouldn't pry."

"Are you sure you can afford it, Mr. Grail?" Every line of Miss Diller's face registered shock. And eagerness, as if the Lord had dropped Jack straight down from heaven.

*Maybe He had,* Lilly thought. After all, God worked in mysterious ways.

Jack sported a rueful grin. "I put aside money for a sailboat, but there's no reason why that can't wait until next season. Why it's nearly August, so I wouldn't have much use for it anyway, with autumn so soon upon us."

Jack's lighthearted explanation didn't quite cover the disappointment he must feel. Lilly gripped her hands and resisted the urge to throw her arms around him and kiss him for his selflessness.

He twisted the top hat in his hands. "Well, uh, I'll see that you receive the funds tomorrow, Miss Diller. Good day, ladies." He headed for the door.

Miss Diller stopped him. "Please stay and eat supper with us in the dining hall. And if you'd like to see our facilities, I'm sure Miss Westbrook would give you a tour."

"Yes, thank you. I'd like that very much."

Lilly stifled a groan. She needed time alone to process all the disconcerting news Jack brought. Instead, he stood close by watching her every expression. And she knew she didn't hide her feelings too well.

She forced her mouth into a smile. "Follow me. I'll show you our classrooms before supper."

As they paused at each doorway, Lilly commented on the different activities. They observed immigrants learning to read, write, and speak English. Another group practiced sewing on the Singer machines, guiding the fabric while their feet pumped the treadle.

"We need several more sewing machines. There's a high demand for seamstresses in the garment industry. It's low-paying and back-breaking work, but at least it's employment. Sometimes I teach sewing."

"You? Now that's a surprise. Socialites are more apt to pore over their embroidery than a machine. Surely your mother didn't instruct you."

Lilly laughed. "No, of course not. I learned

here. I discovered I had a knack for using the machine and I enjoyed it. Believe it or not, I've even made dresses for some of the little girls in the neighborhood."

When they came to the door of the dining hall she gestured toward a black-haired, olive-skinned child carrying her bowl to the table. "I made Angelina's dress from leftover material I bought from my dressmaker." She gazed at the green plaid garment trimmed with white grosgrain ribbon.

"Now I am shocked. And impressed."

Lilly pretended a reprimand. But really his compliment pleased her. "Really Jack, I'm not a helpless woman." But she couldn't keep from smiling at his surprise.

They entered the dining room where a long line was forming along the wall near the kitchen. Volunteers ladled steaming soup into bowls and handed them to children and adults garbed in old and soiled clothes. Mothers steered their little ones to the long trestle tables covered in clean red-and-white checked cloths and reached for the crusty bread piled high in baskets.

"Shall we get in line?" Lilly asked.

"I'd be delighted to take you out to dinner," Jack said, his voice hopeful.

Lilly shook her head even though his invitation tempted her. She couldn't think of anything more pleasant than spending an evening with Jack. "No, I can't leave my friend Miranda Reid. I'm her houseguest while I'm in New York."

"Of course your friend is invited as well." But he didn't look quite as enthusiastic as before.

"No, I think not. I appreciate your thoughtful invitation, but I'd like to eat here. Please join us. The food is quite good. In fact, I helped make the soup."

"Truly? You continue to surprise me, Lilly." His eyes lit with admiration.

She turned her head until her cheeks cooled. They took their soup over to a table where Miranda joined them a few minutes later. Lilly re-introduced Jack to Miranda. They'd met a few times when he'd visited George — and Lilly — during their college days.

Jack finished the generous portion and said, "Excellent soup, though a bit more meat would help."

Miranda put down her spoon, her expression serious. "It most definitely would, but meat is expensive, so we can't serve it as often as we'd like."

Jack nodded. "I can see the need for more money. But I'd say the Settlement House is doing a remarkable job."

"Miss Diller is a tremendously dedicated Christian woman," Lilly said.

"As are you ladies."

Embarrassed, Lilly changed the subject. "Someday, we'd like to enlist the services of another nurse to expand our hygiene program. And we desperately need more supplies."

Jack nodded. "I shall ask Mr. Jarman to consider making a donation once the sale is complete." He grinned at them both. "After all, my pockets will soon be empty, and his will be full."

"Oh, thank you," Miranda said, smiling at him.

Lilly reached for a piece of hot, fresh bread at the same time that Jack reached for one. Both of them stopped in mid-air. Lilly looked up and found him staring at her. Warmth flooded through her. She apologized, took a piece of bread, then continued with the meal. While barely conscious of Jack and Miranda's conversation, she thought about and was shocked at Jack's altruism. He used to covet things for himself without giving the less fortunate much thought. Not that he was any worse than anyone else she knew. In fact, she's always known she'd fallen in love with a generous man with a big heart. How wonderful that this visit caused him to stop and think. *Thank you, Lord.* She couldn't resist smiling along with Miranda, but then a dark thought gave her pause.

"Jack," she said casually, not meeting his gaze, "do you think it wise to purchase Jones and Jarman? Irene mentioned Miss Cole is being hounded by *Talk of the Town,* so your author may wish to stop writing for a while."

He took time to answer. "It's a risk without speaking to Fannie Cole first, but Jones and Jarman is a solid company with great potential for growth, and there's another buyer in the mix. If I don't move now, I might lose the opportunity."

"What about starting your own publishing house?" Lilly asked, her appetite suddenly gone.

"I'd prefer not to begin from scratch. With the newspaper and magazine, I don't have enough time to develop a new company. Besides, Jones and Jarman already has Fannie Cole under contract."

"I see."

Would both Colonel MacIntyre and Jack soon be on her trail? Apprehension spun her into a tight coil. *Dear Lord, don't let them discover Fannie's true identity.*

After Jack departed for his apartment and the other helpers were busy scraping the dishes into the heap for the compost pile, Lilly whispered to Miranda, "What a shock to see Jack. But if I'm vigilant he won't suspect a thing."

"I'm sure you're right. But Lilly, you may have another problem."

"Oh, no. I don't believe I can cope with one more difficulty." She groaned as she washed the last bowl.

Miranda found a dish towel and dried. "A few days ago an awful fellow stopped me on the sidewalk and demanded I tell him everything I know about Lillian Westbrook. He promised to pay me for information. I'm afraid he was one of Colonel MacIntyre's spies. Fortuately, a policeman was coming down the street at the time, so the rogue fled."

Lilly leaned hard against the counter and cradled her forehead in her hand. She glanced at Miranda. "Please pray all this will go away. I'm living a nightmare and I want to wake up."

"Don't fret. I shall pray for you, my friend, without ceasing."

Jack hired a carriage to drive him to the Dakota out on the Upper West Side of Manhattan. As the tall building came into view, he stared, still amazed that he actually lived here among the elite. His four-room space was tiny compared to some of the twenty-room apartments, but that mattered little to him.

Even after residing at the luxurious Dakota for several months, its high gables, deep roofs, and dormers still awed him. The hired cab halted beneath the *porte cochere* and Jack disembarked. Luggage in hand, he strode through the courtyard and rode the elevator to the fourth floor.

After visiting the Settlement House and viewing the surrounding slums, he scrutinized his own rooms with their soaring ceilings, carved moldings, and gilt. He'd come a long way from his childhood home, but maybe this place was more pretentious than necessary. Sitting alone on a brocade sofa decorated with gold fringe, he once again looked over the Jones and Jarman financial statements, satisfied that the company's potential trumped the risk. But the amount of money he'd spent on this residence troubled him for the first time. And he didn't like the feeling. *Lord, I've forgotten where I came from. Please help me to remember.*

Later in the evening his hunger returned, so he ordered a roast beef dinner from the downstairs kitchen, and soon, it was delivered via the dumb waiter just inside the door of his apartment. When he heard the bell, Jack lifted the door and carried his meal into the dining room where he ate sparingly before heading to bed. He wondered if those he had dined with at the Settlement House also suffered from stomach pains and rumblings. He suspected they didn't have nearly enough in their larders.

Sliding between fresh sheets soon after, he pictured the faces of the people he'd seen today. He pitied them, especially the children, and wished he could do something more to help. When he finally fell asleep, it was a restless sleep.

The following morning Jack bought Jones and Jarman and secured a contribution from Lewis Jarman for Miss Diller's fine establishment.

Two days later he finished his work at the *Manhattan Sentinel* and headed for the train terminal, anxious to return to Newport to search for his novelist. As he strode toward the first class section of the train platform, he spotted Lilly and Miranda Reid sauntering toward the back of the train behind Mrs. Carstairs, one of the New York ladies who summered in Newport. On the side of the Carstairses' private rail car, he glimpsed gold letters spelling out the name Beatrice. *Not a bad way to travel.*

Jack watched Lilly, Miranda, and Mrs. Carstairs follow uniformed porters to the door of their car. Lilly turned to speak to two small children, smiling at them as she did so. Miranda paused from the entrance of the car, looking back in her direction. Then without warning a man pushed his way through the crowd and stepped directly in front of Lilly, blocking her path. The fellow said something that seemed to frighten her because she glanced around, no doubt searching for help, then tried to sidestep to the safety of the train. Jack increased his pace, sprinting the last few yards. He feared the stranger in the plaid sack suit and brown derby might grab Lilly's reticule and run.

As Jack approached he heard the man's rough voice, but he couldn't distinguish his words.

Lilly poked him in the leg with her parasol. "Leave me alone at once and don't ever contact me again."

Yelping, the man glared but refused to budge. Jack grasped him by his lapels and pushed him over to a pillar. "You heard the lady. Get out of here."

The man stuttered, "All right. Let me go."

As Jack released his grip, the man broke

away and dashed through the terminal. Jack turned back to Lilly.

"Thank you so much," she said with a shaky voice. "What a horrid rogue."

Jack nodded. "Why was he harassing you? Did he want money?"

"No, actually. Well, it doesn't matter. I'm just grateful you were here to get rid of him."

Mrs. Carstairs came forward. "Are you quite all right, my dear? I thought you were directly behind me! One never knows the riffraff one might encounter . . ." She lifted her eyes from Lilly to Jack. "You're Mr. Jackson Grail, aren't you? I believe you're acquainted with my daughter Eloise."

He bowed. "Yes, ma'am. I am."

"That was very good of you to come to Miss Westbrook's aid. Are you returning to Newport on this train?"

"Yes. I've concluded my business in New York for the moment."

"Please join us in my rail car," she said gesturing toward the *Beatrice*.

Lilly blanched, but added, "By all means. We'd so enjoy your company."

He couldn't pass up the opportunity to ride in a fancy rail car — with Lilly. "Thank you. I'd like that."

Boarding the last car after the ladies, he

gaped at the rococo interior. He noted a frescoed ceiling, tasseled damask curtains surrounding the wide windows, and a blue velvet sofa that matched two sturdy chairs. At one end of the car stood a piano.

"Come with me," Mrs. Carstairs directed. She led them down a passageway with bedrooms on either side. Jack looked into the one she assigned to him, a compact room paneled in mahogany with a double bed boasting a brass head- and footboard, a chest of drawers, and a desk.

"The kitchen and dining room are at the other end," she explained.

For all his altruistic intentions, he had to admit he still craved luxury, though not on such a grand and garish scale. Depositing his luggage on the carpeted floor, he looked about the room fit for a prince, or at least a captain of industry.

"This is quite luxurious," he said.

"Oh, do you think so? I've about decided to refurbish the entire rail car. It's not quite up to standard."

Jack withheld a wry twist of his mouth. Would he soon adapt to this privileged life and fret over the most mundane inconveniences and imperfections? He certainly hoped not.

*Lord, please help me to remember where I*

*came from and where You want me to go. Don't allow me to be sidetracked by things I've never had and don't require.*

"It's impressive as it is, Mrs. Carstairs. But if you do remodel, perhaps you'd consider donating what you don't want to the Settlement House. They're always in need."

"What a splendid suggestion. I shall do it."

"Thank you." Jack grinned. "I guarantee Miss Diller will be grateful for your generosity."

The tiny woman touched his arm lightly. "You are a most unusual young man, Mr. Grail. Any young lady would be fortunate to have you for a husband."

His smile dimmed. He didn't like the gleam in her eye.

# EIGHT

As the train sped through Connecticut, Jack watched the rain splatter against the windows and stream down the glass. Miranda entertained them with several piano pieces while Lilly read a Henry James novel. Mrs. Carstairs focused her attention on Jack until she finally admitted the dreary day had made her sleepy. She adjourned to her bedroom, much to Jack's relief. The lady incessantly chattered about her unmarried daughter, Eloise, whom he vaguely recalled as eager to please but rather clumsy.

"Lilly, would you join me in a game of checkers?"

"Yes, of course." She smiled politely. "Jack, I'm quite eager to help Miss Diller locate funds for the Settlement House. I thought you might be willing to help us. If you wrote an article about their achievements in your newspaper —"

Jack put up his hand. "I'd be glad to. A

bit of publicity would surely bring positive attention to their cause."

"Thank you so much."

He set up the board he found on a small table by the window. The overhead and table lamps burned brightly, dispelling the gloom, and the low, domed ceiling added a touch of intimacy to the car. They each moved their pieces twice before Jack placed his elbows on the edge of the board and leaned across the narrow expanse.

"Lilly, I'd like to tell you about my new venture, if you don't mind. As an avid reader, I'd appreciate your perspective."

"Please, do," she said, then lowered her gaze to the board.

Although her tone wasn't encouraging, he forged ahead. "I've decided to take Jones and Jarman in a new direction. We're holding our own, yet we could be so much more. With a few changes we could become a premier publishing house and far surpass our competition."

He moved his red checker toward her black one. She jumped it. She seemed to be concentrating more on the game than on his words.

"All I need to do is expand one of our lines. It's a matter of which one, the romances or the westerns. Westerns are selling fairly well, but the love stories are floundering — except for Fannie Cole's novels. They've taken off because she's very gifted." Jack moved his checker and jumped Lilly's. Twice.

He watched her stare at the board, holding her breath. Her full lips went white, and a film of perspiration glistened on her forehead. A rather extreme reaction, he noted, to his double-jump — or was it because he mentioned Miss Cole? He pressed on, staring at her. "But Miss Cole's public is clamoring for more of her — more stories, more information of a personal nature. They want to get to know Fannie Cole, the real woman."

Her mouth pursed. "That sounds intrusive to me." She kept her gaze fastened to the board as if those red and black squares held the answer to all of life's problems. But she didn't make a move.

He shrugged. "Perhaps, but it would help us sell books if she came forward and met her public. And I'd see to it myself that she wasn't exploited."

"Going public?" She swallowed hard. "Don't you think that's asking a lot of her? She might cherish her privacy." Fiddling with the jabot of her lacy white blouse, Lilly leaned away from the table, avoiding his stare.

"Our closest competitors, Atwater Publishers, flaunt their star, Mrs. Elna Price, and believe me, it's paid off. Her writing isn't half as good as Fannie Cole's, but she's a star. And that's what I want Fannie to become, the brightest star in the publishing galaxy. She's already a sensation. Stardom, that's what I'm after for her."

Lilly cheeks flared with color. "Obviously she prefers anonymity."

"Yes," he conceded, "right now. But I'm sure if we spoke, I could convince her to change her mind. A little dose of publicity would be in her best interest as well as mine."

"When you locate her, you can mention it."

Jack expelled a long groan. "As I've said before, I don't know who she is. Lewis Jarman tells me even he doesn't know her real name."

Lilly leveled a glare. "Leave her alone, Jack. Obviously she doesn't want to be found."

Why was Lilly so defensive on Fannie Cole's part? What was it to her? Perhaps her sensibilities were offended by the genre. He bent over the board, leaning so close he could drink in her sweet breath and floral scent. Jasmine, he thought. "That's the problem. If she doesn't come forward and agree to some publicity, I'll have to drop our line of romance dime novels and concentrate all our resources on the westerns."

Lilly's eyes widened. "You'd do that without consulting her first?" Seemingly flustered, she moved her checker piece with little consideration.

He raised his hands in frustration. "If I can't find her, I can't explain the importance of her cooperation, now can I?"

He slapped his checker down and jumped her black ones again and again and again. Lilly winced.

"All my money will now be tied up in my publications, especially Jones and Jarman. I need Fannie Cole to embrace her fans. Fannie is our only hope of competing with Atwater Publishers. Otherwise, I need to move on to developing our western line."

"You're putting a lot of pressure on her." Lilly's chair scraped against the floor as she pushed it back and rose. "You've always been a shrewd man. Perhaps you can think up another solution — one that doesn't involve Miss Cole."

"Where are you going? Please, sit down. Don't run off."

"I know your publishing house is important to you, but I'd rather spend my time discussing something besides books and authors."

Jack wasn't sure why, but Lilly seemed jittery. And since when had she distained a discussion about books?

She started for the door leading to the bedroom compartments.

He'd take one more stab at obtaining her assistance. "Lilly," he said softly, reaching for her arm. As soon as she turned, he dropped his hand. "Please — do you know Fannie Cole?"

If Fannie were her friend, Lilly wouldn't want to disclose her name. But he also knew that the unfortunate matter with *Talk of the Town* wouldn't vanish all on its own. Fannie needed an advocate and who better than her publisher?

Lilly grabbed the top of the chair with unsteady hands. "I don't know why you'd think I would know Miss Cole. Now you must excuse —"

"I was counting on you to help me find her. You know so many in the New York and Newport set. I thought you might at least have an idea about who she might be."

"As you've said yourself, Fannie Cole's identity is a mystery. Let it stay that way."

Jack studied her flushed face. Lilly knew Fannie Cole. She had to know her, by her reaction. "Lilly, I must locate her. And soon. It's not just for my sake. She may need advice about handling Colonel MacIntyre and *Talk of the Town.*"

"I'm sorry, Jack, but I can't help you." Starting toward the door, she glanced over her shoulder. "One more thought. You might consider curtailing your ambition somewhat. Do you really need to be the biggest and the best publishing house in New York?"

He touched his cheek, feeling like he'd just been slapped.

More than anything he wanted to explain, but he refused to pour out his heart to a woman who apparently had no comprehension of his struggle against poverty and the nagging fear of its return — a battle he had fought, partially on her account. Without ambition, a poor man would never rise in this world to a position of substance and respect. Without ambition, he would've never returned with the idea of winning her heart again.

Of course many others were far more deprived than he had ever been. At least he had a loving family who walked with the Lord, a gift from his beloved pa and his mama. But was it wrong to seek a better life? He'd worked hard to acquire Jones and Jarman and now he'd work even harder to make it prosper.

Jack watched Lilly retreat into the hallway, head held high, shoulders stiff. He'd have to find a way to change her mind.

He sat down heavily and stared out the window. Elna Price strung together cliché after cliché, but nobody seemed to care. Her readers reveled in her penchant for scarlet dresses with plunging necklines and outrageous remarks that made her fans blush and laugh all at the same time. She gave romantic dime novels a bad reputation. Fannie's dialogue was crisp, her narrative filled with imagery. She evoked emotion, not melodrama. Yet she wouldn't reach the heights of Elna's popularity without acknowledging her public.

As Jack gathered the checkers, he wondered if he really had a chance of either winning Lilly's heart or finding out who Fannie Cole really was. Harlan was about to propose marriage and Lilly appeared poised to accept. Jack felt like an intruder, an unpleasant reminder of the past for Lilly. Was it fair to her to tarry? To hope? To pine?

Lilly returned to the bedroom Mrs.

Carstairs had set aside for her, thankful for the solitude. Jack's presence threw her thoughts into turmoil. She picked up her Bible and turned to Psalms, but she couldn't focus her mind on the words. Glancing at the rain streaming down the window, she blew out a sigh. A knock on the door startled her.

A quiet voice said, "It's Miranda. May I come in?"

"Please do."

The train swayed, pushing Miranda off balance. She staggered into the compartment and dropped onto the double bed covered with a mauve satin spread, laughing at her graceless entrance.

"My, you look upset," she said, her laugh fading. "Tell me what's troubling you." Miranda unlaced her walking shoes, kicked them off, and curled her legs beneath her forest green skirt. She unbuttoned the fitted jacket of her travelling suit. "It wasn't Jackson Grail, was it?"

"Actually, yes."

Miranda looked askance. "He saved you from a ruffian not two hours ago. One of Colonel MacIntyre's horrid spies, I believe. You were so grateful for Jack's intervention. What happened to change your attitude toward him?"

Lilly groaned as she buried her head in her hands. "He's pushing me to help him find Fannie Cole so he can convince her to promote her dime novels."

"Oh my. You can't very well do that."

Lilly nodded. "You're most definitely right. I'd like to help his business succeed, but without exposing myself to ruin, I can't do a thing."

"I have to say that his work ethic is quite admirable. Most of the men we know would have taken that Klondike fortune and made themselves professional men of leisure. And he is assisting us at the Settlement House . . ."

Lilly shot her a look. "I'm well aware of that. But so am I, as Fannie Cole! And if he forces me to embrace my public, then it will destroy my private life. How do I possibly choose that? Can you imagine my mother's reaction? My father's?" She laid back on the bed with a sigh.

"You're falling for him again," Miranda said, eyes wide.

"Of course not," she retorted. "What we had was purely in the past." Lilly glanced at her and then threw up her hands. "I just told him he ought to curb his ambition, set his goals upon lesser heights. Does that sound like a woman in love?"

"It sounds like a woman striving to keep a man at bay. Jack's always been determined to succeed in business. You know that, Lilly, better than anyone."

"I know that he's always put his goals for stature above his heart. That's what I know." Lilly sighed again, heavily. "I can't see what's best here. Should I confess to my true identity and then plead for his understanding? That's the easiest solution, but I don't know if I can trust him to keep my secret. He might very well place his best interests above my own."

"He seems . . . changed. Grown, somehow. Can't you give him another chance?"

Lilly eyed her. "As my publisher or as a beau?"

Miranda's eyes widened, considering. "God forgive me, Harlan . . ." she whispered to the ceiling, as if her cousin could hear her. "Maybe . . . both?"

Lilly held her breath a moment and then shook her head. "I don't think I should chance it. On either front."

The memory of Jack proposing and then leaving her evoked unending sorrow, as deep as a grave. How could she know if he'd cheat her of happiness once more?

"If I were you, I'd pray long and hard." She took Lilly's hand in hers. "God will

127

show you the way. Wait upon Him."

"Yes and I draw comfort from knowing I'm doing the Lord's will with my writing. Somehow I'll avoid detection, even if I have to deal with Jones and Jarman entirely by mail. I can't risk meeting Jack in his office. When I return to New York in September, I'll rent a post office box."

Time would tell whether or not that would work well. Yet it was the only plan she could conjure up as her world began to slowly squeeze in on her.

Lilly avoided Jack for the rest of the journey by remaining in her room. On the carriage ride from the depot to Summerhill, Miranda generously kept up a constant chatter with Jack while Lilly gazed at the scenery. Once home she vanished to her bedroom and spent the rest of the day and evening working on her newest novel, *A Garland of Love*.

The following afternoon she wandered into the deserted library ready for a respite after a morning walking along Bailey's, Newport's most exclusive beach, picking her way among the heavy seaweed, arm in arm with Miranda.

She picked up a copy of the local newspaper from a marble table and settled into a cushioned chair.

The newspaper headline jolted her like an electric shock. *Elna Price to Autograph Books.* Mrs. Price in Newport? She reread the boldly printed caption and then skimmed the article. *The ever popular author of dozens of dime novels will autograph her latest title at Aquidneck Books and Stationery, Thames Street, this afternoon between the hours of two and four o'clock.*

Lilly dropped the newspaper onto her lap. She'd love to glimpse what a famous novelist endured, dealing with her public. Did Mrs. Price enjoy chatting with her readers while she inscribed her name in books until her hand grew numb? Or did she grit her teeth and pretend to thrive on the jostling along with the admiration?

She'd wager Jack would like to organize a similar event for Fannie Cole and capitalize on her popularity for his own profit. No doubt he'd try to force her into the limelight just to sell more books. But in case she was wrong about the horrors of publicity, she really ought to go and see for herself — not that anything would change her opinion.

The grandfather clock in the foyer chimed one-thirty, time for Mama to send a maid to fetch her for a luncheon engagement at Beechwood, the summer home of Caroline Astor, the widely acknowledged queen of society. Lilly rose. She either escaped now to Elna's signing or not at all.

Quick footsteps in the hallway signaled Mama was nearby, no doubt in search of her daughter or daughter-in-law. Without a second thought, Lilly peered out the library door and spotted Mama entering the conservatory. Lilly flew up the staircase to her bedroom, grabbed her hat and reticule and hurried back down. She rushed out the front door into the sunshine, her heart beating double-time. As she strode across the lawn to the stable, she pinned the nondescript straw boater to her head with shaking hands. She didn't dare glance over her shoulder in case someone waved her back home. If only Miranda hadn't gone to the Redwood Library for a lecture on the effects of poverty, they could've ventured to the book shop together.

Once the carriage rolled out onto Ocean Avenue, Lilly's nervousness abated. She'd successfully escaped from Mama and all her questions and social rules. Lilly grinned, satisfied at her accomplishment. It would do her good, professionally speaking, to understand how other authors coped with public exposure. Of course she'd faint if any of her friends or acquaintances spotted her pushing through the crush of dedicated fans, especially after denying any interest in sensationalist fiction. But she didn't expect to see anyone she knew at the book signing. Society ladies claimed romantic dime novels were written for servant girls, not for refined women who appreciated literary works.

She'd heard Mrs. Price included no moral precepts in her stories which reduced them to titillating trash. That was hearsay, however. She'd never read any herself. Fortunately Fannie Cole provided an alternative to Mrs. Price's type of dime novel, although many people lumped all the books together into one category — disreputable fiction. Mama certainly did.

Lilly's coachman reined in the horses and pulled up to the curb in front of the book shop. A line of women snaked around the entrance to the store. Laughter, loud Irish brogues, and clipped Yankee accents mingled with the clatter of carriages and carts. Everyday dresses made from inexpensive cloth without ribbon or lace defined most of the women as average townsfolk. As the crowd inched forward, Lilly scanned the unfamiliar faces. Although they'd never recognize her, she kept her eyes down and yanked her short mesh veil to the tip of her nose.

Ten minutes later she passed the plate

glass window and entered the busy store. Mrs. Price sat straight ahead, bent over a copy of her book, pen in hand. Lilly caught a glimpse of her plum satin dress, cut low, and titian hair frizzing beneath a large hat trimmed with silk violets, black lace, and an immense purple plume. Suddenly the author rose to her feet, chin jutting forward, arms spread wide. A hush fell over the audience.

"Ladies," she boomed, her gaze traveling from one fan to the next, "my publisher, Mr. Sterling, and I are most appreciative of your overwhelming hospitality." She gestured toward the white-whiskered man beside her. "When we came to your fair town today we had no idea how kindly you'd treat us. Your support for my novels brings tears to my eyes." As if on cue, her eyes glistened. A few teardrops rolled down her slightly shriveled cheeks. "Thank you so much for your outpouring of love."

Hands clapped in a deafening roar.

Elna raised her palms and the crowd quieted. "As I meet you and autograph your books, please write your name and address on the slip of paper we've provided. At the end of the signing, I shall pick a name out of my hat." She pointed to her headgear. "The lucky winner will receive a copy of one of my most beloved books, *Flames of Love.* However, if you don't win the prize, we have copies you may purchase. I know you don't want to miss this thrilling tale which I have penned just for your enjoyment."

Another round of applause broke out. Women rushed forward, jostled each other for position, and snatched books off the table, thrusting them at Elna for signature. Her laughter rang above the voices of the crowd. "Thank you so much for your affection, ladies."

Lilly stepped aside, ready to leave this theatrical event. She'd seen more than enough to convince her that she didn't find mob adulation appealing. She shuddered to think this was the kind of publicity Jack wanted Fannie to embrace. Raucous crowds, tours in strange cities, shaking hands, and signing autographs would rob her of her privacy. She'd never take part in such a distasteful task. And Mama would die of humiliation to see her daughter make a public spectacle of herself.

Turning, she made her way out the door just as the line surged forward. A nudge from behind pushed her off balance and she stumbled into the back of a gentleman. Jackson Grail.

"What are you doing here?" she muttered. Her legs wobbled and her hands shook.

Jack chuckled. "I could ask you the same question." He hiked an eyebrow, obviously amused by her discomfort.

"I came to buy — Irene — an autographed copy of Mrs. Price's new book. I thought she'd appreciate the addition to her library of — dime novels." A stack of cheap novels hardly qualified as a library of any sort. Would he believe her? Her excuse sounded so ludicrous. "And you? Did you come to purchase a book?" Picturing Jack engrossed in an Elna Price story brought on a broad smile, in spite of herself.

Jack leaned forward and murmured in her ear, "I do have to keep up with the competition, you know. I'm here to see how well publicity works for Atwater Publishers. I expected to find crowds of fans lined up to fill the coffers and I was right." His face split in a satisfied grin. "A book tour would work equally well for Miss Cole."

Lilly gave a grudging nod, then spoke softly. "I can see publicity is effective. And Mrs. Price thrives on the attention. Your Miss Cole may not." Lilly wove through the congestion and out into the warm, briny air of Thames Street. Her gray serge walking suit felt much too hot for the afternoon

134

weather.

Jack followed one step behind as she headed toward her carriage. "I also wondered if Fannie Cole would appear."

Lilly's breath rushed out of her lungs. "Well, did she?"

He shrugged his square, muscular shoulders encased in a navy jacket of the finest merino wool. "I thought Miss Cole might come out of curiosity. Unfortunately I didn't see any cottagers here, unless she arrived incognito."

"I didn't spot anyone I know, either."

"Then that leaves you, Lilly."

Taken aback, she coughed up a nervous laugh. "Do I look like a novelist to you?"

He tilted his head and narrowed his eyes, much like a dressmaker gauging measurements. "Perhaps you do."

"Nonsense. I'm a would-be poet. Please excuse me. I must go." Lilly headed down the sidewalk. She waited on the corner while her driver made his way down the congested street, weaving through a knot of carts and carriages.

Jack must have lengthened his stride because he reached out and lightly touched the sleeve of her jacket. "Lilly, I was joking. I'm sorry I offended you."

She breathed with relief at his half contrite, half mischievous smile and didn't brush off his hand. "That's all right, Jack. I'm afraid I'm on edge lately. Do enjoy your afternoon."

With Jack's help, she boarded her carriage and sunk into the plush cushion. Despite the shock of running into him, she felt glad she'd come to the book shop. Seeing the flamboyant and rather common Mrs. Elna Price reinforced her determination to remain out of sight. Never would Jack convince her to become a sideshow, a Lillian Russell of the literary world.

As the carriage jolted forward, Lilly closed her eyes and let her worries temporarily diminish.

# NINE

Half an hour later Jack found Lilly crossing the foyer on the way upstairs. He bowed and handed her Elna's newest bestseller. "Here you go. I noticed you forgot to purchase a copy for Irene. It's even autographed."

Lilly's eyes widened, but she quickly recovered with a polite nod, her social mask securely in place. "Oh dear, I did forget. In my haste to get away from the crowd, I forgot all about Mrs. Price's novel." Then her taut shoulders relaxed. "Thank you so much for your thoughtfulness, Jack. I'm sure Irene will enjoy the book."

"No doubt." If Irene didn't care for Mrs. Price's story, Jack knew the servants would. "But won't Irene be shocked you ventured down to Thames Street on your own and mingled among the townspeople?"

Lilly blanched. "Yes, she might, though knowing my sister-in-law, I'm sure she'll be amazed I had the gumption to go by myself. She thinks I'm afraid of my own shadow — or at least, of Mama's disapproval — which, of course I am, most of the time." Her mouth curved in a wry smile.

Others might consider Lilly timid, but Jack felt sure beneath her shy exterior lay a woman with a steel backbone. A lady strong enough to write a book her family and friends would disparage . . . Jack considered this a most interesting possibility.

Avoiding Jack wasn't as easy as Lilly hoped. Even in a "cottage" with twenty-two spacious rooms, she seemed to bump into him every time she turned around, unless she hid in her bedroom. He began to shadow her, obviously hoping to change her mind about helping him locate his authoress. Lilly sighed. Annie brushed Lilly's thick hair in preparation for the evening's frivolity at the van Patten's, then secured it with silver combs.

This was one of the many social functions Mama insisted she attend. In the spring when Harlan had first introduced the family to the upper echelons of society — truly the most elite — Lilly had enjoyed the novelty of extravagant balls and dinners along with her family, but as the round of entertainment pressed on night after night, she'd grown weary. With less time and energy for writing, she knew she was beginning to fail at the one important task God had given her.

Lilly bowed her head while Annie, her maid, clasped a double string of pearls around her neck.

"You look lovely, miss."

Lilly examined her reflection in the dressing table mirror and found it wanting. She'd thought the yellow silk with lace overskirt suited her well enough when she'd chosen the fabric two summers before. Now it appeared not only outdated, but wrong for her pale complexion. Too fussy with too many bows, the frock would better suit an eighteen-year-old experiencing the last days of girlhood. She sighed. Nothing could be done about it now.

Only four other ball gowns filled her wardrobe and she'd worn them all this season. If she'd accepted Mama's earlier offer for a few more frocks, she could have replaced this with one simpler and more elegant. But she hadn't cared for fancy dresses even a little bit until Harlan began to court her. And she hadn't anticipated so many dinners and dances that required an extensive and fashionable wardrobe.

Mama, seated beside her on the slipper chair, patted Lilly's long white glove. "Don't fret, my dear. You've never looked more beautiful."

She smiled, embarrassed at the compliment. "Thank you, but I'm not so sure."

As soon as Annie withdrew to Lilly's dressing room, Mama tilted forward. Her round eyes grew even rounder. "I hope you don't mind my asking, but did Jackson go to the city after you? You left to help at the Settlement House, and next thing I know, he's off as well."

"No, Mama. He merely needed to be in New York at the same time. It was a coincidence that his purchase of Jones and Jarman happened at the same time."

Her mother studied her intently for a moment, then sniffed and adjusted a lock of Lilly's hair. "Years ago when you were young, I was convinced he was smitten — that is, until he suddenly left. You never told me exactly what happened."

Lilly adjusted a few strands of her hair, avoiding Mama's probing gaze. "It wasn't just you, so don't feel slighted. Besides, whatever was between us is long over."

"Oh Lilly, why are you so secretive about everything? We're mother and daughter, we should share intimacies."

"Perhaps, but there's little to share about Jackson Grail." She trusted Mama but still knew she tended to chatter too freely with her friends.

Mama's eyes sharpened. "You're not going to cast aside Harlan for Jackson, are you? He certainly doesn't have the same entree into the best society that Harlan has."

"I understand that." Lilly gave her mother a small but reassuring smile. If she mentioned she wasn't interested in society, Mama would get upset and try to change her mind.

Her mother rose and with a sigh of resignation glided toward the door. "I must go. Do enjoy the ball."

Lilly gathered up her reticule and fan, and then made her way to the foyer to wait for the coachmen to bring around the carriage. The grandfather clock struck ten. No one in the family had appeared yet, so she wandered off to the library, where she met her father. He spent much of his time perusing the classics along with current mystery novels and, against doctor's orders, puffing on his pipe. The sweet aroma of expensive tobacco greeted her as she entered the room.

A wisp of white gossamer hair stood straight up on his shiny scalp. The once formidable tycoon looked old and shapeless, though his suit was perfectly tailored, as always. He slouched in his favorite leather chair, worn and crinkled like Papa himself.

"Off to the ball, my dear?" Cast in the shadows of the gaslight, his face looked mellow but his eyes glistened, as observant as ever.

Lilly's spirits lifted. After suffering several asthma attacks during the spring, Papa's fragile health worried her though he claimed the sea air cleared his lungs. "We're all going, except for Mama, of course."

"She's not very interested in dancing. Never has been. That's fine with me." Papa leaned forward. "Lilly, I don't catch many opportunities to speak to you these days. I'm glad you're enjoying Newport and keeping company with Harlan. He's a responsible man, and he'll provide handsomely for you and my future grandchildren. Now don't go and blush." His soft chuckle changed into a cough from the curls of smoke wrapped around his head. "It's just a matter of time before he asks me for your hand. Shall I agree to his offer? Eh, my dear?"

She couldn't deny Harlan seemed serious about marriage. Hints dropped from time to time had developed into pointed remarks about joining their lives together. Few gentlemen had shown an interest since her breakup with Jack, though admittedly she'd kept every potential husband at bay until Harlan appeared. She hoped that too many years without a real suitor hadn't made her unduly susceptible to Harlan, the first appealing man who'd come along in years.

"Harlan is kind and generous. I could do worse."

Papa nodded vigorously. His lips curved into a smile. "Yes, indeed. And he's giving you and George and Irene an opportunity to meet some of the finest and most influential people in town. They seem very pleased." He took another puff and then groaned with apparent regret. "Your mother and I should have mingled more in society, but we really didn't have the means to keep up with the *nouveau riche.* It's expensive to entertain on such an outlandish scale. Why I heard the costume ball the Bradley Martins held back in '97 cost them hundreds of thousands." He shook his head in bewilderment. "We couldn't compete with that kind of extravagance. But it would've been an advantage to you and George if we'd gotten out a little more."

Lilly kissed him on the forehead. "Oh Papa, you never deprived us of anything.

You certainly gave me all I ever wanted."

He smiled. "Thank you for saying that, but I'm not so convinced George — and Irene — would agree with you." He reached over and gave her hand a quick squeeze.

"Yes, they would. Now put out that pipe before Mama catches you."

He slowly removed the offending object from his mouth, but she knew the moment she left, he'd start smoking again.

"Is there anything I can get for you before I go?"

"No thank you, Lilly. I'm just fine. Now run along and have a wonderful time with your young man."

She nodded. Without Harlan, her family would've received only a handful of invitations over the summer from their stuffy, tradition-bound set and no invitations from society's top drawer. But now even Mama was caught up in the whirlwind of constant entertainment, though she joined in the society's amusements with more reticence and less frequency than George and Irene.

Yet, was thankfulness to Harlan a firm enough foundation for a successful marriage? It certainly seemed to be for many in her clique. But was it sufficient for her?

Vanessa Westbrook strolled into the library

as her daughter departed in a swirl of lace and jasmine scent. Most becoming. No wonder George's old friend Jack seemed as taken with Lilly as Harlan was. Vanessa approached her husband, waving away a fog of aromatic pipe smoke that she secretly loved to inhale. Settling into the wing chair beside Thomas, her feet poked out beneath her beige silk frock and dangled a few inches above the oak floor. She frowned at the pipe resting conspicuously on the ashtray but refused to say a word. Thomas knew her opinion on smoking and asthma and never appreciated a reminder.

Grasping her hands as if to ward off any approaching lecture, he asked, "So, Nessie, are you enjoying your summer in Newport?"

"Yes, indeed. Newport society is a little too rich for my blood, but the sea air is delightful and doing us all a world of good. How's your breathing?"

Thomas drew in a mouthful of air, released it, and then repeated the process. "My old lungs are pumping just fine."

She slipped her hands from his gentle grasp. "Good. If your health is improving, then our season is a success." Vanessa nodded with relief. "The children are having a grand time too. At least George and Irene are taking every opportunity to enjoy themselves."

Thomas quirked a brow. "But not Lilly?"

"Hmm." Vanessa's fingernails clicked against the marble end table. "She's come out of her shell since Harlan started courting her. So much of her shyness and self-restraint have disappeared this summer. But after Jackson arrived, she withdrew again."

"It could be a coincidence."

"Perhaps, but I wonder." Should she confide in Thomas when he'd most likely dismiss her fears? Always the optimist, his disagreement with her observations often led to little spats about the children. "I worry she may be falling for Jackson once again."

"What? How can you think that, Nessie? Lilly is a serious, devoted girl. She'd never throw off Harlan for an old beau. Or was Jackson just an old friend? I never knew."

Vanessa sent him a dry smile which he disregarded. Thomas seldom noticed the subtleties of emotion. "She's certainly been distressed lately. But if it's not about Harlan, then what could be wrong?"

"Nothing, dear Nessie, not a thing." Thomas combed his fingers through his patch of hair. "You worry too much."

"How can a mother worry 'too much'?

146

They're our children and our responsibility."

"They're both adults. Lilly is practically an —"

*Old maid.* Neither of them wanted to say it. "Exactly." Vanessa agreed. "That's why I'm so concerned about her future."

"Lilly can take care of herself. She doesn't need our interference."

Vanessa grumbled, "I'm afraid she really does need our advice."

After thirty-one years of marriage, she realized Thomas purposely ignored any family dissension by pretending she exaggerated. He'd never admit Lilly and Harlan's relationship might be at risk because of Jackson Grail. She'd have to mend any fissures on her own, just as she'd always done.

"Thomas, it's getting late and I'm going off to bed."

"I'll be up in a few minutes after I finish one more chapter in this mystery novel. Crackling good plot. Do you mind?" He propped his book on his paunchy stomach.

"Not at all."

Vanessa strode through the empty hallway, up the stairs and down the corridor toward the bedroom she shared with Thomas. Low gaslight cast deep shadows across the paintings that lined the papered walls. No sound disturbed the hush of the night. The servants were off duty, except for her maid and Thomas's valet, so she had most of the rambling old house to herself.

After passing Lilly's bedroom, Vanessa paused. Did she dare turn the doorknob and intrude upon Lilly's sanctuary? For several seconds she stared at the closed door. No one would ever know if she slipped into her daughter's room. After all, Summerhill was her temporary home. Didn't she have the right to enter any space she pleased? Buoyed by her reasoning, Vanessa gripped the glass knob and twisted it. She pushed the door. It opened easily.

Stepping inside, her heartbeat pounded in her ears. She gulped in fresh sea air blowing through the screens. At first she thought of shutting the windows so Lilly could return to a warm, comfortable room. But if she did, her daughter would know someone had invaded her privacy. Better to leave well enough alone.

Vanessa's eyes quickly adjusted to the darkness. Vague forms sharpened to pieces of familiar furniture. She reached into the drawer of Lilly's night table for matches. With trembling hands, she lit the kerosene lamp. The light banished the eeriness and eased her fears.

As she expected, Annie kept all of Lilly's belongings in perfect order. Where should she search for a clue to Lilly's puzzling behavior? Intuition whispered it must be more than Jack's sudden visit that sent Lilly to her bedroom on every possible pretext. She seemed so distracted lately, definitely not herself. Vanessa yearned to help, but how could she unless she discovered the cause of her daughter's peculiar moods?

Vanessa riffled through the chiffonier scented with floral sachet. In the wardrobe, she searched the gowns, hats, and accessories but found nothing unusual. Disappointed, her curiosity ebbed. She rolled back the cover of the desk and peeked through the cubbyholes, the last possible place to look. She still wasn't quite sure what she was looking for.

Pens, a bottle of black ink, stationery, and several envelopes caught her eye. The return addresses identified an assortment of Lilly's former school chums who had married and moved away from New York. Tempted to pull out the letters and read them, she hesitated only a moment before moving on.

Yanking on the center drawer, she was surprised it didn't budge. Locked. Could Lilly have hidden something important inside?

She opened the lid of a small keepsake box resting on the desk. Guilt mingled with a mother's instinct to help her daughter. Shutting her eyes, she tried to quell her conscience. But her hand continued to touch the mostly inexpensive objects — a scalloped seashell, an unframed photo of Harlan and Lilly taken with George's box camera, a silver cross on a chain. Just personal paraphernalia. She ran her fingers along the velvet lining, ready to give up and snap the cover down. But a lump beneath the bottom sent a shiver of hope through her. She pulled out a key.

Vanessa's hand shook as she slipped it into the desk lock. A quick turn and the drawer released. Her hand grasped the pull. One jerk of the handle and she'd learn whatever Lilly had concealed inside. Gingerly, she gave a tug.

What if Lilly found out? She would never condone prying, even for her own sake. Discovery would prompt an irreparable rift between them. Vanessa knew she couldn't withstand the humiliation of being labeled a snoop by her family. She slammed the drawer shut, locked it, and returned the key. Quickly extinguishing the lamp, she flew toward her own bedroom as if the devil himself were on her heels.

Half an hour later when Thomas arrived, Vanessa still tossed and turned in bed, unable to stop her ruminations.

"Can't sleep, Nessie?" With a soft groan, he lowered his bulk onto the feather mattress. "Ah, this feels good." Propped up with pillows, he turned a sharp eye toward Vanessa. "You aren't worried about the children again, are you?"

Denial lay on the tip of her tongue, but she couldn't fib. "You know I am. I've always fretted over them and I probably will until the day I meet my maker." Vanessa squeezed his wrinkled hand. "You can't expect me to act otherwise."

Thomas heaved a weary sigh. "Oh, Nessie, I know it's your nature to cluck at your chicks."

"But what? You haven't finished your thought."

"You know me too well. Our children need to spread their wings and fly." He grinned, obviously pleased with his own metaphor.

"You dare not say I'm an old hen who dreads an empty nest."

She pretended to elbow him. He squirmed away, chuckling.

"I wouldn't dare, Nessie. But if you henpeck them, they won't thank you for it."

Thomas leaned over and gently kissed her on her lips with the lightness of butterfly wings. "Good night, my love."

He was right, as usual. Yet, she couldn't stay quiet when she saw her children careening down the wrong path.

If they'd only confide in her and accept her advice, their lives would run more smoothly. She saw no need for any of them to make mistakes they could easily avoid. Unfortunately, they rarely sought her counsel.

# TEN

Miranda declined the invitation to the ball, claiming fatigue. But Lilly knew how her friend disliked ostentation. Lilly envied her. She too would've preferred reading a novel or writing her own. But of course Mama wouldn't hear of it.

The Westbrook party arrived fashionably late at Ocean Vista, a limestone "cottage" designed to resemble a scaled-down French chateau. Light from crystal chandeliers blazed through the French doors and curved Palladian windows, revealing a crowd of dancers swirling to the distant strains of the Grand March.

As Lilly emerged from the family carriage, a liveried footman opened the massive front doors to expose the foyer of one of Newport's most celebrated mansions. She gasped at the wide staircase carved in stone and carpeted in red. A fountain, centered in the squares of the black and white marble floor, cascaded like a miniature waterfall.

"My, this is magnificent." She stared at the crystal chandelier hanging from the high ceiling and the antique furniture that must have come from a European castle.

Harlan shrugged as he tossed her an indulgent smile. "How would you like to live in a place like this someday?"

"Oh no, it's far too regal for me," Lilly said before she had a chance to think.

A shadow of a frown crossed his even features and then vanished into a tight smile. "I'm sure you could become accustomed to a bit of luxury if you tried."

"Of course."

The Santerres' mansion, situated on an expensive block of Fifth Avenue real estate, was equally as ornate as Ocean Vista. Harlan took such extravagance for granted. On the other hand, the Westbrooks' shabby old townhouse couldn't compare in either size or grandeur. Yet Lilly preferred its coziness, even if it was a bit on the worn side.

She left her wrap, along with her maid, in the ladies' dressing room and accepted a card imprinted with the program of dances and a space for filling in the names of her partners. Harlan, as her escort, wasn't allowed to monopolize all her time, so with her permission, he signed up for the first set of quadrilles, the last dance before supper, a march, and the final waltz of the evening. As soon as Harlan finished, Jack stepped forward.

He bowed with mock gravity that made her laugh. "May I have a waltz or two, Miss Westbrook?"

Harlan scowled.

"I'd be delighted." The words slipped through Lilly's lips, though the familiar flutter of her heart warned her to decline.

Why did Jack have such a disconcerting effect on her? From the time they'd first met, he'd swept her into his orbit through the force of his dynamic personality. His dark eyes had lit like firecrackers in the night sky, captured her attention, and stirred her desire for more. No one else had caused her to look twice — except Harlan, of course, though to be honest, he didn't ignite quite the same intensity. No doubt he would, as soon as Jack left Newport and she got to know Harlan better.

The line into the ballroom inched forward until the Westbrook party finally greeted their host and hostess at the ballroom entrance. Lilly proceeded inside, arm-in-arm with Harlan. From the corner of her eye, she glimpsed Jack edging closer. A grimace spread across his face. She stifled a smile as she turned away from him. She rather liked the novelty of having two men compete for her attention.

Strains of "The Blue Danube" filled the spacious ballroom and blended with the hum of dozens of conversations. A rainbow of color flashed through the room as young society ladies in pastel gowns danced round and round with partners dressed in black tailcoats and starched white shirts. Satin slippers and polished shoes lightly touched the floor as couples glided past the watchful eyes of the matrons.

"How nice to see you again, Lilly."

She glanced down into the fox-like face of Nan Holloway, the oldest daughter of Mrs. Beatrice Carstairs. An acquaintance since childhood, they'd once suffered through dreadful dance and deportment lessons. Only Nan loved the tedious instructions. Her small feet hadn't tangled up like Lilly's, nor had she stumbled into boys half a head shorter.

Tonight she wore a gown of peach satin heavily embroidered with silver thread and seed pearls. Her pale blue eyes glittered as brightly as her diamond necklace and earrings.

"Nan, how are you?" Lilly asked.

Nan stretched up and leaned closer to

whisper behind her Oriental fan. "I must say Mr. Santerre is taking a keen interest in you. You must be delighted — even a bit relieved." Nan's tiny eyes widened. "Mr. Santerre is quite the catch." Her lips puckered with obvious envy.

Heat blasted through Lilly's skin. "I've been waiting for the right gentleman."

Lilly looked away, humiliated by the rarely spoken truth. No one had to explain she was indeed fortunate to have Harlan as a prospective husband. No one needed to emphasize she'd been left on the shelf far too long in favor of prettier girls with livelier dispositions. But she wasn't to be pitied. She might not possess the skills and attributes prized by society, but she was a good Christian woman with God-given talents. And that counted for something.

Harlan sidled up to her. "You look lost in your own private world."

Lilly pinned on a smile. "I was."

"Our quadrille set is next."

She followed him onto the gleaming floor where they joined three other couples in the intricate steps of the dance.

His small, grayish eyes, nearly on a level with hers, glinted like new dimes. "I spoke to Kip Tareyton this afternoon and told him in no uncertain terms what I thought of his proposed merger."

Lilly forced a smile. "Of the New England Railroad?" Titans from every branch of American industry converged this evening at Ocean Vista.

"The very same."

Lilly smiled politely as he rambled on, but her attention drifted off as his words folded into the music. "Perhaps we can discuss this later when I can hear you more clearly."

He nodded, but his lips pressed together. As soon as the orchestra stopped playing, Harlan continued right where he'd left off. Commerce seemed to be the only topic to sustain his interest. Strange she never noticed that before.

Dressed in white tie and tails, Jack looked every inch the prosperous gentleman. He claimed her for the next waltz and much to her dismay, she found her spirits rising. With his arm clasped tightly about her waist, Jack whirled her around the edge of the dance floor. Lilly's heart raced as she followed his expert lead.

She loved the pressure of their hands entwined, and even though they both wore gloves, a current of excitement surged through her. The flash of his eyes suggested he might feel the same thrill. His warm breath fell upon her cheek and sent a quiver of delight sliding down her spine.

She hadn't tingled like this since before he'd left her.

He dared to press her even closer and she didn't resist. She remembered how they'd sometimes danced at Christmas balls during Jack and George's last year of college. Only eighteen years old and just out in society, she'd worn new gowns in cranberry taffeta, emerald velvet, and winter white. Yards of lace and ribbon decorated the exquisite fabrics. She'd waltzed in delicate slippers dyed to match her frocks, sipped punch, and ate a midnight supper with Jack.

As they whirled around the floor, Lilly remembered talking with Jack for long hours in quiet corners — of everything and nothing. She'd believed they were soul mates and nothing could mar their romance. But she'd been so very wrong. Hadn't she?

As they spun around the ballroom, she noticed the flash of Irene's sapphire and diamond necklace and the royal blue satin of her gown. Irene's broad smile focused upon her partner, a young man with a beard the color of cinnamon and a fringe of curls semicircling his balding head. Lilly didn't know him, but that wasn't surprising.

When the music ended, the little man with the reddish curls retrieved two glasses of champagne and led Irene over to a gilded corner. In moments they were obscured by a profusion of lacy ferns and palm fronds.

"Do you know that gentleman's name?" Lilly asked Jack as he guided her from the dance floor. Irene looked more absorbed in conversation than she ought.

"You're asking the wrong person." Jack shrugged. "I know many people from school or business here, but not the man speaking to Irene."

"It's not important. I was merely curious."

Jack frowned at the unlikely pair. "Maybe you think Irene looks a bit too — absorbed — in the man."

Lilly blushed. "I should deny it, of course, because it's shameful to think the worst of anyone, especially your brother's wife. But the thought did cross my mind."

They wove their way over to the punch bowl, leaving the couple head to head behind the greenery. Lilly sipped the sweet liquid as they retreated to the relative seclusion of an open door leading out to the terrace. A welcome sea breeze swept inside, cooling off the overheated ballroom. In the inky blackness outside, lit only by a half moon and the glow of Japanese lanterns, Lilly noticed a few couples daring to slip away into the night. If they were caught, they'd pay a heavy price for their foolishness. The matrons who controlled the New York elite that migrated to Newport for the summer would cut off an offender by denying prized invitations.

Jack's soft wool tailcoat brushed against her bare upper arm and long glove. She inched away, but his magnetic attraction kept her much too close for comfort.

"I noticed Harlan Santerre has taken a strong interest in you. Since you and I are old friends, might I ask if he has serious intentions?"

"You're still quite blunt, even after all these years." She met his stare. He had no right to pry. "The answer is yes, I believe his intentions are serious."

"He's a fine fellow, I hear. I don't know him well myself, except from school. We don't run around in the same circles." Jack's smile was dry.

Lilly chuckled at Jack's expression. "Neither do I, usually. He's provided George, Irene, and me an entrée into fashionable society and we're grateful for his kindness."

Jack's eyebrows arched. "You never used to seek society's pleasures."

Did he think she was a prim and proper spinster with only books to keep her company? Perhaps she was, but she needed no reminding. "I do like dances and dinners every once in a while, though I'll admit, I'm more introverted than most ladies."

"Then you'll be in for a great upheaval if you marry Mr. Santerre. He'll expect you to entertain lavishly and often."

"No, you're quite mistaken. He likes a quiet life as much as I do."

"Oh? George told me you've attended every social event in every cottage throughout the summer. I don't suppose that was your idea."

"Actually it wasn't, but I wish you wouldn't gossip about me with my brother. It's true I'm out nearly every night, but that's primarily to please George and Irene — and Mama." Her voice rose. "Neither Harlan nor I care one whit for this extravagant kind of life." She gestured toward the marble and gilt ballroom. "I enjoy society from time to time, but it's not a priority in my life."

"And what *is* important to you?" he asked, inviting intimacy she wouldn't accept.

Her lips tightened, thinking of one part of her life that must remain unspoken. "My family and friends are most dear to me — along with my work at the Christian Settlement House. Social events are a distant third."

Jack touched her shoulder and blew out a sigh. "I'm sorry, Lilly. I've lost my good manners and my good sense. It's obvious you're fond of Harlan. In all sincerity, I wish you all the best — or at least, I'm trying to."

She pulled away, but lowered her voice. "Then why does it seem like you are criticizing me?"

"I only want to warn you that this fashionable world is far removed from what you've ever experienced or ever wanted."

"You have no idea what I'm like now, Jack, or how I wish to live in the future. Don't assume you know me better than I know myself." At her raised voice, several people glanced their way.

Jack blocked her from the onlookers' stares. "I apologize for invading your privacy. Your affairs are none of my business. However, I'm concerned about you. I want you to be happy."

"I wish I could believe that." Lilly's voice wavered and she blinked back tears. Drops of her pain, bottled up like poison, began to spill out. "You once asked me to marry you, and then that very night you withdrew your proposal. You walked away and I never heard from you again. Now you expect me to believe you want me to be happy?"

Jack winced and turned pale. "I'm sorry. I never should have left like that. I did want to marry you, but you know your father would never have allowed it."

Her heart hammered so fast she feared it might burst through the bodice of her gown. All the hurt and anger she'd suppressed poured out with hurricane force, sweeping away all sense of propriety. "How do you know that's true? You never even asked him. Why did you give up so easily? How could you walk away?"

"I'm sorry." Jack's eyes reflected compassion and a plea for understanding. It was clear the love was still there between them. It had never died. But as he shook his head, staring at her, she realized that wasn't the case. Just when she'd caught the eye of Harlan Santerre, Jack had burst onto the scene, stirring up dormant feelings, ripping open old wounds. Jack didn't want her, but neither did he want her to marry someone else.

"If you're not going to account for your" — she bit back the word *cowardly* — "inexplicable behavior, then let's end this conversation right now." She'd make a fool of herself and lose all her dignity if they spoke any longer. Lilly leaned against the stone pillar, trying to calm her shaking legs.

Jack paused and then released a weary sigh. "I'm sorry for causing you so much distress. It certainly wasn't my intention. Please forgive me."

He turned and receded into the blur of black evening attire and shimmering gowns. Standing motionless in the shadows, Lilly wished with every fiber of her being he'd never come to Newport.

She turned away, staring out through the dark windows. Why had he abandoned her when she'd loved him so completely? Why did he not pursue her now? In no way could she compare favorably with society's beauties, the fashionable, rich, flirtatious. She'd never competed, sparing herself hurt and humiliation. But she'd opened her heart to Jack and he'd crushed it and tossed it away like a sheet of foolscap.

Then Harlan rescued her from the shame of fading into the wallpaper. He deserved every ounce of her gratitude and loyalty. He treated her with the admiration accorded the most sought after heiresses, raising her self-assurance, diminishing her shy awkwardness. She had felt cherished and esteemed for the first time since Jack's abandonment.

Yet, was it enough?

The luster of the evening dulled. Suddenly, the French furniture set against priceless tapestries seemed overdone and the rococo details of the ballroom pure ostentation. Even if the other guests were delighted to prance around the dance floor or indulge in the rich delicacies served in the supper room, she wanted the seclusion of her home and her own bedroom. She knew this wasn't the abundant life Jesus spoke about in Scripture.

Tears stung the back of her eyes as she stood alone in the midst of the crowd. How ironic that Jack had returned right after she'd finally gotten over his betrayal and found the man to take his place. Was she so superficial she couldn't appreciate Harlan's steadfast devotion? Why did Jack still attract her as no one else ever had? She buried her head in her hands.

*Lord, please help me to banish Jack from my life. I can't seem to do it on my own.*

With a frown furrowing her brow, Irene approached from the noisy ballroom. Harlan trailed behind looking equally upset.

"Is something the matter, Lilly?" Irene drew close and Lilly caught a subtle whiff of her sister-in-law's gardenia corsage.

Harlan's rather bland face squeezed with equal concern. "I saw Jackson storm off. I hope he didn't upset you in some way. He

166

hardly has the manners of a gentleman, given his upbringing."

Lilly flared. "I assure you his manners are impeccable. And he comes from a respectable family, even if they aren't rich."

Harlan shrugged his sloping shoulders, looking bored. "Perhaps you're right. I certainly don't wish to quarrel over *Jackson Grail.*" He emphasized the name with a roll of his eyes.

Glancing back toward the ballroom with unconcealed longing, Irene sighed. "Do come. The evening is young and there's so much more dancing to do."

Lilly shook her head. "I'm sorry." She lifted a hand to her forehead. "I suddenly have the worst of headaches. I'd like to return to Summerhill." At Irene's crestfallen face, she softened. "Please don't offer to go home with me, either one of you. I'm fine, only dreadfully tired. You two enjoy the rest of the evening."

"If you're sure . . ." Irene clasped Lilly's hands. "I would love to stay a while longer. Dancing is such fun. Harlan can ride home with George and me and Mr. Grail."

"Splendid."

Harlan hesitated. "Are you certain, Lilly? I'd be delighted to escort you home. In fact, I really ought to."

"Thank you, but I refuse to cut your evening short." She tossed him what she hoped was a warm, reassuring smile.

Excusing herself, Lilly wound her way toward the ladies' dressing room. Dozens of maids clustered in the area, ready to repair ripped gowns or smooth disheveled hairdos.

In front of the doorway she spotted Annie shaking her head as she inched away from the fellow with the reddish curls — the same man who'd cornered Irene among the plants. Lilly slipped behind the fountain. Through the spray of crystal droplets, she saw only a blurred outline of their faces, but by squinting, she could distinguish Annie's furtive glance around the foyer. Why was this man pestering her maid?

While Lilly considered whether to approach the pair, Annie disappeared into the dressing room and he slunk back to the ballroom. What a strange little man, bony and white as a corpse, ogling her sister-in-law and now her maid.

Lilly crossed the vestibule and found Annie packing up her sewing kit. "Who was that man you spoke to a few moments ago?"

Annie frowned. "I don't know, miss. He didn't say." She rearranged a pin cushion and an assortment of colored threads.

Lilly tapped her fan against her skirt. "I'm

curious. What did he want from you?"

"He stopped at the door and asked for Mrs. Westbrook's maid. Since I help both you ladies, I came forward."

Lilly held her breath. "And?"

Annie avoided Lilly's steady gaze and fussed with her sewing kit. "He said Mrs. Irene Westbrook needed a pin to mend a tear in the hem of her gown."

"Don't you think that was unusual?"

"Why yes, miss, I most certainly do, but the gentleman explained she was dancing and didn't want to take the time out to get it fixed proper like."

Lilly nodded. That sounded like Irene, though it still seemed odd she wouldn't pause for a necessary stitch or two. It seemed a task more appropriate for a husband than a stranger.

On the drive back to Summerhill Lilly leaned into the plush cushion of the carriage, exhausted from the last few days. Could she believe the girl's explanation? Because of Annie's sweet, guileless nature, Lilly couldn't imagine otherwise.

# Eleven

Jack wandered the perimeter of the ball-room, restless and anxious to leave now that Lilly had gone home. Stepping carefully, he sidled between the twirling dancers and the overdressed and overstuffed matrons who lined the walls in their gilded chairs. He surveyed the ocean of faces and recognized quite a few. Though several were school chums, many were business associates from the city who had taken him up as the season's newest bachelor, a dance partner for their sisters, a challenge for their mothers. Only George qualified as a true friend.

Filled with remorse for firing off at Lilly, Jack refused to play the gracious gentleman and make small talk with the ladies. His disgruntled mood would show right through a congenial façade and he'd fool no one. Better to bow and move on.

After so many years of holding back his opinions, he'd finally blurted out the truth.

He'd earned the right to occasionally pontificate now that he had made his money and apparently won the respect of society. But good sense dictated he remain silent when nothing could be gained by spouting off. Criticizing Lilly's beau was stupid, especially since he was a guest in her home. And it displayed a streak of envy he'd rather deny.

From now on he'd curb his impulse to spew unwanted advice. But Lilly's attraction to the man seared Jack's insides.

Late the following morning Lilly's heart fluttered when she spotted Jack leaning against the veranda railing, engrossed in a small leather Bible. Surprised by his open display of faith, she tugged at Harlan's sleeve. "Let's say hello to Jack." She ought to stay far away from him, especially after late night's spat. But his interest in Scripture sparked her curiosity.

"He looks too busy to be disturbed. What about our walk?" Harlan grumbled, glancing toward the rose garden.

"We'll go in a minute."

He gave a long-suffering sigh. "If we must, my dear."

She led him around the corner of the house where the veranda semi-circled into a spacious porch, open to the sea breezes beneath its conical roof. Why didn't she wave a casual greeting and stroll off to the garden with Harlan? Nothing required her to speak to Jack, now or ever again, but even after their heated exchange, an invisible force pulled her toward him.

She'd first noticed him the summer he visited her family in Bar Harbor. Her brother George often invited friends, but none were as handsome or as attentive as Jackson Grail. They spent many sunny afternoons swinging on the porch glider, flirting, and playing board games. Jack spun out wild adventures that caught her imagination. One day he planned to sail around the world in search of lost treasure, the next day he expected to mine for gold or silver. He constantly looked for future opportunities to make his fortune. She lost herself in the gleam of his dark eyes as they sipped lemonade and nibbled tea cakes. She didn't doubt that this scholarship student at the top of his college class would someday succeed at anything he set out to do.

Jack looked up from his Bible and smiled warmly at Lilly. "Hello, Lilly. Harlan. Come join me." Apparently Jack didn't hold a grudge from last night's quarrel.

"Good day. I see you're reading Scripture." Lilly and Harlan climbed up the shallow veranda steps. Slipping into a rocker set on a wide Persian carpet, Lilly rearranged the potted palms to catch a better view of him.

Harlan thudded down beside her. As his fingers drummed on the arm of the wicker chair, Lilly struggled to control her annoyance.

Harlan never seemed comfortable around Jack; he fidgeted, fussed, and fumed. She tried to keep the two men apart, but this time curiosity about Jack's Bible reading overcame her better judgment.

Jack sat beside them, his dark eyes glowing. "I was reading Luke, chapter twelve. Do you mind if I share it with you?"

"If you must," Harlan murmured.

Lilly ignored him and stared at Jack. "Please," she encouraged. Lilly leaned forward, curious to learn more about his faith. Years before when they courted, they'd seldom discussed the Lord, but apparently Jack's interest had increased over the years. After Jack left her, she'd clung to the Lord because she couldn't face the loneliness and the hurt by herself. Apparently, he'd discovered God's goodness as well.

Jack looked down at the Bible. "And he said unto them, Take heed, and beware of covetousness: for a man's life consisteth not in the abundance of the things which he possesseth."

"Do you find that comforting?" Harlan smirked. He crossed his legs and swung the right one back and forth like a metronome.

Lilly searched Harlan's rock-hard face for a spark of interest but found only boredom. "Harlan, please."

"I'm just wondering," he insisted.

Jack's steady gaze held no guile, nor self-protective wariness. "No, it's not a comforting verse." He placed the Bible on the table. "I see too many people who value their material goods far above their spiritual treasure. And I'm not exempting myself."

Lilly winced. Most everyone she knew fell into that category. Though she didn't care as much for earthly treasure as some, she suffered from other faults. Keeping her light hidden under a bushel came to mind. Perhaps Jack was starting to have doubts about the riches he seemed to crave. She hoped his values were shifting.

Harlan grunted. "It's easy to criticize wealth when you don't have many earthly treasures. As for those of us who do, yourself included of late, I say all we have to do is acknowledge our good fortune and thank the Lord for His graciousness."

*And excellent judgment,* Lilly finished his unspoken thought. Harlan, like most in society, believed God blessed him with such earthly abundance because he deserved God's generosity.

Pushing back into the cushion, Harlan folded his arms across his chest.

Alarm boomed in her mind like a thunder bolt. "You're a committed Christian, aren't you, Harlan?" She could never marry him if he weren't. Oil and water didn't mix.

"Of course I'm a Christian. How can you doubt that?" His face hardened as he swung his leg even faster. "I confess I don't know much beyond what I learned in Sunday school as a child. While some men in college were reading Scripture or washing dishes, others gambled and courted women. I, on the other hand, studied business. It's stood me in good stead — at least in this life — and I'm sure I'm headed in the right direction for the next."

Lilly squeezed her eyes shut for a moment, blocking out Harlan's pomposity, and then glanced at Jack. His mouth arced downward.

Jack tapped the flimsy, gold-edged pages. "I highly recommend God's Word. Nothing is more enlightening. You might consider it a form of post-graduate studies."

Harlan eased back against the cushion. "Yes, I'm sure you're correct."

His words were right, but his tone was clear — he thought it foolishness. Lilly hid her distress behind a perfunctory smile. After spending months with Harlan, she'd thought they shared common beliefs. Although they'd never discussed their faith per se, she'd assumed, apparently incorrectly, they both cherished their relationship with the Lord.

She touched the sleeve of Harlan's jacket. "It's so important to study the Bible. Don't you agree?"

He patted her hand as if she were a child to be pacified. "Of course, my dear."

Her chest tightened at his patronizing attitude and she struggled to contain her irritation behind a half smile. He didn't understand Scripture and didn't care to learn. Should she marry a man when they were unequally yoked?

The obvious answer jolted her for a moment before she remembered that the Lord often softened the hardest of hearts and the most difficult of people. It was all in His time, not her own. She trusted Him to guide her into the future — whatever it might hold — though sometimes she felt sure He was ignoring her and withholding His wisdom.

She held on by a thread that threatened to break. No, the Lord wouldn't allow their connection to sever. His patience overcame her impatience. She felt sure He would direct her footsteps when the time came.

Lilly rose, unwilling to listen to any more of Harlan's drivel. "Shall we go for our walk now? Excuse us, Jack."

As they descended the veranda stairs to the back lawn, Lilly twisted around. "I do hope we can discuss the Bible sometime."

Jack nodded. "I'd like that very much."

Her family, while churchgoers, seldom read Scripture except during a worship service. Harlan surely couldn't object to her discussing spiritual things, even with Jack. Yet she looked forward to a discussion with him more than she should.

"The three of us can all mull over religious matters — sometime — if that's what you want," Harlan conceded as he smoothed the yellow hairs of his mustache.

But she doubted that with all their social activities, she and Harlan would ever find the time to discuss the Bible in any depth. And that rankled her.

Jack watched Harlan and Lilly stroll arm-in-arm across the lawn toward the gazebo. Jack closed his Bible and stared at Harlan's back. George joined Jack on the porch and he knew he should tear his eyes away, but he found it impossible.

"What's wrong?" George asked, looking quizzically between Jack and the couple in the distance. "Did Harlan say something to anger you? Or maybe Lilly?"

"Lilly needs a husband who understands her faith and devotion to the Lord, not some snobbish rich boy who presumes his money will buy his way into the hereafter." If Harlan treated her convictions so lightly, he wasn't worthy of her. And they were headed toward marital misery.

"Hmm, I suppose you're right. Lilly does have strong spiritual ideals. I doubt Harlan has ever given the Almighty much thought."

Jack shook his head. "My parents showed me the importance of sharing deeply held beliefs with one's spouse. Without that bond, a relationship skims the surface at best."

George pulled on the tip of his goatee. "You have a deep mind, Jack. Deeper than I thought."

Jack chuckled. "No, but I understand the obvious."

His father instilled in his sons a love for learning and for the Lord. He taught them the satisfaction of working hard at a job you enjoyed and that benefited others. Money was always in short supply, but if they were deprived of anything, they didn't realize it. The love they shared for God and for each other compensated for what they lacked.

"I imagine Lilly hopes for more than Harlan can ever provide. He'll shower her with more riches than love and eventually disappoint her," Jack said.

"You paint a dismal picture for her future."

"I do, indeed. But that's what I envision."

Sadness for Lilly compressed Jack's lungs, leaving a dull ache inside his chest. "Still, Lilly is a grown woman who has made up her mind to be courted by Harlan. She wouldn't appreciate my interference." He'd tried to subtly warn her against settling, but she'd bared her claws at his comments and he'd retreated.

Why was he torturing himself about Lilly's future happiness? She neither paused nor hesitated to run straight into Harlan's outstretched arms. This was her life to ruin. He couldn't stop her, though he ached to talk some sense into her.

As the sun rose high over the ocean, Jack watched Harlan lead Lilly into the garden.

After he secured Lilly's help in locating Fannie Cole — and convinced her to come out of hiding — he'd return to New York, his job completed. No more moping over the "happy" couple and wishing for a different ending. He had a publishing house to run and no time to waste on a dead romance.

That afternoon all the Westbrooks and their houseguests attended a garden party at Grassy Knoll, the Carstairses' summer cottage on Bellevue Avenue. With cups of punch in hand, Lilly and Miranda wandered the grounds with a few hundred other guests. They stopped beneath the wide skirt of a maple tree when Mama spotted them and strode over, a determined set to her mouth. Lilly breathed deeply and then gave a tentative smile.

"Grand party, isn't it, Mama?" she asked as her mother joined them in the shade. Her mother looked especially lovely in her burgundy silk frock, matching hat, and parasol.

Mama's eyes narrowed. "It is," she said without enthusiasm. "While I have the opportunity, I must share some disturbing news. One of my friends — who shall remain nameless — spotted you at an Elna Price book signing with Jackson Grail. Well, naturally, I informed her she was mistaken.

But she insisted she was not. What do you have to say for yourself, Lillian?" Mama had a difficult time putting outrage or authority into her voice, but Lilly heard the high note of panic. No one could survive socially if one's name was bandied about town.

"I did go to the book shop. I know Irene enjoys her dime novels. Jack happened to be there as well. But we certainly didn't go together or plan to meet. Your friend needs to stop telling tales, Mama."

Her mother's hunched shoulders relaxed and her usual smile returned. She glanced nervously at Miranda. "I am quite relieved. I was so afraid you'd compromised your reputation. What would Harlan think if he heard you were off with Jackson?"

Lilly stiffened while Miranda turned away, obviously embarrassed to witness such a private discussion. "Harlan would believe me because I'm telling the truth about Jack."

"Be that as it may, he might not overlook damaging gossip. Certainly his mother wouldn't. Guard your reputation, Lillian."

Lilly choked back an unkind comment about Dolly Santerre, keeping in mind that she was Harlan's mother — not to mention Miranda's aunt and Mama's friend.

A gust of wind lifted the brim of Mama's

hat and stirred the silk flowers, greenery, and tulle wrapped around the crown. "I've noticed how Jackson follows you all over Summerhill. I'm not accusing you of encouraging him. But you must not give him any reason to hope you'll return his affection. I'm quite sure Harlan will propose soon, yet he seems a bit unsure about your feelings. Don't give him cause to doubt you."

"No, of course I won't."

Mama leveled a serious gaze. "You do want to marry Harlan, don't you?"

"Yes, of course I do."

She couldn't marry Jack. Even if he wanted her, she'd have to tell him about her writing. He'd insist she make Fanny Cole a household name and face. The publicity would ruin them all. Not that she could ever trust him —

"Splendid. Then discourage any pursuit on Jackson's part and introduce him to some of the eligible young ladies. That will help take his mind off of you." Mama's features eased back to their normal pleasantness.

Lilly nodded. "Yes, Mama."

"I'm glad we have that settled. If you'll excuse me, I'm going to fetch one of Beatrice's most delicious desserts. A chocolate torte. It's very similar to the ones we had several years ago at the Sacher Hotel in Vienna." Mama strolled back across the lawn, across the stone terrace and into the mansion.

"My goodness, Lilly. I've never seen your mother so upset," Miranda said.

"But she's calmed down." She sipped her punch. "She'll be watching me carefully, so I ought to speak to Jack now."

Miranda tilted her head and whispered so none of the couples strolling by could hear. "Lilly, do you think Jack may still love you? Your mother isn't the only one to notice how he glances at you and follows you —"

Lilly laughed. "Nonsense. He doesn't care for me. He thinks I'll lead him to his authoress, that's all there is to it."

Miranda shook her head and the plume on her hat dipped. "Well maybe, but I don't believe so."

"Why not marry Harlan? He isn't perfect, but no one is, including myself. We're suitable and I'm sure we'll have a satisfying marriage."

After the disappointment George inflicted upon her parents with Irene, a stranger from San Francisco, Lilly was eager to give them something to be happy about. She leaned toward Miranda and spoke softly, "There is one thing that worries me. Do you think Harlan would accept my writing ministry — if he found out?" Writing in secrecy tugged at her conscience more and more as an engagement became inevitable.

"He's too busy with his railroads to ever consider that you might have an outside interest."

Lilly nodded. "Yes, men are so involved in their work they usually pay little attention to their wives' activities." She'd eventually do what was right and tell Harlan about her writing — but not quite yet.

She'd cut Jack loose from the entanglement of the past so he might walk into the future a free man and she a free woman. No more looking back. Only forward.

# TWELVE

Lacking a plausible excuse to skip the garden party, Jack dutifully joined the Westbrook entourage for a few hours of meeting and greeting friends they saw every day. He stayed to himself as he wandered the extensive grounds but kept his eye on Lilly, who chatted with Miranda beneath a shade tree. The crowd of guests dressed in their afternoon finery reminded him of peacocks on parade. Ladies in pastel dresses with matching parasols raised high above their hats acknowledged him with overly bright smiles and an endless stream of chatter.

Only a short time ago he'd envied these brightly plumed birds. They possessed everything money could buy and most had the leisure to enjoy it. Yet their needs were greater than his own. They required a flock of admirers, dozens of servants, expensive clothes, and showy carriages to incite envy among their friends and foes. Ever since he'd gone to St. Luke's on a scholarship, he'd wanted the money and privileges his classmates claimed as their right.

If his parents were still alive, they'd frown at his misplaced ideals and wonder why he'd grown overly ambitious. After visiting the Settlement House and seeing so much poverty firsthand, he had to agree. It was something to ponder.

As Jack meandered about the grounds, his gaze swept the emerald lawn sloping down to the shore in gentle hillocks. It suggested the name of the cottage, Grassy Knoll. Yet there was nothing bucolic about the mansion, a pile of limestone formed into the most hideous, ornate, rococo palace he'd ever seen. Still, the Carstairses served a grand spread of sandwiches and cakes which easily redeemed their taste in architecture.

He watched Mrs. Beatrice Carstairs, Eloise and Nan Holloway's sharp-nosed and sharp-eyed mother, flit from guest to guest, ensuring everyone took pleasure in her lavish gala. The Westbrooks chatted with their oldest and dearest friends, leaving him to his own devices. With George at the dessert table, Irene flirted with the young bucks and old codgers who trailed after her like courtiers in the footsteps of their queen. Jack kept his distance.

Wandering over to one of the many enormous umbrella tents scattered across the grass, Jack felt a shadow move behind him. He glanced over his shoulder and nodded politely to Eloise, Nan's younger sister. He judged Eloise to be about twenty and, from the desperate look in her hooded eyes, in search of companionship or possibly more. Husband hunting was an obsession with her age group.

He wished he could reassure her with frank words. *You're young, you're rich. Don't worry. You're in no danger of becoming an old maid.*

He thought how nice it'd be to see every worry line disappear from the flat planes of her rectangular face. Taller and plumper than her mother and sister, Miss Carstairs lumbered as she came toward him. The slight hunch to her back ruined the effect of her pink-and-white gown, striped like a candy cane. Yet her vulnerability endowed her with a certain charm.

"Good afternoon, Mr. Grail," she said hesitantly.

"Good afternoon to you too, Miss Carstairs." He stopped until she caught up. Holding a glass of iced fruit drink and a plate piled high with cucumber sandwiches and vanilla layer cake, he couldn't offer to carry her dish of strawberries dipped in cream. They passed an open-sided tent where a five-piece orchestra played soothing music for an elderly group. He noticed how the older folks shuffled across the polished dance floor and flirted as if they were forty or fifty years younger. When he and Miss Carstairs reached the only umbrella tent still unoccupied, they sat on chairs nestled around a small table. The bright blue canvas shaded them from the late afternoon sunshine, curtailing the sea breeze but not the briny scent of the sea.

"Lovely party." Jack nodded. "And lovely weather." Jack tried not to gobble his food as she nibbled morsels of her own. Nearby, conversations rose and fell and laughter rang out above the hum.

"Yes, it is a beautiful day." She grinned, showing a fine set of even teeth but too much gum. "My mother wouldn't stand for it any other way."

"Then she must have remarkable powers."

Miss Carstairs giggled until tears spilled from her little round eyes and rolled down her florid cheeks. "Indeed, she has. Well, at the very least, she always gets what she wants."

Jack nodded. Most of these grande dames

could purchase anything they wished, including a husband for their daughters. Some even bought European noblemen as sons-in-law to boost their family's status and evoke the envy of their friends. The impoverished duke or earl received an enormous financial settlement, and the American heiress, an illustrious title. When he examined Eloise's eager face he realized beyond a doubt that he was the object of her desire — or her mother's marital scheme. What had taken him so long to notice?

Yet, a bachelor on the fringe of society hardly qualified for the hand of a wealthy young lady — even if she weren't pretty or poised. He must be mistaken about Eloise Carstairs's designs. *Come on, Jackson. Since when have you become the fool?* But perspiration seeped through his pores and his crisp white shirt began to wilt beneath his black jacket.

With his back to the mansion, he gazed over the lawn to the Atlantic Ocean. He watched the small boats cut into choppy water. How he wished he were out there working the sails and feeling the spray splash against his face and clothes. To be anywhere but here. He'd listened to Miss Carstairs's prattle for quite awhile before allowing his mind to drift toward the sea and the sailboat he might never own.

"Don't you think so, Mr. Grail?"

"Excuse me. I didn't quite hear you," he apologized.

"You're staring at the sea. Do you like the water?"

"I love to sail."

She lowered her voice. "A sailboat would make a man quite a nice wedding present, don't you agree?"

He jerked his head around to meet Miss Carstairs's hesitant gaze. Was this merely an awkward attempt at flirting? Her eyes betrayed such a yearning for love and romance that she evoked his sympathy along with a sudden urge to run.

He fumbled for words. "Yes, but certainly a sailboat is too extravagant a gift."

"Not if one is in love." Her smoldering eyes made him squirm. Sweat poured in rivulets down his spine.

Out of the corner of his eye he noticed Mrs. Carstairs and Mrs. Westbrook glancing his way and communing behind their open fans. Conspiratorial smiles clung to their faces. Were they plotting his marital future or was he reading far too much into an innocent conversation? Surely, Mrs. Carstairs would focus her eye on someone better heeled; he lacked nearly every attribute elite society prized. Still, he reluctantly admitted to himself that he'd come to find out the "top drawer" considered him newly "minted," a gentleman with a fortune, a thriving publishing empire, and a future.

Why wasn't he happier? After all, he'd achieved his goal.

Jack looked into Eloise's eager eyes. "I was recently in New York, and I saw more poverty than I ever thought possible. For the cost of a sailboat, you could feed hundreds of hungry people at the Christian Settlement House for months, if not a whole year."

Eloise tilted her head. "Are you implying I should donate funds to charity?"

"Yes, I suppose I am. Excuse me for being so audacious." Would she take umbrage at his little sermon?

She nodded slowly. "I appreciate your honesty. And I'd be delighted to contribute."

"Thank you. They'll certainly appreciate your generosity." He saw Lilly approach and recognized his means of escape. "Miss Westbrook will be pleased to give you the details. If you'll excuse me, Miss Carstairs, I'd like to try a piece of that chocolate cake I saw on the tea table." He rose and glanced toward the veranda and the dining room inside the open French doors.

She gripped his arm. "Do stay. Please. I'll send one of the footmen to fetch it for you."

Jack sunk back into the wooden chair, trapped, but feeling sorry for a young lady forced to resort to physical restraint in order to hold a potential suitor. A sad sign of desperation. Eloise signaled a footman carrying a silver tray laden with breads and sweets. As luck would have it, the tray held chocolate cake. Jack chose a piece, which he didn't actually want, and took a bite. Toying with the rich dessert, he watched Lilly slip into a chair on the opposite side of the table.

"So, you've met Miss Carstairs, I see." Lilly beamed like a search light. He detested her artificial smile.

Eloise nodded. "We've met on several occasions — at the opera, at a reception last spring, at a house party in the Adirondacks. Isn't that right, Mr. Grail?"

"You have a keen memory." From her deep blush, Jack realized he'd made a faux pas and hurt her feelings. "Of course, I remember meeting you, but I'm amazed you recall meeting me."

These situations often drew a man into a verbal minefield where one misstep could send him flying into the air like an exploding bomb. Pleasant bantering held hidden meanings beyond his comprehension.

"Miss Carstairs has decided to contribute to the Settlement House. Isn't that wonderful, Lilly?"

"I am so thrilled, Eloise." Lilly beamed.

Eloise giggled. "Mr. Grail is terribly persuasive."

"On behalf of the Settlement House, I'd like to thank both of you," Lilly said.

George and Irene sauntered over to the table. "How about a game of croquet? The footmen are setting up the wickets now." George gestured toward the side lawn.

The ladies rose all together followed by a reluctant Jack. He'd jump at the suggestion of tennis, but croquet was about as appealing as scrubbing a floor. Lingering, he found himself last in the starting order, far from Eloise who was lured away by the sight of another bachelor. Jack stood right behind Lilly. *This might not be so bad after all.* Though at second glance she didn't look overly friendly.

"Are you enjoying yourself?" Lilly asked, her plaster-of-Paris mask still firmly in place.

They strolled side by side to the first wicket. "It's a grand party and the food is exceptional," he said.

Jack's heart thudded. Did he still have a chance to win her back? Lilly's pull on his heart never eased up. Consumed with thoughts of her, he couldn't concentrate on anyone or anything else.

"Where's Harlan this afternoon?" He fought to keep his tone genial.

"He's not feeling well, so he left early."

It didn't surprise him that she didn't appear to mind his absence. When she and Harlan were together their expressions looked stilted, their voices overly polite. A typical society couple. Jack groaned inwardly. He could offer Lilly unending love and devotion. Instead, she'd choose the approval of her parents — wouldn't she?

Lilly tilted her head topped with a flower-laden hat. "I've noticed you're quite popular with the ladies and their mothers. I've heard you're the 'catch of the season.' "

Jack grunted his displeasure as he looked toward Eloise, flirting with a young swain while they waited for their turn to play. "I'm hardly a catch. I'm still the same small-town boy I've always been."

His limp shirt continued to lose its starch.

"You are a good catch, Jack. You're just too modest." Lilly's steady gaze didn't mock and she didn't seem to take pleasure in his discomfort.

He chuckled with more ease than he felt. "No, I'm not a suitable match." If he were really acceptable, why didn't Lilly respond to him?

Lilly persisted. "Mama says all the mothers are eyeing you for their daughters. Surely you're aware of their interest."

He grimaced. From the flurry of invitations he'd received in the last several months, his social status had soared upward. Perhaps Lilly was right and he was now acceptable, though certainly not truly desirable. And apparently, he was still too little, too late, in the Westbrooks' minds. If only he'd arrived six months earlier, before Harlan Santerre entered the picture . . .

With a mallet and wooden ball in hand, Lilly waited beside a blue hydrangea bush as her brother made the first hit. Each player took a turn, leaving Jack alone again with Lilly at the first wicket.

"Eloise Carstairs is quite fond of you, Jack. I'm sure she's donating to the Settlement House because of you." Though the other players ambled out of earshot, Lilly kept her voice low. "People say she's set her cap for you."

"If you were teasing me, I'd laugh it off. But you're not, are you?" His chest knotted.

"I'm serious. I don't joke about important matters. She flirts now, with that one, solely to make you jealous."

His jaw clenched. He didn't like the link between Miss Carstairs and himself. Eloise wasn't his type, but apparently Lilly wished to match them up.

"So, what's your opinion? Should I court her?" Jack sent her a sardonic grin.

"Of course you must get to know her before you begin to court her. I don't believe in love at first sight."

Jack stifled a chuckle. He'd fallen in love the moment he'd seen Lilly stride across the quadrangle of St. Luke's on a crisp fall day during his senior year. Though she was only about fourteen or fifteen, scarcely older than a child, he remembered how she attracted him with her straightforward manner and natural laugh. She treated him like an older brother, one to share jokes with and even tease. Smitten, he'd waited impatiently for her to grow up.

"In my experience, Lilly, love can strike instantly." He tightened his grip on the mallet.

She raised an eyebrow. "Then you must be a romantic."

"Once maybe, but no longer." He moved toward the stake. "I'm more of a cynic than a romantic." Yet he stubbornly clung to his dreams, impossible as they were.

"I thought perhaps you might be charmed

by Miss Carstairs. She's so taken with you. Eloise is delightful." Lilly's voice gathered speed. "She'll make someone a splendid wife."

"No doubt she will. I hope she finds the right gentleman."

"But you're not the one?"

"Definitely not."

"I dare say she'll be disappointed."

He couldn't tell from her bland expression if Lilly felt let down or relieved. He hoped relieved. He listened closely to see where she'd lead the conversation and fought to keep his disappointment from showing.

"I'm sorry if Miss Carstairs will be disappointed, but I doubt her heart will break. I never led her to believe I was a prospective suitor. We're barely acquainted." He'd danced with Eloise a few times, but that was the extent of their acquaintance.

Lilly moved closer and he felt the warmth of her compassion. "Jack, I know you'd be happier if you fell in love and married."

Stunned, he stared at her. "Other than Miss Carstairs, do you have someone in mind?" He tried to smile, but his face froze in a grimace.

"I know many eligible young ladies who would enjoy your attention."

Obviously she didn't include herself on the list. His harsh laugh rang out, drowning the background music of a string quartet. "If I need a matchmaker, I'll be sure to call on you." He tipped his silk top hat as his world collapsed.

Lilly drew out a long sigh. "I'm only trying to help."

"I need no assistance with matters of the heart." He could ruin that all on his own. "But I *would* appreciate assistance in locating Fannie Cole." His eyes narrowed as he waited for her reaction. If she wanted to be all business, so could he.

Lilly spun away. "I believe it's my turn." She swung the mallet like a golf club. The ball flew through the wicket and well past the next one.

Jack tapped his ball through the curved wire. Then with one powerful stroke his ball followed hers across the lawn. "You can't evade me that easily," he muttered.

He followed Lilly until they reached their croquet balls. She faced him, her forehead crinkled in a frown. "I don't understand why you're so opposed to marriage," she said softly, avoiding the topic of Fannie Cole.

How did their conversation become so personal? He exhaled a breath rising from the depth of his lungs. Lilly bit down on her lower lip.

He regarded her, drinking in her beauty. Bathed in the gold of the late afternoon light, her flawless skin glowed. The pink satin of her gown shone like a brilliant sunset. Her white hat trimmed with carnations lent her a becoming femininity she rarely exhibited in her tailored skirts and shirtwaists. He wanted to take her in his arms and kiss away everything that kept them apart. But she'd never let him. Not now, not ever.

He tapped his ball through the next wicket. They were far behind the other players and well out of earshot. "I'm not opposed to marriage, per se. But it's not for me, and it never will be."

Her voice quivered. "Surely the right lady will come along and change your mind."

Jack shook his head. "No. She won't." His lips tightened. He wouldn't marry anyone other than Lilly. And clearly, she wasn't interested in him.

While they waited for the others to take their turns, Jack leaned against a copper beech tree and propped his elbow against the rough bark. He chipped a piece and rolled it between his fingers. He scrutinized her lovely face to see if she truly meant the message she was sending. She flinched beneath his steady gaze, but her eyes radiated sincerity he didn't wish to acknowledge. So he really had no hope of winning her back.

"I can't believe you're set on remaining single." Lilly cocked her head at a most becoming angle.

He shivered in the afternoon warmth and then pulled away from the force of his longing to take her into his arms and kiss her until she remembered. "My whole adult life, I've tried to gain admission to the upper echelon — but now that I'm here — I know it's not where I belong. I'd make a miserable husband for any of these women here."

Her voice shook. "Why do you say that?"

He stared at her, wishing he could read her mind. Why did she tremble? Because he offended her? Because she honestly hoped he'd pursue Eloise? He shook his head. "After seeing all those poor people at the Settlement House I realized I want to spend my earnings on helping others less fortunate. Do I sound like a do-gooder? If so, I'm not ashamed of it. For a long time I managed to forget my roots and everything I used to believe in." The truth had nagged the edges of his conscience since his visit to New York.

"I'm glad," she murmured, gazing toward the breakers crashing over the cliff.

"Truly?"

"Truly. And no, I consider your intentions admirable."

He paused, wondering if she had just opened a door to him. "Lilly, are you going to marry Harlan?"

"Yes, if he asks me I shall." Her voice rang strong and clear, though without enthusiasm.

"I see." He swallowed hard. So it was done. "My time at Summerhill is soon over. But before I go . . . I must beg your forgiveness for all the pain I put you through."

Lilly spoke softly, her eyes sparkling with what? Tears? "You have my forgiveness."

"Thank you."

She turned and walked toward Miranda, her shoulders slumped, her head down.

He let out a low groan. So that was that.

Even as his heart tore apart — releasing all the hopes and dreams he'd cherished over the years in a painful rush that left him breathless — he wondered why he wished for her to turn and glance in his direction once more. *Give me something, Lilly. Some reason to cling to this idea of us . . . together.*

But Lilly walked on, up the hill, and did not turn.

# THIRTEEN

The next morning Mama burst into Lilly's sitting room, grinning broadly. "Harlan would like you to join him on the veranda. I'm sure he's going to propose." Unable to contain her glee, Mama clutched her hands to her bosom and gave a sigh of delight.

"All right, I'm coming."

Lilly smoothed her skirt and followed her mother down the deserted hallway. She hated to admit her heart's infidelity, but it was true she'd wavered in her devotion. Now was the time to renew her commitment, if not for her own sake, then for the benefit of her family. She'd veered off course, but yesterday Jack had steered her back on track.

Her mother frowned. "You look like you're going to your execution."

"That's nonsense, Mama. But marriage is serious business and I don't take it lightly."

Mama waved a hand. "Marriage is about

love and happiness. It's not somber like a funeral."

Lilly sighed. "You're right, I'm sure. But it's also about commitment. That's worth pondering."

"Naturally." Mama lowered her voice as they descended the stairs.

Lilly pictured marriage to Harlan as a contract between two like-minded individuals who understood and respected each other. That was how most of her friends viewed matrimony, too, though a few held out for romance. And love. Despite their ups and downs, Mama and Papa lived comfortably in a union based on a combination of love and commitment. She envied them.

With a clean handkerchief Lilly dabbed at Mama's wet cheeks. "Now don't get all sentimental about this. Harlan may have no intention of proposing today."

As Lilly opened the doors to the veranda, she took a fortifying breath. What she needed was a strong dose of courage. She spotted Harlan, his back hunched, pacing the length of the veranda. Looking up, he flicked an uncertain smile. "Thank you for joining me." He motioned her over to a chair.

Her every nerve ending tingled with anxiety.

Awkwardly he thrust a bouquet of pink roses into her hand.

She sniffed the delicate fragrance and gathered the blooms to the bodice of her silk blouse. "Thank you, Harlan. They're beautiful."

He jerked his head up and down. "I'm glad you like them. Shall we walk over to the garden? I have something important to ask you." Swallowing hard, his Adam's apple bobbed.

Obviously this meeting was as difficult for him as it was for her. Lilly gave a reassuring nod as they strolled arm-in-arm toward the rose garden. Harlan led them to a stone bench at the end of the arbor deep within the shadow of tall, manicured hedges. It was cool here under the arms of a sturdy oak, and dew still moistened the grass. Sitting side by side, an uneasy tingle skipped up Lilly's back. For the sake of propriety, she scooted over a few inches to the edge of the bench, inhaled the fragrance of rose blooms, and waited.

Harlan jumped up like a jack-in-the-box, and then bent his knee to the crushed stone path. He took hold of her hands and gently rubbed her knuckles. Anguish puckered his features.

"Lilly, we haven't known each other for a long time, but during the last few months, I've come to admire you — as you undoubtedly know. And I've grown to love you." He paused as if trying to recall the words of a speech. "I've considered our friendship, and I believe we could be content together."

He looked up and studied the clouds as if they could infuse him with courage.

Releasing a deep breath, Harlan met her gaze. "Would you do me the honor of becoming my wife?"

Lilly's voice snagged in the back of her throat. Harlan had declared his love just as she'd anticipated; he'd knelt and followed the proper form. By all rights, she should be bubbling with joy. She hadn't expected fireworks or an explosion of passion, but she had anticipated some appropriate emotion, not this . . . numbness.

He dug into his pocket and snapped open a tiny box. A diamond ring glittered on black velvet like a shower of stars. Lilly blinked at the multifaceted gem. Ostentatious, though not vulgar, it caught the slits of sunshine streaming through the tree branches and flashed its brilliance.

"Oh, my. Harlan, it's magnificent."

He pushed the ring onto her finger. "Do

you accept my proposal?"

Words failed her. She had waited for this invitation since last spring, but now . . . "Yes," she said before she had time to reconsider.

He'd make a steady, companionable husband which was all that mattered. Months ago she'd decided they were compatible. There was no need to hesitate just because Jack had flashed into her life like a meteor. He'd vanish just as quickly. Or so she hoped.

Together she and Harlan returned to the cottage and searched the library and game room before finding the Westbrooks gathered in the drawing room. All eyes turned toward them. No one spoke.

"Mama, Papa, everyone, Harlan has asked me to marry him and I've accepted." Lilly offered her left hand for her family to examine.

A chorus of congratulations erupted. Papa and George thumped Harlan on the back. Even Jack shook his hand, although the scowl clouding his face belied his best wishes. He shot her a glance filled with regret and let it linger for several long moments. Then he turned away toward the window.

She tightened her grip on the back of the sofa to steady herself.

Jack still loved her.

For the first time, she'd read it in his eyes along with sadness and dismay. How could she have been so blind? All his talk about never marrying meant nothing. The truth was there, all along. She turned away, unable to look at such naked pain.

"Is something wrong? You look pale." Irene glanced from Lilly to Jack.

"No, I'm all right," Lilly mumbled.

"She's merely overcome with happiness." Mama raised Lilly's hand to examine the jewel. "My, what a lovely ring."

"Exquisite." Irene briefly frowned at her own diamond, not much bigger than a chip.

Mama pecked at Lilly's cheek. "I'm so delighted, my dear." She dried her tears with an embroidered handkerchief while she giggled with embarrassment at her own excessive emotion.

"You must excuse my exuberance. I'll pray you'll both be very happy, just as your Papa and I have been all these years."

"Thank you." Lilly forced a smile while her mood spiraled downward. She couldn't imagine her marriage to Harlan resembling her parents' marriage at all. But if it was sanctioned by the Lord, then He'd see to it they were happy. Or at least content.

"When will the wedding take place?"

Mama beamed. "Fall is a beautiful time in New York. Or perhaps winter, if you don't mind waiting."

Harlan strutted over and slipped his arm around Lilly's waist. "How about late in August?"

Lilly's stomach lurched with nausea. "That wouldn't give us enough time to plan properly, would it, Mama?"

Her mother's gaze darted from her daughter to Irene. "That's very short notice, but perhaps we could manage." Mama's eyelids fluttered.

"A wedding at Summerhill is a splendid idea." Irene's face lit up as she patted her mother-in-law's arm. "I'll help with the planning. I adore weddings. I only regret George and I had such a small one. It's a pity we missed out on a grand celebration. But perhaps a gala anniversary party might do. What do you think, George?"

George shrugged. "Whatever you wish, my dear."

Harlan pressed Lilly's fingers. "The sooner we marry, the better."

Fighting the urge to pull her hand out of his grasp, panic swelled inside her. Everything was happening too fast. She needed more time to consider the wedding — and most of all the marriage. Dizzy, she dropped onto the nearest chair. "I'm afraid I'm . . . overwhelmed."

"That's understandable, my dear." Mama rang for a glass of water and then took a seat beside her. "But we should set a date or at least decide on the season."

Lilly glanced at Harlan, whose look of delight caused her pangs of remorse. She appeared to be the only one besides Jack not sharing the euphoria of her own impending nuptials. Excited faces glowed with anticipation. Lips moved, but she barely heard any words.

"Perhaps we should consider the date carefully and take our time." Lilly forced a weak smile.

Harlan casually swept a glance from Lilly to Jack and back. "And why is that, my dear?"

A parlor maid handed Lilly a tumbler of water. She took a sip as she searched for an acceptable reason. "Weddings take meticulous preparation. Besides, I've always wanted to marry in the spring." She was simpering, batting her eyes to gain her own way, a trick she'd never in all her life employed before.

Mama rose. "We'll leave it to you two to decide the date. In the meantime, I'd like to ask Mr. and Mrs. Santerre to visit us here at Summerhill. Harlan, do you think they'd like to come?"

Lilly's jaw clenched. Dolly Santerre, with the thunderous voice and imperious manner, intimidated and annoyed her as few people did. Lilly held her breath, hoping Harlan would decline for his mother.

"My father rarely takes a day off. But Mother would be delighted, I'm sure."

Lilly closed her eyes, though ignoring reality didn't alter it.

Harlan nodded. "She can offer suggestions for the wedding too. She'll have lots of ideas."

Lilly tried to relax the tight press of her mouth.

When the joyful group finally dispersed, she slipped off to her favorite retreat by the sea. Alone among the rocks, she listened to the crashing breakers and watched the seagulls soar and dip in the deep blue sky.

The hiss of the surf foaming over rock drowned out her sigh. The very idea of allowing Jack into her heart again was unthinkable. Yet she couldn't erase him from her mind. Thinking of his broad shoulders in his well-cut suit coat, dark brown eyes that slanted in merriment, and the heartiest laugh she'd ever heard, sent waves of heat surging through her body. Memories of their times together were as sweet as they were bitter.

But all her reminiscing wouldn't bring Jack to his knee with a proposal of marriage. He might care for her, but a life together as man and wife wasn't in his plans. He'd said so himself. *I'd make a miserable husband for any woman here.* Lilly scooped up a pebble and tossed it into the surf. He could easily hurt her again. She wouldn't take a chance. Besides, even if she wanted to, the threat of him exposing Fannie Cole's true identity always lurked in the background.

Settling onto a boulder, she watched the sunshine spray thousands of shiny sequins across the waters. For once, the scent and sound of the sea failed to calm her spirit.

Poor Harlan. He deserved a loyal, adoring wife, not one who harbored a secret desire for another man. She should end their engagement before wedding plans gathered a momentum of their own, yet she couldn't bear to disappoint her family. And undoubtedly Harlan would make a fine husband and father to her future children. They shared common interests and a similar background and he seemed to truly care for her. Their marriage might lean toward the dull side, but it would be solid and, hopefully, fulfilling. She shouldn't expect the kind of romantic love she wrote about.

The sound of boots scraping against rock gave her a start. Jack jumped over to the ledge and lowered himself to the narrow spot beside her. A black curl blew across his forehead and the steady breeze billowed his tie out from under his navy jacket.

Lilly touched her bodice. "You startled me."

"I apologize. I merely wanted to congratulate you on your engagement. At the ball I advised you to think long and hard about marrying Harlan, but I trust you've done that. You have my best wishes for a happy life together."

"Do you mean that, Jack?" She held her breath, waiting for his answer.

His tie flapped like a sail. She leaned over to tuck it in, then thought better of it.

"Of course I mean it. If Harlan is your choice, then I approve. He's an outstanding gentleman and eminently suitable. Your family seems delighted." He looked her squarely in the eye and gave a bleak smile.

"Quite so."

She waited for him to speak, to open up and admit he still loved her, wanted her. For those few moments in the drawing room when he'd let down his guard, she'd felt sure their love had never truly been severed, even through the mist of time and circumstance. But his congratulations made her doubt her assessment. Maybe she wanted him to love her so badly she saw emotion that wasn't there. If he truly loved her, he'd speak now, before it was too late. Instead, he gazed at the roaring breakers and said nothing.

Apparently she'd misunderstood. "I'm going back to the cottage. It's too chilly to stay out here."

Jack nodded and followed her across the lawn.

And Lilly felt his shadow every step of the way.

From the back veranda, Vanessa watched the pair return to the cottage. Jack lagged behind, his head lowered. How peculiar they didn't walk together and chat. Well, there was no telling what splendid thoughts were spinning through Lilly's mind on the happy occasion of her engagement. Perhaps she didn't appreciate the interruption while she was trying to plan her wedding festivities. Maybe she just wanted to be alone to relish her triumph. But as Lilly approached, she noted her daughter looked glum, her shoulders slumped.

"What could possibly be the matter with Lilly?" Vanessa asked George, seated by her side on the porch glider. "This should be one of the most joyful days of her life."

He shrugged. "Nothing, I'm sure. You shouldn't read dire predictions into a person's every expression."

Vanessa wrinkled her brow. "I don't do that. Do I?" More than once Thomas had accused her of smothering their children with too much unwanted attention.

George hesitated. "No, Mama, not really. But sometimes you probe too deeply. Lilly is probably just overcome with emotion. It's not every day someone proposes to her."

"That's unkind. Lilly is a lovely girl. She's never been a wallflower. It's just that no one caught her eye before Harlan, except perhaps Jackson when they were very young. You don't suppose —"

"No, Lilly's not interested in Jack. Thankfully. Lilly is sensible. She knows Harlan is imminently suitable." George patted Vanessa's arm. "She'd never do anything to upset you or Papa."

Vanessa looked away, her lips pressed tight. Lilly was so unlike George, her mercurial, irresponsible, yet cherished son. She didn't want him to think for a moment how much he'd disappointed her with his choice of a wife — or in his lack of business acumen. He had so many redeeming qualities, though at times they were overshadowed by his poor judgment and lackadaisical attitude.

Climbing the veranda steps, Lilly glanced up and flashed a strained smile. Vanessa peered closely. She'd have to get to the bottom of this.

"Do join us, my dear." She gestured toward a nearby chair. "You, too, Jackson," she added as he approached, his face as serious as Lilly's. And even more dour.

Lilly sat down between a fern and a large pot of red geraniums. Jack mumbled an excuse about reading manuscripts and disappeared inside with George at his heels.

"How about a game of tennis? Too much work will only dull your brain and ruin your disposition," George said as he trailed behind Jack.

Vanessa reached across the wicker table and squeezed Lilly's cold hand. "I'm so thrilled for you, my dear. I pray you'll always be as happy with Harlan as you are today. You waited so long for the right man."

Nodding, Lilly folded her hands on her lap. Her violet dress with white lace on the bodice and skirt was most becoming. If only she'd relax her pinched face, she'd be quite a beauty.

Before Lilly found a reason to leave, Vanessa continued. "I was fortunate. I fell in love with your father when I was barely eighteen and we married soon after. I'm confident Harlan will be a grand husband as well." Lilly's complexion was as white as a clamshell. "Are you getting jitters already, my dear?" She spoke in a lighthearted tone, gone flat and critical.

Lilly took several seconds to answer. "Perhaps I'm a bit nervous."

"That's perfectly normal. All brides are apprehensive. But remember, my dear, marriage is a gift from God. He wants you to be joyful with your spouse."

Tears brimmed in Lilly's eyes. "We shall be. I'll see to it."

Vanessa laughed. "It's not quite that easy. It takes both partners to make a marriage work. But with enough love . . ."

"I'm determined."

Vanessa grinned broadly. "You've always been one stubborn girl, even when you were young. You'll accomplish whatever you set out to do. Remember when you decided to win your piano competition even though you'd taken only a few lessons? You practiced your heart out and we were so proud of you when you won first prize. I never doubted you'd win."

"Thank you, Mama."

"But marriage isn't a matter of the will. It's a matter of the heart. You understand that, don't you?"

Lilly nodded, but her lower lip trembled.

Vanessa leaned closer. "Of course, affection grows. It can start with fondness and then blossom into love, even passion. Sometimes you must be patient and allow it to develop over time." That's what she'd heard from her friends. Yet she'd loved Thomas right from the start when he'd strode into her life as a tall, strapping man with a twinkle in his eye and quip on his tongue.

"Do you have doubts, my dear? Perhaps we should talk."

Lilly shook her head as she rose. "Just pray for me, Mama. I want to do the right thing."

"I know you do. And I shall certainly ask the Lord for whatever guidance you need."

Blinking back tears, Lilly stepped into the cottage.

Vanessa sighed as she watched her lovely daughter leave. These were the most intimate moments she and Lilly had experienced in the last several years. Maybe if she prayed more the Lord would show them how to draw closer together. She'd like that very much.

■ ■ ■ ■

The next morning Jack leaned over the balcony of the Newport Casino, the clubhouse and gathering place of the elite summer crowd. He gazed down upon the grass tennis courts, not particularly interested in the match between two fellows he knew only slightly from Yale. Mingling with society appealed to him less and less. On close inspection, these people seemed surprisingly ordinary, bored by their idle lives and, actually, just plain boring.

"Would you rather be alone or may I join you?"

Jack recognized Irene's feathery voice tickling his ear. He tensed. "You can stay, if you'd like. That's entirely up to you. Where's George? I'd think you'd be together."

Irene shrugged as she lowered her yellow parasol that matched her frilly outfit. "I don't know, but I imagine he's watching the tennis match. I'll go search for him in a little while. But tell me Jack, why are you alone and looking so glum? Is it because of Lilly's engagement?" Her eyes mocked him with their gleam.

Jack bristled. "You get right to the heart of the matter, don't you?"

Irene flashed a grin, showing her pearl white teeth. She seemed to think he was paying her a compliment. "I do indeed get straight to the point. There's no use in beating around the bush."

"I wish Lilly and Harlan all the happiness in the world." He tried to muster some enthusiasm, but his voice sounded false and flat.

She cocked a thin blonde eyebrow. "Come now, Jack. I can tell when a man's in love. Do tell," she prodded. "I'll wager you and Lilly were once lovers — quite respectable lovers, of course."

Jack clutched the balcony rail. "We're old friends. It's not a secret." Their true relationship was a secret, however, unless Lilly had confided in others. But he doubted the very private Lilly would advertise an engagement that ended so abruptly, except possibly to Miranda.

Irene rolled her eyes. "It's a shame she's chosen to marry Harlan. I'm sure she still fancies you."

Jack stiffened. "I doubt it — not that it matters."

"You're right." Her voice thickened with sarcasm. "Lilly is engaged to Harlan and that's that." She cast a cynical eye at him as one corner of her mouth curled in a smirk.

"I'm disappointed in you, Jackson. I mistook you for a man determined to win at all cost. Now I see I was mistaken."

"When it comes to business, I'm in the game to win. But love isn't a sport with an enemy to vanquish." He glowered at this woman who apparently enjoyed another's misery.

"Hmm. To me, love is a game. Winner take all."

And that's what she'd done — taken all of George's money and boundless love, giving little in return. "You're heartless, Irene."

She tossed back her head and laughed until tears glistened in her eyes. "No, you misunderstand me. I'd never marry without love. My point is: there's more to marriage than mere emotion."

"Marriage shouldn't be as calculating as a business proposition."

"Where I come from, a woman has to watch out for her own welfare," she said.

"Quentin Kirby's niece shouldn't fret about fending for herself," Jack snapped back.

Irene frowned and all the beauty drained from her face. "I didn't become his ward until after my parents died."

He suspected they shared a common ailment. "Did you grow up poor?"

Irene's eyes widened. "Yes, I was raised on a pig farm, if you must know. I don't take my privileged life for granted, not for a second. And neither do you."

Jack nodded, not surprised she tagged him as a fellow with *nouveau riche* credentials. "I count every blessing the good Lord gives me." He stepped farther away from Irene as several cottagers joined them on the balcony. "Didn't your Uncle Quentin help your family when times were hard?"

Irene smoothed her gloved fingers, her eyes averted. "No. He and my mother were never close. I — I didn't meet him until my parents died from diphtheria. But that's in the past — a very sad one, to be sure. I only think of the future." She leaned so close he was surrounded by her cloying scent.

"Odd. I can't imagine Mr. Kirby abandoning anyone in his family. He has more than enough money to lift countless relatives out of poverty." Known for showering his mistresses with lavish gifts, Jack wondered why he neglected kin.

"How do you know my uncle?"

"Everyone in San Francisco knows Quentin Kirby. I met him once or twice when I lived in San Francisco, just before I headed for the Alaskan gold mines."

"I see. Perhaps I ought to be going. Good

day, Mr. Grail." Jutting out her chin, Irene hurried down the stairs without glancing back.

Instinct raised his suspicions. Perhaps Irene Westbrook was not all she seemed. It wouldn't take much to set a reporter on her tail and find out what she was hiding.

As soon as he got back to New York, he'd make sure his old friend hadn't made a tragic mistake in his choice for a bride.

# FOURTEEN

Seated on a chair by the edge of the well-tended grass court, Lilly watched the tennis players languidly bat a ball back and forth across the net. Dressed impeccably in white from head to toe, their peaked caps protected them from the glare of the scorching sunshine. Several rows of seats and bleachers lining the court held Newport's prominent cottagers. Beneath ruffled parasols, the ladies displayed fine summer wardrobes, light colored and lacy, and the men, white trousers, dark jackets, and straw boaters.

Squeezed between Nan Holloway and her younger sister, Eloise, Lilly caught little of their silly prattle until Nan slipped a copy of *Talk of the Town* from her reticule. She spread the latest issue across her sage green lap. Lilly leaned over to catch a better look.

Her back tensed as she skimmed the text. At the top of the column she spotted the name Fannie Cole. With her hand shaking,

Lilly pulled her spectacles from her reticule and slipped them on. The letters swam on the page. She took the news sheet from Nan and blinked until her eyes focused. *Miss Fannie Cole, will you please come forward and identify yourself to your Newport friends and acquaintances? Or are you fearful of criticism from a certain young man's family, along with your own? Don't hesitate to satisfy society's curiosity, because for the sake of your readers, your true name will soon be revealed.*

Lilly gaped at the threatening words. Would *Talk of the Town* actually print her name? The paper had divulged secrets countless times before and damaged many a member of good, respectable families. She couldn't think of any reason why they'd protect her reputation. She'd heard rumors it was possible to stop the colonel from disclosing personal information, but she didn't know how, short of boldly walking up to him and demanding an end to this nonsense. But the colonel was undoubtedly in New York writing his scandalous rag for the next outrageous edition, not here in Newport — not that she'd find the nerve to confront him in person.

Lilly dragged her gaze from the offensive sheet, unable to banish the man from her mind. Would he demand hush money and chain her to years of blackmail? She wiped her upper lip with her lace-trimmed handkerchief.

Nan brightened. "Mother and I tried to guess Fannie's true identity, but we can't imagine who among us would have the temerity to write such books."

"Hmm." Lilly opened her fan and peered at the hand-painted images of exotic birds without really seeing them.

Nan lowered her voice. "I shouldn't admit it, but I do find Miss Cole's dime novels immensely entertaining. Truth be told, everyone adores her books, your sister-in-law included. They're not just for maids and factory workers, you know. Though they are rather down-to-earth stories, they're not nearly as racy as Mother claims."

The flutter of Lilly's fan stirred a mild breeze. "It's rather hot today," she mumbled, trying to change the subject.

Nan's mouth twisted in a vindictive grin, undeterred. "If Fannie Cole has a young man, I presume she's young herself. Do we know any writers with a sweetheart?" Her eyes widened. "Lilly, you're the only one who writes. But come to think of it, you're a poet, aren't you? That's not quite the same as a renowned novelist."

225

Lilly gulped. "No, it's certainly not. And I'm not a terribly gifted poet, at that."

Why did Mama brag to everyone about her sophomoric verses? Couldn't her enthusiastic mother employ some discretion and curb her pride? Of course, with a son like George who couldn't find his place in the world, Mama couldn't resist boasting of even the minor accomplishments of her daughter. Lilly loved George's mild manner and kind heart, but he hadn't achieved anything during his twenty-nine years that Mama could crow about.

Nan closed her eyes and shook her head. "Goodness gracious, can you imagine what your mother would say if she thought you were actually Miss Cole? And Mr. Santerre too?" She gazed down with envy at Lilly's engagement ring. "Old Mrs. Santerre wouldn't stand for that."

Lilly twisted her diamond ring around her finger and then replaced her glove. "No need to worry."

Harlan slid into the empty seat next to Nan. "Good morning, ladies. Lilly, is that *Talk of the Town*?" His lips pursed.

He sounded so scandalized Lilly had to muffle a laugh. "It's Mrs. Holloway's copy."

Red blotches colored Nan's skin. "It's a pleasure to see you, Mr. Santerre. Congratulations on your engagement." She looked like she'd swallowed a sour pickle. "As for *Talk of the Town,* a friend gave it to me because it contained some fascinating tidbits." She pointed to the Fannie Cole item. "Read that."

He bent over the page and scanned the article. "So the woman is a cottager, I take it. Do you know who she is?"

"No, we don't have a clue," Nan replied.

Lilly despised herself for remaining silent; it felt like a lie. *Lord, please forgive me.*

Nan leaned across her, pushing the brim of her hat into the corner of Lilly's eye. "Mr. Santerre, there's only one writer I know in all of Newport. Can you guess who?"

"No, I don't know." A net of fine lines wrinkled his high forehead.

Nan clapped her hands. "This writer is a poet. Perhaps you can name her now."

"Lilly?" His mouth fell open.

"None other." Nan dissolved in peals of laughter.

Lilly rapped Nan on the arm with her fan. "That's ridiculous."

Nan glared back. "You're the only one I know who could possibly be the mysterious Fannie Cole, unlikely as that may seem."

"Then you don't know young society ladies as well as you think you do. Many keep diaries and write poetry for their own enjoyment. It's quite common."

Lilly glanced at Harlan, who didn't look convinced. His steel-gray eyes still demanded a denial. She turned away and frowned at Nan. "Stop your silly speculation. It's unbecoming to gossip."

Harlan rose stiffly. "Please excuse me, ladies. I'm going sailing this afternoon and I'll be late if I don't leave now." He bowed then strutted off without stopping to speak to anyone.

Nan sniffed as he vanished into the crowd. "Your fiancé doesn't have a sense of humor."

Lilly rose. "I don't find your humor any more endearing than Mr. Santerre's. I must be leaving as well."

"Well, I never . . ." Nan said, her wily fox-face drooping with surprise.

"Good day." Lilly didn't want her name connected to Fannie Cole, even in jest. After a while the busybodies might start believing she *was* Fannie and then nothing would quell the gossip. Unfortunately, Nan was the best purveyor of innuendo and rumor in Newport.

Lilly headed for the casino entrance and wove through the crowd of well-dressed spectators. She saw another copy of *Talk of the Town* sitting on a bench as if forgotten, and quietly pulled it into the folds of her dress. Many cottagers craned their necks to see the game over and around the hats, while others ignored it altogether for a chat with their friends. Thankfully, none paid any attention to her. She passed the lawn tennis courts and continued down the path near the clock tower until Jack's voice stopped her.

"What's wrong, Lilly? You're white as a ghost."

She stifled a groan. He was the last person she wanted to see. "I'm perfectly fine, thank you. If you'll excuse me, I'm on my way home."

She brushed by, but Jack caught up with her before she'd taken half a dozen steps. Before she could stop him, he grabbed *Talk of the Town.*

"I didn't realize you enjoyed gossip." As he glanced down the columns, his eyes gleamed with merriment. "What's this about Fannie Cole?" As he read the item, his face lost its cheer. "She's being threatened." He thumped the paper with his knuckles. "Look at me, Lilly." He reached over and lifted her chin.

She pulled away. "Please don't touch me, Jack." Fortunately the walkway was deserted so they weren't in danger of being seen or heard.

He dropped his hand to his side. "I'm sorry. But if you know Fannie Cole, and I believe you do, you need to understand she's in serious trouble. I can help her." Slipping her arm into his, he led her toward the wide tunnel which led out to Bellevue Avenue. "Who is she, Lilly?"

"Listen, Jack, I know you need to know who Fannie is. But I am not at liberty to disclose her identity."

Jack groaned. "I understand why you don't wish to divulge a friend's name, but Colonel MacIntyre is a ruthless man. Don't underestimate him. He'll defeat her thoroughly."

Lilly flinched. "Fannie can look out for herself."

"But she need not. As her publisher I have a duty to protect her from predators like MacIntyre."

Lilly squeezed his hand. "You're very kind, Jack, but I think you worry far too much about Fannie. I'm sure she'll contact you if she needs assistance." She strode down the walkway, wishing Jack would leave her alone to sort out her problem.

He exhaled a groan. "There's one more thing."

"Yes, what is it?"

"Tell me why Fannie is not at liberty to come forward."

Lilly returned his level gaze. "If Fannie Cole is a society woman, she's breaking the code she's bound to live by. She cannot write dime novels or earn a living. If she's discovered, she and her family will be ruined. Think of her untenable situation."

"I understand." But he sounded unconvinced. "When you see her please convey my offer to help."

Lilly nodded as she opened her parasol against the glare of the sun and Jack's steady gaze. He sincerely wanted to protect her. Involuntarily, she shuddered at the possibility he was right about the colonel.

Jack looked her squarely in the eye before she glanced away. "Lilly, tell me the truth. Please. Are you Fannie Cole?"

"What gives you that idea?" She dared to give him a disdainful look, but her voice trembled.

"Many small things point to it." His skeptical stare bore into her eyes.

Lilly turned to leave before he asked her to plainly deny his suspicions. He knew the truth, but she wasn't about to confirm it. Then her attention fell upon her sister-in-law, walking arm-in-arm with the man with the fringe of reddish curls curving around his bowler. "Look. There's Irene and the gentleman she flirted with behind the potted palms! At the van Patten's ball. Do you remember?" Although they weren't doing anything entirely inappropriate, they looked oddly intimate, engrossed in conversation.

Jack grimaced at the duo. "I do remember. I've since learned his name is Theo Nottingham."

Lilly frowned. "You don't think he's trying to woo Irene away from George, do you?"

Jack seemed unsure. "By the looks of it, I'd say that's certainly possible. But we don't know."

"True." Lilly brightened. "We're merely speculating and not giving them the benefit of the doubt — which is quite unfair."

He eyed her carefully. "Is that what you're asking me to do? Give you the benefit of the doubt?"

"It would be nice," she said. Lilly looked up at him with pleading eyes.

"All right, Lilly," he said. "But know I'm here, ready to assist you, in any way you need."

As he tore himself away and walked back to the tennis courts with sloped shoulders, Lilly wondered if he spoke merely as a publisher . . . or as a spurned lover too.

Later in the afternoon, Jack entered Mr. Westbrook's quiet office and lifted the telephone receiver. The operator soon connected him to the *Manhattan Sentinel,* the newspaper he'd purchased when he'd first returned from out West. He drummed his fingers against the desktop and waited for the editor to come on the line.

"Mr. Hayes, I'd like one of the reporters to check up on a gentleman named Theodore Nottingham from the city. It's not an investigation. The man hasn't done anything wrong. It's just a hunch I have about him."

"What kind of information are you looking for?"

"News about his family, financial status, anything unusual or odd."

"Got it, boss. I'll get back to you as soon as I can."

"Thank you."

If Irene were involved with Nottingham, Jack wanted to know before George got wind of it. He'd try to soften the blow for his friend — not that anyone could dull the pain of rejection or infidelity.

He had one more important call to make. His chest constricted when he thought of the harm Rufus MacIntyre could cause

233

Fannie Cole and indirectly, Jones and Jarman. He soon had *Talk of the Town*'s secretary on the line.

"I'm sorry, Mr. Grail. The colonel left for Newport yesterday."

"Newport? Do you know where he's staying?" He never expected MacIntyre had the gall to come here when half the town despised him.

"I'm not allowed to divulge that information."

Jack bit back a sharp retort. It wasn't the hireling's fault. "Thank you, ma'am." He'd find the old scoundrel all on his own.

He spent the rest of the afternoon searching. But the wily rogue evaded his best efforts. Tomorrow he'd scour the town until he'd located MacIntyre.

Steering the horses down Summerhill's driveway, Jack noticed an older woman climb down from the Westbrooks' gleaming black carriage parked in front of the veranda. Even from a distance, he recognized the lady. She motioned the coachmen toward the steamer trunks secured in the carryall. Jerking her head up and down, she pantomimed how carefully she wanted the luggage to be handled. Mrs. Dolly Santerre, Harlan's formidable mother, in action.

She peered at Jack through her pince-nez

spectacles. It was possible, though highly unlikely, she recognized him from St. Luke's, the school he'd attended with Harlan and George years before. Jack shuddered at the memory of his first day at the prestigious institution.

On his way to class, he'd been flagged down by Dolly Santerre, who had insisted he lug Harlan's belongings up to the third floor of the dormitory as if he were one of her servants. He ignored her then and he would ignore her now. He remembered she'd informed the headmaster that the new scholarship student was insolent and completely unworthy of financial assistance. When Mr. Elliott called him into his cavernous office, bigger than Jack's entire house, he realized he'd made a mistake by not acknowledging Mrs. Santerre's superiority. But she wielded no power over him now.

Gritting his teeth, Jack headed for the front veranda.

# FIFTEEN

"Welcome to Summerhill, Mrs. Santerre. I'm delighted you've come." Lilly pasted on her most hospitable smile as her future mother-in-law grabbed her hands and squeezed the blood right out of her fingers.

When Mrs. Santerre released her grip, she glanced from Lilly to Miranda to Mama. "It's delightful to see all of you. But where's my dear Harlan?"

The door opened and Harlan stepped onto the veranda. "I'm here, Mother." He gave her a quick hug and pecked her on the cheek.

"Shall we all go inside?" Mama asked.

"Come along, girls," Mrs. Santerre directed with a lift of her chin. Dressed in a chocolate brown traveling suit, she wore a fashionable cocoa colored hat with dark feathers rising from the brim.

"In a few moments, Aunt Dolly," Miranda said.

Lilly grimaced as Dolly Santerre sailed into the foyer. A female version of Harlan, Dolly was stick-thin except for her remarkably prominent bosom accentuated by a sturdy corset. Her blue eyes reflected the same winter chill as Harlan's.

"How I dreaded her arrival," Lilly whispered to Miranda when the door closed. "She intimidates me so."

Miranda gurgled with laughter. "Aunt Dolly intimidates everyone. I'd like to say she's completely harmless, but I'm afraid she does have a bite. From time to time." She squeezed Lilly's arm. "Don't look so distraught. I'm exaggerating."

But Lilly knew the truth when she heard it.

The crunch of a horse's hooves on the pebbled driveway distracted her from anxiety over her future mother-in-law. The gig halted at the veranda and Jack jumped out of the driver's seat. She braced herself as he sprang up the steps and halted by her side.

"Good day, ladies." He bowed. His gaze rested on Miranda. "Did I just see Mrs. Santerre?"

"Yes, indeed. She's my aunt — my mother's sister."

"You are Harlan's cousin?" His tone began as incredulous, but then he collected himself. "I had no idea you were related. How fine to have more of your family here with you at Summerhill." He leaned against the porch rail and studied Miranda, ignoring Lilly. "Miss Reid, I've been meaning to ask you a question. Do you happen to know Miss Fannie Cole, the authoress? Since you bought her books for the women at the Settlement House, I thought it's quite possible you're acquainted."

Lilly froze.

Miranda tossed him an easy smile. "None of my acquaintances is named Fannie Cole. As far as I know, there aren't any Coles in society."

A slight smile on his lips, he looked from Miranda to Lilly, then back again. "It's a nom de plume, of course. But it's apparent you'd rather not speak of her." He raised his bowler. "Have a splendid afternoon."

After dinner at home, the ladies gathered in the elegant drawing room while the men drank brandy and smoked cigars in the dining room. Lilly hoped she and Miranda could wander off unnoticed, but Mrs. Santerre peered through her spectacles when they rose to leave.

"Stay, my dear girls. We must discuss the wedding. There's no time like the present, I always say. Harlan and I feel the sooner the marriage takes place, the better. It's merely a matter of setting the date." Dolly Santerre flashed a smug smile.

Overwhelming a high-backed chair with her presence, though not her size, Dolly resembled a dowager duchess. Her neck stretched back, tilting her small head and sharp chin upward. Through her pince-nez, she peered down upon her subjects. Critically. Her steady gaze swept across the ladies on the settees and rested on Lilly. "So, how does the last Saturday in August sound to you, Lillian?"

Lilly inhaled sharply. "The bride always sets her own wedding date." She could scarcely believe she'd found the gumption to equivocate with the commanding Dolly Santerre.

"Naturally, I'm giving you that choice. You're not objecting to August, are you?" One eyebrow arched dangerously.

Lilly's hands twisted her crepe de chine skirt. "I had my heart set on a spring wedding. May is a beautiful month in New York."

Mrs. Santerre snorted. "May is unlucky for weddings. June is far more suitable. But why wait so long when you can have a lovely summer affair here at Summerhill?" She studied her for a moment. "Lillian, I don't understand your reluctance. Is there some reason you insist upon delaying the ceremony?"

All eyes rested on Lilly. She shrank back into the sofa. "No, except that I love the spring."

Dolly chomped back, "Spring weather isn't dependable."

Mama offered a cautious smile. "Actually, Dolly, summer in Newport is also unpredictable."

Lilly looked eagerly to her mother, an unexpected block against Dolly's intimidation. A frown flickered across Mama's face like a flash of pale heat lightning and then faded.

Amusement raised the corners of Irene's mouth. "Personally, I'd choose August for my nuptials. What month does your son prefer, Mrs. Santerre?"

"August. Definitely August." A curt nod punctuated her pronouncement.

Lilly gritted her teeth. "I'll agree to next June." She couldn't allow her future mother-in-law to grab the upper hand or the woman would soon control every aspect of her marriage. "I'm so relieved that's settled." She forced a smile and then reached out to squeeze Miranda's hand, as if all was perfectly well and she was merely an excited bride to be.

Mrs. Santerre clicked her tongue then spoke in her sweetest, most reasonable voice. "I'm sorry my dearest, but I forgot to mention the most important consideration."

Holding her breath, Lilly waited with a sinking heart while the older woman scrunched her face into a counterfeit look of regret.

"My dear mother, Mrs. Langley, wishes to attend. She's eighty-five and in poor health. So, it's imperative we have the wedding as soon as possible." Mrs. Santerre expelled a long sigh, as mournful as a foghorn. "She may not live through the winter. Her heart, you know." She thumped the deep curve of her breast, upholstered in moss green brocade.

Lilly paused a moment, then stood and faced her future mother-in-law. "I've dreamed of a spring wedding ever since I was a little girl. However, I understand your situation. I too would like Mrs. Langley to attend." Lilly smiled graciously through clenched teeth. "So, I have the solution; the wedding will take place on the second Saturday of September here in Newport."

"As you wish." The blood drained from Mrs. Santerre's face. With her grimace frozen in place, she resembled an ice sculpture.

"Is that an acceptable date for you — and for your mother?" Lilly knew she'd crossed the line. Dolly Santerre refused to tolerate defiance. For Harlan's sake and probably for her own as well, she needed to stay in the woman's good graces. A difficult task when Mrs. Santerre resisted any ideas other than her own. Yet Lilly vowed not to give in to the woman's every whim.

Dolly gave a brusque nod. "Mother will live until September, though the last weekend in August would be more convenient."

*As if Mrs. Santerre determined the dates of life and death.*

Lilly knew Mrs. Langley, the family matriarch, suffered from failing health. She couldn't make it out the door of the home she shared with the Santerres no matter when or where the wedding took place. It was all a farce, a blatant attempt on Dolly's part to wield control.

Mama's eyes fluttered. "There's one other thing we need to discuss — the engagement party. Since the wedding is in the near future, we need to announce the engagement as soon as possible."

"Whatever you decide will be fine with me," Lilly demurred.

Mrs. Santerre brightened. "You can count on my help, Vanessa. After marrying off five daughters with only one more to go, I know a little something about parties and wedding receptions."

"Thank you so much." Lilly headed for the door with her friend at her heel. "Miranda and I are going for a walk down by the beach. Would anyone care to join us?"

When all the ladies declined, she and Miranda hurried outside into the setting sun. Blood-red streaks blended into hues of rose and orange, glowing across the western sky.

Miranda glanced sideways. "I can see trouble ahead for you and Harlan. Aunt Dolly will try to control everything you do."

They crossed the shadowed lawn. Lilly stopped by the boulders reaching down into the cove. Giant waves washed over the rocks below, thrusting fingers of seaweed into the crevices. She led Miranda down the wooden stairs to the small strip of beach she called her sanctuary, holding her skirts above the damp silver sand.

"I do hope you're wrong. Oh my, I'll certainly have my hands full." Lilly gave a wry smile. "Do you think Harlan will stand up for my point of view?"

They stood side by side on the beach

watching the sun sink toward the horizon. Miranda exuded so much compassion and concern, Lilly wondered if she should take Mrs. Santerre even more seriously than she already was.

Miranda tossed a pebble into the roaring surf. "You must understand, although Harlan loves you, he's always taken his mother's part. Aunt Dolly adores him and he appreciates her loyalty. I doubt that he'll change." Miranda stamped her shoe in the firm gray sand and looked sorrowfully in her direction. "Now I've gone and upset you, Lilly. Forgive me. Remember, my cousin Harlan's a good man. He'll put you on a pedestal, just as he does Aunt Dolly. I'm sure he'll make you happy." But Miranda's voice wavered.

"You're really not sure I should marry him, are you?"

"Oh, Lilly. I truly don't know what's best for you. Think about it long and hard. You must be sure of your love before you walk down the aisle."

Miranda's words reflected the doubts Lilly harbored in her heart. Could a mama's boy ever bring her joy? "If I didn't believe we'd be content, I'd never marry him." Yet, she'd have to assert herself with her future mother-in-law and insist her marriage remain off limits. No acquiescing to keep family peace. Unfortunately, she lacked experience standing up for herself and defending her own opinions.

Miranda patted Lilly's arm. "Don't fret about Aunt Dolly. You'll find a way to deal with her. Just think — we'll soon be related. Won't that be fun?"

"Yes, I'm looking forward to it." Then Lilly frowned. "But I do worry I'm not temperamentally suited to the Santerres' social set."

"Of course you won't take up my aunt's tiresome schedule. You'd detest those boring get-togethers."

"Indeed. I try my best to avoid them even now." Lilly lowered herself onto a boulder and cocked her head. "Do you think Harlan will allow me to follow the Lord's plans for my life? You know, my writing, my visits to the Settlement House. He's already told me I should find another charity to support."

Miranda rolled her eyes toward the darkening sky. "I'm sure he'll leave you to your own devices."

"But is it right to keep my ministry from him?" Lilly sighed. She valued her privacy, but she didn't like living a double life. "I still feel such dreadful guilt about deceiving Harlan — and my family as well."

"I'll pray that the Lord will arrange the right time and circumstance for you to tell everyone." Miranda gave her a warm hug.

"Please do pray for me. I want to be honest and open. Keeping this secret is eating away at my soul. And I know it can't please the Lord." Lilly shuddered. "But I'm so afraid exposure would ruin my family."

"Lilly, God's light shines through your work — just not through your name. The Lord will show you a solution."

The sun melted into the horizon. Stars twinkled dimly in the luminous blue sky as the moon ascended. Lilly folded her arms around her chest to stave off the chilly night air.

*Lord, please show me what You wish me to do.*

Lilly knew if she failed to appear for afternoon tea in the drawing room Mama would roust her from the sanctuary of her bedroom where she'd spent the last two hours catching up on her writing. Headed down the hallway, she was stopped cold by shouts from George and Irene's room. Despite the rise and fall of angry voices, her brother and sister-in-law's quarrel penetrated the walls loud and clear.

George spit out his words in a barrage of

verbal bullets. "Irene, for months you've shopped to your heart's content and played cards into the small hours of the morning. But fourteen hundred dollars lost in a bridge game! Where on earth will I find the funds to pay your debt?"

"I simply don't know. But I'm sure you'll find a way, my dearest." Irene sounded petulant. In her mind's eye, Lilly pictured her sister-in-law's pout, one of her standard weapons aimed at anyone who crossed her.

"That's impossible. I have very little money of my own."

"Do keep your voice down, George. Maybe you can borrow money from your parents. They wouldn't want your reputation soiled."

George grunted. "It's really your reputation, not mine. Everyone knows I don't gamble."

"Nevertheless, I imagine your parents will help us. They'll want to preserve the family's good name."

"I refuse to ask. It's not their problem."

"Well then, I'll speak to them myself." Lilly heard belligerence in Irene's voice coupled with a shrill note of fear. Lilly almost pitied her sister-in-law, though the careless woman obviously hadn't worried about consequences when she'd played cards for high stakes.

"Ask your Uncle Quentin," George boomed.

"I can't. He's traveling in Europe and I don't know how to get in touch with him."

"Telegraph his office in San Francisco. They'll give you his schedule."

Irene's sigh dragged into a groan. "Please, George, stop badgering me. Tracking him down is out of the question. Uncle Quentin isn't responsible for my debts. You are."

"All right, Irene. I'll think of something to help you. But never again. Do you understand?"

George's barely restrained anger shocked Lilly. Her lackadaisical, easy-going brother seldom raised his voice or showed irritation, let alone fury. Lilly knew she shouldn't listen to a private conversation, even one loud enough to be labeled a shouting match. But her shoes were riveted to the carpet runner. She'd never heard Irene and George bicker before, though lately they seemed to spend more time apart. Irene often played hand after hand of bridge while George frequented billiard tables and the golf links. They seldom showed affection or laughed at each other's jokes as they had only a few months ago.

Once in the hallway, Lilly headed for the

staircase. Jack emerged from his bedroom next to George and Irene's and whispered, "Loud, aren't they?" with an unhappy twist of his mouth.

"And angry. I do hope Irene's gambling won't ruin their marriage," Lilly added, realizing it most likely already had.

Lilly had heard Irene seldom won at bridge, but she hadn't suspected the extent of her sister-in-law's losses. Didn't Irene realize George's modest income needed frugal management which excluded every type of gambling and reckless spending? Together she and Jack quietly descended the staircase.

"That was a terrible row," Jack said as they approached the empty foyer. "I feel bad for George. Irene is the wrong woman for him, though there's nothing he can do about it now." Glancing at Lilly from the corner of his eye, Jack shook his head sadly. "Choosing the right spouse is crucial. If love is missing, there's little chance of happiness."

*Dear Lord, please don't let my marriage to Harlan be like Irene and George's.*

If Jack hadn't come along she'd never have questioned her feelings for the man who offered her so much. But Jack *did* appear and change everything. He flipped her world upside down. He pointed out the shallowness of her affection for her suitor and perhaps the shallowness of his fondness for her. But Jack offered her nothing more than book contracts and fame.

"A penny for your thoughts, Lilly." Jack leaned toward her as they strolled down the back hallway past the empty billiard room and library.

She sniffed a small chuckle. "They're not worth a penny."

He leaned closer and whispered, "Tell me anyway."

"I think not."

Jack shrugged and halted by the conservatory.

"Excuse me. I believe I'd like to take a short walk before tea." Lilly stepped out onto the veranda.

A swirl of mist swept around her as she strolled across the wet grass. Ahead, the clouds thickened and smudged the line between the cliffs and the ocean. Seagulls shrieked and the sea roared, but everything blurred into the fog.

"Why are you following me?" Lilly asked after they'd taken several steps. She should have stopped him at the veranda and gone on alone. His presence certainly didn't bring her any comfort, but when he walked by her side, she felt so alive.

"I'm following you because I like to be

with you, Lilly." Before she could object, he continued. "Do you remember when I gave you a small silver cross on a chain?"

"Of course." She stopped herself from pulling it from beneath her collar and showing him. She wasn't sure why she wore it every day, other than it seemed to remind her of love, hope . . . if not here on Earth, in the hereafter. Her heart beat with the force of the sea pounding against the rocks. She pressed her hand to her silk bodice to stop the painful rhythm, but it continued. "Your gift meant so much to me. I kept it as a remembrance."

He gave a sad chuckle. "It was my Christmas present to the girl who charmed me and stole my heart. I was grateful for your many kindnesses."

"Perhaps it was more like infatuation." The words slipped out. She'd admitted too much. If she weren't careful he'd capture her in his spell all over again. "I must go. I'll be late for tea."

"No, stay with me and talk awhile. We still have so much to say." He reached for her hand, but she snatched it away.

"I can't."

"Lilly, please stop running away from me. I thought we were still friends."

But she rushed back to the cottage, pant-

251

ing for breath. Her head ached, but so much less than her heart. She was already lost and so afraid the past would soon repeat itself if she weren't more careful.

As she passed the billiard room, she heard the click of wooden balls and smelled the stench of cigar smoke wafting through the open door. Curious, she peeked inside and saw her brother racking the balls, a smelly cigar protruding from his mouth.

"Do come in, Lilly. I'd like to have a word with you, if you don't mind."

# SIXTEEN

She hesitated. He looked so miserable with his long face. Dispirited herself, she felt unprepared to cheer him up. "You look despondent, George. Is it Irene? I couldn't help but hear your argument."

He jerked a nod. "Irene and I don't agree about anything." Bending over the carved table, George took aim with his cue stick and broke open the pack of billiard balls.

"I'm sorry I overheard. I didn't mean to listen."

George shrugged. "Everyone heard us, I'm sure. Irene and I disagree about finances, as usual." He stood up straight. "I'm sorry to burden you with my troubles, but I do have a favor to ask."

She stepped away from the stink of the cigar and fanned the smoke. "What is it, George?" Lilly braced herself for the worst, knowing her brother's propensity toward asking for assistance.

He bit his lip. "I need to pay off Irene's gambling debts as soon as possible, before Mama gets wind of it."

"Then ask Papa to loan you the money."

"I told Irene I would, but I reconsidered." George gave a mournful shake of his head. "You know how Mama opposes gambling. She'd never allow Papa to loan me the funds. And he wouldn't hand over a penny without her approval. So there's no point in asking."

Lilly nodded. "Yes, I'm sure you're right about that."

He cocked an eyebrow. "I have a better plan."

"Go on."

Extinguishing his cigar, he leaned toward Lilly, but not close enough to subject her to his tobacco breath. "Since you're going to marry Harlan, I thought you might ask him for a loan — which I'll repay as soon as I begin working. In September, right after your wedding."

"Why don't you ask him yourself?"

He pulled on the point of his goatee. "Because he might not want an employee who can't manage his finances — or his wife." He raised his eyebrows. "But he loves you, so he's more apt to agree to a request from you than from me."

The sag of George's jaw and downturned mouth drew out her sympathy. Even in his late twenties he was as vulnerable as a little boy. And that was the problem. She'd often provided the cushion to soften the blows George would otherwise receive.

"Please, Lilly." He clasped his hands in mock supplication.

"Oh, all right, but please don't ask any more favors. I hate to be indebted to anyone." Especially Harlan.

Relief spread across his long face and his tight shoulders relaxed. "You're the perfect sister."

Lilly flicked a wry smile. "Of course I am. I've always done what you've asked. But from now on, you must take care of your own problems."

Just as she had to.

That night Harlan whirled Lilly around the dance floor to the strains of a lively march. She brushed aside a few carefully arranged bangs that stuck to her forehead in a small mass of frizz. Her new champagne-colored gown felt cumbersome and her white kid gloves clung to her fingers like a second skin. The humidity from a light drizzle seeped beneath the Palladian windows and permeated the crowded dance floor.

Three hundred and fifty costumed guests chattered in the gold and white ballroom of Rocky Ridge, unable to spill into the courtyard where the storm had washed the stone slick. Lilly had come as Elizabeth Bennet, one of her favorite literary characters. Her costume paled in comparison to some of the more elaborate get-ups. Eighteenth-century French courtiers and Renaissance nobility were among the most popular choices.

"Would you care for some supper?" Harlan called over the roar of voices as soon as the music ended. He glanced toward the dining room where half a dozen servants scurried around, preparing the tables for the famished dancers.

The aroma of the midnight supper drifted in from the dining room. It mixed with the pungent odor of the sea and the fragrance of corsages.

"Yes, I'm rather hungry," Lilly said.

This might be the ideal opportunity to mention her need for fourteen hundred dollars. As they strolled together through the tangle of guests, her heart skittered. How would she tactfully broach the topic of money? And how would she convince him to loan it to her? She hated to cajole or flirt, the usual feminine weapons, though she doubted the straightforward approach would work. She had tried that with the Settlement House . . .

They passed a gilded mirror and Lilly caught sight of her reflection. With her mouth pinched and eyes drawn together, she looked terrified, like a trapped rabbit. So much for the self assurance she tried to project.

Harlan led her to a small round table bathed in the softness of candlelight and decorated with puffy blue hydrangeas, one of Newport's favorite flowers. Since the late-night supper would be served continually for three hours, most of the guests lingered on the dance floor. Only a few trickled into the immense, high-ceiling dining room transported piece by piece from a French chateau, like so many other salons in Newport.

While Harlan delved into the Lobster à la Newberg, Lilly sat stiff and silent staring into her clear terrapin soup. Her appetite vanished when she considered her task.

She tried to smile. "Harlan, I have something to ask you. A favor, actually." Her voice emerged like a croak.

Starting on the tomato aspic, he glanced up from his gold rimmed plate. "Anything at all, my dear. What would you like? My grandmother's pearls or perhaps one of her ruby rings?"

Lilly winced. How could he be so crude? "I'd never think of requesting a piece of family jewelry. That's for you to give me as you see fit."

"Well then?" He laid his fork on the dinner plate and gave her his full attention.

A formally dressed waiter refilled Harlan's glass.

Lilly sipped water to sooth her parched throat. "Something has come up and I need a large amount of money. My monthly income won't cover it all, or even most of it. I was hoping you'd loan me the funds, if you don't mind. Of course I'll repay you as soon as I can." She inhaled a deep breath and held it.

Harlan folded his arms across his chest. His eyelids dropped to half mast like the visor on a knight's steel helmet. "You haven't lost money on bridge, have you? I certainly hope I'm not about to marry a gambler." He chuckled at his attempted humor and then gave the ends of his waxed mustache a nervous twist.

"I don't play cards, Harlan. You know that."

"Naturally I know you abstain from such things. It was just my little joke."

"Of course." She waited for his answer that wasn't forthcoming. "I would greatly appreciate a loan, if you wouldn't mind." She wished she could have added, "a small loan" to minimize its importance.

Harlan paused for several seconds. Why couldn't he say yes without pursing his lips and scrunching up his face?

He stroked her hand with his clammy fingers. "If it's money for your trousseau or even for the wedding, I'll be glad to speak to your father. The ceremony is to be rather intimate and informal, so I'm sure he can afford it. But if he's short of cash, I'd be delighted to help."

The music emanating from the ballroom faded into the background as the drone of conversations grew louder. Couples and small groups wandered into the supper area and found places at the empty tables. If anyone joined them, Lilly knew their discussion would immediately end.

She glanced around, careful to avoid eye contact with anyone searching for a table and a friendly chat. "No, that's not it. Please, don't ask me to explain. It's a personal situation I'd like to resolve soon, before we're married."

Harlan tapped her hand and smiled condescendingly. "You must tell me. As your future husband I have a right to know how my fiancée plans to spend my money."

"Yes, of course you do. But I'm not at liberty to say."

He scoffed. "No? And why not?"

"Because — it's private and somewhat embarrassing. Doesn't a girl have the privilege of keeping a secret or two?" Her words emerged more like a challenge than a request. She was so horribly inept at employing charm, let alone womanly wiles. She should drop her chin and look up flirtatiously like a coquette, but her jaw jutted and her gaze locked on his. "I wish I could explain since you do have every right to know the details, but unfortunately . . ."

Harlan tossed his serviette on the table. "In any case, I'm afraid I must decline."

Lilly held up her hand. "Then I withdraw my request. It was impertinent of me to ask. No need for you to worry." *I will not beg.* Her cheeks flamed, but she kept her voice low and soft.

For a moment he looked surprised she'd given in so easily. She asked, "You're not angry with me, are you?"

A long-suffering sigh answered her question. "I thought we would always be honest with each other. But I can see you're secretive. I hope you'll be more forthcoming after we marry. Or am I to be disappointed about that too?"

"Harlan, can't you trust me? I promise you'll get your funds back."

"How can I fully trust you when you won't confide in me? A husband should be privy to each and every financial transaction his wife wishes to make. We must not keep anything from each other, financial or otherwise. I expect you to share all your concerns and always seek my advice."

"And follow it, too, no doubt," Lilly muttered.

"Naturally." His eyes narrowed. "Do I detect a note of sarcasm in your voice?"

Lilly stared at him. This wasn't love, this thing between them. It was a business arrangement. How could she marry for reasons she would never allow her own characters to marry for? How could she accept anything less than love?

A crowd swept into the supper room and headed their way. Others soon followed. The noise level rose and all their privacy ended.

Harlan bowed low and offered his arm to escort her back to the ballroom. Lilly accepted and retreated to a vacant chair beside her mother. With curiosity etched in every crease of her round face, Mama opened her mouth as if to pry then slammed it shut. For once she didn't ask any questions, though from the flutter of her eyelids Lilly knew she was tempted.

*Thank you for leaving me alone.* Too tired from the stress of the day and Harlan's intransigence, Lilly pushed into the stiff back of the gilt ball chair, glad it hugged the far wall by the screened-off orchestra. No one could converse with the beat of the polka pounding in her ears. She felt invisible and glad of it. As the dancers twirled around the herringbone floor, Lilly closed her eyes.

She'd hoped Harlan would lend her the money without demanding specifics, but she hadn't really expected it. Still, worry shifted down her spine. What other disappointments were in store for her? Not too long ago she'd thought his attentiveness suggested a thoughtful spirit, not a calculating mind. This new side of his personality chilled her.

Lilly opened her eyes and focused on the gentlemen in knee britches, satin waistcoats, and white powered wigs, King Louis the XIV, XV, and XVI look-alikes dancing with their ladies. Even in Little Bo Peep and Alice in Wonderland costumes, the cottagers sparkled with jewels.

She noticed Queen Elizabeth marching toward her, her head weighed down by a crown, a scepter in hand. No doubt as intimidating as the original monarch, Dolly Santerre could cause knees to quake. Dressed in purple velvet, Harlan's mother stared at her without a polite smile. Lilly braced herself. Unfortunately the seat to her left was empty. Mrs. Santerre brushed past her and descended onto her throne.

"My son tells me you need money, but you won't explain why." Mrs. Santerre's nostrils constricted as if she smelled horse dung. "Why don't you ask your parents for help? That would be the proper thing to do." She glanced over at Mama, who smiled beatifically since she couldn't hear a word above the music.

Lilly gulped for fresh air, breathing in the overpowering sweetness of Dolly's perfume. It hadn't taken Harlan long to tattle to his mother. "I regret that I can't explain."

Dolly's thin lips tightened. "Then you must have done something shameful. Tell me what it was so I can judge for myself. Out with it, my girl."

Lilly clutched her hands in her lap, pressing on her knuckles until they hurt. No one had ever spoken to her in that tone of voice. She was the "good daughter" who brought credit to her parents and never caused them a moment of concern.

But spilling the tale of Irene's gambling debt wouldn't endear the Santerres to either George or Irene, and they were counting on a job for her brother.

"I told Harlan I regretted asking for assistance. Please forgive my boldness." Her apology nearly strangled in her throat.

Dolly wagged a finger in Lilly's direction. "One word of caution: don't ever try to take advantage of my son again or you will have to deal directly with me. Is that understood?"

Lilly dared to stare back into her eyes. "Yes, you're perfectly clear."

Dolly snapped her head in a nod. "Then that's settled. I'll overlook your disgraceful behavior this time. In the future, remember who you are and who you're marrying." Her eyes glinted. "You'll be grateful to know I do have a solution to your problem."

Tensing, Lilly swallowed hard. "Yes?"

"I'd be pleased if you and Harlan would share my residence on Fifth Avenue. If you agree, I will advance the money tomorrow. Harlan hopes we can all live together rather than waste funds building a smaller place out in the middle of nowhere, as you seem to prefer."

Lilly grimaced. Harlan had promised her a home on the outskirts of fashionable New York, not in the hub of the city. Sharing the Santerre mansion with Dolly and dozens of servants would bode poorly for the success of her marriage — that is, if she really went through with a marriage. Their Renaissance chateau had all the warmth of a bank.

Lilly stood and stared at her future mother-in-law. "Your generosity overwhelms me, but I'm afraid I must refuse. As a new bride I'd like my own home, even a modest one." Her voice rang with strength and firmness she didn't realize she had. "Thank you kindly for your offer, but I must decline."

Dolly's face turned almost as purple as her gown. Lilly bit the inside of her cheek to keep from laughing. Relief rippled through her. She hadn't secured the funds she sought, but she'd cut the strings that bound her to Dolly Santerre — and perhaps her son.

Lilly rose and looked for George. Unable to find him, she wove through the clusters of guests until she located Irene in the secluded picture gallery near the foyer. Irene was murmuring in Theo Nottingham's ear. Sweet nothings, no doubt. Lilly's satin slippers pounded across the marble floor.

"If you'll excuse us, Mr. Nottingham, I'd

like to speak to my sister-in-law." She didn't care that her voice carried censure.

He slipped away, leaving Lilly with the open-mouthed Irene. Her face, hard as her emerald necklace, glared with indignation. She smoothed her taffeta skirt, a brilliant green, and thrust out her chin.

"Why did you send Mr. Nottingham scurrying away when we were merely having a pleasant conversation?"

"It's inappropriate for a married woman —"

Irene cut her off with a disdainful wave. "It's also inappropriate for an engaged woman to allow another man to follow her around like a lovesick puppy. Don't look so shocked, Lilly. It's very apparent Jack is in love with you." Irene laughed as humiliation sent a blast of heat to Lilly's face. "It's also very apparent you're in love with him."

Lilly fought the urge to escape. She swallowed hard and said in her most controlled voice, "Please tell George that Harlan refused to give me a loan. You'll have to find someone else to pay your bills."

Irene's smirk dissolved. "Did you mention the money was for George and me — for personal expenses?"

"I did not. I thought it best to keep your names out of it."

"Hmm." Irene flicked a sly smile. "You do love your little secrets. Anyhow, George will find another way to pay our debts."

As Irene stepped away, Lilly touched her arm. "You must stop gambling at once. If this becomes common knowledge, you'll bring disgrace upon my entire family."

Irene's eyebrow arched. "I'm surprised *you're* so concerned about propriety." Her mocking laugh echoed through the dark, deserted gallery as she strode back toward the ballroom.

# SEVENTEEN

On the ride home Lilly stared into the foggy night sky from the back seat of the crowded carriage. She tried not to think of Irene's cutting remarks about her relationship with Jack. Was it really obvious he held a torch for her — and she for him? Or had Irene exaggerated to make her worry? She couldn't help but wonder if others had noticed. She'd hate to be the object of gossip and innuendo. Her cheeks warmed with heat though a chill had cooled the night air. She was grateful for the shroud of darkness.

As the horses trotted toward Summerhill and her fellow passengers recounted the evening's entertainment, Lilly closed her eyes. With an avalanche of wedding presents arriving each day and the engraved invitations ready to be posted, it was too late for second thoughts, wasn't it? She should have pondered her marriage long and hard weeks before. Instead, she'd allowed events and family expectations to engulf her.

*Lord, please show me what to do. I have no answers of my own.*

Jack read another set of manuscripts by the glow of the fireplace and the sputtering gaslight. He'd declined tonight's invitation in his quest for a new authoress. He strongly suspected Lilly was his dime novelist, but since she wouldn't admit the truth or help him in his search for Fannie, he had to find another author to propel into the public arena, and quickly. A star. Preferably an attention hound. Unfortunately, none of these manuscripts were up to par.

He sighed and put down the last of the stories. Not much had gone right lately.

Footsteps sounded in the hallway before he saw Miranda at the door. She peered into the room.

"Do you mind if I join you while I look for a book? I was much too tired to dance this evening, so I decided to stay at Summerhill." She grinned. "Actually, I don't like dancing very much."

"Do come in, Miss Reid." Jack rose part way before she motioned him to sit.

She strode across the carpet, removed a copy of *Anna Karenina* from the bookshelves, and regarded Jack with pursed lips and a furrowed brow. Book in hand, she came closer. "May I speak frankly?"

"By all means."

Miranda slid into the leather chair opposite Jack and leaned forward, her long fingers entwined on her lap. Unlike most society ladies, she wore no jewelry except a gold watch pinned to her tailored shirtwaist. "I'm not sure how to begin or if I should even broach the subject of — your relationship to Lilly."

Jack gulped and his pulse quickened. Were his feelings for Lilly so obvious even Miranda noticed? He didn't wish to answer, but the woman looked resolute. "Miss Reid, Miss Westbrook and I have no relationship. We did once, as you probably know, but that ended years ago."

"Lilly and I have been friends since childhood and we do confide in each other. My point is: your presence at Summerhill upsets her and reminds her of your past together. May I be blunt?"

Jack gave a sardonic grin. "I think you're already blunt. But yes, please continue."

"Thank you." She steepled her fingers and seemed to weigh her words. "If you have no romantic interest in Lilly, please leave her alone and quit playing with her emotions. Let her marry Harlan in peace, without second thoughts. She deserves to be happy, especially after the pain you caused her several years ago. She's barely recovered from your — betrayal."

He winced. Miranda's words stung. "I've tried not to interfere with her engagement, but it's hard to remain silent since I find them completely unsuited. Please don't take offence, but I think your cousin Harlan is an arrogant popinjay who'll never make Lilly happy."

Miranda sputtered with laughter. When she sobered, she stared at him with dark blue, direct eyes. "Then do something about it. Don't just fret. Win her back — if that's what you actually long to do."

Jack felt his face and neck blaze from embarrassment. Seldom had a woman spoken to him so candidly. "I do want to win her affection, but I hesitate because I failed her once — and I hate to disrupt her life again. Her parents might feel I'm not a good enough match for her —"

"Nonsense, Mr. Grail. Perhaps that was true once, but no longer. You've proven yourself and you've established your place in the business sector. The Westbrooks want their daughter's happiness, and they believe Harlan is the right man. But I don't really believe he is. I've known him my entire life so I understand his virtues . . . and his faults." Miranda's eyes locked onto Jack's. "They're a dreadful match. And more to the point — Lilly loves you."

"Did she tell you this?" Jack felt the room spin.

"Not in so many words, but she didn't have to. I know her well." Miranda didn't let her comment digest before she asked, "Now what are you going to do about it?"

Miranda's question remained in the forefront of Jack's mind for the rest of the evening as he waited for Lilly to come home from the dance. He heard the hall clock strike midnight, shattering the silence of the nearly empty house. Lilly might be gone for several more hours, so perhaps he should retire now and search for her in the morning. He rose from the leather chair, then dropped down again. No, he'd stay. His anxiety would never permit him to sleep. He'd wait here in the library and listen for Lilly's return.

Jack read Mr. Westbrook's latest edition of the *Wall Street Journal* until his eyes blurred with fatigue. Unable to settle his mind, he paced in front of the crackling fire, threw another log on the burning wood, and watched it blaze.

■ ■ ■ ■

"Harlan, may I speak with you in private?" Lilly trailed the group, lingering in the foyer as George, Irene, and Dolly climbed the stairs to their bedrooms. "It's important."

Now was the time to break their engagement. *Lord, please give me strength.*

Harlan glanced over his shoulder as he paused on the first stair. "I'm tired. Can't it wait until morning? I said all I intend to say about the matter you mentioned this evening. Just let it drop."

Lilly's eyes widened. The loan was the least of her considerations. "Please, Harlan. We're always too busy during the day. Now would be much better."

He expelled a long exasperated sigh. "No, not tonight. We'll talk tomorrow, after I return from sailing."

"All right," she mumbled. She watched as he climbed the rest of the stairs, never looking backward. Did he have so little regard for her? Or did he fear what she had to say?

She sat on the stairs, burying her head in her hands

Jack strode into the foyer.

"Lilly, may I speak to you for a few moments?"

Looking up, she gave a weary smile. "Of course. For a few moments." She arose and followed him into the library, her champagne-colored skirt swishing as she walked. Standing with her back to the mantle, she waited with her head tilted.

His voice grew husky. He clasped his hands behind his back and stood with legs apart. "Lilly, I've wanted to tell you something ever since I arrived at Summerhill, but the time never seemed right. And then you became engaged to Harlan, so I kept quiet." Jack took a deep breath.

Her small nod encouraged him to continue.

"May I tell you now?"

"I believe so, Jack."

"I came to Summerhill to ask for your forgiveness, even though I don't deserve it. And I hoped you'd let me back into your life." He paused as if looking for some hint of encouragement.

Her eyes welled with tears.

"I love you, Lilly," he said in a hoarse voice barely above a whisper. "I should have married you long ago. I should have never left you. I should have trusted that you could make your way, alongside me."

Lilly's heartbeat roared in her ears. Had Jack actually admitted he should have married her? Slowly, Lilly gazed up at Jack, unsure whether she ought to let go, give in. In a flash their past love flared with life, with fire. She needed to think, not let her feelings overwhelm her. But love so filled her heart she couldn't think clearly.

Lilly sunk into the nearest sofa. "Then why did you leave me?"

He breathed out an anguished sigh. "I was humiliated. I thought your parents would laugh at my audacity. And I felt certain that in the cold light of day you'd reconsider and turn me away. So I took the coward's way out before either you or your father told me in polite terms that I wasn't an acceptable match. I couldn't face the rejection."

Her throat constricted and she could hardly speak. "Your love was all I ever needed." Why hadn't he realized that?

Jack's features pulled down with misery. "But your parents wanted so much more for you."

Lilly pressed her hands to her forehead. "Perhaps you're right, but you should have asked Papa anyway. I would've begged him for his blessing and I might have won him over." Her argument sounded weak, but didn't he think their love was worth fighting for?

Jack shook his head mournfully. "Your

father would've rebuffed me. Who could blame him? If only I'd found the gumption to ask anyway." His voice dropped as he held her gaze. "My pride wouldn't let me accept outright refusal. I couldn't bear hearing I wasn't good enough for you."

"Oh Jack, I believed you proposed hastily and then regretted it." How could she have so misunderstood his abrupt departure? "I was shy and awkward, too conventional and dull to hold your attention." She blushed at her admission. "My family didn't have a large fortune, so I thought you were searching for an heiress who could help you with your career. Someone more fitting for a man on the rise."

His self-mocking laugh shocked her. "No. You were the young, beautiful heiress while I was the unworthy pauper."

Jack leaned so close she could feel his warm breath caress her cheek. "I left you with every intention of making my fortune and returning in triumph, a rich man, if not a grand catch."

"Why didn't you tell me?" Lilly stammered. "I would have waited for you as long as necessary."

"I didn't want to confess how inferior I felt. I had nothing but a good education and I didn't know if I could actually use it to my advantage. It wasn't fair to ask you to wait on the off chance I might succeed." Jack paused. "I railed against the unfairness of life. I hated my fear of failure. I despised myself for not telling you the entire truth. I am so sorry."

He dropped down onto the sofa beside her. He reached for her hand and this time she let it rest in his. "Do you want me to continue?" he asked.

"Yes, I need to know everything." She'd waited for this moment for so long. Lilly knew it cost him dearly to voice his failings. She squeezed his hand and he pressed back with a warmth that shot through her.

"The day after you and your family sailed for Europe I returned to Washington Square to ask you to take me back. I decided to throw myself on your father's mercy and leave the solution in his hands. But you'd gone for the year." He groaned. "So I left for California, and then a few years later, Alaska."

"Oh Jack, I wish I'd known."

"I wanted to write to you, but it all seemed . . . insurmountable."

She sat perfectly still, unable to speak.

"Lilly, I have no right to ask, but do you think we still have a chance together?" Jack gently touched her shoulders with fingertips that sent silky shivers down her spine.

She wanted him to crush her in his arms and feel his cheek burning her own. But as she faced him, her answer stalled. Should she follow her heart regardless of the consequences it would have on the people she loved? She already knew her answer. Yet she had to consider the dilemma of Fannie Cole.

Lilly closed her eyes. "Let me think, Jack. We can't erase the past. Or the present. So much has happened."

"Then let's start fresh. I love you with all my heart." He took a deep breath. "Will you break your engagement to Harlan and marry me, Lilly?" His smile lifted with a glimmer of hope.

Not trusting her voice, she paused, barely able to comprehend his words. "I want to say yes — but I can't — at least not now." Tears welled and she tried to blink them back. She'd so often imagined Jack proposing again, but now his words seemed as unreal as a dream.

Her heart cracked in two. One piece belonged to Jack, but the other belonged to her family — and so much of their future hinged on her union with Harlan. Jack could heal the fissure and make it whole, but should she let him try? Would Jack expect her to publicize Fannie Cole's dime novels for the sake of his publishing house?

"Before I do anything else, I must speak to Harlan." She looked at him, hoping for understanding and patience, but instead, she caught him staring over her shoulder. She turned around to find George striding into the library. Why did her brother have to interrupt at a most inopportune time?

"Jack, please allow me a few days. I don't wish to make another mistake. Let's not speak of it again until I can come to a decision."

"Of course. Take all the time you need. I won't rush you." His ardor had cooled, or perhaps George's approach had hurled Jack back to earth.

"I have splendid news," George heralded. "I'm not interrupting, am I?"

Lilly sighed. "No, go right ahead."

George beamed. "I just saw Papa in the billiard room. He told me that this afternoon Harlan gave him a tip about some land for sale in upstate New York. It's the last piece Harry Morrison needs for his rail line into Quebec, but the old skinflint wasn't willing to pay a fair price. The owner of the property wasn't about to take anything less than he thought it was worth. So, when Harlan got wind of it, he met with the owner and they agreed on a low but reasonable price. Harlan wants Papa to make the purchase in his stead."

"Why doesn't Harlan buy the land himself if it's such a bargain?" It made no sense to Lilly, though it obviously did to her brother.

George rolled his eyes as if she were an idiot. "Because he loves you and wants to help our family. When Papa sells the tracts of land to Mr. Morrison, we'll make a killing."

"That's very thoughtful of Harlan," Lilly murmured.

George harrumphed. "He's more than thoughtful. He's far beyond generous. We're quite fortunate he's joining our family."

Jack's crestfallen face harbored disappointment even George could detect if he were looking beyond the Westbrooks' good luck. But loose-limbed George was jumping around like a grasshopper too excited to contain himself.

"What does Papa think of this?" Lilly headed for the door. Jack stood by the fireplace.

"Papa's thought it over and he's ready to buy. He's anxious to end his recuperation and get back to the business world. I should think he'd enjoy it. I certainly do." George stroked his goatee.

"I should go find Harlan and thank him myself." Lilly swept into the hall, leaving Jack and George behind. She glanced back at Jack. "But it's terribly late, so I'll speak to him tomorrow. Good night. I hope you both sleep well."

"Nothing to say?" George asked.

Jack looked his friend squarely in the eye as they strolled across the Persian carpet. "I can see how much Harlan benefits the Westbrook family, so I should keep my mouth shut and congratulate you on Harlan's offer."

"But —"

"I'm in love with Lilly." Jack looked sideways, waiting for George's reaction.

"Well, I'll be. You're sweet on my little sister. Does she know how you feel?"

Warmth rose into Jack's neck and face. "Yes, I told her."

"And?" George halted.

"She's going to consider my proposal."

"Proposal?" George anchored his hands on his narrow hips and shook his head in obvious bewilderment. "She's engaged! Have you forgotten? Or do you want her to break off her engagement to Harlan?"

Jack could imagine the fear invading George's mind. No high-paying job with the Santerres' railroad, no windfall profits to augment the family bank account, no more hobnobbing with ultra-fashionable society, no solution to Irene's spending crisis. Things that would be running through Lilly's mind too.

Jack paused, disappointment knifing through his heart. "I don't believe you have to worry. She'll make a decision advantageous to your family. I won't like it for one second, but I understand her position."

George frowned, drawing heavy lids down over his eyes. "It sounds cold and calculating when you put it in those terms."

"It is, George, it is." Jack lengthened his stride, leaving his friend to mull over the situation.

Lilly hesitated before knocking on Miranda's door. It was late and her friend was probably already asleep. She gave one soft rap. "Miranda, it's me, Lilly."

The door creaked open. "Do come in." Miranda yawned and rubbed her eyes.

Lilly ventured inside the small, darkened room dimly lit by only one bedside lamp. She boosted herself onto the four poster bed while Miranda slid back beneath the covers, then reached over and turned up the light.

"I'm sorry to bother you, but I so need to tell you about this dreadful evening." Lilly spilled out her story of Harlan and Dolly and then ended with Jack's declaration and George's announcement of a land deal. "What am I to do?"

Miranda picked at the lace edging the neck of her white cotton nightgown. "I'd say you should end your engagement to Harlan without delay."

Lilly nodded. "I know you're right. We're not as compatible as I once thought and tonight convinced me we're truly mismatched." She smiled wryly. "I tried to ignore the warnings in my heart, but I can't any longer. I'm a bit sad it didn't work out for us."

"Yes, but it's much better to acknowledge it now before you marry than live to regret it." Miranda reached across the bedspread and squeezed Lilly's hand. "You must tell him soon."

"He's retired for the night, so I'll speak to him tomorrow morning. But Miranda, what about my family? They'll be so disappointed."

"Yes, that's probably true. But your parents love you and don't want you to marry the wrong man. And George can fend for himself. He ought to stand on his own two feet for once. He lets Irene lead him around by the nose."

Lilly giggled. "I shouldn't worry about Irene, should I?"

"Goodness, no. *She* can take good care of herself."

Lilly hesitated, then whispered, "What about Jack?"

"I know you love him, and he loves you as well."

"He said he does."

"But?" Miranda asked.

A cool breeze stirred the curtains and wrapped a chill around Lilly's bare arms. "There's the problem of Jones and Jarman and Fannie Cole."

"Then maybe you should tell him the truth."

Lilly shook her head. "I can't take the chance he'll insist I go public, in spite of my wishes."

Miranda remained silent. Apparently, she wasn't sure Jack would curtail his ambition either.

"But Lilly, you must tell Jack before he discovers the truth on his own."

# EIGHTEEN

The next morning Lilly looked for Harlan at breakfast. But he didn't appear. She waited in the dining room until the food on the sideboard grew cold and everyone finished their meals and departed. She'd catch him before he left for the casino. In the meantime, she'd continue her research for her next series of dime novels.

Lilly paused at the library door when she saw Jack inside. *My, but he looks so devastated.* "What's the matter, Jack?"

Slumped in a leather chair with his head buried in his hands, Jack glanced up and tried to smile, but then gave up the half-hearted attempt. "Mr. Jarman telephoned. Henry Reynolds, our best-selling and most prolific author of western dime novels, just suffered a stroke."

"How terribly sad. Is he expected to recover?" Lilly hurried inside and sat on the matching wing chair.

"It's too soon to tell. His family is understandably distraught. They promised to let us know how he's progressing."

How unfortunate for Jack to lose such a successful writer so soon after he'd purchased the publishing house. "I don't suppose Mr. Reynolds will be able to write for quite some time."

Jack shook his head. "No, probably not. I'll need to find a new author for the westerns right along with a new romance writer I might promote."

Lilly paused, then reached over to touch his hand. "I'm sure you will. There are bound to be many talented novelists in search of a publisher."

He gently pressed her fingers and smiled. "You're right. I won't be discouraged."

Lilly heard a booming voice as Harlan swooped in through the open doorway. "What is the meaning of this?"

Jack dropped Lilly's hands. "There's no meaning at all."

They both rose. Lilly stared at the red-faced, apoplectic Harlan as he raised his fists in front of his narrow chest. Was Harlan going to throw a punch?

"Calm down, Santerre. I was just leaving." Jack bowed and stepped out of his range, yet only a few feet from Lilly.

Harlan glared. "Both of you owe me an explanation. I find you holding hands like lovers and you have nothing to say for yourselves. Well, I can't tolerate that."

Lilly sighed with exaggerated patience. "I assure you, we were merely discussing one of Jack's writers. He's suffered a stroke. That's all there is to it." Lilly straightened to her full height and looked Harlan directly in the eye. "Stop snickering at Jack and stop questioning me. Your jealousy is unseemly."

Harlan blubbered, "How dare you accuse me of jealousy toward Jackson Grail. The very idea is preposterous."

Jack's jaw tightened. Fists clenched at his side, he glanced toward the door but didn't move.

"Harlan, we must talk." She spoke softly.

Harlan jerked a nod. "Of course. You should leave, Grail. My fiancée and I need time alone."

Hesitating, Jack looked to Lilly for confirmation.

"Yes, that's a good idea." She sent him a brave smile.

Without muttering a protest, Jack departed.

"You're not taken by that man, are you?" Harlan sputtered, as if the question was truly beyond the realm of possibility.

Lilly gulped. "Mr. Grail and I were merely discussing his challenges —"

Harlan sneered. "Well, I'm not surprised he's having a problem. He's not accustomed to managing a business, coming from such humble circumstances. But he should've complained to George, not to you. I don't like to see my fiancée alone with another man." Harlan pulled at the waxed tips of his mustache, and Lilly squirmed under his appraising gaze. A satisfied smirk settled on his face. "I never really thought you had any interest in Jackson Grail, but I know he holds a torch for you."

She couldn't deny it and wouldn't try. Lilly perched on the edge of a chair and gestured to the settee next to it. "We need to talk."

He sat down, stiff and straight. "Yes, we most certainly do. Last night my mother made you — us — an extremely generous offer. She wishes to share her home after we're married." His glacial eyes bore into Lilly's. "I understand you refused."

"I thanked her for her kindness, but no, I couldn't accept."

"Mother means well. She's lonely with Father gone to the office all day. I believe she craves companionship. Shall we grant her this one small wish?" His voice was as smooth as ice and equally as cold.

"Harlan, she's out and about in society. She doesn't need me to keep her company."

"But she loves you, my dear. She'd like to keep you close by."

*She'd like to control me. That's not love or affection. How could Harlan be so blind?*

"When we live with Mother, she'll introduce you to everyone in her set. You won't be stuck in a shabby old townhouse twiddling your thumbs."

What admirable qualities had she ever seen in Harlan? His disdain for her family was becoming increasingly evident. Her parents' home on Washington Square might be old and unfashionable, but it was certainly comfortable. She'd like to wipe that smirk right off Harlan's face.

Clasping her hands at her waist, Lilly stared at him. "I enjoy the quiet life you disparage and I don't envision myself changing my routine to suit society or your mother."

His eyes froze. "I won't allow you to hole up in your room when you're my wife. You'll have social obligations to fulfill. I hope you'll appreciate your new position and make the most of it."

He expected her to waste countless hours

on small talk and tea parties when she could be writing.

Lilly sighed. "Harlan, when we started keeping company last spring, did you think I was interested in constant socializing? While I'm not a recluse, I'm happiest at home with my family and friends. Surely you've noticed."

Harlan frowned. "I assumed you'd be anxious to join society if given the chance. But now I wonder if I misjudged you."

Lilly nodded. "Yes, perhaps you have. For me, dinners and parties and the opera are diversions, not everyday life. Harlan, tell me what attracted you to me in the beginning?"

He paused, obviously not expecting such a question. "You're a conventional, sensible woman, not like those flighty girls who think only of fashion and parties."

Just as she'd assumed. "But you want me to become one of them, don't you? Maybe not as silly and shallow as some, but just as social. Am I not right?"

"I chose to marry a woman, not a girl, who would fit into my life. I thought you were that woman."

Past tense. His pale face registered shock. He must have recognized their union would be a jigsaw puzzle with pieces cut to the wrong sizes and unable to lock together.

He gave a conciliatory smile, reluctant to accept the inevitable. "You'll adjust, Lilly. Mother thinks you're anxious about the wedding. But you'll overcome your nerves if you try harder and leave the important decisions to me."

Though Harlan's words were full of conviction, Lilly saw doubt reflected in his eyes.

"No, Harlan, I won't adjust and I don't wish to."

His eyes widened with disbelief. "What are you saying, Lilly?"

She took his hands in hers. "I'm so sorry, but surely you know we're not right for each other. We're too different. Our interests aren't even the same."

"You're ending our engagement." He slid his hands out of her grasp.

"Yes, I am. I'm so sorry, Harlan. But it will be better for both of us. You'll make a wonderful husband for some young lady."

His face sagged with shock and he paused for several moments. "Well, I don't suppose there's anything more to say. I best tell Mother."

Within an hour the Santerres departed for a visit with the Carstairses.

After Mama returned home from the casino, Lilly gathered the family in the drawing room along with Jack and Miranda.

"I have an announcement you might find difficult to hear." She took a deep breath. This was every bit as hard as she feared it would be. "After much prayer and thought, I've ended my engagement to Harlan. I'm convinced we'd never bring each other happiness. He understands and perhaps even agrees. Anyway, he and his mother left Summerhill for Grassy Knoll."

"That's quite a boon for Eloise Carstairs," Irene said with a glint in her eye.

"Oh dear." Mama's eyelashes fluttered as she stared at her daughter, obviously bewildered. "Are you sure you made the right decision, Lilly?"

"Of course she is," George said shifting his weight on a chair too small and delicate for his long-limbed body. "Lilly is hardly impulsive. She knows her own mind."

She gave her brother a grateful smile and focused on Mama. But out of the corner of her eye she saw Jack's relief.

Mama pursed her lips. "I wish you'd consulted me first, but since it's probably too late to reconsider, I hope and pray you thought this through carefully."

"For goodness' sake, Nessie, our daughter knows her own mind."

Lilly smiled at Papa, then frowned. "But what about the tip Harlan gave you yesterday — about land for sale. I'm sorry if this ruins your plans."

"I bought the land first thing this morning."

Irene cocked an eyebrow. "Lilly, Harlan is a generous man and I believe you've made a dreadful mistake sending him into the arms of some other silly girl. But I'm sure you had your reasons." Her leer slid from Lilly to Jack.

"You did the right thing," Miranda said quietly.

Lilly knew she had. She should never have agreed to marry Harlan in the first place, but at least she'd finally ended it before things had gotten out of control.

*Thank you, Lord, for giving me courage.* Now if only she could summon the courage to tell them about her writing.

Jack wanted to speak to Lilly about her broken engagement, but she disappeared into her bedroom and remained secluded all day. He read a few manuscripts Lewis Jarman had sent him, but he couldn't concentrate on anything but Lilly. Now that she'd ended her relationship with Harlan, would she turn to him? Or was it too presumptuous to even hope?

Jack slipped the pages back into a large

293

envelope and placed it on the wicker end table beside a pot of ferns that bobbed in the late afternoon breeze. With a sigh, he rose. A brisk walk might improve his mood.

As he clattered down the veranda steps, he heard Lilly's voice. Glancing over his shoulder, he spotted her emerging from inside the cottage.

"Jack. If you're not too busy, could we talk for a bit?" Her voice sounded weary.

He waited for her to join him on the stairs. "Of course."

Together they strolled down the pebbled path toward the rose garden set behind high stone walls on the far side of the lawn. Jack opened the wrought iron gate and they made their way into the garden. Silently they passed beneath the arbor. He inhaled the fragrance of roses tumbling over trellises in wild abundance; none were half as sweet or intoxicating as Lilly herself.

She lowered to a bench, smoothed her ivory skirt, and laced her fingers on her lap. A shiny blue sash accentuated her tiny waist. It took all his self-control not to wrap his hand around it — or lean over and kiss her satin-smooth lips. Dropping down beside her, he kept a respectable distance between them. He waited for her to begin, but she seemed to hesitate. He'd wait forever if he had to.

He noticed a pair of cardinals splashing and dipping their beaks into a nearby birdbath, shaded by the branches of a sugar maple. From the overhead limbs several birds he couldn't identify warbled and sang on and on like a long sequence of arias. And still Lilly stared down at her hands. Finally she looked up and spoke.

"Jack, I ended my engagement because I realized I didn't love Harlan enough to marry him. I was truly fond of him, but that's not enough for a marriage to be happy."

He nodded. "I agree." Should he ask if she'd decided in his favor, or would that be pushing her too far, too fast? He clamped his mouth shut.

Lilly reached for his hand. "I thought about your proposal all afternoon. I believe that you love me —"

When her voice broke, he thought his heart would stop. "I do love you with every fiber of my being."

"Yes, but sometimes love isn't enough."

"What's keeping you from me, Lilly? I've felt your love — and I still feel it."

She looked away.

"Tell me you don't care and I'll leave you alone." He knew she couldn't say that with any conviction. "Is it Fannie Cole? Is she the problem?"

Lilly's eyes blazed. "Please stop bringing her into every conversation."

"I'm sorry. Let's forget I ever mentioned her name." When would she tell him the truth about Fannie? Why did she hold back, even now?

She stood and glanced toward the gate. "Jack, I need more time. I'm deeply honored by your proposal, but I can't give you my answer now."

Before he could respond, Lilly was gone.

Jack leaned against a tree and pulled off a piece of bark. How stupid and insensitive could he be? Of course she was Fannie Cole. But she refused to admit it because she couldn't trust him yet. Maybe if he let her write anonymously as she always had and he relinquished his dream of building Jones and Jarman into a major publishing enterprise, she'd agree to marry him.

He sat alone in the garden for quite a while before giving in to the distraction of locating Colonel MacIntryre. He borrowed the Westbrooks' gig, a light two-wheeled carriage, and drove uptown where several small inns, guest-, and boardinghouses were located. Most of the summer people built their own cottages and eschewed hotels, leaving few establishments exclusive enough for the rich or nearly rich. He doubted whether one of the nicer establishments such as the Coastal Inn would allow the likes of an infamous publisher/extortionist even inside their door.

At his last stop, a respectable gray clapboard house with a "Rooms for Rent" sign, he expected the proprietor to repeat what he'd heard several times before. "I'm sorry. Colonel Rufus MacIntyre isn't registered here." But this innkeeper confirmed the man was indeed a guest. Unfortunately, he'd gone out without mentioning his destination or time of return.

Disappointed, Jack climbed into the buggy and headed across town toward the harbor where he suspected he might find the blackguard. Jack had heard all the stories from his reporters. After extorting money from the millionaires to suppress their secrets, Rufus MacIntyre could hardly show his hated face around Bellevue Avenue, Newport's fashionable section of mansions and exclusive shops. And yet he constantly needed new fodder from among their circles to feed his paper.

Jack soon reached Thames Street, a thoroughfare far too narrow for all the bustling traffic along the waterfront, he decided.

Behind the row of stores that blocked a clear view of the water, he glimpsed long wharfs, a ferry steaming toward its landing, and the masts of tall ships rolling in the breeze. As he jumped down from the carriage, he sniffed the tang of seaweed at low tide. And he remembered the last time he'd been on this street — when he had spied Lilly at Elna Price's book signing. He clenched his teeth. It was for her, first and foremost, that he must see through this task.

He looked around, unsure where to begin. Would MacIntyre go to a restaurant, tavern, clothing store, apothecary, or bakery? He didn't know him and he couldn't guess the man's tastes or habits. Peering through the plate glass windows of each successive business, Jack slowly progressed down one side of the street then up the other. He strode beneath the storefront awnings and through the mist. A foghorn moaned as the clouds thickened to a gray mass and swirled to the ground.

The glorious day had gradually turned dreary, darkening the windows of the shops and making it difficult to see inside. After nearly half an hour he'd glimpsed only sailors and housewives, but no one who could be the colonel. Though ready to return to Summerhill before a downpour soaked his new pin-striped suit, he was drawn inside Celeste's Patisserie by the smell of freshly baked cookies and pies. He spotted a batch of jelly donuts displayed among the éclairs, rolls, tarts, and tortes. Unable to resist, he bought a cup of black coffee and half a dozen of his favorite treats before glancing around for an empty table. Four lined the wall; three were occupied. As Jack took the only vacant spot, a lone man at the back table looked up at him.

Big and bulky, he wore a plaid sack suit. The yellow and black fabric stretched to the limit across his belly and looked ready to rip apart at the seams. A plate piled high with petit fours lay before him. A cigar stub burned in his ashtray, sending spirals of smoke up to the ceiling. Fanning the stinking air, Jack took a closer look. A red carnation in the fat man's lapel caught his eye. This was Colonel Rufus MacIntyre, the bloodsucker himself, sporting his signature flower. With his appetite gone, Jack abandoned the donuts and coffee and eased over to the colonel's table.

MacIntyre reared back, then continued to shove cake into his mouth. He patted his lips and double chin with a napkin. "May I help you with something, sir? Have we met?" His voice, smooth as oil, oozed with phony charm.

"I'm Jackson Grail, the publisher of Jones and Jarman. I know who you are, so there's no need to introduce yourself."

The colonel stuck out his hand, but when Jack didn't offer to shake, MacIntyre frowned and folded the sausage-like digits on his rounded lap. "Is there something I can do for you?"

"I want you to stop harassing one of my authors — Miss Fannie Cole."

MacIntyre's smirk matched the menace in his eyes. He puffed on his cigar, then slowly blew a stream of smoke into Jack's face. "If you mean those little items in *Talk of the Town,* you're way off the mark. I might tell my readers her real name, but that's perfectly legal. Just a bit of gossip that titillates the public."

"The lady doesn't want her identity revealed." If she did, she'd allow him to promote her, wouldn't she?

MacIntyre shrugged. "Of course not. I understand that fact very well." He snickered. "If I print her name, she'll be humiliated. She's playing a risky game. Chances were always great she'd eventually get caught. Fannie did it to herself, so I don't worry about the consequences."

"But I do." Jack balled his fists and planted

them firmly on the table. "Are you going to expose her?"

The colonel sneered. "That doesn't concern you."

"She's one of my writers, so it most definitely concerns me."

"Fannie's a big girl — she can take care of herself." The man shoved another petit four into his mouth.

"You can at least refer to her as Miss Cole."

Doffing his bowler in a mock bow, MacIntyre leaned on the table and heaved himself to his feet. "Good day, Mr. Grail."

"Listen, Colonel, you'd better not blackmail Miss Cole, because if you do, I'll —"

"You'll do what? Nothing, I'll wager."

The fat man's nasty laugh sent fury through Jack's chest. "You'd better leave Miss Cole alone, or you'll have to deal with me."

MacIntyre snorted. "I'm quaking, Mr. Grail." Grabbing up his remaining petit fours, he sauntered from the bakery.

Jack followed him out the door into the rain that slanted down in cold sheets. MacIntyre heaved himself into a hired carriage and vanished. Shielded by the awning flapping in the wind, Jack stood against the shop window. If he'd driven an enclosed carriage instead of an open one, he could've returned to Summerhill right away. He stepped back into the warmth of the bakery, munched on a donut, gulped his tepid coffee, and waited for the rain to let up.

Misery engulfed him. Out of solutions, Jack weighed his mounting problems. Fannie Cole — Lilly? — about to be exposed. Reynolds in a sickbed, unable to write. Nothing of worth in his stacks to publish. He expected the road to success would wind as it climbed up steep mountains, but not dead end. If his luck didn't return, he'd soon find himself in the grip of poverty — right where he began.

He felt alone and out of luck. No, out of grace.

Jack sighed. He lacked a solution to his troubles with Fannie. It was time to humble himself before the Lord. Long past time, really. He finished his donut and sat staring out at the sheets of rain coming down the window, praying with a need sunk deep into his bones.

*Heavenly Father, I've been working on my own far too long and striving for fame and fortune. I'm building a business, but I'm encountering more problems than I expected. The woman I love hesitates to marry me. She won't reveal her identity, and I can't see a way to help her stand up to an extortionist. Lord, I need Your guidance and I'm ready to listen. Amen.*

He sipped the dregs of his coffee and listened for some sort of response. Not words whispered in his ear, though that kind of assurance would certainly help, but a new insight, a practical solution. Really he wanted anything that suggested God was in His heaven and He cared for His people. For him in particular. Jack bought another cup of coffee and waited for the rain to end.

Slowly a peace he hadn't felt for years spread through him. The Lord would guide him if only he would follow.

In his quest for money and respect, he'd put aside the fervency of his childhood faith in exchange for self-reliance. Gradually, over the years, he'd neglected his relationship with the Lord. He'd ended up weak and out of clever ideas.

Jack arose from the rickety chair. The struggle wasn't over yet. He'd find his authoress and protect her from Colonel MacIntyre, whether she appreciated it or not.

# NINETEEN

Raindrops sent Lilly and Miranda scurrying from the tennis court. Rackets in hand, they pounded up the veranda steps to find George talking to Papa.

"Dreadful weather." Miranda shook the moisture from her skirt and glared at the gray mass of clouds reaching down into the rough waters. "I believe I'll go inside and dress for tea. If you'll excuse me."

"I'll head inside as well. A short nap would do me more good than staying out in this dampness," Papa said as he followed Miranda inside the cottage.

Lilly dropped down on the rocker while George leaned against the porch rail, his long legs crossed at the ankle.

"George, I assume Irene told you Harlan refused to loan me money the other night. I'm so sorry." She knew George was counting on her; he always had, though at his age he ought to stand on his own two feet.

"Thank you for trying. I'm sure you did your best. Harlan was always tight with a penny and this is quite a sum." He cocked his head. "You didn't end your engagement over the loan, did you? I'd hate to think my problems ruined your happiness."

"Goodness, no. I should have realized how ill-suited Harlan and I were right from the start." Lilly paused. "But if I may ask, how do you plan on paying Irene's debts?"

As the rain slanted toward the veranda, George moved away from the railing and took a seat beside Lilly. The wicker chair squeaked as he sat down. "I was desperate, so I told Papa about Irene's gambling and he gave me all the funds I needed — without much of a lecture. Of course, I wanted to keep my difficulties from him, but I had nowhere else to turn. He asked me to speak to Irene about her spending habits and I did this afternoon." He pulled on his goatee and grunted. "She claimed she is normally a much better bridge player but she'd had a streak of bad luck. She missed the point."

Lilly sighed. "So your problem isn't solved."

George made a woeful face. "Not at all." Then he brightened, looking more hopeful than she'd seen him in a long while. "Since she's not going to change, I decided I had to."

"Oh? What will do you differently?"

George straightened his slumped back. "I'm going to find a job. Now, don't raise your eyebrows, Lilly. I've wanted a job for a long time, but I never found one I thought I might enjoy. And then there's the added problem of needing a position that pays well."

She'd never heard her brother so enthusiastic about working for a living. "What do you have in mind?"

"I've applied for a teaching position at several New England preparatory schools. I hope I have a knack for instructing young boys. At least I have a keen interest in youth and in history. You probably think Papa's bank would be ideal, but to learn the business inch by inch, sitting behind a desk for ten hours a day, sets my nerves on edge."

"I understand. And I agree you should do a job you'd enjoy. But have you considered a modest salary won't satisfy Irene?"

George sighed. "I have, indeed. She'll be unhappy, but I'm hoping and praying she'll adjust. It'll be a year's experiment to see how we both like it."

"A year is not too much to ask."

George grinned, apparently heartened.

"That's what I thought. I won't tell her until I receive an offer, but I'm hoping to hear soon. And then I'll break the news — gently, of course."

Irene would undoubtedly complain about exchanging her life in society for the position of faculty wife, even for a mere ten months. But if she truly loved her husband, she'd concede.

When Lilly and George arose, Lilly grasped her brother's hand and gave it a tight squeeze. "I'm proud of you."

"Thank you." An embarrassed grin spread across his face. "I do believe I'm proud of myself as well."

As the rain intensified, they left the veranda for the warmth and comfort of the cottage. In need of a few more hours of writing time, Lilly headed upstairs to her bedroom. She passed through the foyer as Mr. Ames opened the front door to Jack. He burst into the entrance hall, dripping water from his hat to his suit. He removed the wet derby, shrugged off his jacket and shook them over the area rug, avoiding the expensive Oriental carpet.

Lilly shot him a sly smile. "You must remember to carry an umbrella. It often doesn't just rain in Newport, the very heavens themselves seem to open up."

Jack ignored her playful advice. "Lilly, I need to speak to you after I change clothes. It won't take long. It's important." He sounded so serious her heart lurched. No doubt, more bad news.

Lilly nodded, curious about the urgency of his appeal. "All right. I'll be in the library."

As usual, she found the reading room deserted. Needing a reference book about France, the setting for her current manuscript, *A Garland of Love,* she searched the stacks until she discovered a text filled with photographs of cathedrals, palaces, and monuments. She turned up the gaslight to dispel the gloom and sank into the sofa.

Ten minutes later Jack entered the library dressed in dry clothes. The worry etched in his brow gave her a jolt.

"What's the matter?" Lilly placed her thick tome on the end table and turned her full attention to Jack. "You look agitated."

His gaze swept the room. Apparently satisfied they were alone, he spoke in a rush. "Colonel MacIntyre is in town. I tracked him down this afternoon."

She gasped. "He's in Newport?"

"Unfortunately, yes. That means he's going after someone and, given the articles we've seen, I suspect it's Fannie Cole."

Lilly's knees weakened, but she tightened her muscles so she wouldn't fall at his feet and give herself away. "Oh my. How do you know?"

Jack groaned. "I have learned how he operates. It's common knowledge he's extorted money from dozens of Newporters over the years. They pay dearly to keep their secrets out of *Talk of the Town*. They're left with no other choice unless they're so rich and powerful they can't be cut from society." He leveled a deadly serious stare. "Almost no one escapes his grasp."

Lilly closed her eyes against her worst nightmare. "Are you quite certain?"

"I'm convinced of it. I'd like to help Miss Cole fend him off."

Avoiding Jack's steady, almost sympathetic gaze, she looked out the window at the shroud of hydrangea bushes shadowing the room. She'd burst into tears if she succumbed to his compassion.

"Lilly, please tell me Miss Cole's real name."

When she remained mute, he dropped onto a nearby chair by the roaring fire. "Will you tell her that together, we can face this?"

She nodded.

He looked as if he wanted to say more, but instead he opened his leather satchel

309

and spread its contents on the cushion. "I'd like you to take a look."

"All right. What are these?" she asked, eager to change the topic of conversation. Obviously, the pile of handwritten notes weren't manuscripts.

Jack leaned toward her. "I'd like you to hear some of the comments in these notes. They're written by fans of Fannie Cole who —"

"Oh, I'm afraid I don't have time." She tried to move, but her body still wouldn't cooperate.

He rushed on undeterred. "You might find these letters enlightening. Miss Cole's readers sent them to her via Jones and Jarman. They're full of praise for her writing and for Fannie herself." He pulled out one of the notes and handed it to her.

She waved it away.

He sighed. "All right then. If you won't read it, I'll read it to you.

"Dear Miss Cole,
Your lovely book, *My Lady's Fan,* set my heart to humming. How I nearly swooned at the hero's rescue of his true love. It made me think maybe I'll find my very own hero someday. I decided I should wait for a tenderhearted man

who treats me like a lady and not settle for one of the clods who has pursued me. The good Lord wants us girls to keep our standards high and remember we're His children, loved and protected by Him. Thank you ever so much for reminding me of that. It would be grand if I could meet you in person, Miss Cole. That would give my friends and me so much pleasure.

Sincerely,
An Ardent Fan, Sadie Smith"

Lilly drew her arms across her chest and trembled. "No doubt Miss Cole would enjoy such adulation from a reader."

The rain trickled to a stop. Jack rose and walked to the window, opening it wide. Fresh air flooded the room. "Are you moved by that note?" He turned around and searched her face.

"Yes," she answered in a voice barely audible.

"The rest are similar. Miss Cole has garnered an appreciative audience."

Lilly's cheeks flushed before she reached over and opened more of the letters. Minutes ticked by as she skimmed one letter after another. "Miss Cole is succeeding, isn't she? She's reaching the girls she's writing for. She's doing some good."

Despite the risks and the consequences of penning dime novels, her work for the Lord was bearing abundant fruit. She wanted to shout for joy that all the risks she'd taken were well worth it. She was walking down the right road, and the Lord was truly directing her path. A sense of relief calmed her spirit which had been troubled for such a long time. In fact, ever since she'd begun to write, she'd questioned whether secrecy was the proper way to conduct her ministry. Yet, she hid her work and lied by failing to tell the truth. She couldn't bear to stop scribbling her stories. And the money helped the Settlement House operate. *Lord, if You want me to admit this ministry You've given me, You also must give me the strength.*

Jack looked at her, his head cocked at an angle, as if he understood how deeply the letters were affecting her. "Yes, indeed, Fannie Cole is performing a great service. By pointing these young ladies to God, she's had a profound influence on their lives. Many have little guidance."

Lilly coughed to cover the happiness swelling in her chest. Her efforts actually made a difference. "You're probably exaggerating. But I'm glad her dime novels benefit those they're designed to help." She wanted to laugh and cry and throw her arms around Jack and thank him for the opportunity to publish. But she sat with her hands folded demurely in her lap, her gaze averted so he couldn't view the tears she fought to hold back. Nervously, she picked up another letter, trying to focus on the words.

Jack returned to sit beside her, watching as she read it.

After a moment, she gave up on the letter, unable to concentrate with him sitting so near.

She stood. "I know Miss Cole will seek your help — if she needs it."

"Thank you," he said with more weariness in his tone than hope.

She saw the web of lines around his eyes deepen and his mouth droop. Protecting Fannie and his publishing house apparently drained him of his usual spark. And she was to blame for his difficulties.

*Lord, help me to keep my faith and trust in You. I know You won't abandon me. Please don't punish my family because of my secret. Give me courage to confess to them when the time is right — if You feel it's absolutely necessary, which I hope You don't. And Lord, is there something I can do to help Jack with his business other than promote myself? He's worked so hard. Please, don't let him fail and especially not because of me.*

Nothing came to mind, but she hoped the Lord would answer her soon.

Though Mama was still upset about Lilly ending her engagement, she insisted they visit Ocean Vista, the van Patten's chateau on Ochre Point. As usual, Lilly preferred to remain at home, but Mama objected.

Mama gawked at the mansion's gilt and marble decor as they passed beneath soaring ceilings and down wide hallways on their way to the oceanside.

"I've never seen such beauty outside of Europe." Mama's eyes sparkled.

Lilly followed a step behind, amused by her mother's childlike amazement. Except for the Santerres' Fifth Avenue mansion, Mama hadn't seen many of the millionaires' homes, although she could have if she made even half an effort to secure an invitation. No one, especially the *nouveau riche,* turned down the interest of a Knickerbocker, a group of "old money" New Yorkers with *cachet,* if not cash.

The butler led the Westbrooks to the small circle of overdressed ladies gathered on the stone loggia facing the sea. Mrs. Winnie van Patten, seated at its center, was fiftyish and frumpy and the wife of Philadelphia's most aggressive real estate speculator. With a broad smile she came forward, arms outstretched. "I'm so delighted you could join us this afternoon." Like Mama she wore lace over silk, hers in pale pink, Mama's in periwinkle blue.

After introductions and greetings, Mrs. van Patten poured tea and passed tarts and cake on hand-painted china plates. The visitors settled into conversation with several matrons familiar to Lilly, mainly old acquaintances of her mother's from New York. Lilly sat primly, balancing her delicate cup and plate.

She hoped the call would pass quickly so she could return to her manuscript. Far behind on her writing, she needed to concentrate and turn out more stories at an assembly-line pace. So far she'd made little progress. She couldn't remember when she'd last had a carefree day or a peaceful night's sleep.

"Miss Westbrook, you're looking so lovely this afternoon," drawled Rhonda Wooten, wife of the West Virginia coal king. New to society, she spoke in halting phrases, apparently well aware she was still on social probation. The influential Winnie van Patten had taken her up, but negative opinions from the other ladies could permanently send her back to Appalachia. Or, if she were spunky, she and her husband might try another resort less exclusive, like Bar Harbor or Saratoga Springs.

Mrs. Carstairs jutted her pointed chin as if a compliment made to anyone other than one of her daughters was in bad taste. "You do look remarkably well, Lillian, considering the unfortunate end to your engagement. But I'm sure you'll recover quickly. My daughter Eloise and I are taking excellent care of the Santerres, so you need not worry about Harlan." She pinched a smile and quickly changed the subject. "The only other interesting news I've heard lately is from my maid. It seems that Miss Fannie Cole is *one of us*."

Gasps escaped pursed lips and eyes glowed.

"So I've heard."

"Such an outrage."

"*Talk of the Town* knows these things." Mrs. van Patten gave a sage nod. "Servants tattle, you know."

All the plumed hats bobbed in agreement.

Lilly tried to look concerned and innocent. "Perhaps *Talk of the Town* is mistaken."

Faces drooped, taffeta bottoms shifted

uneasily in their chairs.

"Oh no, my dear, they usually get it right." Mrs. Carstairs frowned as she twisted a curl of gray hair loosened by the breeze. Her tiny face was overwhelmed by the turned-up brim of her hat trimmed with peacock feathers. "Eventually the truth will emerge, and we'll all learn who the culprit really is."

Mrs. van Patten inclined her head. "When we discover her identity, I for one will never speak to her again or anyone in her family. She'll be treated exactly like Thomasina Jones. Do you remember her?"

Mama blinked. "Indeed, I do." She finished the last crumb of her strawberry tart. "Her family fled to Italy after . . ."

Some indiscretions were so egregious one could only allude to them.

The crash of the sea seemed to crescendo as the ladies paused, apparently to recollect the scandal that rocked society five years before. Remembering the incident brought a film of perspiration to Lilly's face and neck. She dropped her gaze and sipped her tea as if it were delicious nectar from the gods.

Mrs. Wooten glanced from one lady to the other. "I'm afraid I don't recall . . ."

The ladies leaned into their circle.

Mrs. Carstairs lowered her voice. "Addy

Jones's daughter ran off with a married man. One of the Stockman brothers — a money-grubbing rogue. Thomasina eventually returned home alone, but she was ruined."

"How dreadful." Mrs. Wooten sucked in a mouthful of air, the lines of her worn face drawn into a scandalized frown. "What happened to her?"

Mrs. Carstairs sighed. "She was unrepentant and brazen as a showgirl, if you'll pardon my comparison. Everyone ignored her from then on."

"Is that when her family left?" Rhonda pressed.

Mrs. van Patten shook her head. "Oh my, no. That came later. First, Thomasina had a breakdown of her nerves. She howled and screamed and carried on until most of the servants quit. It was a horrid situation for the family, losing both their daughter and their staff at the same time."

"Her father committed her to an asylum where she's confined to this day," Mama murmured, blushing flames of red. "The family fled to Europe. No one has seen them since."

"The Joneses were quite influential," Mrs. Carstairs added, "but even they couldn't survive the scandal."

A long pause let the weight of the tragedy sink in.

"But writing dime novels isn't nearly as dreadful as going off with a married man. Is it?" Lilly cringed and wished she'd kept quiet. To these women, one sin was equal to the other. A major breach of society's rules and customs was punishable by exclusion. Period.

Mrs. van Patten grimaced. "Lillian, we object to more than just the books. It's Fannie Cole herself. Someone from a good family just doesn't work. She demeans herself, her relations, and her friends by stooping to the level of her servants. It's one thing for a penniless immigrant girl to earn a living but quite another for a society woman to rely on herself instead of on her father or her husband. Surely you must understand this?"

Mama's eyes fluttered again and Lilly knew she'd gone too far. "Of course she understands, Winnie. My daughter is perfectly aware of what constitutes responsible behavior and what does not."

"Oh dear, Vanessa, I certainly didn't mean to imply otherwise." Winnie gave Mama a conciliatory pat on the hand. "Please, have another tart."

"They are delicious," Mama agreed, mollified.

Lilly smiled contritely for her mother's sake, though her face ached from the effort. These pampered women had nothing more to do than entertain themselves and shun each other for trivial infractions of their silly standards. She shouldn't take them seriously. Yet their disapproval would destroy the Westbrooks' social lives and even their business prospects. Maybe she didn't care very much, but the rest of the family did.

Just as Lilly thought Mama was ready to leave, the butler announced the arrival of Nan Holloway and Theo Nottingham. Looking up with interest, Lilly saw the familiar semicircle of reddish waves. He bowed low before accepting the empty seat beside her. Mrs. van Patten introduced him to the group as the Holloways' houseguest from the city. The ladies soon resumed their chatter.

Lilly studied his slight build and old man face. How could Irene find him attractive? He must be terribly rich, though he certainly didn't look like much of a catch — not that good looks counted for a lot.

Lilly flashed her brightest social smile. "I remember seeing you at the ball here at Ocean Vista."

He mumbled, "Oh, yes."

Apparently he hadn't noticed her. That didn't surprise Lilly. She tended to fade into the crowd, but that didn't bother her at all. Observing others without being observed herself brought more satisfaction than holding the center of attention.

"You danced with my sister-in-law, Mrs. George Westbrook," she said. And she and Jack had also seen them at the casino as well. What would her poor brother think of those two huddled behind a post like a pair of guilty lovers? *Oh, Lord, I do hope I am jumping to the wrong conclusion.*

He swallowed hard and his Adam's apple quivered. "I don't think I recall. I danced with so many ladies that night."

"She's a lovely blonde with emerald green eyes." No one ever forgot the stunning Irene.

His hollow cheeks sank into his skull. "Ah, now I remember Mrs. Westbrook — a delightful woman — and an excellent partner." He tapped the carpet with the toe of his polished shoe. "We only danced one waltz, so we aren't well acquainted."

But what about their time together hiding behind the ferns and potted palms? Or was she dramatizing an innocent conversation?

Perhaps Mr. Nottingham was truly interested in Irene, though Lilly still couldn't imagine what engaging qualities her sister-in-law saw in him. They were an odd two-some to say the least. She couldn't shake off the feeling that there was more there than met the eye. But he deftly changed the subject, ending Lilly's fruitless attempt at probing. At least for now.

The Westbrooks' Victoria crunched down the pebbled drive of Ocean View, passed under the wrought iron arch, and rolled onto Bellevue Avenue. With the carriage's low body and calash top folded back, Vanessa and Lilly had a fine view of the other equipages parading up and down the town's most exclusive street.

The ladies wore their best Parisian frocks made of silk or chiffon and trimmed with lace. Flounced parasols rose above their flowered hats and vied for space in the small carriages. Vanessa adjusted her own hat as a feathery wisp escaped from the ostrich plume attached to the side of the wide brim. It landed on her nose and tickled.

She brushed it off and nodded to the ladies in the other carriages as they passed by. The only socialites Vanessa couldn't identify were some of the newcomers who weren't able to trace their social lineage to the days before the war.

"Mama," Lilly began slowly, "why didn't society forgive Thomasina Jones? Ostracizing seems too harsh a punishment."

Vanessa met her troubled gaze. "That's obvious, isn't it? She broke the rules and failed to live up to accepted standards."

A small sigh escaped Lilly. "But as Christians, shouldn't we forgive?"

"Well, I suppose so, but Thomasina never repented. She acted as if she'd done nothing wrong. She was quite the rebel and set a dangerous example to impressionable young ladies."

Lilly persisted. "But what if she'd asked for forgiveness? Would society have accepted her apology and taken her back?"

Vanessa pulled on her pearl earring while she considered her answer. "Probably not. But when she ran off with that horrid man she knew what the consequences would be. At the time, she didn't care."

Lilly pursed her lips. "But what about her parents? Why should they be shunned because of their daughter's behavior? They weren't at fault."

"No, of course not. The Joneses were a lovely family and I miss Thomasina's mother to this day. Addy and I were girlhood friends. She only lived a block away growing up."

"Did you defend Mrs. Jones when everyone else ostracized her?" Lilly asked with a quiet intensity that caused Vanessa to scrutinize her more closely.

"No, I'm afraid not. Perhaps I should have stood up for her publicly, but it never crossed my mind." Vanessa squirmed on the plush seat cushion. Had she let down her friend? The guilt of her disloyalty pressed on her. Of course she had.

"But why didn't it occur to you to support her?"

Lilly looked so sincere Vanessa couldn't end the conversation by accusing her of impertinence, as she'd so often done. It wasn't a tactic that worked well with an adult child. "I suppose I didn't question society's norms because no one I know ever questions them. If they're accepted standards, then they must be worthy. At least that's what I've always thought."

"But do you think perhaps they're too stringent?"

"No, never." Somehow her complete honesty made her sound like an uncaring fool. No one she could possibly like or respect. Vanessa sniffed. "Abiding by standards should be applauded, not condemned. But you seem to disagree. What exactly are you trying to say, Lilly?" She wanted to draw closer to her daughter, not pick a fight, but the girl was needling her on purpose.

A warm breeze rustled the tree branches arching over the sidewalk and dislodged another bit of feather.

"We should forgive others who transgress and allow them back in our circle. We don't have to approve of their actions to accept them as weak sinners in need of God's grace. Every one of us falls short."

"Yes, indeed. But there's no need to preach. I understand what forgiveness means. But you're not talking about the Joneses, are you?"

"No, Mama. I believe the rules of our set stifle our freedom to express our true ideas and opinions. We become dull and complacent and all alike. Individuality is denigrated."

Vanessa's temper rose to the tip of her tongue, but then cooled. She had every right to resent Lilly's criticism of her long-held beliefs, but there was more than a grain of truth in what the girl said. "Lilly, I warn you, if you spout off your radical ideas, you'll lose your friends. Do take care."

"Of course, Mama." Lilly rolled her eyes and looked away. "Haven't I always?"

"Yes, my dear. You're a dutiful daughter

and I appreciate it." Not wishing to end their talk on a sour note, Vanessa added, "I shall ponder this and possibly reconsider some of my assumptions. And I shall write to Addy Jones and ask how the family is faring in Europe."

"Thank you, Mama."

The surprise in Lilly's voice irked her, but Vanessa had to admit she wasn't as open-minded as she might be.

# TWENTY

The following morning Lilly rose two hours early to write before the start of the day's social activities. After a full morning at Bailey's Beach and luncheon at Cliff House, Lilly retired to her sitting room, hoping to spend a few more minutes working on her latest story.

Before Lilly could lock her door, Annie delivered a stack of letters.

"Your mail, miss." The maid bobbed a quick curtsey.

Lilly nodded her thanks as she settled into a soft chair by the window. She'd scan the mail before beginning chapter two of *A Garland of Love.* She opened one invitation after another and then tossed them aside to consider later. Two letters arrived from friends touring France and Italy. She eagerly read their notes filled with descriptions of places she'd also visited and loved. Very romantic if you were with the man you adored. Her mind filled with an image of Jack. She couldn't stop thinking of him.

She appreciated his willingness to battle Colonel MacIntyre, but she was a grown woman responsible for defending herself against her adversaries. She'd decided to embrace an unacceptable career and now she'd have to extricate herself from its complications. With the Lord's help. But where was He? His silence frightened her.

*I trust you, Heavenly Father. Please don't let me down.*

He'd never failed her, so why was she starting to doubt His protection? She needed Him as never before.

She flipped through the remaining envelopes and noted several more invitations from the best cottages of Newport. The last envelope stuck out like a cold sore. Her name and address were printed in bold block letters.

Her hand shook as she slit open the crease. A sense of foreboding slithered through her body. No respectable person neglected to cite the name of her cottage or return address. She pulled out the letter. A stiff breeze blowing through the screens fluttered the paper. She tightened her grip. The short note held few words.

My dear Miss Westbrook:

If you wish to keep your name out of Newport's most popular news sheet, I suggest you contact me without delay. Although it is not my intention to cause you distress, I strongly advise you give this request serious consideration. May we meet and discuss the unfortunate situation in which you find yourself? Send your reply in an unmarked envelope. Deliver it to Baxter and Dunne Book Shop, Bellevue Avenue, and place it in the copy of Mr. Whitman's *Leaves of Grass.*

Sincerely,
An interested party

Who had sent the letter — Colonel MacIntrye from *Talk of the Town*? Who else would have the audacity to demand a meeting? Of course Jack had a great interest in luring his authoress out of hiding, but Jack was hardly this devious. Direct and outspoken, he wouldn't stoop to such an underhanded tactic. Unless he was desperate to meet Fannie — and force her to the truth. She'd have to take a chance.

"Annie, I need my pink and burgundy parasol, the one that matches this gown, and my hat with the silk roses." Lilly piled the mail on her desk except for the colonel's note.

The girl placed a stack of folded nightgowns in the white bureau and turned toward Lilly. "Are you feeling all right, Miss Lillian? You look piqued. Perhaps an aspirin might help. They say they're awful good medicine."

"Thank you, Annie, but I'm all right. Just fetch my things, please." She tried to smile as if nothing were amiss. But her entire life was off kilter and it apparently showed in her face.

Annie headed for her dressing room. While Annie searched for the requested items, Lilly scratched out a response agreeing to meet with Colonel MacIntyre. She stuck it in an envelope and then shoved it into her reticule along with the threatening letter.

"Lillian, are you ready to leave for a few hands of whist at the Holloways'?" Mama strode into the bedroom, dressed in a blueberry-colored silk frock that flattered her plump figure and a frilly, flowered hat.

"Must I go? I'm feeling out of sorts."

Mama fitted white gloves onto her hands. "I'm sorry to hear that, but yes, you must come along. You cannot turn down invitations at the last minute or you'll be deemed unsociable. Oh dear, please don't cry. Do take an aspirin tablet. Annie will fetch one for you."

Lilly knew that she'd lost. She'd deliver the note after they returned.

Five minutes later, as she climbed aboard the carriage, she spotted Jack carrying a chair across the front lawn, book in hand. She yearned to sit beside him, let the sun's warmth surround them, and listen to him talk about literature and more. His smooth voice would surely be better than Mama's cheerful jabber.

Jack placed his wicker chair beneath the shade of a wide-skirted maple. He calculated he could read several chapters of *Dorothea's Dilemma* before George dragged him to the tennis courts. Jack liked to play, but work came first. During his short tenure as publisher, he'd read two of Miss Cole's dime novels but hadn't found time to go through any more.

He settled into the soft cushion, swatted a bumblebee, and read the first seventy-five pages surprisingly fast. Before long he'd discover if the heroine had escaped from the villain's clutches and accepted the marriage proposal of the most dashing fictional hero he'd come across in ages. Another hour or two flew by. From the corner of his eye, he saw the Westbrook carriage roll up the driveway and halt in front of the veranda. Back from their calls, the ladies emerged and waved to him before they disappeared inside the mansion.

He turned the page and came to a scene where the heroine, Ada Brown, fell through a crack in the ice and slipped beneath the surface of the pond. Jack skimmed the text. Of course the hero, Lawrence Macon, plunged in after Ada and grabbed her before she sunk to the bottom. He'd pulled her onto the ice, gasping for breath, yet thrilled he'd saved the life of his true love.

*"Thank you, Lawrence," she gasped. "Oh dear, I've lost my emerald ring in the pond!"*

Without a second thought, the hero leapt back into the frigid water and brought up the treasure, still gleaming through the mud. Ada grasped the ring, threw her arms around her beau, and planted a kiss firmly on his frozen cheek.

A satisfying, romantic scene that stirred long-forgotten memories. Jack straightened his back as he placed the book in his lap and stared up at the cottage. He smiled in satisfaction. This was proof that Lilly was indeed his sought-after authoress. He'd once saved Lilly from drowning at her cousin's country estate in the Adirondacks. This was no coincidence. Lilly was Fannie.

He studied her bedroom window. She'd never come out of hiding as long as he insisted she promote her dime novels like Elna Price. Her reserved nature held her back. Frustrated, he slapped his palm against the wicker arm rest and let out a long groan. How he wished Fannie Cole was anyone else but Lilly. He didn't have a chance of coaxing her into the public eye.

Is this what held her back from him? Ever since she had broken her engagement with Harlan, she'd kept him at arm's length. Was it because she feared he'd force her to tell the truth, force her into the limelight?

He'd find her and hash this out now. Rising, he spotted her with her maid on the front veranda. Jack tossed *Dorothea's Dilemma* onto the cushion of the wicker chair and rushed across the lawn. He tipped his bowler and bowed. A frown flashed across Lilly's face before smoothing into a faint smile.

"Where are you off to?" He masked his guile behind a wide grin, or so he hoped. "I thought you'd just returned." Unveiling Fannie would require tact and patience, two qualities he consistently lacked but needed to acquire in a hurry. "If you have a few minutes, I'd like to speak with you."

She glanced toward the stables, her mouth tightened with obvious anxiety. "I have a few errands to run in town."

"Coincidentally, so do I. May I join you?"

She shook her head and the plume on her large hat fluttered. "I'm sorry, but I'm driving the runabout and there won't be enough room."

There was enough space even with her maid and several packages. "All right. I'll go alone. When you're finished perhaps we can meet for tea or coffee."

"Thank you for the invitation, but I'm afraid I can't."

"You mean you don't wish to." Exasperation swamped his chest.

Lilly let out a sigh. "I'm afraid I'm too busy this afternoon." She spoke with exaggerated patience he didn't appreciate.

Jack blew out a groan. "I need to discuss something important with you."

As the runabout turned onto the drive, Lilly flew down the veranda steps. "I'm sorry, but that's impossible right now," she called over her shoulder. "Maybe we can talk for a few moments when I return. I'll not be long."

She and Annie scrambled aboard the small carriage. She flicked the reins. The roan trotted down the long driveway, turned onto Ocean Avenue, and vanished. Jack stepped inside Summerhill and found Mr. Ames near the door.

"Did Miss Westbrook mention where she planned to go this afternoon?" Jack asked without preamble.

"I heard her say something about Baxter and Dunne's, the book shop on Bellevue Avenue."

Jack thanked the butler and raced to the stable where he requested a gig. Lilly couldn't avoid him forever, try as she might.

Lilly urged the horse around Ocean Drive, past the seventy-five or so cottages gracing Bellevue Avenue, and on to the small shopping district near the casino. She wished Miranda was with her, but her friend hadn't yet returned from the library.

As soon as they arrived at Baxter and Dunne's Book Shop, Lilly's breath escaped from her lungs in one long *whoosh*. What if she couldn't find a copy of Mr. Walt Whitman's *Leaves of Grass*? What if she was caught by someone she knew? Pausing before the store, she steadied her breathing while she pretended to examine the book titles in the window.

She could send Annie to insert the note

into the book, but Annie was a curious girl and might peek at the contents first. No, she'd do the deed by herself.

As she and Annie passed through the shop door, the soft tinkling of a bell announced their presence. A clerk who was shelving a stack of books glanced over to the door and asked if she required assistance. Lilly declined and he continued with his task. She strolled down the first aisle flanked by rows of religion and philosophy books. She easily found the poetry section and scanned the book spines for "W" and then for "Whitman."

It was there — a tall, brown tome with gold lettering on the spine. Relief slowed her heartbeat. Glancing around, she noticed the store bustled with customers she recognized. Fortunately, the poetry aisle remained empty, except for herself and her maid. She turned away from the main aisle, hoping no one would identify her.

"Annie, would you please run over to the children's shelves and try to find *The Adventures of Tom Sawyer*? If you can't locate it, ask the proprietor."

"Yes, miss." Annie hesitated. "Is this for your cousin, Mrs. Templeton's boy?"

Lilly nodded, anxious for her maid to disappear. Annie ambled down the row of books, scanning the titles. Though always respectful to the Westbrooks and their guests, her curiosity bordered on nosiness. Lilly's mother often claimed the servants knew all about their employers, including their tastes and preferences. Often, even their secrets.

Once the maid was out of sight, Lilly reached up to the top shelf for *Leaves of Grass.* Her fingers brushed the bottom of the spine, and she grabbed for it. But it stood too high. She rolled onto the balls of her feet but couldn't get a grip on the book. In a final attempt, she leaped up and slapped it with the palm of her hand, dislodging the next volume. It tumbled to the wide pine floor with a crash.

"May I help you, Lilly?"

Lilly gasped and she turned. "Oh my, you startled me, Jack. I didn't hear you sneaking up on me." She paused. She planted her hands on her hips. "What are you doing here? Are you following me?"

"I confess I am. I'm hoping you'll lead me to Fannie Cole."

"Don't be absurd." Flustered, Lilly bent forward to retrieve the book. Jack leaned over at the same time and they nearly bumped heads. His face came so close he could have kissed her. Why had that image suddenly popped into her head? Lilly thought she might faint.

"Are you feeling well? You look flushed."

She inhaled the fragrance of his woodsy cologne, then stood up with the errant volume. "Yes, I'm perfectly fine. Only I can't reach the book I want. Perhaps you can get it for me. It's called *Leaves of Grass* by Mr. Walt Whitman."

An easy reach for him, he handed Lilly the only copy and returned the other book to the shelf. "Do you enjoy Mr. Whitman's poetry?"

Lilly let out an uncharacteristic giggle. "I haven't read any of his poems, but I'm open-minded. I'll let you know what I think after I read it." What was she babbling about? There was only one copy of the book and it wasn't coming home with her. She'd have to borrow the volume from the library in case Jack asked her opinion of it.

"I understand *Leaves of Grass* might not be suitable for young ladies," he said.

His hearty chuckle pushed her off stride. "Dear me, I hope not. But maybe I should choose something else . . ." She pretended to peruse the shelves.

She waited for him to leave so she could reclaim her dignity and finish her task. But Jack didn't move, as if he was seeing right through her. And now he expected her to choose another title or head for the counter and purchase the book. Irritatingly, he perused the shelves beside her, pulling out one book after another.

"Would you mind checking up on my maid? I sent her over to the children's section to find a book for my cousin's son. She's taking quite a long time."

His eyebrows shot upward toward his thick black hair. "At your service." His lopsided grin set her teeth on edge. What was wrong with him? Why was he acting so peculiar?

As soon as Jack left, Lilly dug into her reticule and pulled out her note to Colonel MacIntyre. Drawing in a deep breath, she slid the envelope into the center of the pages. It stuck up beyond the top edge of the book. She grimaced as she reached to return the volume. She jumped and flailed to shove it back, but even stretching her arm nearly out of its socket, she couldn't touch the shelf.

"Oh, dear," she muttered, panting from her efforts.

Afraid that Annie and Jack might return at any moment, she compromised and pushed the volume into an empty space one shelf below the W's. The recipient of the letter would just have to search for the book.

Jack rejoined her. "The shop is all out of *Tom Sawyer*. It's very popular."

That was a blessing since she hadn't brought enough money to purchase it. "Thank you for looking."

"You're not buying the *Leaves of Grass*?" Jack looked down at her empty hands.

"No, I decided against it. I'll pick a more appropriate work some other time."

"An excellent decision, I'm sure."

He nodded as Lilly stepped away from the stacks. She passed him when she noticed his long arm snake around her to the misplaced copy of Whitman. She spun about and watched in horror as Jack grasped the book. He reached to the top shelf. The pages fanned out and the letter dropped to the floor.

"What do we have here?" He grabbed the envelope before Lilly could snatch it away. His sardonic grin infuriated her.

She rubbed her forehead and tried to hide her fiery hot and, no doubt, scarlet face.

He leaned against the bookcase. "Well, Miss Westbrook, are you going to explain or must I guess what this is all about? Your choice."

Lilly tensed. She met his mocking appraisal with a defiant stare. "I don't owe you an explanation. This is strictly my business."

"I'm sorry to have to do this," he said as he moved to open the envelope, "but I have no other option."

Lilly grabbed for the letter and missed. "Return it at once."

He held the letter above his head. Pulling on his arm with all her strength, she found hard muscle beneath his navy blue jacket. She jumped and swatted to no avail.

"Stop this ridiculous game, Jack. You're making fools of us both."

"If you don't wish me to rip this open and read it out loud, tell me what it's about." His eyes glared with exasperation. "Are you sending a love note to someone?"

"Don't be ludicrous."

"Exactly the point." Jack stuck his index finger into the air. "But then, you must have something else in mind. Does this concern Miss Fannie Cole?"

"Please stop badgering me." Lilly glanced about and noticed a friend of her mother's at the end of the aisle examining the religion books. "And do keep your voice low."

Jack swept a finger to his lips and whispered, "I won't say a word about Miss Cole if you tell me the truth about her."

Smoldering anger quickly flared. "Jackson

341

Grail, you've exhausted every bit of my patience. If you continue, I shall call the clerk and have you thrown out of this book shop on your ear."

His raised his arms in mock fear as Mrs. Leontina Radcliffe, staring openly at Jack's antics, hurried toward them.

"If you answer a few questions I have about my most popular authoress, I won't tell Mrs. Radcliffe who you really are."

His stage whisper could easily reach the lovely and stylishly dressed woman.

"Do stop talking or I'll scream."

"Then are you coming with me to the tea shop?"

Through gritted teeth, she hissed, "Yes, if you insist."

Jack bowed. "I do, indeed."

Annie appeared without a book. "There's no *Tom Sawyer* in stock, miss."

Lilly steadied her nerves. "Then look for *Adventures of Huckleberry Finn*. Surely they have some books by Mark Twain. Take your time. I'll be back in a short while."

After greeting Mrs. Radcliffe, Lilly marched out of the shop and followed Jack to a deserted café a short way down the street where he ordered tea and petit fours. As they waited to be served, their silence thickened.

"That was quite a show you put on." Lilly flared.

Jack chuckled and poked his head around the vase of roses in the center of the table. He moved them off to the side. "I thought I was quite effective."

"You would," she conceded with a rueful twist of her mouth. "Out with it. I don't have all day to spar with you."

The formally attired waiter laid their dessert on the white damask tablecloth and poured tea into thin china cups rimmed in gold. When he departed, Jack leaned closer to Lilly, his full attention riveted on her. Instinctively she edged away. Folding her hands in her lap, she clasped them tightly.

"Lilly, I know you are Fannie Cole."

His firmness shattered her resolve to do battle. "Why do you believe that?"

He leaned across the small square table, his dark eyes probing. "Because you're the only writer who could have known about our tryst at Cooper's Pond."

Perspiration beaded her forehead as she met his gaze. "What does that have to do with Miss Cole?"

Jack shook his head and the merriment in his eyes faded. "You aren't going to make this easy, are you? All right, if you don't remember what you wrote, I'll refresh your memory."

# TWENTY-ONE

Lilly tensed as Jack continued. "In *Dorothea's Dilemma,* a young lady is saved from falling through the ice by her beloved." He continued, reciting her favorite scene in her favorite book. He leaned closer. "Ice skating, upstate New York, stealing time away from the rest of the group. Does any of this sound familiar?" All traces of humor left his face.

Lilly trembled, but she managed a dry smile. "Your story is a bit melodramatic."

"That's how I remember it — melodramatic, terrifying. I like to picture myself as your Sir Galahad — without the white steed, of course."

Despite herself, Lilly laughed nervously. "You're outrageous, Jackson Grail."

"Perhaps, but I'm also serious. Lilly, please listen. I can help you deal with MacIntyre. He's in the midst of blackmailing you, right?" His eyes narrowed and he glowered. "Is that what your note is all about?"

She took a sip of tea and ignored his question.

"I can see that it is." He paused for several seconds. "Now that I've discovered your identity, I hope you'll reconsider." His voice was gentle, but his eyes sparked with determination.

"You've established nothing, except that life is fraught with coincidences." Lilly pushed back the heavy gilded chair and rose. "If you'll excuse me, I must leave. Good day."

"Lilly, stop denying the truth. Admit you're Fannie Cole."

She held out her hand. "Return my letter or I shall tell the waiter you stole it from me. I'll ask him to fetch a policeman." She glared at the envelope he clutched tightly.

"You wouldn't dare."

"Don't force me, Jack. Just give me back what's mine."

Grimacing, he thrust the letter into her hand. "You win — for now."

Leaving behind a plate of sweets, she strode into the bright afternoon sunlight. Her neck ached, her temples throbbed. If only Jack understood she couldn't possibly introduce herself to Fannie's readers —

even if she were so inclined.

Without her family's approval, she'd never divulge her secret. And even if the world turned inside out and her parents bestowed their blessing, she refused to relinquish her privacy and take on a role for which she was so ill suited. Accommodating Jack was impossible. He'd have to accept no as her final answer and find another way to build his business.

He looked so forlorn she pitied him and wished he didn't depend so completely upon her cooperation. Yet, she couldn't do as he asked.

Glancing up, she watched Jack board the gig and head south down Bellevue Avenue toward Summerhill. Quickly, she returned to the book shop and asked the clerk for a step stool. She placed the note into *Leaves of Grass.*

Too bad she hadn't thought of a step stool earlier.

Snapping the reins, Jack let the horse fly around the twists and turns of Ocean Drive. Her chestnut back glistened with sweat as her legs stretched into a gallop. The carriage careened to one side and threatened to overturn and smash into the stone wall bordering the long perimeter of Summerhill. He pulled back on the reins, slowing the horse to a more manageable canter.

*Careful, Jack. No point in breaking your neck over the fate of a publishing house or Lilly's intransigence.*

He'd driven around for over an hour in the sea breeze and sunshine, hoping to ease his frustration. But his financial worries spun through his mind. With every dollar he had now invested in his three enterprises, he felt curiously at the mercy of the world again — much like when he had nothing at all. He'd thought wealth would provide security and a sense of well-being. And to a certain degree it had, yet along with the benefits came the fear of losing it all. A frequent roiling in the pit of his stomach proved just how vulnerable he felt.

He'd opened his soul to Lilly and she'd still refused to help him. Not that he really faulted her for her stubbornness. He'd treated her so shabbily six years ago, he deserved punishment. But it would be generous of her to forget the past and finally forgive him. And to trust him to treat her fairly.

He turned onto Summerhill's drive and forced Lilly from his thoughts. Back to business concerns he *could* control, at least for the time being.

Jones and Jarman needed Fannie Cole more than ever. But he had little chance of changing Lilly's mind about a publicity campaign. Jack grunted. Lilly Westbrook writing as Fannie Cole. What bad luck. He'd never really considered her courageous enough to buck society and churn out popular novels, though he'd had his suspicions. Of course, she actually hadn't crossed society. She'd sidestepped and concealed her profession. She'd hidden her light under a bushel and it was undoubtedly torturing her.

But if he were a good Christian he'd leave Lilly alone and not compound her problems. He undoubtedly was adding to her misery just like Colonel MacIntyre. Well no, perhaps he wasn't quite that despicable. At any rate, he'd treat her with more kindness from now on and handle *Talk of the Town* on his own. Somehow.

The next morning Jack waited for the coachman to drive the carriage up to the veranda. After a late night at yet another fancy ball, most of the household were probably still curled up in their soft feather beds, too exhausted for Sunday service, Jack assumed.

The front door flew open and Lilly

stepped outside, adjusting a flowery hat that dipped becomingly over her forehead. Her maid trailed at her heels. Jack bowed low to Lilly and let his face stretch into a broad grin. A lovely sight in pale blue and white lace, she stopped short at the threshold and fussed with the bow at her neck.

"Good morning, Jack. I'm afraid I'm late. I thought the carriage might be gone by now." As she spoke, the open landau arrived with a coachman sitting straight and tall in his box. She pulled on a white glove, carefully fitting her fingers into the kid. "I suppose we're the only ones going to church this morning. I checked with my friend Miranda and I'm afraid she's a bit under the weather and won't be able to join us." Her voice sounded a little too bright and high pitched.

"I'm sorry to hear that. So where do you usually worship?" Jack offered his hand and boosted her into the vehicle as the maid scrambled up beside the coachman.

"Trinity — when we attend. I'm afraid church is the last thing my family thinks about during the summer season. But they do prefer Trinity to all the others. I often go with only Annie."

Just as he'd guessed. The elite belonged to Trinity, the imposing white colonial structure where George Washington had worshipped when he'd visited Newport. Jack heard many of the members decorated their soft pew cushions in their family colors to match their coaches and footmen's livery.

"Would you mind a less fashionable church with a pastor who gives exceptional sermons?" That would be a departure for Lilly and a challenge to her conventional attitudes. He wondered if she'd decline.

"I'd be delighted to go."

"Good." He suppressed a chuckle. Lilly was proving to be far less conventional than he'd ever thought.

"What church shall we be attending?" she asked.

"Calvary, if you don't mind."

Jack gave directions to the driver and the carriage jerked forward. He wanted to edge closer to Lilly but knew she'd shift toward the door. What happened to his honorable intentions of remaining as far away as possible?

"I'm afraid I've never heard of Calvary," Lilly said as she scooted to the far side of the carriage seat.

Why would she? Calvary wasn't remotely fashionable. Mr. Ames, the butler, had recommended it as the house of worship favored by the staff and that was sufficient for Jack.

They rode in silence around Ocean Drive, inhaled fresh sea air, and gazed at the rugged coastline swept clean by the wind. Once they reached town they wound through a maze of narrow, leafy streets bathed in deep shade. Their horses' hooves and carriage wheels ground over gravel and dirt, disturbing the bird song and the occasional bark of a dog.

When the small, stone church came into view, the coachman slowed the horses and pulled up to the curb. Jack and Lilly climbed down and followed the other congregants into the building.

Once inside, Jack's eyes quickly adjusted to the dimness. The wooden floor, partially covered by a faded red runner, creaked as they walked down the center aisle. A stained glass window above the pulpit filtered the morning light and added a touch of warmth to the cool, dark interior. He liked the smell of furniture polish and the mustiness of age and climate.

It reminded him of the little church he'd attended with his parents, a welcoming place he'd tucked into his bank of childhood memories. Odd to be with Lilly in a spot so reminiscent of his past and so different from her own. The wide, impenetrable chasm that separated them widened and grew deeper; Lilly was accustomed to luxury and he wasn't.

He glanced over the congregation without recognizing anyone, not that he expected to. From the look of the patched clothing worn by the worshippers, he assumed Calvary was packed shoulder to shoulder with towns-folk, probably shopkeepers and laborers. None of the summer people would think of patronizing any church without their friends.

Sidestepping into the pew, Jack felt strangely at home. But did Lilly? Dressed in her finery, plain by society's standards, she stood out as a very rich lady indeed. Both men and women stole curious glances at her. She smiled politely before settling into silent prayer.

When the organ finally poured out its music, Jack rose and sang with his usual gusto. He made a joyful, robust noise to the Lord, and that was what counted, he hoped, not the dismal quality of his voice. Lilly flashed a crooked smile when he reached for a high note and missed by a mile. Her grin, half hidden behind the brim and veil of her pearl gray hat, pierced his heart with a sad sweetness.

Mercifully, the plump pastor with a

canyon-deep voice hooked his attention and pulled him back to the present. Jack opened his Bible to Romans 12:1–2 as Reverend Minter read the verses.

"I beseech you therefore, brethren, by the mercies of God, that ye present your bodies a living sacrifice, holy, acceptable unto God, which is your reasonable service. And be not conformed to this world: but be ye transformed by the renewing of your mind, that ye may prove what is that good, and acceptable, and perfect will of God."

*Hmm.* Now those were words to ponder. Did Lilly understand she shouldn't worry what the world would say about her writing career? Her decision to follow the perfect will of God ought to relieve her mind and renew her heart. Jack glanced sideways, but her profile betrayed no reaction to the verse. He felt sure she needed the pastor's message, just as he did.

And then Reverend Minter boomed Joshua 24:15. "And if it seem evil unto you to serve the LORD, choose you this day whom ye will serve; whether the gods which your fathers served that were on the other side of the flood, or the gods of the Amorites, in whose land ye dwell: but as for me and my house, we will serve the LORD."

Would this convince Lilly to follow God

instead of her parents and her social circle? Only He deserved her undivided loyalty. Jack hoped she'd serve the Lord even if it didn't benefit Jones and Jarman.

The pastor's voice resonated throughout the packed church. "Always remember, you can not serve both God and man. You must choose." He glanced down at the open Bible resting on his pulpit and read aloud. "Jeremiah 45:5 says: 'And seeketh thou great things for thyself? seek them not: for, behold, I will bring evil upon all flesh, saith the LORD; but thy life will I give unto thee for a prey in all places whither thou goest.' "

The preacher's eyes gleamed as his gaze swept across the congregation. "Proverbs 11:28. 'He that trusteth in his riches shall fall; but the righteous shall flourish as a branch.' Value the Lord, not your earthly possessions."

Jack squirmed. Why would the man preach against riches when most of his flock looked like working-class poor? These people were hardly burdened by an overabundance of material goods. Of course, riches came in many forms, not merely hard currency. To serve yourself and not the Lord was the crux of the matter.

Perspiration seeped under his tight collar and trickled down his back. Perhaps the sermon was meant for him *and* Lilly. That was the strangest thing about Scripture — it spoke to everybody in a clear, disconcerting way, leaving no one boastful or unaffected.

On the way out they shook hands with Pastor Minter and his wife and then boarded the carriage. It rolled toward Summerhill at a fast clip. He and Lilly sat across from each other, but neither of them spoke. He wanted to discuss the sermon and his suggestions about Fannie's career, but she looked lost in her own thoughts as she stared at the countryside flying by. Was she pondering the sermon or her troubles as a dime novelist? He sighed. She wasn't going to divulge whatever was on her mind, though he wished she'd take a chance and confide in him.

As the carriage rolled down Ocean Drive, Lilly turned her head and half-smiled. "I've been mulling over what Pastor Minter said. And I have a confession to make."

He swallowed hard. "Yes?"

"As you've long suspected, I'm your authoress, Fannie Cole. However, I'm afraid my identity won't change anything for you. I'll continue to write my dime novels, but I won't allow you to promote me as Fannie, in any way. I'm sorry, Jack."

He paused. "I'll respect your wishes, Lilly. But you'll be passing up a wonderful opportunity to make more money for the Settlement House."

Lilly nodded. "Maybe you're right. But I couldn't promote myself like Elna Price. She reminds me of a Vaudeville star, though I admit I've never seen one actually perform. But I've heard tales of how they flaunt themselves. And I've seen Mrs. Price. That was more than enough to dissuade me from ever going out in public to sell my books."

"I'd never ask you to blatantly promote yourself. I'm only asking you to reveal your name and sign a few autographs."

He bit back his dismay. He needed so much more from Fannie, but even a small amount of publicity would help Jones and Jarman inch toward the top of the publishing heap. But from the firm set of her jaw, she wasn't about to budge. "I promise not to exploit Fannie Cole."

Lilly shook her head and pressed her lips. Yet her eyes begged for understanding. "I want to help you, Jack, but I won't admit I'm Fannie. My family's humiliation would be more than they could bear." She placed her hand over his. "Please try to forgive me."

He shrugged. "All right, I forgive you." He couldn't add enthusiasm to his voice because between her refusal and Reynolds's stroke, all his hopes of building Jones and Jarman into a prestigious publisher were fading like a distant dream. "I won't badger you anymore."

Her small smile conveyed her appreciation. "I'm sorry to cause you such disappointment, Jack."

He suppressed a low groan as the horses' hooves pounded against the dirt road. "There's one more thing, Lilly. I want to help you handle Colonel MacIntyre. He's a man without scruples and you shouldn't deal with him on your own. Please, let me assist you."

She hesitated for only a moment. "Thank you, Jack, but if and when it's necessary to confront him, I can do it on my own."

He shook his head and groaned. From the determination in her eyes, she wasn't about to change her mind.

# Twenty-Two

Early Monday afternoon Mr. Ames stumbled through the library doorway and offered Lilly a letter lying on a silver salver.

Lilly recognized the bold, black handwriting of Colonel MacIntyre. She reached for it slowly as if it were a flaming ember. "Thank you." She accepted the letter opener from the butler, slit open the envelope, and pulled out a single page with a trembling hand. As soon as Mr. Ames departed, Lilly read the note in a whisper to Miranda, who sat in a chair beside her.

My dear Miss Westbrook,
Please meet me at O'Neill's Café on Thames Street, Monday at three o'clock. We have important business to discuss. If you wish to keep your secret safe and your reputation intact, it behooves you

to accept my invitation. Come alone.

Sincerely,<br>An interested party

The note dropped from Lilly's hand and fluttered toward the floor as a breeze wafted through the screens and blew it across the Persian carpet. As luck would have it, Jack strode into the library, scooped up the paper and held it up. His eyes twinkled with curiosity.

Lilly lifted her chin. "It's mine, Jack. May I have it — if you don't mind?" She tried to keep panic from capturing her voice, but she sounded like an ill-tempered shrew. Hadn't they just had this very conversation?

Jack's forehead pleated. "There's no need to be so touchy. What's the matter? You look terrified. Did the letter frighten you?" His right eye twitched as he glanced at the stationery.

"No, of course not." Lilly held out her hand.

"It's rude to read other people's mail, Jackson," Miranda added softly.

Jack paused. Would he dare peruse her note? Lilly couldn't breathe as the seconds slowly ticked by. Appraising her as if he heard her thunderous heartbeat, his eyes narrowed. But instead of glancing at the letter, he returned it to her. Reluctantly. His better angels had won out.

Lilly nodded, suppressing relief. She snatched the colonel's message and slid it into her skirt pocket. "Thank you, Jack."

He nodded and excused himself. "If you need me, I'll be nearby."

Lilly waited until Jack left the library before she leaned closer to Miranda. "That was a close call. Do I dare meet with Colonel MacIntyre?" she whispered.

"You must. Unless you want your name smeared all over *Talk of the Town,* you have no other choice."

Lilly buried her face in her hands for several seconds before looking up. "Writing under a *nom de plume* seemed such a clever idea when I first began scribbling romances. But now I know it was the worst mistake I ever made. Of course, I couldn't write as Lillian Westbrook, either. Oh, Miranda, what am I to do?"

"Meet with the man and don't act frightened. Stand up straight and tall and stare him directly in the eye. Glare at him. I shall accompany you."

"But Colonel MacIntyre specifically directed me to come alone."

"I'll wait in the carriage. You don't have to do this on your own. And remember the

Lord is always with you."

Lilly wrapped her arm around her friend's shoulder and gave her a hug. "Please pray for me, Miranda."

Miranda grinned. "I always pray for you. The Lord will give you the strength to do what you must."

"I know. I won't allow that horrid man to get the better of me." For a moment Lilly almost believed her words.

A short time later she returned to her bedroom to dress for her meeting with the colonel. Already behind schedule, she only had a few minutes to escape Summerhill before Mama captured her for a carriage ride, then tea at the Breakers, Alice Vanderbilt's Italianate villa on Ochre Point. Later, Mama and Irene would ask why she hadn't joined them. She'd worry about a reasonable explanation later when she returned home.

Lilly rushed down the staircase. "Do hurry, Miranda," she urged as she glanced over her shoulder.

"I'm coming as fast as I can. The hem of my skirt ripped, so I must be careful. Perhaps I ought to change my clothing." Miranda grasped the rail as she gingerly descended the wide, carpeted steps.

"There's really no time."

The grandfather clock in the foyer struck two thirty-five. If no one at Summerhill waylaid them, they'd arrive by three, right on time. Grateful for the empty hallway, Lilly strode toward the door and peered through the glass side panels. The lawn looked deserted except for her carriage waiting by the veranda steps. She took a long, steadying breath. They'd make their escape before anyone had a chance to catch them.

A piercing shriek and series of thuds sent Lilly spinning around. Head over heels, Miranda tumbled down the stairs and landed on the Persian rug that covered most of the foyer floor. Slowly she righted herself, groaning.

Lilly rushed to her side and stretched out her hand. "Let me help you up."

"My ankle, I think it's sprained. Oh my, it hurts." Miranda gasped as she leaned against Lilly and thrust herself to one foot.

Hobbling, Miranda turned pale. With Lilly's help she lowered herself onto a stair-step. She examined her ankle and winced.

Lilly bit her lip. "Do sit still. Don't try to move. I'll have Mr. Ames fetch a doctor. You may have broken a bone."

"Perhaps some ice . . ."

Mr. Ames appeared out of thin air and

sized up the situation. "I'll telephone for Doctor Hansen." He shuffled toward the office.

"I'm afraid I shan't be able to accompany you. That fall was so clumsy of me. I'm terribly sorry, Lilly."

"Don't worry about my meeting. I can handle the man on my own. It's your ankle I'm concerned about." Lilly bent down to get a closer look at the injury.

"You must leave right now. The entire household will be down here in a minute. They'll all be so distressed about my fall they won't even notice you're gone. Do hurry. I promise I'll be fine."

Lilly hesitated, but she knew Miranda would soon be in capable hands. "If you really think you'll be all right . . ."

"Go." Miranda gently pushed her away. "At once. I'll pray everything turns out well."

Lilly pressed her in a hug, then dashed to the carriage. The driver jumped down from his seat and helped her inside the open landau. An enclosed vehicle like the phaeton would draw less attention, but there was no time to exchange carriages. They drove the length of the long driveway and out onto Ocean Avenue. Heavily veiled, she prayed she wouldn't be recognized. If she were spotted by a friend of her mother's, the lady might ask why she was out and about on her own without a chaperone. Fortunately, none of the Westbrooks' equipages had a family emblem on their side. Thank goodness her parents weren't as pretentious as most of the cottagers.

Lilly's carriage rumbled toward the waterfront. The air hung heavy with dampness as fog and storm clouds blew across the harbor. The humid breeze curled her tendrils and fused her starched shirtwaist to her back.

Lilly gulped in the soggy air and struggled to stay calm. If only Jack were here beside her she'd feel more confident. The prospect of confronting Colonel MacIntyre all alone coated her stomach with nausea. But she had only herself to blame for this entire disaster. She hoped she wouldn't falter when she met him eye to eye.

*Lord, please give me the words I need to confront the colonel and the strength not to flee.*

The landau wove through the congestion of Thames Street, past buggies and drays and every type of equipage imaginable. Once they reached the small café named O'Neill's, the carriage pulled up to the curb. Her driver helped her step down. She smiled as if stopping at a working class eatery were commonplace. "Stay put, please. I'll be detained for only a few minutes."

The coachman's expression betrayed no interest, but Lilly knew he must wonder why she directed him here. Bellevue Avenue shops and restaurants catered to her set exclusively. She seldom needed to travel to the waterfront where the townspeople conducted commerce. Mama would faint if she knew Lilly planned to meet New York's dreaded extortionist . . . on Thames Street, no less.

She took a fortifying breath, but nothing calmed her agitation. Straightening her shoulders provided a small measure of self-confidence but not enough to stop her teeth from chattering. She pushed open the glass door and stepped inside the dark café. Her eyes rapidly adjusted to the dim light. Scanning the customers, mainly locals by the look of their clothing, she spotted a fat man sitting at a back table smoking a cigar. He waited, his hands folded on the faded tablecloth, an exaggerated, clown-like grin splitting his face. Then he waved her over.

Lilly swallowed her revulsion and lifted her chin. As she strode toward his table, the heels of her boots beat against the uneven wooden floor. "I assume you're Colonel MacIntyre."

His menacing smile stretched even wider. "Yes, I am the colonel, at your service. And of course, you're Miss Westbrook. Please be seated." He pointed to the other side of the table with thick fingers decorated with gold, silver, and diamond rings. "I'm honored you've deigned to meet with me."

Did she have any other option? "Let's not pretend this is a social call." Lilly sharpened her voice, amazed at her sudden bravado. Never would she or her family receive him as a visitor. "Let's get on with whatever it is you want to discuss." As if she didn't know.

His smarmy grin faded and took a downward turn. "Splendid. But first, would you like a cup of tea or perhaps coffee?" He continued his pretence of good manners.

"No, thank you." Lilly squirmed in the hard chair and waited for the colonel to scrape up the crumbs of his cherry pie.

"Miss Westbrook — or may I call you Lillian?" His piggy eyes shone with mockery.

"No, you may not."

"Then I should like to call you Fannie Cole, the name you're so anxious to keep hidden. Now then, Fannie. You've been most indiscreet writing for publication without informing your parents or friends.

They'd all disapprove of your occupation, as well they should."

She gulped, holding back a torrent of anger. "What do you want? If you don't tell me at once, I shall leave." Focusing on the man's gleaming eyes, Lilly started to rise.

"Sit down. I'll get to the subject at hand." He glanced around the café. Obviously satisfied no one was listening, he leaned forward across the table. His tobacco breath struck her like a cloud of poisonous gas. "In order to keep your name out of my news sheet, I require three thousand dollars. Now don't look so stunned. That might seem like a large sum to you, but I'm sure when you think it over, you'll agree it's a small price to pay for silence. I'll tell my readers I was misinformed about Miss Cole's identity, but I'll continue my diligent search."

Lilly clutched her hands to stop from slapping his face. Where would she obtain that amount of money? Her own bank account, managed by Papa, had a modest sum. Of course Papa possessed substantially more, but he'd never loan her any of it without knowing all the details. Perhaps Miranda could help. No, Miranda's father controlled her funds also — giving her little more than pin money.

"I'm afraid I can't come up with that

amount. It's out of the question."

The colonel spread out his hands in a gesture of helplessness. "Then you're out of luck, miss. Perhaps your father or your publisher could help. Explain you need to pay for some gowns or a few trinkets. You're creative. Use your imagination."

Lilly stood and found her bones too soft to hold her up. She grasped the back of the chair to steady herself and dug her fingernails into the wood. "You're the most despicable man I've ever had the misfortune to meet."

Colonel MacIntyre chuckled and bowed. "Thank you for your kind words."

As she turned to leave, his warning resounded in her ears. "I expect to meet you here in two days at the same hour. Bring cash or you'll see your reputation destroyed in the next issue of *Talk of the Town.* Good day, Fannie."

Where could she possibly locate such a vast sum in such a short time? Out of ideas, Lilly climbed aboard the carriage and buried her head in her hands. She didn't know how she'd conceal this scandal of her own making, but she had to find a way.

*Help me, Lord. Only You can provide me with a solution to the mess I've made.*

Jack wanted to help. Full of clever ideas

and bravado, he'd devise a solution that would rid her of *Talk of the Town* forever. But she needed to face the consequences of her choices without dragging him into it. If possible.

*Heavenly Father, what should I do?*

Lilly returned to Summerhill and found Miranda waiting on the front veranda, tatting in hand. Laying the ivory shuttle on her lap, Miranda motioned her to the porch swing.

"How does your ankle feel?" Lilly asked, frowning at her friend's foot which rested on a tapestry footstool.

Miranda grimaced. "It's still a bit sore, but better. Now tell me all that happened with the colonel," she whispered as Lilly dropped beside her.

"It was dreadful. He's a vile extortionist, just as Jack claimed. He demanded three thousand dollars to keep my name out of *Talk of the Town.* I have absolutely no way of obtaining that much money." Lilly's voice quavered as she covered her face with her hands. She feared she might cry, but after one sniff she blinked back hot tears.

Miranda squeezed Lilly's hand. "I'm so sorry."

"Every last dime of my inheritance is

controlled by Papa, not that I cared until now. But I can't obtain any of it without his permission, and he'd want to know why I need it."

Miranda nodded. "Do you have money left from your publisher?"

"Not one cent. I donated all of it to the Settlement House. Of course, I'm glad I did because they're in such desperate need of funds."

"Only now you're desperate too." Miranda drew out a sigh.

"Yes, I'm afraid I am."

"If I had the money I'd gladly give it to you, but I don't. Neither does my father."

"Thank you, anyway. I know you'd help if you could." Miranda was poor compared to the Santerres, her prosperous relations, but she donated what she did have to worthy charities.

"Perhaps I can ask Jack for an advance on my newest dime novel. A sizable advance." Lilly laughed at her absurdity. "What am I thinking of? Jack knew the colonel would blackmail me. It was I who thought otherwise. Sometimes I can be so simpleminded."

"Ask him anyway." Miranda leaned down to rub her bandaged ankle.

"No, that's not a good idea. Jack doesn't want me to pay to suppress my real name.

371

He'd balk at paying blackmail money."

Miranda looked skeptical. "I don't think you give Jackson enough credit. He loves you and wants to marry you."

Lilly unpinned her straw hat and placed it across her skirt. She toyed with the silk carnations and ran her fingers over the mesh of the veil. "Yes, I believe Jack does care for me — in his own way. But he loves his business equally, if not more. And he's quite unhappy I didn't tell him the truth about Fannie Cole earlier." Lilly shook her head. "No, I most definitely can't ask Jack."

"I truly believe he'd help you."

"If he loaned me the money, I'd be in his debt. He might expect me to promote Fanny in return for his favor. And I couldn't do that."

Miranda sighed. "Oh Lilly, don't you think it might be better if you confessed to your family? I know it would be difficult, but then you'd be forever free of the colonel. It might be worth swallowing a bitter pill."

How could Miranda suggest such a thing? "If I only had myself to think of, I might consider it. But my parents would never understand my writing dime novels. And to think of what it might do to them, and our reputation . . ." Lilly sighed.

"I certainly sympathize with your reticence. But to be practical, you'll have to find the money somewhere. If you refuse to ask Jack or your father, who can you ask?"

Lilly shook her head. "I don't know. I promise to consider asking Jack, but I really doubt I'll change my mind." Lilly stood up. "I believe a walk by the sea might clear my head."

She left Miranda with her tatting and walked around the side of Summerhill toward the rocks. Over the blue hydrangea bushes and porch spindles she spotted Mama resting in a wicker chair. Mama looked up and over her spectacles.

"Hello, Lilly. Out for an afternoon stroll?"

Lilly nodded as she climbed the veranda steps. "Why Mama, is that *Dorothea's Dilemma*?" Her voice shook, but Mama didn't notice.

Mama's fingers spread across the title, but it was too late. Lilly recognized the cover immediately. She forced a laugh, but feared she couldn't hide her displeasure. "I can't imagine you'd enjoy a *dime novel*."

Mama jutted her chin and then chuckled. "I'm surprised myself. But I'm enjoying it. The story is splendid. I'm almost half finished."

Before long Mama would come to the scene with Ada Brown plunging through the

373

ice and Lawrence rescuing her along with the ring. In an instant she'd put two and two together, just like Jack had done, and realize Lilly wrote as Fannie Cole. She'd have to misappropriate the book as soon as Mama left the porch — if Mama didn't take the book with her.

Lilly frowned as her mother clutched the volume to her bosom. "You mustn't waste your time reading books when you could be visiting your friends."

"When I find a few more spare minutes, I most definitely will read more of this enchanting story." Mama leveled a quizzical stare at Lilly. "I'm afraid I've misjudged all dime novels as worthless. *Dorothea's Dilemma* is certainly not trash, as I first thought. Would you like to read it when I'm finished?"

"No thank you, Mama." Lilly glared at the cover and wished the novel would vanish into thin air.

"You're scowling. What is the matter with you, Lillian? You haven't been yourself in weeks."

Lilly lowered her gaze. "I'm fine, really I am."

She waited for her mother to leave the veranda, but just as Lilly feared, Mama departed with her book in hand.

# TWENTY-THREE

Lilly came downstairs the next morning to discover a trunk and a valise in the hallway. "Is someone coming or going, Mr. Ames?"

The butler cupped his ear. "What was that, Miss Westbrook?"

Then she spotted Jack striding in from the breakfast room and predictably, her pulse quickened.

He avoided her stare as he grabbed his bag. "Good morning, Lilly. I looked for you at breakfast — to say good-bye, for now. It's time to return to New York."

Her heart plummeted with unexpected dismay. "I see," she murmured.

Two tall footmen silently appeared and carried his trunks outside to the carriage.

Jack sighed. "Work never ends, and I have some business to take care of. I enjoyed being with you here, more than you can ever imagine. And I hope to return as soon as I can."

"Were you going to leave without telling me?"

He pinched a smile. "No. I was searching for you when you came downstairs."

She nodded. "You'll allow me more time to decide about — marriage, won't you?"

She was in such a quandary she feared her decision wouldn't come quickly or easily. Yet she wanted to throw her arms around him and reach up to feel the fire of his kiss upon her lips. That would answer the question better than mere words.

"I'm giving you as much time and space as you might need. But I have to tend to business. A publishing house doesn't run by itself." He bowed, picked up his valise, and headed to the front door. Then he halted and leaned toward Lilly. He gently touched both her shoulders as he'd done last night. "I hope you'll accept my proposal, but I understand if you don't." He stepped onto the veranda.

"Jack. Wait."

Fortunately Mr. Ames was out of earshot.

Words hardened in her mind and wouldn't break loose. So much had passed between them, binding them together. "I confess, I'll miss you."

He expelled a short, self-conscious laugh. "Yes, you'll miss me like a wart."

"That's not true."

He stepped closer. She could feel heat rising from his skin. She inhaled the light scent of his cologne and a tingle danced up her back. If only this pleasure could last forever.

"If you find yourself in trouble with Colonel MacIntyre, and I know you will, remember to call upon me. I'll help you any time, any place." He bent over and kissed her cheek.

A ripple of excitement skipped across her heart. "I know you would. Thank you, but I'm sure that won't be necessary."

"I have an hour before the boat leaves for New York. If you have time, shall we take a short stroll?" Jack offered his arm.

She couldn't resist. "Yes, I'd like that."

Together they stepped into pale sunlight and sauntered across the damp grass filmed with morning dew. Surf rushed against jagged rocks, rising in a spray of crystals. Lilly watched a seagull soar overhead against the opal sky and envied its freedom to be just as God intended.

At the edge of the lawn, Jack stopped short. "Lilly, please, tell the world who you are. Don't be ashamed of your work just because some old biddies find it scandalous. If they actually read your books, they'd approve."

"I hardly think so." But if she truly loved him, wouldn't she take a chance? She stayed secluded in the bedroom writing her little stories, afraid to venture out into the world and face the petty people she allowed to control her. If she showed a bit of courage, she could possibly help Jones and Jarman and perhaps even find genuine love.

"Maybe you should stop ignoring the Lord's will for your life. He wants you to write the stories He gives and acknowledge them."

She stopped by the side of a giant rock jutting into the surf. The wind stiffened, whipping blue-gray waves against boulders, forcing her to raise her voice. "Jack, you're simplifying a complicated problem. My worst fear is what my family will think of me."

"Are their opinions that important?"

"Yes. I've always tried to be a good daughter and make my parents proud. They were so distraught when George ran off to California. I tried to compensate by pleasing them. I refuse to hurt them."

Jack nodded, conceding her point. "But you write dime novels anyway."

Her conscience pinched. "I do," she said. "I never expected anyone to find out. Naïve, I know, but since writing is my ministry, I felt sure the Lord would protect me. And to be honest, I couldn't control the urge to write. I *have* to write." She eased her fingers away from his soft touch. "My family would be crushed if they learned of it."

Jack groaned, obviously exasperated. "This won't be the last time that Colonel MacIntyre demands money. He'll come back 'round, and ask for more than you'll want to pay, or be able to. And then he'll expose you. It's best you do so yourself, now. And not give that lout a single dime. But the choice is yours, Lilly."

She swallowed hard. With nothing more to say, she turned to leave. Jack touched her sleeve.

"Lilly, what about us? Have you thought any more about marrying me . . ."

She eased her arm away. "I've thought of little else."

His dark eyes bore into her. "Follow your heart, Lilly. Stop fretting about other people's opinions. They don't matter. And I believe your heart has given you the answer."

She straightened. "Jack, answer me one question. Has success brought you all the happiness you expected?"

Jack reared back, apparently not anticipating that question. "Not yet, but I believe it will in the future."

"What has prosperity given you besides business worries? Was all that striving worth the cost?"

He hesitated. "I don't know. Maybe not." His voice grew testy. "Look, Lilly, we've both made mistakes. But let's not continue to make them."

He leaned over and pressed his lips against hers. Shocked by the intensity of his sudden affection, she tried to push away. But the sweetness of his mouth paralyzed her resistance.

"Lilly, let's get married right away." He wrapped his arms around her in a protective cocoon.

She didn't want to move; he was casting a spell over her. Struggling to speak, her words emerged weak and hesitant. "I love you, too, but I'm not free to do exactly as I wish. I'm sorry, Jack, but you'll have to wait a while longer for my decision. I wish I could say yes right now, but I can't."

She wrenched away from his grasp and fled across the grass toward Summerhill, unshed tears burning her eyes. Jack followed, lifted his luggage into the carriage, and said his farewells.

She watched him depart and listened to the sound of horses' hooves fading away.

"He's a nice young man, that Mr. Grail," the butler said.

"Yes he is," Lilly agreed.

She didn't know how long she'd stared at the deserted drive when Miranda's quiet voice broke into her thoughts.

"Jackson left, didn't he? You'll surely miss him."

Nodding, Lilly hunched over the porch rail, hanging her head. "I shall." She looked up and readily absorbed Miranda's sympathy.

"Embers can flicker long after the fire has died. I believe they've flared once again and you shouldn't try to put them out." Miranda wrapped her arm around Lilly's rounded shoulder. "You must soon decide whether or not you can let go of the past and trust Jackson."

"I know." Lilly choked back tears.

Miranda embraced her with a hug.

"Confound that Lilly," Jack railed to the wind that swept his complaint out to sea in one powerful gust. He leaned over the side of the steamship as it cut through the choppy waters of Long Island Sound. All the way from Newport to New York, Jack replayed his confrontation with Lilly, never once letting her image slip from the forefront of his mind.

He pictured her beautiful oval face etched with worry, the flutter of her hands, the pearl gray walking suit, tailored, yet so feminine on her slender frame. He wanted to hold her in his arms and shield her from her enemies, but she wouldn't let him protect her. He wasn't one bit surprised she refused his help. But even a smart young woman couldn't battle the likes of Colonel MacIntyre on her own. Lilly would wither under the pressure and cave into that rotter's inevitable demands — though where she'd find the funds to pay extortion remained a mystery.

*Lord, don't let Lilly rely on her own wit and courage. Help her to understand only Your wisdom and strength will get her through this crisis.* God was in control and Jack was glad, because He was their only hope. *Thank you, Father, for being faithful and thank You for forgiving me for all the years when I wasn't faithful to You. Lord, if it's Your will, please bring Lilly and me together. If You don't intervene, I'm afraid it won't happen.*

He stood alone by the rail and allowed the wind and salt spray to wash away some of his tension. When the steamship docked hours later, he felt almost refreshed and ready to tackle the business that brought him back to the city.

At his newspaper office, he met with Albert Hayes, the editor of his weekly newspaper which, by all accounts, was prospering. With circulation rapidly heading upward, Jack hoped the *Manhattan Sentinel's* success would help offset the impending decline at Jones and Jarman. Only time would tell if the publishing house had been a smart investment or put him over the edge.

After years of experience assisting his father at their town paper, Jack felt comfortable running the *Sentinel.* Yet, his interest lay with novels since becoming an avid fan of adventure stories during his boyhood. And, he had to admit, the love stories of one famous author in particular.

Seated at his office desk, he composed an editorial, but his mind wandered back to Colonel MacIntyre. What could he do to help Lilly defeat the blackmailer? The wily old scoundrel was accustomed to lunging for the jugular. Alone in Newport, Lilly couldn't defend herself against a man known for outmaneuvering his cleverest opponents during the war. Jack regretted leaving her despite his urgency to return to the city. He couldn't continue to neglect his fledgling businesses.

Maybe he should write an editorial denouncing *Talk of the Town*'s extortion schemes, but the colonel would undoubtedly retaliate by exposing Lilly's identity. If only she trusted the Lord enough to confess her ministry to her public, then MacIntyre wouldn't wield power over her.

"Mr. Grail, I have the information you requested when we spoke on the telephone." Albert Hayes handed Jack a summary he'd typed up.

With a nod of thanks, Jack skimmed the information, hoping Theo Nottingham, Irene's unsuitable friend and possible beau, was actually as bland as he looked.

Albert clasped his hands behind his back. "Theodore Nottingham is a bachelor from a prosperous San Francisco family which recently fell on hard times, although few know about that. Mr. Nottingham keeps up appearances. He's been quietly courting a Louisa Thornton for five years, but no engagement has been announced."

Jack tensed. "Hmm." If Theo hadn't proposed yet, it seemed likely his feelings toward Louisa were lukewarm at best.

"Miss Thornton comes from lots of money, but rumor says their reservoir was drained dry a few years ago."

Albert cleared his throat. "Mr. Nottingham has a secret habit. He owes thirty thousand dollars in gambling debts and his creditors are not all gentlemen."

"Ah. I would think he'd be eager to marry the lady before her father got wind of his financial difficulties." Theo Nottingham kept his problems well hidden.

"From what I hear Miss Thornton hopes to announce their engagement sometime during the next year — if he proposes by then."

Perhaps Theo was still searching for a wife, one with more to offer than merely a distinguished name. If Nottingham were a romantic, Irene might fill the bill nicely, except for the inconvenient fact of her marriage and empty bank account. Lovely, charming, and discontented, she wore an invisible sign on her neck which announced, "I am available to the highest bidder." Not for one moment did Jack doubt Irene would leave George for a better situation, either for love or money. Irene couldn't eliminate Theo's debts, but he probably didn't know that. And she was one of the most stunning women in society — if one liked the shallow, sensuous types. Her beauty might be enough for Nottingham to convince Irene to shed George and marry him.

But what would Irene gain by divorcing

385

George and marrying Theo? She probably thought he possessed a fortune. Certainly she wasn't attracted to his skeletal looks or solemn personality.

"And what about Mrs. George Westbrook? Did you discover anything interesting in her past?" Perhaps he should feel guilty about checking up on his best friend's wife, but he didn't, not in the least.

Albert's expression brightened like an incandescent lightbulb. "Yes, indeed." He gathered a set of notes from his desk and scanned them.

Jack's pulse quickened. "Go ahead."

"Irene Frampton comes from a small farming town in California. After her parents died, leaving her practically destitute, she made her way to San Francisco where she worked in a dance hall as a can-can dancer."

Jack felt the blood drain from his face. "A can-can dancer?"

He'd thought she looked familiar, but George's wife bouncing around in the chorus line? That was absurd. Yet, somewhere from the back of his memory he pulled up a picture of a striking blonde kicking long, shapely legs, turning cart wheels, and jumping into high-flying splits. The image focused. He remembered Irene in a low-cut bustier, feathers, and a frilly skirt she swished around in front of a room full of raucous men. He'd seldom frequented dance halls, but during his short stay in San Francisco, he had visited one. Obviously Irene's striking beauty stood out among the rest of the dancers' good looks and fine figures.

His stomach flipped over. Poor George must have married Irene unaware of her past. He'd never bring home a former showgirl to his straight-laced family.

"Tell me about her relationship to Quentin Kirby."

Albert shuffled his feet. "He claims Miss Frampton is one of his nieces, and most people believe him. But the rumor is that he found her in a dance hall, fell for her, and took her home with him. None of the local gossips suggest any impropriety since Mr. Kirby is well past his prime, though he was quite a ladies' man in his day. A few say he's a foolish old man still infatuated by a beautiful and talented young woman — even though she ran off with George. However, the majority accept the story of the family kinship."

Should he tell George what he'd learned? George deserved to know, and Irene deserved to be exposed as a fortune hunter and a can-can dancer. Yet, his friend still loved the woman. Jack sighed. Did he have a heart cold enough to disillusion George and disrupt his marriage? No one appreciated the bearer of bad news, even if it came from a friend with good intentions. He just couldn't tattle to George no matter how he might be tempted.

Albert continued. "Miss Frampton lived with Kirby for nearly a year before she met Mr. Westbrook. She was visiting a friend in Stockton when they were introduced at a soiree. Within two months George Westbrook and the young woman were married and on their way back East. The wags in San Francisco say Mr. Kirby was hopping mad for a while, but he eventually cooled off."

"I always suspected she had a secret," Jack muttered, angry that he'd been right.

Albert chewed his lower lip. "I'm afraid there's more."

Hayes's frown sent a spasm of apprehension through Jack.

"Go on." Jack leaned into the hard back of his chair and braced himself for the worst.

"When I looked into Mrs. Westbrook's background I discovered a close connection to a man named Hiram Wilson. Yesterday afternoon I received more information about them from San Francisco." Albert handed Jack a telegram.

Jack scanned it and slumped down in the chair. "Oh my. This is a most shocking revelation."

# TWENTY-FOUR

Right after luncheon, Lilly joined the rest of the ladies in the drawing room for a half an hour of needlework before they paid their afternoon calls. Seated beside Miranda on the settee, Lilly began a new counted cross-stitch pattern.

"My goodness, listen to this." Irene pointed to an item in *Talk of the Town*.

Lilly's heart knocked against her rib cage as it did whenever the scandal sheet appeared. She avoided it but wondered if she were the only one in Newport immune to its appeal. For a moment she considered leaving the drawing room to the others, but curiosity and fear nailed her to the stiff sofa.

Irene glanced up at her captivated audience with a gleeful smile.

*"News from the book publishing industry — Mr. Davis Sterling of Atwater Publishers has confided to several colleagues that he is currently seeking to purchase dime novels from*

the best-selling and beloved authoress Miss Fannie Cole, who is currently summering incognito in Newport. Much to his chagrin, he is unable to contact her since her true name and whereabouts remain a mystery.

"But in the next edition of Talk of the Town, we hope to announce Miss Cole's true identity within these pages. We so hope this revelation will delight her readers.

"If Miss Cole has the good sense to peruse Talk of the Town, she may learn of Mr. Sterling's splendid offer and call upon this old and highly respected publisher at her earliest convenience. We shall be fascinated to hear what Mrs. Elna Price has to say about this development."

Lilly gripped the carved arm of the settee and pressed her fingers into the white and gold padding. Miranda glanced at her, her lips pursed. Lilly lowered her gaze, afraid she might reveal her apprehension to anyone with sharp eyes.

"How unfortunate." Mama shook her head. "Poor Mr. Grail. I do hope his business won't suffer because of Miss Cole's decisions."

Arching her brows, Irene flashed a malicious grin. "Why shouldn't Fannie Cole be paid handsomely for her books? It's business, after all."

Mama's hand thumped against her chest. "But what about her loyalty to Jackson? Jones and Jarman made her famous, I understand. Don't they deserve some consideration?"

Irene shrugged. "Not necessarily. Now I know you're fond of him because he's a friend of George's, but Miss Cole must put her own interests first. That's only natural. Jackson Grail can fend for himself."

Lilly's heartbeat roared in her ears. She could scarcely hear the conversation. To leave Jones and Jarman would smack of the worst kind of treachery. She didn't need the additional funds personally, but they would help ease the financial difficulties of the Settlement House.

Atwater Publishers might provide anonymity, allow her to continue her dime novel career, and end her conflict with Jack once and for all. It was oh so tempting to feel the relief that would bring. It might solve all her problems — except it would end their fledgling relationship.

And she had to remember Jones and Jarman had always treated her with the utmost fairness. They'd bought her books and paid generously. She must consider that.

She felt a headache coming on again. Lilly closed her eyes and rubbed her temples as the voices of indecision droned on.

Mama sighed. "Well at least no one we know would ever dream of writing dime novels."

Irene beamed a smile. "But someone in our midst has done just that. Colonel Mac-Intyre will reveal exactly who she is in the very near future."

Lilly rose from the settee. "Will you all excuse me? I'd like to — find a book to read."

Irene frowned. "You read too much, Lilly."

Lilly ignored the remark and hurried to the deserted office before going to the library. Dropping onto the hard wooden chair, she stared at the telephone as if it offered a lifeline. Atwater Publishers might be willing to keep her name secret and pay a large advance. Then her immediate problems would vanish. She could probably pay Colonel MacIntyre and have enough to donate more to the Settlement House. . . .

With a shaky hand she picked up the telephone receiver and asked the operator to connect her with Atwater Publishers in New York City. Her heart thudded as she waited for the publisher's operator, and then the publisher himself, to come on the line. When he greeted her, she quickly explained her position.

"I am so delighted you chose to inquire about my proposal, Miss Cole. Now I'd like to offer you very generous terms."

His "very generous terms" sounded so advantageous she scarcely believed the numbers he quoted. He agreed to pay an enormous sum for a three-book contract and even change her pen name if she so desired. He wouldn't expect her to promote herself or her dime novels; she could remain anonymous. Tempted to agree without further thought, she took a deep breath and tried to steady her racing heartbeat.

"I'll consider your offer carefully and give you my decision within a few days. Thank you so much for your interest in me, Mr. Sterling."

"And thank you for your interest in Atwater Publishers. Good day, Miss Cole."

After she hung up the telephone, she crumpled into the desk chair. Could she turn against Jack for the promise of a new beginning? Mr. Sterling offered everything she wanted except the most important thing: Jack.

*Lord, please show me what I ought to do — soon because time is running out.*

Jack took a cab to Jones and Jarman Publishing. A secretary ushered him into Lewis

Jarman's office. Jack was relieved yet again that he'd asked Mr. Jarman to continue working because of his invaluable publishing experience.

They shook hands before settling into chairs set by an unlit fireplace. A high forehead touched Lewis's badly receding hairline, now wrinkled with worry. "Shall we have a cup of tea or coffee?"

"Coffee, please. Is something wrong?" The hair on the back of Jack's neck prickled.

"I'm afraid so."

The day was unusually humid and Jack's starched shirt immediately wilted.

"What's the problem?" Jack wiped his brow with a crumpled linen handkerchief.

Lewis cleared his throat. "During the last quarter, sales of the dime novels have decreased. I attribute the decline partially to poor-quality writing. Mr. Reynolds's and Miss Cole's books made the majority of the company's annual profit. But not enough to offset our losses."

Losses. It was much worse than Jack anticipated. A short time ago, he'd hoped to surpass Atwater Publishers — but it wouldn't happen without several star writers.

"How is Mr. Reynolds doing? Have you been in contact with his family?"

Lewis gave a solemn nod. "Yes, his wife telegraphed me not an hour ago. I'm afraid he passed away last night."

"I'm so sorry to hear that. What a terrible loss for his family." And of course, for Jones and Jarman as well, though insignificant compared to the sorrow of his loved ones.

"More than ever, we need Miss Cole to turn out additional books in less time. Have you had any success finding her?" Lewis asked.

Jack grimaced as the secretary delivered cups of coffee, cream, and sugar and then quietly departed. "I found our Fannie. She's Miss Lillian Westbrook, daughter of Thomas Westbrook, the banker and the owner of some very nice New York real estate."

Lewis shook his head, obviously flabbergasted. "My goodness. I never suspected."

"Neither did I, at least not at first. She certainly didn't want to admit her identity. I promised to let Fannie remain anonymous, but without her or Mr. Reynolds, I'm not sure where to go from here."

Lewis groaned. "This is a bad turn of events, indeed." He bit his lip. "I'm afraid I have some more bad news."

"Tell me. Things can't get much worse."

"I dare say they can."

Jack blew out a groan. "I'm listening."

Lewis ran his hand over his shiny bald head. "My wife showed me the latest issue of *Talk of the Town*. It seems Mr. Davis Sterling wants to add Miss Cole to his stable of authors by paying her substantially more than she's earning with us."

"How does MacIntyre know what Davis Sterling is up to?"

"His spies, no doubt. They're everywhere in society. I do believe Atwater Publishers is trying to steal her away from us. Sterling intended to purchase Jones and Jarman, principally to gain Miss Cole's titles, past, present, and future. The question is: will she switch?"

Jack's lip twitched as he nodded. "I don't believe she'd want to, but she may find their offer difficult to pass up." *Especially if she sees the cash she needs to pay off MacIntyre.*

He hoped Lilly would think through the repercussions of accepting Sterling's offer. Elna Price was a publicity hound, intolerant of any competition. Jack remembered how she'd once feuded with a popular writer who tried to steal her limelight. He'd heard the other woman changed her pen name and switched to another publisher rather than compete with the likes of Elna. He wondered how this would play out if Lilly accepted the offer. She might not understand how formidable Elna could be, but if he warned her, she would probably think he was self-serving.

"I need to speak to Miss Cole myself — or should I say Miss Westbrook." Jack grimaced. "If she doesn't remain loyal to Jones and Jarman, we've got a terrible problem."

Mr. Ames scuffed into the room, bent over like a willow branch in the wind. "There's a telephone call for you, Miss Westbrook."

Lilly frowned. Few people contacted her except in person or by post. "Thank you." If it were Colonel MacIntyre, she'd hang up immediately. He wouldn't have the temerity to telephone her, would he? Of course, a man adept at blackmail had no scruples.

"I'll return directly," Lilly promised Miranda as she exited the room.

Closing the office door behind her, Lilly picked up the receiver as if it were a burning coal. "Good afternoon. This is Miss Westbrook speaking." Her voice squeaked like a timid child reciting for her teacher.

"Good afternoon, Lilly. It's Jack. You sound frightened. Is something wrong?"

Her laugh rang hollow. "Of course not.

Why would you think such nonsense? How was your trip to the city?" When he didn't answer immediately, she pushed ahead. "I do hope the weather was pleasant. It's lovely here today except for the oppressive heat. On second thought, it's quite possible it might rain later."

"Lilly, please stop babbling and tell me what's upsetting you. It's MacIntyre, isn't it? He contacted you again. Tell me the truth."

She didn't have the energy to keep up her charade, but she couldn't involve Jack in her troubles. This was her dilemma, not his, and she needed to solve it on her own. He'd only exacerbate the problem. "Please don't worry about that horrid man."

"I don't worry about him, Lilly. I worry about you. You're my only concern."

Her heart flared with warmth. "I know. Thank you." She needed him now, but she couldn't let on or he'd take the next steamship back to Newport, her white knight eager to do battle. Sorrow and regret bubbled up and blocked her throat.

"Lilly, I imagine you've read that Davis Sterling wants you to write for him." Jack hesitated. "Have you given it any thought?"

"To be honest with you, I have. But I haven't decided yet."

He paused for several seconds. "I see. Well, I hope you'll tell me as soon as you make up your mind."

She heard disappointment in his voice and she regretted her forthright answer. "Yes. Of course, I will. Jack, Jones and Jarman has been so good to me over the last few years and I won't forget that for a moment. So please don't fret about my decision."

"I finished my most pressing work here in New York. I have a mind to return to Summerhill immediately — just to ensure MacIntyre stays away from you. Do I still have an invitation to visit?"

She mustered all her enthusiasm. "Of course you do. But maybe now isn't the best time. We're in the middle of —"

"I get your point, Lilly." He sounded more sad than miffed. "Have a good afternoon."

To her surprise, he hung up the telephone receiver before she could say anything else.

She leaned back in the chair and drew out a long moan. Why hadn't she been more tactful, less rude? Yet, he seemed so determined to rush to her rescue, she had to find a way to stop him. She couldn't allow his kindness to break down the barriers between them.

Jack boarded the steamer for Newport, to

convince Lilly that she needed his help. He'd planned on staying in the city a few days more, but he couldn't dismiss the feeling that something was amiss. He'd wager it involved more than which publisher to write for. It had to be the colonel. He'd deal with MacIntyre himself without involving Lilly. If she knew, she'd fight his every step. She'd tell him to mind his own business. But where would she find the money to pay the blackmailer? Surely no one in her family would loan her funds without expecting a reasonable explanation.

Should he offer her the little cash he had, despite his displeasure at caving in to blackmail? He feared he'd be feeding a lion that would come roaring back. He slapped his palm against the metal railing and leaned forward to let the stiff sea breeze cool his face.

When the Fall River Line vessel finally docked at Newport's Long Wharf, the sky loomed low and gun-metal gray. Stepping off the boat, he quickly hired a carriage.

All the way to Summerhill he thought of Lilly. He pictured her on the piazza, dressed in one of her frothy silk or chiffon dresses, greeting him with a wave. But he couldn't expect an open-armed welcome from the woman who often found him aggressive, irritating, and untrustworthy.

The drive from the waterfront was too short and the cab arrived before he felt ready to face her. Had he steel-plated his emotions against her rejection? A bitter laugh escaped his throat. He had no defenses.

When he entered the foyer, he saw her coming down the staircase. "Hello, Lilly."

She stopped short. "Welcome back." A tentative smile flickered, then faded.

His grin gave away his pleasure even though he probably was the last person she wished to see. "I thought you might need some assistance. You understand my meaning, I'm sure."

She inclined her head. "I do, but let me reassure you, everything is fine."

"Stop play acting, Lilly. You're in serious straits and I'd like to help." He wanted to kick himself for blurting out the truth. "I'm your publisher and your friend. At least I hope I am."

Her glance darted around the deserted front hall. "Keep your voice down. Please."

Jack inclined his head. "I'm sorry."

"If you've returned to Summerhill for my sake, then I'm afraid you've wasted your time."

"Why won't you let me help? I'm able to

deal with MacIntyre in ways you can't."

She grabbed his arm, pulled him into the reception room, and shut the door. He stayed close as she tried to step away. Only inches apart, his urge to lean down and kiss her nearly overwhelmed him, despite her less than enthusiastic greeting. But instead, he gently ran his hands up and down the silky fabric of her long-sleeved blouse in what he hoped was a sympathetic, non-threatening gesture. She half-heartedly attempted to brush off his fingers, then stopped and looked up, her expression serious.

"Jack, if I allow you to confront the colonel yourself, I'll owe you a debt of gratitude I won't be able to repay." She stared at him, pleading for understanding. "I'd feel obligated to go public with my writing and I can't do that. I must consider my family. We'd all be shunned," she continued. "Mama and Papa would never forgive me and I couldn't blame them. Mama might enjoy reading my dime novels, but she'd never approve of me writing them. There's a world of difference."

Slipping her hands into his, Jack felt her resistance strengthen. Lilly's determination was born of stubbornness and a shy nature. Along with concern for her family, her fear of taking center stage suffocated her wish to help him out.

Despair suffused his chest. "I do understand."

"Thank you, Jack." Relief seemed to relax the tension in her shoulders. "I'm truly sorry I can't help you with Jones and Jarman. I sincerely wish I could."

He grunted. What more could he say? For the last few weeks he'd tried his best to change her mind, but to no avail. Finding a solution without involving Lilly might be impossible, yet what other choice did he have?

He gently pressed her fingers, hoping to convey his surrender. But she slipped them from his light grasp, turned away, and fled. Jack shook his head. He'd search for MacIntyre and try to solve this situation without Lilly's blessing.

*Lord, show us both how You want this to end.*

# TWENTY-FIVE

Thunder rumbled in the distance. From her favorite spot on the back veranda, Vanessa Westbrook glanced across Summerhill's darkening lawn toward the sea. Granite gray waters met the sky and blended at the horizon. Yet the tangy air remained warm and humid. She calculated she could read another ten or fifteen pages of *Dorothea's Dilemma* before the clouds burst open and forced her inside.

Seated on the chair next to gently bobbing ferns, Vanessa resumed reading. Only fifty more pages and she'd discover if the heroine escaped from the villain's clutches and accepted the marriage proposal. He reminded her of a younger, more handsome, and more perfect Thomas. She understood why the shop girls, in fact any woman, would love this story. *Trust in God to help you find your way.* She remembered the Bible verse she'd memorized in her youth,

"Trust in the LORD with all thine heart; and lean not unto thine own understanding. In all thy ways acknowledge him, and he shall direct thy paths."

An excellent lesson to learn. But did she trust the Lord to help her navigate the murky waters of motherhood? Or did she interfere too often? Perhaps she ought to let Him guide Lilly and not carry the burden herself, even though she was accustomed to managing her daughter from the time the little one came into the world. Yet, to allow the Lord to help Lilly would bring such blessed relief. She'd mull over the idea later, after she finished the chapter.

Vanessa peered through her spectacles. She turned the page and came to a scene where the heroine, Ada Brown, fell through a crack in the ice and slipped beneath the surface of the pond. Vanessa's heart flip-flopped as she skimmed the text. Of course the hero, Lawrence Macon, plunged in after Ada and grabbed her before she sunk to the bottom. Lawrence pulled her onto the ice, gasping for breath, but thrilled to have saved the life of his true love.

How gallant. Vanessa ignored the growling thunder followed by a flash of lightning. The scene wasn't over so she couldn't bear to tear herself away from the pages.

Why did that last scene stir up long-forgotten memories? Of course! Several years earlier Jackson Grail had saved Lilly from drowning at her cousin's country estate in the Adirondacks. He'd also retrieved her ring from the pond where they'd gone skating. How unusual that Fannie Cole imagined the entire scene so realistically.

Could Lilly be the authoress? No, that couldn't be right!

Vanessa closed her eyes as the first drops of rain splattered off the roof into the open veranda. Fannie Cole couldn't possibly know the exact details of the skating accident unless she was Lilly. No other explanation made sense. So Lilly had written *Dorothea's Dilemma,* just as she'd authored all those other dime novels. No wonder she girl so often vanished to her bedroom. Where else would she find the privacy to compose fiction in such a lively household?

Vanessa grasped her book and headed inside on rubbery legs.

"Where are you running off to?" Thomas asked as she strolled past the game room door. "Come sit by the fire."

"Later, Thomas, later."

Vanessa rushed up the stairs, caught her breath at the landing, and climbed as fast as she could to the second floor. She strode down the darkened hallway to Lilly's bedroom, relieved that the upstairs maids were finished with their chores and gone from the area.

She knocked on Lilly's door, expecting a response. Where else would her daughter be on a dreary day when the weather prohibited the usual carriage ride and afternoon calls? She wasn't in the library, her other place of refuge. "Lilly, are you there?" she called quietly.

Several seconds passed. The silence convinced her that the room was empty. Vanessa pushed open the door, took a deep breath, and stepped inside. Even without the gaslight casting its yellow glow, the room looked the same as usual, tidy and rather impersonal. Quickly, she crossed the carpet and reached beneath the lining of Lilly's treasure box. Her heart bumped against her bodice as she grasped the key in her trembling hand. Before she had time to feel guilty about invading Lilly's privacy, Vanessa unlocked the desk drawer and jerked open the secret compartment. There, in a neat stack, were typewritten papers labeled *A Garland of Love.* Another dime novel typed up for publication. Her hand pushed against her bosom as she dropped into the nearest chair. All her energy drained from her body, leaving her limp as a rag doll.

So, Lilly's hobby of composing poetry had developed into the career of notorious authoress. It was one thing to read a dime novel and enjoy it but quite another to discover her own daughter worked furtively in an unsavory profession. How could Lilly have placed herself in such an awkward position? If she were caught she'd become a laughingstock and a pariah. The implications of Lilly's deception robbed Vanessa of oxygen. She could barely breathe. Slowly she rose, locked the drawer, and replaced the key.

Back in her own bedroom, Vanessa rang for her maid and a cup of hot milk. For once she wished she drank whiskey. Something to soothe her nerves might help now, though she realized a temporary fix wouldn't provide a permanent solution.

She'd obviously failed as a mother. Never once did Lilly confide in her about her writing or ask for advice. Did the girl think her mother was an ogre incapable of understanding her love of storytelling? Vanessa sighed. If only they'd discussed this together, maybe they could have come to some sort of consensus. Well, perhaps. Vanessa groaned. If she were scrupulously honest, she'd have to admit she never would have accepted Lilly's literary career. She'd have done everything in her power to dissuade her daughter from penning such trash. Yet *Dorothea's Dilemma* was hardly trash. A superb story, well told; she wished to read all of Fannie Cole's dime novels.

Should she confront Lilly with her newfound knowledge and admit she'd snooped?

Then the items in *Talk of the Town* came to mind and replayed with horrifying clarity. What would Lilly do when she was exposed as Fannie Cole? What would the family do? Before she could absorb the crisis looming directly ahead, Thomas appeared.

"You're sitting there in a stupor, Nessie. Why aren't you dressing for tea? You must have someplace to go this time of day."

"Well, I do, but I don't feel like moving." Should she tell him the news or keep mum until she could puzzle out the situation?

Thomas grunted. "That doesn't sound at all like you. Is something wrong?"

Shrugging, Vanessa walked to the window overlooking the ocean, pulled back the sheers and stared into the fog and drizzle. "I have some thinking to do."

"Oh?" His bushy white eyebrows shot upward. "Would you care to discuss it? I'm a good listener, Nessie. Haven't I listened to you all these years?"

She tossed him a crooked smile. "Yes, you have and the Lord has blessed me for it." She so appreciated his efforts. And his love.

She'd confide in him, but not just yet.

For the rest of the afternoon Jack searched Newport's likely hangouts for the colonel, returning to his rooming house, the bakery and then other establishments. Annoyed at finding no trace of him, Jack drove the carriage back to Summerhill, still intent on trailing Lilly whenever possible. Eventually she'd lead him to MacIntyre.

Daylight faded into the sunset as Jack dressed for dinner. The Westbrooks were having dinner guests. He preferred to stay out of Lilly's way, but he needed to follow her every move. If she noticed, she'd object with every stubborn fiber of her being. But if he were discreet she might not observe his scrutiny. Who was he kidding? No one, least of all Lilly. Whenever they were in the same room they watched each other with probing eyes. Jack slipped on his black tailcoat, straightened his bow tie, and headed downstairs.

A few dozen cottagers arrived promptly at eight and strolled into the candlelit dining room with the Westbrook household. Crystal vases of red roses graced the long table between tall, silver candelabras. Jack looked for Lilly and saw her seated at the opposite end of the large table, her lovely face as stone cold as a statue's.

She glanced his way once, then turned toward another gentleman and never looked back. Was this a subtle refusal to his proposal? Or was he reading too much into a simple turn of the head?

Annoyed his place card located him beside Irene, he politely bowed to her before they took their seats. Resplendent in green satin with a diamond necklace around her slender neck, Irene grinned with amusement at the seating arrangement.

"I'm sure you'd rather sit beside Lilly, but that wouldn't be appropriate." Irene's tinny laugh set his nerves on edge.

Jack ignored her remark, resisting the urge to glance at Lilly, so lovely in a blue and silver gown. "Your jewels are beautiful, Irene. Has George seen them yet?"

Her mocking smile slipped into a frown. "They're a gift from my Uncle Quentin." She sipped her water and returned the goblet to the white damask tablecloth.

"Are they? How interesting."

His comment wiped the smirk off her face. Surprise and uncertainty flashed in her glittery eyes.

"Whatever do you mean? Do you doubt these are from him? He's very fond of me and I of him."

Jack laughed. "I'm sure that's true." He plunged his spoon into the consommé.

"Now what is that snide remark supposed to mean?" she whispered.

Jack's glance swept the dining room. Beneath the soft glow of chandeliers and flickering candles, conversations hummed and jewels sparkled. Satisfied no one would overhear, he leaned closer to Irene. "Aren't diamonds a rather expensive and unsuitable gift from an uncle to a niece?"

Her delicate fingers twisted the napkin in her lap. "Not at all. I'm offended you'd think so." She ladled the clear soup into her heavy silver spoon, paused, and then poured the liquid back into the bowl. "You must have a very poor opinion of me. Why is that?"

Though her voice was as light as the tinkling of a piano, perspiration appeared above her upper lip.

He inclined his head. "Perhaps your relationship to your uncle is different than you let on."

"Indeed, it is."

She had purposely misunderstood his

irony. *Clever little witch.*

Irene reached inside her mesh reticule and retrieved a letter. "I do believe you doubt my connection to Quentin Kirby. This proves it." She unfolded a sheet of expensive cream stationery. Reading softly, her voice was steady.

"My dearest niece Irene,
I do hope this note finds you in excellent health and fine spirits. Your absence has caused me much loneliness. Perhaps you would take pity on me and return to San Francisco for an extended visit. The necklace from Tiffany's is just a small token of my esteem.
Your loving uncle,
Quentin Kirby"

Her self-satisfied smile rankled.

"No regards to your husband?"

"I'm sure that was an oversight on Uncle Quentin's part."

"Indeed. I find it very strange."

Irritation crept into her expression. "Not really. Uncle Quentin and George have never met."

Jack leaned back into the throne-like chair. "No?"

"I met George while I was visiting friends

in Stockton. We married soon after we were introduced." Irene's smile deepened as if she were remembering a whirlwind courtship. "We loved each other too much to wait any longer."

"But your uncle approved of your marriage?"

Her confidence faltered. "He — he didn't want me to move to New York. He wished me to stay in California."

A footman served them the next course. Irene stabbed her fork into the duck, then looked toward the gentleman on her left.

Before she could begin a new conversation, Jack asked, "Are you planning to visit your uncle soon, as he requested?"

She glanced sideways. "As a matter of fact I am. I do miss the dear man. He's my only living relative." A soft sigh escaped her lips. "I have such fond memories of him."

Jack's chest tightened at the lies that so easily rolled off her subtly painted lips. "Have you told George about your plans? He may object to such a long trip."

She shrugged one sloping shoulder. "He'll find a position soon I'm sure, so of course I don't expect him to accompany me. That would be selfish."

Jack lowered his voice again. "You're going to leave George, aren't you?" Sucking in his breath, he watched Irene flinch. Tiny lines around her mouth and eyes deepened.

She coughed up a nervous laugh. "Don't be ridiculous. I'd never leave my husband."

"Oh?" Jack said, his eyebrow raised.

Irene's fork dropped and clattered against the china plate. Several heads turned toward her, but apparently misunderstanding fear for clumsiness, quickly looked away.

"Whatever do you mean?" she blustered.

"I know your background. All of it. Before you sneak off, have the decency to tell George about your life in San Francisco."

Her thick lower lip trembled for an instant before she raised her chin. "That's all in the past, over and done with. I'll admit I wasn't always discreet, but there's no point in tattling to George. It would only hurt him. I've been a faithful wife and will continue to be."

"Then why are you returning to Quentin Kirby? Are you in love with him?"

A peal of harsh laughter rang above the din of the conversations. "Don't be absurd. He's a decrepit old man. I love George and I'm coming back just as soon as I can."

"Then if you're not going for love, you're going for money."

Irene looked at him as if he were a dunce. "Of course it's for money. Why else would I give an ancient roué the time of day?"

In her own selfish way she probably did care for George, but Jack suspected her feelings lacked any depth. Loyalty and integrity were alien, worthless qualities she neither recognized nor respected.

"I can never confess my — compromises — to George because they would wound him too deeply."

"You're afraid he'd toss you out."

Irene moaned. "That too. But you won't tell him, will you?"

He hated to keep the truth from his friend, but he also hated to cause him misery. Yet, there was that other insolvable problem.

Irene's lips curled with triumph. "You hesitate, so I know you'll stay mum." She seemed to breathe easier.

Jack glared and leaned so close he could smell her wine-laced breath. "But that doesn't eliminate the problem of Hiram Wilson." He watched the color drain from her face. "Inconvenient, isn't he?"

Irene jumped to her feet but then sank back into her chair, obviously defeated. "How did you find out about him?"

"My newspapermen did some investigating. I could ignore your dance hall career, but Hiram is another kettle of fish." One in which she might drown.

"Don't you dare mention that man's name to George."

Jack shook his head. "I'll make no promises."

"How dare you!" Her hands trembled. "If you'll excuse me, I'm not feeling well." Eyes clouded with fear, she looked about for a quick means of escape.

The footman pulled back her chair and she sauntered away without her usual flourish. She apologized to Mrs. Westbrook and then disappeared through the archway, her golden head bowed, her shoulders hunched.

He pitied the young woman, despite her money-grubbing ways and lying heart. She'd tried to better her life through a prosperous, respectable marriage, the only avenue of real success for a female. He gave her credit for that. But she'd tricked the guileless George with charm and dishonesty, which tossed her into Jack's debit column.

Jack stifled a weary groan. He wished he could be excused from the festivities, too, but a plausible reason wouldn't come to mind. He watched Lilly for the rest of the dinner and noted strain in her serious eyes and the tight line of her lips.

Why did she insist on going through this crisis alone?

# TWENTY-SIX

Lilly suffered through the long, tedious dinner, trying to carry on a pleasant conversation with Richard Calloway, a widower she'd known for years. Miranda helped keep the discussion flowing while Mama sat across the table staring at Lilly, her eyes wide but oddly unfocused. Light from the flickering candles and crystal chandeliers couldn't erase the bewilderment stamped on Mama's pinched face. Lilly squirmed beneath her scrutiny, yet she couldn't figure out the cause of her mother's strange expression.

As soon as the evening's festivities ended, Lilly hurried to bed. Neither a warm bath nor a cup of hot milk soothed her enough to induce sleep. Her eyes finally closed when the chill of early morning blew through the screens. She dreamed of Colonel MacIntyre's nasty laugh and his cigar smoke choking her lungs. Well past noon she awoke to recall her meeting with the editor of *Talk of the Town* was only a few hours away. And she had no money to pay his blackmail.

Her empty stomach curdled with bile, but she forced herself to get up and dress. She donned her least conspicuous black skirt and a plain white shirtwaist, a combination she hoped would help her blend in with the other women on Thames Street. She headed for the door when shivers suddenly twirled down her spine and sweat erupted on her face and neck. Lying back down on her bed, she waited several minutes before attempting to rise. Slowly she walked to the window and gulped in cool, revitalizing air.

*Please Heavenly Father, You've taken me this far. Make me strong enough to face the consequences of what I've thoughtlessly brought on myself. I can feel Your presence and Your comfort. Stay with me and guide me because I still don't know what I ought to do. But You know, Lord.*

She wished she had time to read Scripture, but the minutes were ticking away. Descending the staircase, she gripped the rail to steady her shaky legs. Where was Jack? She searched Summerhill from top to bottom. Her heart plummeted at the thought he might have gone to Bailey's Beach or the casino. She hadn't time to traipse all over

Newport hoping to find him. Finally, she glimpsed his tall, broad-shouldered form striding across the back lawn toward the small beach cove she loved so well. Sprinting across the grass, she was out of breath as she hurried down the wooden steps.

The tide rolled to shore, leaving a narrow band of dry sand edged with lacy, hissing waves. Jack stood by the water watching the breakers crash against the rocks. Lilly sucked in a deep breath and then slowly let it out.

*Please help me, Lord.*

As if Jack sensed her presence, he looked over his shoulder and smiled. The heels of her black leather shoes sunk into the soft sand as she joined him. Her carefully arranged hair escaped from its pins and brushed against her cheeks.

"Jack, may we talk?"

"Of course." His grin encouraged her to continue.

"I — I'd like to borrow some money from you, if you have it to spare right now. I hate to ask, but you said if I needed help, come to you. So, here I am," she finished lamely.

"Is this for Colonel MacIntyre?"

She swallowed her hesitation and fear. "Yes."

Jack ran his fingers through his thick hair

and stared out to sea for several seconds before he turned and looked her in the eye. "If you pay him, he'll only demand more. It might never end. Lilly, this extortion has to stop now."

It took all her self-control not to burst into tears. "I know you don't approve of paying blackmail — and neither do I — but I must take the chance he'll demand money only this one time. You know I don't have a choice unless I go public. And I won't do that."

"Lilly, I love you and I want to help you. Please let me handle MacIntyre. I'll find a way to deal with the problem. Don't do this on your own. You need not get involved. Blackmail is a nasty business."

"Jack, I appreciate your concern, but I can face the colonel alone. Please, will you loan me the money? I will pay you back with interest in Dec—"

"It's not the money, Lilly. It's the idea of paying a scoundrel to keep a secret he'll never honor. Don't you see that?"

She saw he wouldn't help her, though he'd promised he would. He might be right about the colonel, but at least the funds would give her more time to decide the best way to handle the situation. Jack was leaving her in the lurch, just as he'd done six years before — right when she'd begun to believe he'd never abandon her again. Miranda had been so sure he loved her enough to help in any way.

"I understand your point, Jack. And it was wrong for me to ask." *And foolish.*

"No, Lilly. I'm glad you asked because I do want to help. I love you."

She nodded, then turned away.

He spun her around, paused, and then kissed her.

Woodenly, she returned his kiss, but couldn't pull away from the strength of his embrace. It pained her to know he wouldn't come to her aid, but she understood why. He thought he was helping her face her dilemma head on, though he was actually forcing her to look for the funds elsewhere. But despite her frustration and hurt feelings, she melted in his arms and buried her head in the softness of his jacket. He loved her.

Then she broke away before she lingered too long, her eyes stinging with tears.

Only one option remained. She'd ask Papa, her last hope. Lilly hurried upstairs and grabbed her straw hat and reticule before returning to the main floor.

Huffing and puffing, Mr. Ames tottered into

the library. "I thought I might find you here, sir. You've a telephone call from Mr. Lewis Jarman."

"Thank you." Good news, Jack hoped. He hurried to Mr. Westbrook's seldom-used office and put the receiver to his ear.

Lewis got down to business immediately. "I've been reading manuscripts all morning, and low and behold, I believe I've discovered a winner. A writer of westerns. She told a tale so exciting I couldn't put it down."

"Excellent. That's the best news I've heard in a long time. Did you say 'she'?"

"I did, indeed."

Jack lowered himself into the hard desk chair. "Interesting. Have you contacted her yet? Could you send me the manuscript? We need to work fast before Sterling gets a hold of her."

"Of course, I'll send it today. And I'll telephone her right away. She lives in the city."

When Lilly heard Jack's voice coming from the office, she stopped short near the half-open door. He must be speaking on the telephone, probably to Mr. Jarman. They seemed to stay in close contact. She knew she shouldn't eavesdrop, but as she took a step down the hallway, Jack's words grabbed her attention.

"And when we speak to her, we must make it clear we'll have a large promotional campaign, much like the one Sterling has for Elna Price. No more anonymity for Jones and Jarman writers. If she doesn't like being the center of attention, then she's not the authoress for us. We must insist she understand that. I can't allow her to hide in her garret."

Lilly covered her mouth with her hand. Fannie Cole was disposable now that she refused to allow Jack to take charge. Well, who knew what he might do in the interest of his company? Just when she'd begun to trust him, he'd turned against her. She'd thought he'd changed for the better and relinquished some of the raw ambition that had consumed him for years. But apparently, he hadn't.

Well, he had to make his choices, and she needed to do the same. She'd borrow the money from Papa, pay off the colonel, and pay her debts with the proceeds from signing a deal — a deal that would allow her to preserve her anonymity — with Atwater.

On wobbly legs she slowly walked toward the game room where she hoped to find Papa. She'd worry about Jack's promotion plan and a switch to Atwater after she'd secured the funds. But when she reached the foyer she dropped into a gilded chair. Could she truly leave Jack in the lurch after all they'd been through? No, even after the conversation she'd just overheard, she couldn't show Jack such disloyalty. She'd stay with Jones and Jarman.

Lilly heard soft footsteps on the carpet runner right behind her. She increased her pace, but Jack quickly caught up and gently grabbed her elbow.

Spinning around, she wrenched free of him. She tried to speak with cool detachment, but her voice shook with emotion. "Jack, please excuse me. I'm pressed for time."

"Lilly, I have news to tell you. Mr. Jarman and I were just speaking —"

She shook her head. "I'm afraid it will have to keep for a while. I'm in a bit of a hurry. We can talk later."

Jack narrowed his eyes. "You look upset."

"No, I'm all right." She wasn't all right, but with no time to waste, she couldn't explain. With her head cast down, she strode toward the game room, blinking back tears. She stood at the door for several seconds until she composed herself and then looked inside. Papa was stretched out on his favorite leather chair by the fire, book in hand.

A roaring fire crackled and hissed then tossed up a shower of red and yellow flames. Papa's pink face glowed even pinker in the heat and light.

Lilly prayed no one else would wander in. *Heavenly Father, please give me the right words to say to Papa. Soften his heart. And Lord, guide me to do the right thing and follow Your will.*

"Good morning, Papa." Lilly perched on the edge of the footstool by her father's feet.

He placed his book on his lap and smiled expectantly. His downy hair rose in one thin peak, lending him a benevolent and slightly comical appearance. But Lilly knew he was shrewd and nobody's fool.

"You look a bit tired today, and your eyes are red. You're not coming down with something, are you? I can call the doctor, you know. It's no trouble at all."

"No, I'm fine." *Only a severe case of grief and nerves.* "I have a favor to ask of you, Papa." She paused, momentarily losing her courage. But with no other option, she plowed ahead. "Something has come up and I'd like an advance on my trust fund. I don't have much money in my bank account right now, but by December I'll have enough to pay you back with interest."

"Of course, my dear. How much do you need?"

She swallowed the dust in her throat. "Three thousand dollars."

"That's quite a sum." Papa said in a light tone, as if he wouldn't inquire any further.

Could she dare breathe a bit easier? "It's a private matter or I'd explain." She gave a nervous giggle. "Don't worry, I haven't gambled or bought gems. Nothing like that."

He looked puzzled for a moment before he patted her hand. "I never thought you'd be that foolish. But if you're in some sort of scrape, tell me about it. Surely I can help."

"Loaning me the money is more than enough." If only she had the gumption to confess why she needed the funds and, above all, why she wrote her dime novels. His smile was so inviting, she could almost imagine him accepting her career. But right now she hadn't enough time to explain properly and defend her position.

"You're not trying to pay Irene's gambling debts, are you? She and George probably think your mother and I don't know about her losses at bridge, but we do. Don't ever bail her out, Lilly. Those two need to grapple with their finances, and I intend to hold them accountable myself."

Lilly half-smiled. "No, the money isn't for them."

Papa heaved himself off his chair and padded over to a concealed wall safe. He dialed the combination, counted out the money, and frowned. "Oh Lilly, I'm so sorry. I forgot I gave George quite a bit to cover Irene's debts and then I paid your mother's dressmaker's bills just this morning. So I'm temporarily short. I'll wire the bank for more funds and they should arrive within the next few days." Papa handed her a one-hundred-dollar bill. "This is all I have for now. I hope you can wait."

She couldn't wait, but she couldn't explain either. "Thank you, Papa."

His eyes sharpened. "You took like you might cry. Do tell me what's the matter."

Lilly managed a small smile. "No, I'm fine. Really. George told me he asked you for money. I was surprised at his gumption."

"I gave him a spirited lecture about overspending, but he took it well. I was also shocked he found the nerve to ask."

Lilly started for the door before she found herself breaking down and confessing. "Thank you again, Papa, for your generosity and for not questioning me." Would the colonel take this paltry amount as a down payment and wait for the rest? Or would he splash her identity all over *Talk of the Town?*

Lilly's hands shook as she stuffed the cash into her skirt pocket. Papa's steady gaze signaled curiosity, but he didn't question her. "It's really your money, not mine. I have no business asking you how you spend it."

"Nor do I." At the sound of Mama's voice, Lilly spun around.

Mama sailed across the carpet and slipped her hands into Lilly's warm palms. Lilly glanced down at her mother, startled to find Mama's dark eyes brimming with affection.

"I've treated you as a child for too many years when I should have acknowledged you're a grown woman. And a very capable one at that. But it's been so hard to let go of my children." She gently pressed Lilly's fingers. "I want to keep you and George from making mistakes that you'll regret. So I always try to protect you and maybe even manage your life. I'm so sorry. Will you forgive me, my dear?"

"Why of course, Mama." Lilly bent down and hugged her mother for the first time in months. "But why are you telling me this all of a sudden?"

Mama pulled in a deep breath, then blew it out slowly. "Because I have something to confess."

The grandfather's clock in the hallway chimed the hour. One o'clock.

Lilly frowned, bewildered by Mama's abrupt change. Distressed she couldn't stay, Lilly apologized. "I do wish we could speak right now, but I have an appointment which I must keep. If it's all right with you, may we talk when I return? I believe we do have a lot to discuss. In fact I have something I need to tell you too." But was she really brave enough to admit the truth about her writing? She wasn't sure.

"That's fine." Mama beamed a cherubic smile. She seemed relieved at her temporary reprieve.

"I'll be on my way. Thank you again, Papa."

Lilly pecked at his cheek and hurried to the foyer.

*Dear Lord, I have no way to pay the colonel and no one else to turn to. I'm begging for Your help and I'm relying completely upon You for a solution. I've looked to myself instead of toward You and I've found no answers. Please forgive me.*

She took a deep, cleansing breath as she walked into the foyer. She stopped short and gasped. Harlan and his mother stood at the front door with Jack and George nearby.

"Good afternoon, Lillian. We've come to

431

pay your mother a short visit and collect my niece, Miranda." Dolly's glare could crack glass. "Mrs. Carstairs has extended her an invitation to stay for two weeks and we'd like her to join us now."

Harlan nodded without even a hint of a smile. "Miranda belongs with her family."

"I believe that's Miranda's choice," Lilly said softly.

Harlan rolled his eyes.

Lilly bit back a remark as she swept past the group. She had no time for chatter if she were to meet Colonel MacIntyre on time.

"Where are you off to, Lilly?" Jack followed her toward the door while George waited with the Santerres.

"I'm going out for the afternoon." She tried to sound breezy and calm, but her voice quavered, and she refused to look up at him. "Please excuse me. I must be leaving."

"By yourself?" Harlan's mouth fell open.

Dolly's jaw dropped.

"Would you like an escort?" Jack asked.

"No thank you, but it's kind of you to volunteer."

Parasol in hand, Lilly slipped past Mr. Ames and stepped over the threshold.

The coachman assisted Lilly into the carriage, and within seconds they were swaying down the driveway. Free at last, Lilly expelled a long sigh. She couldn't stop trembling as the carriage rolled toward town.

Her mind volleyed between her mother's puzzling remarks to Jack's decision to make Fannie Cole go public to the look on Harlan's face as she breezed out the door. She shook her head. Right now, she had to concentrate on the task at hand. Eradicating the threat of Colonel MacIntyre. The rest she could deal with later.

Lilly sank back into the cushion feeling disquieted and patted her skirt pocket concealing the cash. She'd pay Colonel MacIntyre part of his extortion money and pray he'd leave her in peace. Yet a nagging doubt tugged at her mind. Would the greedy man be satisfied with just one payment or would he demand countless more? Would she ever free herself from his grasp? Suspecting the answer, she thrust the disconcerting questions out of her thoughts.

She steeled herself for a confrontation. And wished she'd accepted Jack's help.

"My goodness. What has gotten into Lillian?" Dolly peered through her pince-nez from one shocked face to the other.

"It seems to me she's asserting her inde-

433

pendence," Jack said, staring after her. "It's about time."

Dolly squeezed her eyes and her spectacles popped off. "Well I never."

Harlan's face contorted in a sneer. "See here, Grail. If you're implying I tried to keep Lilly dependant upon me, then you're quite mistaken. I merely expected her to behave appropriately and not disgrace my family or her own."

What a pompous fool. Jack stared at Harlan, unable to conceal his dislike. "She's an intelligent, talented woman who didn't want a jailer. She'll always be her own person, not anyone's lap dog."

George stifled a laugh behind a fake sneeze. "Stop it, you two. There's no point in arguing over my sister." He looked bewildered, as if he couldn't imagine anyone dueling over Lilly, physically or verbally. "But Jack is right. No one will mold her thinking. She may be reserved, but she's strong-willed and opinionated."

"Lilly is not the woman you think she is. Actually, she's far superior." Jack returned Harlan's glower.

Harlan veered back on the heels of his shiny black shoes. "And you always thought I wasn't worthy of her. Well, you're not tricking me, Grail. You're in love with her yourself. It's plain as day."

"And I believe she's in love with Jack too," George added. "And I'm happy for them. Harlan, I'm afraid you and my sister were never well matched."

George had just burned his last bridge, but he didn't seem to care that his former future employer scowled at him.

*Good for you,* Jack cheered inwardly. Never mind that he had no earthly idea what Lilly felt.

Both Santerres were chalk white while George flashed a self-satisfied grin.

Dolly pointed toward a stringed purse resting on the mahogany side table next to a vase of yellow and purple gladiola. "Lilly forgot her reticule."

Snatching it, Harlan began to pull open the gathered top, then stopped. "Should I look inside, Mother? Perhaps we'll learn where she's gone off to."

Jack guessed it came from the colonel. "Don't open it, Santerre. It belongs to Lilly, not to you."

Dolly dismissed Jack with a condescending wave. "Yes, but I'm certain her parents will wish to know. Please hand it to me, Harlan. A lady may peer into another lady's purse, if her intentions are pure."

He gave the reticule to his mother. Dolly

435

rifled through the interior, retrieved an envelope and removed the note. Repositioning her spectacles, she scanned the writing and read aloud.

"My dear Miss Westbrook,
    Please meet me at O'Neill's Café on Thames Street, Monday at three o'clock. We have important business to discuss. If you want to keep your secret safe and your reputation intact, it would behoove you to accept my invitation. Come alone.
                                Sincerely,
                        An interested party"

Harlan paled. "What does it mean? I don't understand," he muttered.

"I certainly do," Dolly snapped. Looking more triumphal, she proclaimed, "I believe she has taken a lover. She betrayed you, my dearest boy. How fortunate you ended your engagement when you did."

"Why, I, I . . ." Harlan sunk into a throne-like chair against the wall. "Lilly would never . . ." His voice trailed off. "I find it hard to believe she's that kind of woman."

Dolly's brows knit. "But today is not Monday. She must have already rendezvoused with the man."

Jack snatched the envelope and note from

Dolly's hand. Nearly illegible, a few words were scratched on the back of the envelope. *Wednesday, 3:00 O'Neill's Café.* Today. He tucked it into his waistcoat pocket.

"Come on, George." Jack motioned his friend to the front door.

Leaving Harlan and Mrs. Santerre to condemn Lilly's transgressions, Jack and George sprinted across the lawn to the stable. At their command, the stable boy quickly hitched a lively roan to the gig.

They were soon racing around Ocean Drive with Jack straining to spot Lilly's carriage. He kept up their breakneck speed but didn't see her even in the distance. *Never mind, I'll catch her at the café.*

"Do you think Lilly has a secret beau?" George yelled above the pounding hooves and the whine of the wind blowing off the ocean.

"No, definitely not."

"If she doesn't have another suitor, then who is she meeting?"

He hesitated to tell George the truth about Lilly, but when they arrived at the café, he'd find out anyway. "Colonel Mac-Intyre, the editor of *Talk of the Town,*" Jack shouted.

George blew a low whistle. "Is she in some sort of trouble?"

Jack nodded. "Yes, indeed. She's the dime novelist Fannie Cole. MacIntyre is blackmailing her and she's about to pay him off."

George's eyes widened. "You don't say. I can hardly believe that. But then Lilly writes for you. Didn't you know her real identity? Why didn't you tell me?"

Jack glanced sideways. "She thought her family would condemn her writing, so she kept silent. I wanted her to tell you and your parents, but she wouldn't. It wasn't my place to reveal her secret. Even though she refuses to let me deal with MacIntyre, I can't let her go through this by herself."

George pulled on the point of his goatee. "Neither can I." He shook his head, bewildered. "I never once suspected my little sister was the infamous dime novelist. Imagine that."

"I want to stop her before she turns over the money."

George gave a grim nod. "I hope we make it in time."

## Twenty-Seven

Lilly stepped into O'Neill's Café, pulling her veil over her face. She hid behind a pillar and waited for a well-dressed couple to leave the colonel, ensconced in the back of the small restaurant. What were other fashionable Newporters doing here in a working-class establishment? Perhaps they were paying off the colonel too. As the pair bent over MacIntyre's table, Lilly couldn't identify their forms or hear the hushed conversation. Her chest tightened as she cringed by the entrance attempting to look inconspicuous. If the couple turned around, they might recognize her. Then she'd be doomed. But there were no safe hiding places among the many empty tables and scattered groups of diners.

"May I help you?" A waiter approached from the kitchen carrying a tray.

She gestured for him to leave and then turned back to the colonel. With a shrug, the young man served his customers with pints of beer and bowls of steaming soup. He didn't give her a second glance.

Lilly yanked her veil further down, hoping it was opaque enough to conceal her face. She side-stepped to the next pillar, drawing closer to the trio. Poking her head around the corner, she identified Theo Nottingham as the man huddled with the colonel. Then the woman's hazy silhouette sharpened unmistakably into her sister-in-law.

Lilly gasped. What was Irene doing here? Were she and Theo truly lovers, forced to pay blackmail money just as she was? Lilly couldn't believe Irene would trade George for a bland little man, but that was the only explanation. Her poor brother would be crushed if he discovered his wife's infidelity, if that was in fact the case. Lilly's palm pressed against her bodice in a futile attempt to slow her galloping heartbeat.

MacIntyre's hand jerked forward and thrust a wad of cash at Theo. Why was he giving them money instead of taking it from them? Then the fat man bowed slightly and pushed another stack of bills into Irene's white gloved palm. Irene smiled grimly as she stuffed the money into her reticule.

"For a job well done," the colonel gushed.

Lilly gasped. What was going on?

Colonel MacIntyre glared directly at her. His stomach protruded over the tabletop and his eyes bulged in his doughy flesh. "Ah, Miss Westbrook, you've arrived a trifle early. So glad you could come."

"I don't understand," Lilly murmured as she moved into the aisle between empty tables.

The thud of leather heels distracted her. She glanced over her shoulder, annoyed at the interruption. As Jack and her brother charged toward the group, unexpected relief caught her by surprise.

"I'll explain, Lilly." Jack's eyes bore into Irene and then MacIntyre. He blocked the aisle, preventing anyone from escaping.

But before Jack could speak, George lunged for Theo and jerked him by the lapels. "You're having an affair with my wife, aren't you?"

"No, no, of, of course not," the man stuttered, as if appalled at the very idea of adultery. Theo pushed away from George.

Surprised, George turned to Irene and held her by her shoulders. "You're in love with Theo, aren't you? I've seen you together often enough. I want the truth."

Irene shook free. A nervous laugh spewed from her throat. "George, how can you believe I'd be interested in a puny fellow like him when I have you?" She looked up through the curve of her long eyelashes.

George hesitated. "Then why are you here? Is that scum blackmailing you too?"

"No, no. Theo and I are having a business meeting." Her voice trailed off.

Jack stepped forward. "Tell him the whole sordid story, Irene. Your husband has a right to know."

After several moments of silence, Irene raised her chin. "I don't have to take your rudeness any longer, Jackson." She glanced up at her husband and narrowed her eyes in a sensuous smile. "George, the truth is, I'm returning to San Francisco to visit Uncle Quentin. My stay might be a long one. I was borrowing some money from the colonel for my journey since I know we're temporarily short of funds. Theo introduced us."

Jack chortled and shook his head in disbelief. Then he sobered. "George, I don't know how to break this to you, so I'll just come out with it."

"No, Jack, don't," Irene begged.

Turning his back on the colonel, Jack drew a deep sigh, suddenly somber. Lilly could tell this wasn't easy for him, and with all her heart she wanted to throw her arms around this man. He'd come to the rescue and now he was trying to set things right with her brother and his wife. "Irene isn't really the niece of Quentin Kirby." Jack cleared his throat before continuing. "He found her in a dance hall and brought her to his home and treated her like a princess. But she married you for love, apparently. Though she's doing a despicable job honoring that devotion."

George sunk into the nearest hardback chair. "And now you're going back to your first lover?"

A shocked look swept across Irene's face. "He's an old man. We were never lovers."

"Then why are you returning to him?" George's words strangled in his throat.

Irene's eyes sparked with defiance. "Because he recently offered me marriage and his entire fortune. I can't refuse."

"But you're married to me." George glanced from Irene to Jack. "I don't understand."

"She's not married to you, George," Jack said as gently as he could. "She couldn't be."

Lilly gasped and George glanced upward, desolation etched in every line of his face.

Jack leaned back against a pillar. "Before Irene met Quentin Kirby, she wed a California farmer named Hiram Wilson. They separated but never ended their union. So, they're still legally married. She'll have to search for Hiram to ask for her freedom before she can marry Quentin." He reached out and laid a hand on his friend's shoulder. "Your union was a falsehood."

George buried his head in his hands.

Irene slid into the chair beside him and touched his jacket sleeve. "I never meant to deceive you, George. My marriage to Hiram . . . it was short and so long ago, it simply didn't seem necessary to find him. It was such an ugly, painful situation, I erased it from my mind."

The colonel leaned forward. "You're a fascinating woman, Irene Westbrook. Or should I say Irene Wilson?" He was obviously enthralled by the drama playing out all around him. "If things don't work out with Kirby, I might be interested." His pig-like eyes gleamed with lust.

Irene ignored MacIntyre and clutched George's hands. "I'm sorry, George. I never meant for you to find out. It was just a youthful mistake."

George shook off her hands and rose to his full height. "You're a liar and a bigamist, Irene. Get out of my sight. You've brought disgrace upon yourself and upon my family, though you probably don't understand that concept." Fury flared in his eyes. For the first time in Lilly's life, pride in her brother displaced pity. He refused to crumble in the face of disillusionment.

MacIntyre opened his palms. "If you'll pay me a small sum, I guarantee I'll keep this nasty business quiet and out of *Talk of the Town*. No one except the six of us ever needs to know."

"Why, you *scum*." With fists clenched, George drew closer to MacIntrye, who tipped his chair backward against the wall, his eyes wide with fright. The extortionist cowered, his huge body shaking like gelatin. He shielded his barrel chest with his arms.

"You'll not get a penny from me," George spat out. "If you want to spread your filthy gossip, go ahead. I'll not protect Irene."

Lilly looked at her brother, astonished. He'd confronted society's most dangerous enemy and stood his ground. That was so unlike the weak-willed George she knew. He'd always taken the easy way out of every scrape and avoided any hint of confrontation.

"I'm proud of you, George," she said. If he found the grit to face the greatest shock and disappointment of his life, how could she do any less?

He tossed her a grateful smile.

Standing beside her chair with his arm on the top rung of the ladder-back, Jack added, "There's something else you should know, Lilly."

Her heart lurched.

"Irene was the colonel's spy at Summerhill. That's why she's here. He just paid her for the last of the items she delivered through Theo Nottingham, one of MacIntyre's many operatives in Newport. Isn't that right, Irene?"

Irene's shoulders sagged. "Yes, but I only did it because I needed the money. George and I never have nearly enough, so when I met Mr. Nottingham, he offered a way to pay our bills. I'm sorry, Lilly, but I didn't have a choice."

"So those trysts with him were never romantic?" That explained the attraction between Irene and Mr. Nottingham — money.

Irene's harsh laugh caused Theo to blush. "Goodness no. We were informants, not lovers." Irene glanced around. "Well, I'm afraid I can't stay any longer. I must be off to San Francisco. I'll send for my things once I arrive." She gripped her parasol and reticule.

Lilly's glare made Irene wince, but only for a moment. "You had a choice, Irene, you just made the wrong one. You didn't care how much havoc you caused my family."

Irene adjusted her hat and pulled her veil over her face. "I apologize for all this unpleasantness, but now I must be gone. Good day, everyone." Irene scurried from the café, Theo right behind her.

"You're well rid of her," Lilly squeezed George's arm as they watched his so-called wife vanish out the door and out of his life. "Though I'm sorry things turned out so badly."

George expelled a long sigh and sank into a chair again. "I know I'm better off without her. But still I never expected this."

Without a doubt, he'd miss her for a long while. Love didn't die in an instant.

"How did my sister-in-law and Mr. Nottingham become involved?" Lilly asked. Numbness spread through her from the shock of these revelations. They were more than she could absorb all at once.

The colonel puffed on his cigar, looking rather relaxed now that George was seated again. "Theo has been one of my informants for quite a while. From listening to local gossip, he discovered Irene needed money to cover her gambling debts. He approached her at a party and asked if she'd like to help us. He realized she'd come to know just about everyone in society and might be willing to spill a few secrets for a little cash. She turned out to be quite an observant woman." He chuckled. "It seems you were careless about locking your desk. Irene wanted to borrow a pen and stationery and discovered a manuscript with Fannie Cole's name."

Lilly doubted that. She'd always locked her desk. Irene had snooped around and found the key.

The colonel rubbed his hands together. "I believe Miss Westbrook prefers to speak to me alone."

"I think not, MacIntyre. I have something to say to you." Jack leaned across the worn tablecloth sprinkled with crumbs from MacIntyre's pastry. "I told you that Miss Cole is one of my authors and I take a great interest in her career. A personal interest. Drop your blackmail scheme right now, because she's not paying you one red cent." Jack glanced at Lilly.

"Then maybe you'd like to, Grail."

Jack shook his head. "No. Nothing from me, either."

"I want to hear from Fannie herself. Speak up, Miss Westbrook."

She glared at the colonel as he blew a smoke ring in her direction. "You'll not get a dime from me." Lilly stared at the arrogant man, thrilled she'd finally defied him. "*Or* from Mr. Grail. You can expose my name in your horrid newssheet, but it doesn't matter because I've decided to promote myself and my novels for Jones and Jarman. You have no hold over me any longer."

Jack reached for her hand. She pulled her attention away from the colonel and looked down at Jack's hand. His touch warmed her icy fingers, but heated her heart even more. These were the hands she longed to hold forever — hands that could make her feel secure and safe.

A stinging in the back of her eyes told her that unexpected tears threatened to spill. Had the day's stress gotten to her, or did having Jack here with her touch her beyond belief?

His eyes pleaded with her for understanding — and maybe something more.

"I know how much you want to stay in the background. So if you don't wish to engage in any promotion for any of the titles published by Jones and Jarman, I understand."

"Thank you." Lilly squeezed Jack's hand, hoping he would sense her overwhelming gratitude for his selflessness. The future of his company rested on her doing promotions, yet he'd give her an out for —

"I find your mutual self-sacrificing quite touching," the colonel interrupted her thoughts, "but shockingly unrealistic. Think of the humiliation and heartbreak this will cause your family, Fannie." He looked from Jack to Lilly. "I don't care who pays me, but someone will or Fannie Cole is going to see her true name in the next edition of *Talk of the Town*."

The colonel leaned toward Lilly, his stare hard. His noxious cigar breath drifted across the table. "If you don't pay up, I'll expose you on page one of *Talk of the Town* so nobody can miss it. I'll write how you cheated on your fiancé with your publisher. Oh yes, Irene told me all about you and your *good friend,* Jack here, and his *personal interest* in you. What do you say to that, Miss Cole? Do you want to be cut from every rich and powerful family in New York and Newport? Or would you rather pay a small sum for my silence? You can go on just as you always have, marry Grail or some society swell, and write your stories. What's your answer?"

Lilly tried to speak, but only a croak came forth. "I planned to pay your blackmail because I was afraid our friends would ostracize my family and me." She looked at Jack and George. "Irene's previous marriage will cause a dreadful scandal for George and our family, but we'll face it and weather it. I refuse to do anything less in this matter." She shook her head. "I've hidden my work as if I'm ashamed of it. Well, I'm not. It's time I own up to my career. I won't be timid any longer."

She smiled at her brother. "George, you've given me courage and I'm grateful for your example. And I'm so proud of you." Funny how he was the last person she'd expect to show fortitude in the face of social shunning.

She took Jack's hand again. "And I want to help you build Jones and Jarman into a prosperous publishing house. If I'm going to be unveiled as Fannie Cole, I may as well go a step further. So feel free to introduce me to 'my public.' " She chuckled at her last two words. It would take awhile to adjust to celebrity, but with Jack's help, she'd overcome her reticence. "Just don't overdo it."

Jack blinked, and in a low voice said, "Then you're not going to switch to Atwater Publishers?"

"No, I'm not. I admit I once considered it, in order to preserve my anonymity, but I don't believe so any longer. I've decided to stay with you." She wanted to say "to stay with you forever," but she bit her lip.

Jack's eyes softened. "You're willing to promote Fannie Cole?" Then he added, "For me?"

"I am."

Jack's obvious relief showed in a big smile soon followed by a frown. "But what about your family? It's one thing for them to know you're Fannie; it's another to see you promote yourself as a dime novelist."

His concern touched her deeply. "I trust they'll come to see that my writing is worthwhile and that they can weather the storm alongside us." She focused on Jack, her heart thumping, her throat dry.

*I love you, Jack. I want to marry you!* She wouldn't voice her feelings in this place, in front of Colonel MacIntyre and George, but she hoped her eyes conveyed her heartfelt feelings. How she wished they could be alone so she could tell Jack the true feelings that she'd had for so long, but the moment wouldn't allow that.

Colonel MacIntyre thrust himself to his feet and relit his cigar. "You're making a big mistake, missy."

Jack tore his gaze from Lilly, then stood. He towered over the editor. "It doesn't matter what you do if Miss Westbrook goes public. You have no hold over her." Jack pointed his finger in MacIntyre's face. "But I have the note you sent to Miss Westbrook. There's enough evidence in that to prove you're a blackmailer. If you print one word about her or the Westbrook family ever again, you'll be sued and your scandal sheet will be shut down for good."

MacInyre choked on his cigar and bent over coughing.

Jack frowned. "And for the trouble you've caused, I expect you to make reparations or else I'll take your blackmail letter to the police."

Rufus MacIntyre's tiny eyes narrowed. "No, you wouldn't do that."

"Tell you what. I'll reconsider if you make a large, anonymous donation to the Christian Settlement House of New York. Your kind gesture will be greatly appreciated."

Again, Jack's gesture swept her off her feet. She bit her lip hard to keep from crying, but she looked at him with eyes that said, "I love you for this and for all that you are."

A sneer spread across Colonel MacIntrye's face along with a hint of fear. "I don't find that necessary. They'd never believe a former colonel in the Union Army would do such a thing."

"Shall we find out?" Jack asked.

MacIntyre paused. "All right, I'll do that," he muttered as he smashed his cigar into the ash tray.

Jack stared at the man. "See that you do. I'll be checking up on you. I'll telephone Miss Diller, the directress, tomorrow afternoon to make sure your contribution has arrived."

Lilly mouthed a heartfelt thank-you toward Jack, then let him lead her and George out of the cave-like restaurant, away from the stink of the colonel. Jack took her arm, unaware that his touch sent a surge of love through her. He helped her into her carriage and climbed in beside her, then directed the coachman to take them back to Summerhill. George lumbered off to his gig and drove off, just ahead of them.

As the carriage jolted forward, Jack settled close to Lilly. Her heart swelled. "I truly appreciate what you're willing to do for my company. But wouldn't it be better for you to accept Sterling's offer? He'll give you everything you want — anonymity, a new *nom de plume,* and probably more money than Jones and Jarman could ever afford."

Lilly's eyes widened. "Do you have another dime novelist to take my place?"

He shook his head. "I'm afraid not in the romance area. But that's all right. I'll concentrate on my newspaper and magazine." He paused. "We're on the verge of purchasing a manuscript from a new writer of western dime novels, so I'm sure that will help."

"But tell me, when did you find this new authoress — of westerns, you say? You've never mentioned her before."

"Lewis Jarman telephoned me just an hour or so ago. He's excited about the possibilities of promoting her books."

So the telephone call she overheard concerned their newest find; it wasn't about her. How could she have jumped to such an unfair conclusion?

Lilly grasped his hands. "Since George has shown so much courage, I can't do anything less. I shall go public. And I want to write for Jones and Jarman, not Atwater."

Jack's face lit up. "Are you sure, Lilly?"

"Positive."

"But that's an enormous sacrifice. Maybe I should curtail my ambition, as you once said. It takes so much time and energy to build a publishing empire." Jack tilted his head. He looked nervous, unsure of himself. "I'd like to spend the extra time with you, Lilly."

Joy swept through her body. A smile turned up her lips. "I'd like that as well. But growing Jones and Jarman into a prosperous publishing house is your dream and I'll not ruin it. I want to help you."

"Thank you, Lilly." He brushed a kiss across her hand.

Jack slipped his arm around Lilly's shoulder. She sighed with a happiness she'd only known for a short time six years before.

"I'll never let you down again, Lilly."

She leaned closer. "I tried to forgive you, Jack, at least in my head, but I wasn't willing to trust you with either my career or my heart. I see now that I can. And I do. I couldn't imagine how this dreadful problem would end, but I knew the Lord would find a solution for me. And He did."

Jack grinned. "A solution for us."

She tilted her head toward him and he bent down and kissed her. She accepted the warmth of his lips upon hers and let the sweetness linger. Wrapping her fingers around his, she stroked them tenderly.

"I love you, Lilly."

She realized how deeply she'd craved those words. "I love you too."

"Lilly, I asked you before and promised not to pressure you, but will you do me the honor of marrying me? I need you so very much."

She didn't hesitate. "Oh, Jack, and I need you too. I love you and would be honored to be Mrs. Jackson Grail."

A few joyful tears trickled down her cheeks as he again pressed his lips to hers. Jack flashed a smile brighter than sunshine. They were together at last.

They took the long route back to Summerhill, enjoying the glory of the afternoon and each other. When they arrived home they found George pacing in the foyer.

"I thought we could go in together and explain things to our parents. They're waiting for us along with Miranda. I assume you don't mind her presence, Lilly."

Lilly sighed, not because of Miranda, but because of what was ahead of them. She braced herself for her confession. Dread shot up her spine as she tried to harness her thoughts. *Lord, You've shown me Your will today. Please help me to explain without upsetting anyone too much.*

As if knowing her feelings, Jack took her hand into his and gave it a slight squeeze. Looking into her eyes, he smiled. With a newfound courage she entered the sunny drawing room on Jack's arm.

Lilly cleared her throat. Mama and Papa

were perched on the stiff furniture. Miranda sat beside the unlit fireplace tatting a lace collar. All three looked up at her. "I have something important to say. Actually, to confess." Jack stood close beside her. Lilly took a deep breath and clutched her hands together. "For a long time I've been afraid to tell you my secret because I knew you'd be mortified." She took another breath and steadied her hands. "I write dime novels for Jones and Jarman Publishing. My pen name is Fannie Cole." She heard her father gasp.

"Why Lilly, I had no idea," Papa murmured.

Mama patted Papa's hand and looked at Lilly with kindness. "But I did know. I believe Lilly's writing is a worthwhile endeavor. Her books are beautifully written and convey an uplifting message. What could be more important?"

Lilly let out a gasp. "Oh, Mama, when did you discover I was Fannie Cole?" Tears pooled in her eyes.

Mama smiled shyly. "I recently finished *Dorothea's Dilemma* and loved every word of it. As soon as I came to the scene by the pond, I realized only you could have written it. Of course, I was shocked, but I've had some time to reflect on it. More than anything else, I'm so very proud of you."

Glancing at Papa, whose mouth was opened wide with disbelief, Mama gave a firm nod. "It's past time I let you children fly on your own and accept you both for who you are becoming. I thought I knew better what would make you happy, but I was wrong. That's what I wanted to tell you before you left this afternoon. And one more thing." Mama paused and her eyelids fluttered. "I'm ashamed to admit that after I discovered you were Fannie, I — I found the key to your desk drawer and I opened it. Your latest manuscript was inside. Lilly, I snooped. I wanted to confess, but I didn't have the gumption. I am so sorry. Can you ever forgive me?"

Lilly threw her arms around her mother and hugged her tightly. "Yes, Mama. I too was afraid to confess so I pulled farther and farther away from you. I thought you'd be ashamed of me and I couldn't bear that. I'm so sorry I misjudged you."

Mama laughed as tears escaped down her cheeks.

"I've decided to promote my books to help Jones and Jarman grow as a publishing house. I'm sure it will be hard at first, but with Jack's support I'll get used to it. I'm afraid society will ostracize us and for that I'm truly sorry."

George leaned against the green marble mantle and pulled at his goatee. "And if Lilly's career doesn't end our foray into ultra-fashionable society, surely Irene's indiscretions will." Briefly, he told his parents what had transpired.

Vanessa lifted a hand to her forehead.

"Mama, are you all right?" George asked. Lilly's father reached out to grab his wife's hand. They shared a long look.

"It's only . . . it's a bit much to take in." She looked up to George. "I'm sorry, son. That is a horrible loss for you."

"I'm sorry I brought her into our family. I'm afraid you and Papa will bear the brunt of my foolishness."

"That's all right," she said, looking from her son to her daughter. "Our real friends will stay loyal," Mama said. "Our true friends."

"And I have new plans too," George said. "A position teaching young boisterous boys would suit me well. Just today I've been offered a teaching position at a preparatory school in Connecticut. Irene would hear nothing of it. But now there's nothing to hold me back. I'll begin in September."

Papa lighted up. "Splendid! You always were so good with children. Much better than in the office." He grinned at George.

Late afternoon sunshine flooded the room with golden warmth. Lilly breathed easily for the first time in weeks. Glancing up at Jack, she knew the time had come. She smiled, hoping for support. Jack laced his fingers through hers and gently squeezed.

"Mama, Papa, you may have surmised that Colonel MacIntyre was trying to blackmail me. Jack wanted to confront him, but I was afraid to admit I wrote the Fannie Cole novels. I didn't feel I could trust Jack to keep my secret. But he proved he could and — I also realized I love him." She clasped his hand tightly. "We're going to be married."

The Westbrooks erupted with shouts of approval. George pecked her cheek and whispered, "It's about time." Mama rushed forward with wide-open arms.

Papa thumped Jack on the back. "Best wishes, son. You're getting a delightful girl and, I dare say, she's getting an equally fine man. My best to you both."

Mama raised a finger to her flushed cheek. "When will we have the wedding?"

Jack laughed. "How about the end of August or September at the latest?"

"August sounds best to me." Lilly tossed her head backward as Jack reached down to touch her lips with the loveliest kiss she'd ever tasted.

Joy, fireworks, an explosion of passion — just as she'd always imagined. Perhaps love and excitement weren't too much to hope for after all.

# ACKNOWLEDGMENTS

I'd like to thank all the wonderful people at Thomas Nelson who helped publish this book: Allen Arnold, Natalie Hanemann, Lisa Bergren, and Becky Monds. I'm also grateful to Mary Connealy, Christy Barritt, Anne Greene, all the contest judges who read parts of the manuscript, the Gulf Coast Chapter of RWA, and Karen Solem. An enormous thanks goes to my children, Justin and Alicia, for all their encouragement, my "Seeker sisters," and Beth White and Fran McNabb, two fabulous authors who have helped me most with my writing.

# READING GROUP GUIDE

1. Jack proposed to Lilly without thinking through the objections he'd encounter from her parents. Should he have asked for her hand in marriage even though the answer would certainly have been no? Do you sympathize with him despite his cowardly behavior in leaving Lilly? If not, how could he redeem himself in her eyes?

2. Lilly thought she could keep her writing secret. Do you think she was justified in hiding her career from her family and friends? If she'd chosen to tell them, how should she have handled the situation to make it more palatable? If they continued to oppose her, what could she have done?

3. Lilly saw her writing as a ministry and God's will and purpose for her life. From that perspective, did she have a choice in writing in spite of opposition? Was she brave, prudent, or cowardly in keeping her career secret?

4. As her publisher, did Jack deserve to know the truth about Lilly's writing? Lilly held back and didn't reveal her identity. Should she have trusted him to keep her secret? If so, at what point in the story had he proven himself loyal to her?

5. Jack's faith grew during the course of the story. He read Scripture and took it to heart, but he relied more on himself than on God — until he realized he couldn't find solutions to his problems on his own. Does he have an inner flaw which prevents him from turning to the Lord sooner? Do you see a flaw within yourself? Does it keep you from drawing closer to God?

6. Lilly's social group ostracized its members for defying their standards of behavior. Why would they "shun" offenders no matter how trivial their infractions? Do you think this helped to keep their values intact or just cause people to hide their offences? How does this 19th-century society compare to our own?

7. How did Lilly's and Jack's backgrounds affect their attitudes, values, and behaviors? Who do you think had the better upbringing? Why?

8. In what ways did Lilly's mother change from the beginning to the end of the story? What caused her to open her mind

and begin to think differently?

9. How do you think wealth effected Lilly, Jack, their families, and friends? In what ways did it benefit them and in what ways did it harm them? How did their faith influence their lives?

10. Irene was pragmatic but unscrupulous. Did her childhood poverty explain or excuse her selfish behavior? Was she evil or merely weak? How did her lies hurt the Westbrooks? Did she suffer any consequences for her misdeeds?

The employees of Thorndike Press hope you have enjoyed this Large Print book. All our Thorndike, Wheeler, and Kennebec Large Print titles are designed for easy reading, and all our books are made to last. Other Thorndike Press Large Print books are available at your library, through selected bookstores, or directly from us.

For information about titles, please call:
  (800) 223-1244

or visit our Web site at:
  http://gale.cengage.com/thorndike

To share your comments, please write:
  Publisher
  Thorndike Press
  295 Kennedy Memorial Drive
  Waterville, ME 04901